DRAWING
CIRCLES

DRAWING CIRCLES

JOE BUZZELLO

11-Creative, LLC

ISBN: 978-0-9969503-0-5

I dedicate this book to my father, **Anthony Bailey "Buzz" Buzzello**

*My father left this earth in March of 1987, but before he did, he taught
me how to be a man. He was the gentlest, smartest and kindest person
I have ever met. With his quiet, but strong manner, he conveyed to me
all of the lessons I needed in order to navigate a life full of peaks and
valleys. When I searched for a fitting photograph for this dedication
I couldn't find the right one of him standing alone. I finally gave
up; realizing that in virtually every picture, people were gathered
around him, drawing strength from this person I loved so much.*

Buzz, Joe and Helen Buzzello, circa December 1961 –
Santa's Village, Lake Arrowhead, California

1

Summer 1982

It seemed like summers lasted forever when I was a kid. We ruled our world from the seats of our ten-speed bikes, zigzagging our way through the streets of the hood looking for excitement. We'd have our baseball gear, golf clubs, basketball or football in tow, looking for a game. If we couldn't find one, we'd invent some kind of minor trouble, usually the kind that wasn't serious enough to warrant LAPD involvement.

By the late 70s our bikes morphed into used cars, which gave us enough self-assurance to persuade a few girls to hang out with us. Our enhanced modes of transportation allowed us to escape the oppressive summer heat in the Valley. We staked out a small stretch of sand just north of the Santa Monica Pier. We claimed lifeguard station number 11—and the adjacent volleyball court—as our own.

The summer nights on that beach were magical. There was no end to the simple good times we had as we played volleyball, dug for clams and chased grunion. After most of our energy was spent, we'd dig a big hole in the sand. Then we'd sit there, well past midnight, talking shit and drinking the beer I'd liberated from the liquor store I worked at. Those nights on the beach and the long, hot summer days in the Valley were fruitless, but they always put a smile on our stupid faces.

Our tightly knit group of friends and those good times were everything to me, but that carefree period of my life slowly vanished along with the 70s. By the end of that brain-dead decade most of my friends waved good-bye to their adolescence, and to me, and headed off to college.

Bill Mazal was my best friend. I met him on a basketball court just before my first year in junior high. He was a year older and a few inches taller. Even though the other kids towered over me, he still picked me for his team. Mazal and I had been glued to each other's side since age thirteen, so when he started college, I was a little lost.

By July of 1982, I was twenty-one, and couldn't rightly masquerade as a kid anymore, but that somber fact hadn't discouraged me from trying to milk a little more depravity out of my vanishing innocence. On a scale from one to ten, the hangover I was nursing rated a nine—ten being a near-death experience. The origin of the hangover was a weeklong binge with Mazal and the rest of our high school buddies who were back in town, on break from college. My banging headache rendered me acutely aware that it was time to dry out and get back to work.

I dragged my ass out of bed and threw on a semi-clean dress shirt and a wrinkled tie. I wheeled my Olds Cutlass onto Roscoe Boulevard and snapped on the radio. I needed to take the focus off of my banging coconut.

The deejay apprised the listeners of the Monday morning weather—as if there were actually weather in Los Angeles—stating that the "low-lying valleys" would be pushing past a hundred degrees. The low-lying San Fernando Valley was where I'd spent my lackluster twenty-one years up to that point. The Valley is situated north of Beverly Hills and Hollywood and south of places you wouldn't normally visit if you had a full set of teeth.

Supposedly, some hearty Spanish and Mexican explorers with a hundred donkeys in tow discovered the Valley in 1769. Those brave pioneers probably didn't envision that the Valley would become the soft pornography capital of the free world and a haven for purveyors of inexpensive

Mexican weed and twice-cut cocaine. At the tender age of twenty-one I was beginning to notice the darker underbelly of my birthplace.

The Valley was a poor-man's version of the more affluent life available over the hill. The temperatures were higher where we lived, but the rents were far cheaper. The other upside for anybody with something to sell is that there were several million people dwelling in the low-lying piece of real estate. Any entrepreneur with a dream or a scheme could set up shop quickly and cheaply and they'd have an endless supply of eyeballs. I sold stuff for a living so the bulging populace worked for me.

Starbridge Financial Planning was on the upper floor of a two-story building in Sherman Oaks. I slipped into the front door hoping the residual alcohol in my body wouldn't be noticeable. I reached into the small mail slot that bore my name, Tony DiBona, and I grabbed a stack of envelopes and pink phone memos. I sat down in my tiny cubicle and stared at the pile of stale messages.

Thanks to my recent bender, I was out of money. Well, I wasn't out of money completely; I had seventeen bucks in my checking account. The dismal condition was part of a habitual cycle. I'd close a few deals, collect the commissions and pay some bills. I'd play as much golf as I could and then party away whatever cash was left over. The moment a spare dollar settled in my bank account, I found no need to go into the office. I could usually be found at one of our favorite dive-bars or at one of the local municipal golf courses. I'd wake up a week or so later, realize I was down to rock bottom in my checking account and repeat the sequence.

The reckless routine was becoming more frequent and my gaps of attendance at work were growing longer. It was emotionally draining, living from commission check to commission check, while lying to my parents about how hard I was working. Yet it hadn't changed my ways.

Starbridge wasn't a bad place to work, if you called commission-only insurance sales real work. I'd followed a couple of other agents over to Starbridge after we all bailed out of Pennsylvania Life. Penn Life was my first job out of high school. Starbridge was a half-step up from my previous gig but most importantly, it was a place that would hire a person without a college education, a guy like me. Starbridge had one actual Certified Financial Planner on staff. The place was a life insurance mill, and one of the most successful in California.

I followed Rex Logan over to Starbridge from Penn Life. Rex was a hippie in his late thirties. He concealed his round face behind a bushy salt-and-pepper beard and a pair of oversized prescription sunglasses. Rex never looked comfortable in business attire. His sport coats were always too small and his ties always dangled at half-mast. He escaped chilly Ohio in 1974 for the temperate climate of L.A. Rex was a closet wake and bake—the kind of guy who woke up to a bong hit instead of a cup of coffee. He spent most of his spare time smoking good weed and listening to a non-stop soundtrack of Zeppelin and Floyd.

Rex became my mentor by default. Nobody else wanted the job. I liked his style. He was astute enough to reap the maximum commission out of the least amount of effort. It was an art form and he was expert at his craft. I was captivated by his ability to produce enough to get by with little effort. I believed he had few motivations beyond making enough money to pay the bills; keep his wife Linda off his ass, and keep his bong full. He was also a keen judge of people, a proficiency I hadn't yet refined.

My career path had not been well-charted. I opted out of college life. Surviving high school had been strenuous enough for my parents and me. We quickly reached a mutual decision that the small amount of money they'd set aside for my schooling would be better spent on a reliable vehicle and a few new suits for whatever job interviews I could find.

I answered a blind ad in the local newspaper the summer after I barely graduated high school and was enrolled in the insurance license school the following week. Selling insurance had never proven difficult for me. I could cruise and still post decent production numbers. The label "underachiever" had been tattooed on my forehead since first grade in Catholic school and that hadn't changed as I entered the work force.

I was blessed with two dutiful parents. My father, Buzz, had been an aerospace engineer for more than twenty years but was exiled into the automobile industry after the government ended the space race. My mother,

Helen, was a homemaker. There was an older sister: Regina, the smart one. I was the guy who barely got by in school. We grew up in a post-World War II tract home in Van Nuys: an archetypical and Sixties nuclear family.

After I began my insurance career, I started to grade my parent's financial acumen. They were doing okay financially; but they were not rich, never going to be rich. Wealth wasn't important to them. I'd often hear my mom say, "There's a lot more to life than money." I'd reached the conclusion that this was code for, *we've settled for this level of mediocrity.* I wondered if my lot in life would be similar to theirs, making most of my lifestyle decisions based on money, or the lack thereof.

With my Velcro wallet empty it was hard to ignore those "various reasons" I didn't go to college. I had screwed off in high school. My grades were humiliating and my attitude about them worse. I could hit a golf ball reasonably well but my defiant attitude got me kicked off the high school team. Most of my friends maintained decent grades and had parents with deeper pockets than mine. My best buddy, Mazal, and all of the others were enjoying the benefits of advanced education. While they were setting up lucrative futures, I was hawking life insurance on straight commission over kitchen tables.

While I slumped in my desk chair, massaging my pile of pink messages, Rex Logan waddled over to my cubicle. He propped himself on the divider and stroked his beard.

"Welcome back stranger. You ready to go downstairs for a coffee break?"

I examined the mountain of stale phone messages and underwriting declines as I pondered his offer. I'd been at the office for ten minutes. I was semi-nauseous and not anxious to start cold calling on dead-end leads.

"Sure," I sighed.

The decision to screw off was remarkably easy. Rex and I liked to take what he referred to as "mental health breaks" from work. We headed downstairs to the Valley Donut Palace. The tacky joint served cheap apple fritters, jelly doughnuts and drinkable coffee. The older woman who owned the place liked us and gave us free refills. She had installed a new Ms. PacMan machine and we'd become experts at the game. The establishment had a payphone on the wall next to our regular booth. If we had to call someone we were only a dime away from conducting business. We also used the payphone for incoming calls. Occasionally, the Starbridge receptionist would call down to us and tip us off if Fred Cohen, the owner of our agency, was looking for us.

In our minds, we were kings. We ran our world from a payphone in a doughnut shop. We had one other friend who regularly joined us on these long mental health breaks. Annie Wu was our third wheel.

Annie was also a Penn Life runaway. She fit in with us because she had similar bad habits. Her father raised her after her mother's sudden death due to a heart defect. As an only child, she would often become nostalgic about him while we wasted time at the doughnut shop. He owned a dry cleaning establishment in San Francisco. Raising a daughter to compete in a man's world meant a lot to him. At night, after closing, he taught Annie how to prepare the cash deposit for the bank, telling her, "Take care of your own business. If you don't, nobody else will." Annie told me that story every time my self-pity grew annoying.

The three of us talked for hours in the doughnut shop. Rex professed his liberal hippie philosophies while smoking like a chimney, and Annie challenged him—advocating her free enterprise values—while killing her pack of Virginia Slims. I sat in the middle, in a cloud of smoke, watching them argue while drinking more coffee than Juan Valdez.

Rex ended our screw-off session that day sooner than usual. He signaled, with a point of his cigarette, that it was time to go upstairs. We entered the office, but as we passed the production board, I slammed on my brakes. The weekly commission numbers had just been posted. Rex's name was third with $2,950 in commissions.

He hadn't mentioned his incredible week to me. He'd already shuffled back to his desk and had a phone to his ear making calls. I was frozen in my tracks, staring at the production numbers. I was happy for him, but wasn't sure how he'd gone from zero to hero while I was on my latest two-week binge.

I went back to my cubicle, flopped down in my chair and rubbed my forehead in a futile attempt to suppress the lingering hangover. The sight of other people's huge commission numbers made my headache seem worse: it cemented what a loser I was.

From the vantage point of my cubicle I watched the receptionist complete the weekly rankings. The top producer, Ken Richman, had earned $3,875 in commissions.

Richman was the new star at Starbridge. The owner, Fred Cohen, hired him straight into a vice president's role four weeks earlier. Apparently, Richman's job was to coach the current sales team as well as expand the size of the agency through recruiting efforts. Rex told me that Richman was willing to share his knowledge with only a select few. Because of my lack of attendance at the office and the fact that Richman rarely came in there, I'd never met him.

I broke into a cold sweat, loosened my tie and snatched the dusty stack of lead cards. I began placing calls in a half-hearted attempt to book an appointment. Forty-five minutes ticked off the clock. I was in the midst of a horrid slump when Rex leaned on my cubicle wall.

"Do you have some time on Friday afternoon?" he asked.

I shrugged; knowing all I had was time. I was hoping he wanted to hit our favorite saloon and drink Friday afternoon away, but he had a no nonsense expression on his face.

"You remember the new vice president I mentioned, Ken Richman?"

"Yeah," I said. "I'm hung-over, not senile."

Rex leaned in close as if he was about to deliver the code for the atomic bomb.

"I wrangled you a meeting with him. Here's his home address," he said, handing me a note. "Be there on Friday at 2:00 PM. Wear a suit and tie. Don't be late."

I laid the piece of scrap paper next to my list of failed appointment attempts and mustered up a sarcastic question: "Is this BYOB or will this guy have some cold beers set up for us?"

Rex's eyes narrowed. "Suit and tie," he repeated.

I mumbled, "Thanks" as he hurried back to his desk.

I attempted a few more dials, but quickly grew bored with my labors.

It was only 3:50 PM but I was done. I cleaned up my desk and cruised by Rex's cubicle to say goodbye. I stopped a few yards short of his workspace and eavesdropped on his conversation. He was hyping somebody on Ken Richman. I'd never seen my makeshift mentor so enthused about another person.

Glancing at Rex's desk I noticed a wooden eagle perched beside his phone. Carved below the claws, the inscription read: *Freedom Isn't Free*. I didn't wait to say goodbye. I dipped out the back door, artfully avoiding human contact, especially with Fred Cohen. I was teetering on the edge of dismissal; he was the last person who needed to witness my current state.

I placed the clip-on shades over my prescription glasses, flipped down the visor of my Olds and headed west into the afternoon sun. The pesky hangover was still torturing me as I contemplated Rex's remarkable week as well as the scrap paper address he'd handed me. Had I pegged him wrong? Maybe he aspired to be better than average, or at the moment, just better than me. I was in a horrific hole. Whatever Rex was cooking up with Ken Richman was a secret he could've kept to himself; instead, he was throwing me a rope. I was inclined to grab it.

I never put much thought into production numbers. I wasn't that competitive; well, at least until I saw Logan's commissions that week. Rex's offer made me realize how deeply I had fallen. Humiliation was a circumstance I normally handled with a joke or a crude hand motion.

Alone in my car with my head pounding, there was no audience to entertain. I had to face facts. I'd need to nail down a few juicy life insurance sales fast and then ask Fred for a commission advance. If I didn't pull that off I'd have to admit to my parents that I'd screwed off so badly again that I'd need them to bail me out on my mortgage payment one more time.

The hangover was wearing off but the anxiety was kicking in. I eased my Olds into the driveway of my Canoga Park tract house. I grabbed a cold forty from the fridge. I wasn't sure if I was still suffering from a hangover or if it was simply the discomfort of my life. Whatever it was I was quite sure another beer would fix it.

2

Friday Morning

I'd somehow avoided all distractions and squeezed out the two sales I badly needed. I pulled my ass out of the gutter. Again. I made my first prospecting call by 9:45 AM that morning. A new world record for Tony DiBona. I would've been hitting the phone twenty minutes earlier, but Fred Cohen stopped me short of my cubicle and worked me over.

Fred was an old-school life insurance guy who had done well. He and his wife lived in a mansion in Beverly Hills and he drove a Rolls Royce, Silver Shadow. Fred enjoyed the fruits of his labor, but wasn't all caught up in it. He wasn't interested in personal appearance. Food stains on his shirt were common and it was rare that his ties matched the rest of his attire.

His other distinctive quality was his habit of incessant chitchat. He'd stroll over to your cubicle and ask about your family and hobbies, diving into topics that had absolutely no connection with selling life insurance. If you wanted to be productive you avoided Fred like a bad venereal disease. That aside, he was genuinely kind and offered guys like me the chance to have a job, a desk and phone. He'd even hand us warm leads to call on once in a while.

The other reason I liked the guy was that he'd always help me out with an advance on commission when I was low on funds. I think he liked me, but it was clear he regarded me as an underachiever. He'd tell me, "You're working on half your potential. If I could just get you to work a full week." I'd just smile, knowing that would leave too little time for golf and beer.

This particular Friday was magic. Four appointments hit my calendar before noon. I glanced at my watch and realized it was almost time for my scheduled meeting with Ken Richman. I sat for a moment, wondering if I should even bother to go. The note that Rex had given me the previous Monday sat on my desk staring at me.

Why should I listen to some hotshot tell me his shit doesn't stink? I grabbed my pen and circled the address a few times, scribbling around it. Then I crumpled it up. I'd tell Rex I was busy. Why should I go to this guy's house when I didn't even know what the meeting was about?

The piece of scrap paper landed in my trashcan and sunk into the sea of dead lead cards. Had I just thrown an opportunity away? I dug through the trash, located the note and flattened it out.

Looking across the office floor, my eyes fell on Annie, sitting in her cubicle. I wondered if Rex offered her the same cryptic opportunity I'd almost sent to a landfill. Her commission numbers hadn't been good. She was a single mother of two with no safety net. I knew she would bounce back out of her slump sooner or later. She always did.

Most of the agents on the floor were at least ten or fifteen years older than me. They were slaving away at their phones, trying to sell a policy or two. I couldn't imagine being in my thirties or forties, out every night—sitting at those damn kitchen tables—pretending I liked the wife's home-made lemon cake so they'd write me a check. I put the piece of notepaper with Ken's address in my shirt pocket. I made sure the path to the back door was clear—that Fred was nowhere in sight. I'd go to the stupid meeting. What the hell did I have to lose?

I pulled up to the address just a few blocks south of the Boulevard. I'd driven through the area over the years, admiring the expensive homes, but had never been inside one of them. The Richman home was positioned on a flag lot with a long driveway that snaked back to a secluded property. I approached the front doors and noticed one was slightly ajar.

"Hello!" I shouted. "Tony DiBona here to meet with Ken Richman."

I heard Logan's familiar cackle coming from somewhere inside. I rang the bell and a woman appeared.

"You must be Tony," she said.

I reached out my hand. "Yes."

"I'm Nancy, Ken's wife," she said, shaking it while flashing a saintly smile.

She was attractive, with soft facial features and meticulous makeup. Nancy Richman was dressed conservatively with the exception of a few pieces of show jewelry. She appeared to be in her early thirties.

"Ken and Rex are in the family room," she said.

I stood dumbfounded by my surroundings and a tad uncomfortable with her Sunday school teacher vibe.

"Can I show you in?" she asked with some measure of formality.

I followed Nancy into the large family room. Ken rose and shook my hand. He was well over six feet tall; his hand easily eclipsed mine. At five-foot-eight, his commanding presence towered over me. He was in great physical shape and looked the part of a matinee idol with bleach-blond hair, sturdy facial features and a California tan. He was dressed in a white nylon tracksuit, as though he'd been lounging around his big house all day. I noticed the thick gold bracelet adorned with a gold eagle. It was draped on one wrist; a Rolex Presidential engulfed the other.

"Hi Tony. Heard a lot about you. Good to meet you."

Ken motioned for me to sit. The luxurious surroundings were intimidating. The home featured high ceilings with exposed wood beams. Lavish furnishings and expensive art dominated the room. The most curious piece of art was hung over the stone fireplace. It was massive—an oil on canvas painting of an American bald eagle. The bird was in flight, looking down, a claw stretched out ominously as though it was preparing to pluck a rodent off the ground. It was unnerving. He noticed me staring at it.

"That's my favorite," he said. "Freedom. That's what the eagle symbolizes. Freedom."

I nodded my head in submissive agreement as my eyes continued to wander around. I glanced in the direction of the French doors that opened to the backyard. The sprawling yard housed an enormous pool and Jacuzzi bordered by a grove of palm trees and lush foliage. So this is how rich people live?

"I understand you'd like some mentorship?" he asked, breaking my spell.

I calculated how I might respond. I was rudderless in my career and living in a small tract home my parents helped me buy. I was struggling to cover my monthly mortgage with seventeen bucks in my checking account. I resisted the urge to make a clever comment.

"Yeah. That would be great," I sputtered.

Ken put his size thirteen sneakers up onto his glass coffee table. He rubbed his chin, sizing me up. After his moment of consideration, he launched into one of the better pieces of reverse psychology I'd heard up to that point in my life.

"I'm not interested in working with someone who isn't a hundred and ten percent serious," he said. "I'm also not going to waste time with a person who doesn't follow directions. My goal isn't to mentor every deadbeat at Starbridge, no matter what Fred Cohen expects. If I select you as one of my protégés I will demand your total loyalty and commitment to my full program. As a result, you'll become wealthy."

He let his last thought linger as he took a long drink of his Diet Coke. He smacked his lips and pointed at Rex.

"He's been in my program for three-and-a-half weeks and his life insurance commissions are exploding," he said. "You've probably noticed the production board at Starbridge. His life is changing quickly because of my mentorship. If I bring you aboard I'm going to teach you how to create similar results—knock down three times the insurance commissions you're used to earning."

He had my attention, but it was what he said next that shocked me.

"I'll require you to keep details about our program to yourself around the office. You won't disclose our strategies to Fred. The only people you can discuss our program with are the agents actually involved. And finally...in order for me to teach you how to triple your insurance income, you have to be involved in my home-based business."

Ken stopped talking and clasped his hands behind his neck. He grinned slightly, a cunning grin that I'd come to know well in the future.

"Acceptable?" he asked.

I'd been in the guy's presence for five minutes and in that time he'd asked me to completely commit to his "program" and his other "home-based business" without giving me specifics on either. He had a set of balls bigger than a rodeo bull.

"I've definitely got some questions but you have my interest," I said.

He smiled confidently, and shrewdly, and began to tell me his story.

3

Friday Afternoon

Kenneth Richman grew up in Boise, Idaho. He described a failed marriage that produced a daughter and son. Ken was a high school football coach and history teacher but moved on when he saw an ex-colleague make three times his income selling life insurance. He jumped into the industry and began making good money. Ken met Nancy at a church mixer and they were married within a year.

Soon, Ken started banking big insurance commissions. He began playing racquetball at the club with local business people. One of them offered him exclusive rights to market a new computer software program. The guy convinced Ken he could make millions in the emerging industry. He and Nancy invested all their savings to secure rights to the Arizona sales territory. They moved to Phoenix and kicked off their venture.

Ken was a well-polished storyteller. He leaned forward in his chair as he unwound his past for me, as though he was telling a ghost story around a campfire. I was putty.

"It took a while to make a sale because they were big-ticket orders and there were a lot of decision-making layers," he said. "After we sold our first few deals the software started crashing. Customers canceled. We had an 'out clause' that enabled us to sell the territory back; however, the guy we invested with wasn't returning our calls. We traveled to Boise, got to his office and it was abandoned. After a visit to the bank and a call to the sheriff's office, we found out the investor capital was gone and so was he."

"Nancy and I filed for bankruptcy. We called home to ask our parents for loans to get us through the month. We'd lost it all. Three weeks later I'm involved in a friendly game of park league basketball. This guy low-bridged me while I was going up for a rebound. He didn't mean to hurt me. It was a freak accident. My head hit the ground hard and when I came to, they were loading me into an ambulance. I felt numbness, first in my neck, my upper back, and then it moved down my arms. My neck was broken in two places. They took me to the hospital and screwed a metal halo into my head."

Ken leaned toward me, slowly brushing his blond hair away to reveal several scars where the halo had been attached. He placed the time-line of the accident at just sixteen months prior. I gazed at him. Surrounded by all this—the house, the Rolex, the luxury—I found it hard to believe Ken had been broke less than two years earlier. He explained that a friend with whom he'd coached basketball in Boise came to see him when he was in the hospital.

"He was the only person to offer any help when we were down and out," he said. "The marketing plan he drew for us was a home-based business, a multi-level marketing business."

And there it was...multi-level marketing. I had limited knowledge of "MLM", as the industry is commonly called. Multi-level marketing had been around since the 1940s. These deals enable people to run businesses out of their homes.

People involved in an MLM gig make money from sales they personally generate. They also recruit people, getting little pieces of what they sell. These companies were often criticized due to their similarity to illegal pyramid schemes. During the early 1970s the Federal Trade Commission cleaned house and the worst of the lot were forced out of business, leaving a handful of legitimate companies.

I was aware of some of the more popular MLM companies. The last guy who tried to get me into his deal was driving a 1975 Pinto with bald tires and was living at home with his parents. Ken wasn't living with his parents and he wasn't driving a Pinto. He was living in luxury.

"So he came to the hospital and pitched us," he continued. "The plan seemed logical, but looked small time stuff to me. Nancy was more eager than I was. I wasn't sure what to even say to him in my condition. I was in traction, a halo bolted into my skull. At that point the doctors weren't sure I'd even be able to walk again. My pal and his wife promised me that they'd teach Nancy how to make enough money so she'd have the financial means to take care of me."

I was perched on Ken's couch, listening closely. Ken explained how he and Nancy were sponsored and began building the business. They were working with products such as soap, vitamins, food supplements and personal care items.

"We work with a company that's the best at what they do," Ken said. "Their corporate headquarters are in Illinois. They're called American-Made."

I'd heard of them. They were one of the older, more respected companies. Ken grabbed a piece of note paper from the end table and began drawing circles. He filled each circle with the numerical value of $100. He drew six that directly connected to my name with a straight line. He called these circles "personal width." The $100 represented the amount of product each distributor was asked to move each month. He then drew four new circles below, connecting each one of them to the original six. These circles were distributors who would be sponsored "in depth" underneath my direct recruits. He went down one more level and added two new circles to each set of four.

Ken's pace quickened as he drew the circles. He called the basic example he'd just drawn, "me-you-six-four-two." In his example I would sponsor six people, "in width," and then help each of them sponsor at least four others "in depth," and they'd each get two more people involved. Each circle represented a hundred dollars a month of AmericanMade's product volume.

"What's so beautiful about our way of building the business," he explained, "Is there's no door-to-door, no retailing. We don't do any of that crap. We can sponsor higher-level professionals and ask them to consume the hundred bucks a month. By the time you complete the 'me-you-six-four-two' phase you'll be earning an extra two thousand bucks a month."

My mind flashed on the reality that there were many months I wasn't earning two grand to begin with, let alone an *extra* two thousand a month. That kind of money would change my current condition. He shifted gears and grew excited as he explained the next stage.

"This is just the start, Tony. We're going to teach each of your personally sponsored distributors how to create six of these six-four-two groups underneath you."

He started drawing more circles, shoving numbers and dollar signs onto the paper until it was soaked with ink.

"By the time we duplicate six of these legs under you, you'll be banking a hundred grand a year in walk-away income," he said. "This normally takes five to ten years for the average AmericanMade distributor, but I did it in fourteen months. I can have you making a hundred grand in less than two or three years. I'm going to show you how to take every life insurance lead you run and sponsor those people into your downline. You'll show each lead how to form a home-based business and create tax savings. Here's the best part: they'll use part of the tax savings to fund their life insurance plan."

I glazed over, but I understood the crux of it. He was using the MLM business to help his life insurance business and vice versa. Each one was feeding the other. I didn't understand the fine details, but I didn't need to. I stopped listening when Ken said "a hundred grand of permanent income."

"As I said, no discussion of what we're doing and who's involved around Starbridge. I'll let you know who's in the business and who's not. No discussion, especially with Fred Cohen, got it?"

I nodded, trying to remain cool while sorting out what I'd just been offered. It all fed on itself and was rather brilliant in its synergy.

"You have a glow around you Tony," Ken continued. "You're an underachiever. I can tell. I sense you want to be great, but you don't have a clue how to get there. You've got nobody to follow who knows how to make big money."

There was that word again. Underachiever.

"You need to ask yourself a couple questions," Ken continued. "Where do you want to be in five years? Whom are you following who can get you there? Who has the fruit on the tree to help you?"

His questions hit home. I'd bit hard and he knew it. Ken looked at his watch and abruptly excused himself. He returned a few minutes later in a coat and tie and motioned for us to follow. He told us he was heading to a "house meeting" down in Orange County to "show the plan—draw some circles." He opened the trunk of his Cadillac, revealing hundreds of cassette tapes. He tossed a few of them to me.

"These tapes aren't from AmericanMade. All they do is supply us with products. All of our training comes from what we call our *upline* support system. The guy that sponsored me has a few guys upline from him that formed an alliance. These guys control the support system that supplies us with all the tapes, books and training events we need to build the business. Listen to these cassettes tonight and we'll talk on Monday."

He jammed his key into the ignition, threw us a wave and was gone. Rex lit up a Marlboro. He had a big shit-eating grin on his bearded face.

"What do you think of Ken?" he asked.

I chuckled nervously. I wasn't sure what to say or think. I'd just been run over by a Mack truck of financial opportunity. I spent a few minutes trying to convince Rex that he should sponsor me at happy hour. I finally gave up when he smugly told me he was "drawing circles for a new prospect" that evening.

The tapes Ken gave me sat idle in my passenger's seat for a few miles. I cranked up a Blue Oyster Cult tape in an attempt to silence the noise bouncing around in my head. Eventually I reached over and grabbed one of the tapes. I twirled it around in my hand and pondered what the message on it might be.

The cassette was titled, *Don't Let Anybody Steal Your Dream*. I was curious so I popped it into my deck. The speaker on the tape was a guy named Beau Willis. He had a heavy southern accent, but even with his annoying twang, I found myself sucked in. The content of his message was mesmerizing. He described when he and his wife were broke and had "more month than money each month." He said, "Our typical work week now consists of six Saturdays and a Sunday." I was enthralled. I pulled into my driveway and cut the motor, but left the tape running.

"How many of you are livin' from paycheck to paycheck, makin' every decision on money, lookin' at your parents and wonderin' if you'll wind up just like them? How many of you wanna wake up at the crack of noon instead of wakin' up to that stinkin' alarm clock at 6 a.m. every morning?"

Beau Willis closed out his talk, lowering his voice to a seductive whisper.

"Let me tell you the truth my friends—and it says this in my Bible: 'The truth shall set you free.' Are you willing to pay the price for five years so you can be free for a lifetime? God bless you and God bless this business. Ain't it great!"

I walked through the front door of my home. As if on cue, the phone rang. My mom wanted to know how my week had gone, if I was working too hard and if I had enough food in the fridge. After I put her mind at ease she put my dad on the phone.

"Hey Sport, what's new?" Buzz asked. "When are we going to the driving range to hit a bucket of balls?"

I'd coaxed my dad into trying his hand at the game of golf shortly after I took it up at age thirteen. He had a homemade game. He'd swing so hard he corkscrewed himself into the turf. He didn't care. He loved hanging out with me at the range.

"I'm sorry Dad. I've been real busy the last week or two," I told him.

Yeah, real busy screwing off. I wanted to tell him all about Ken Richman, but wasn't sure how to broach the subject. I wasn't sure how to describe the opportunity to him.

"I had a meeting with a guy today. He's making a lot of money in multi-level marketing," I blurted. "He wants to teach me how to do it."

"Really?" he asked.

"He told me he can get me to a hundred grand in two or three years. A hundred grand of permanent income, guaranteed," I told him.

"I'm sure it all sounds good, Sport, but don't kid yourself into believing it's permanent, and don't count on the income being guaranteed," he said. "Be careful what you decide to chase after. It seems like right now you just need to keep your head down at your job and make sure you have your house payment covered next month."

My dad's words, as well-meaning as they were, cut like a rusty blade. I didn't want fatherly advice at that moment. I wanted a cheerleader. I kept quiet.

"You there, Sport?" he asked.

"Yeah," I replied.

"All I'm saying is be careful. All that glitters isn't gold. Be careful about the choices you make and who you follow. Maybe take a little more time to research this guy and his operation."

I'd just finished listening to the tape. At one point Beau Willis mentioned that if you get excited about the business and tell your family or friends about it, they are likely to be negative. He said they'd try to "steal your dream."

"Thanks for the advice," I said. "I've got to go."

I slammed down the phone without saying goodbye and as soon as I did I felt horrible. I tossed my briefcase on the imitation wood dining room table and trudged into my bedroom. I rattled some spare change out of my blue ceramic pig. The pig was my lone source of emergency funds at that juncture in my life. It coughed up three bucks. With a few singles in my pocket and the coupon taped to my fridge, I had enough for a cheese pizza with no extra toppings.

I placed a delivery order and grabbed a cold forty. I flipped on the stereo, opened my sliding glass door and flopped down on a rusty beach chair that sat in my dirt-patch tract-home backyard. I commenced my solitary version of happy hour, floating away in the music. As hard as I tried, I couldn't switch my brain off. I began asking myself those questions.

Where do I want to be in five years?

Who am I following that can get me there?

Who has the fruit on the tree to mentor me?

As much as I loved and respected my father, he couldn't teach me how to make real money. He'd never earned more than $36,000 in a year. I had an intense fear of waking up some day, thirty something, broke. Like those guys in the other cubicles at Starbridge—still selling life insurance over the kitchen table. Making a lot of money would make me happy, fix things, change my life. I believed that. For the moment I was fixated on the circles Ken drew.

I heard the doorbell and scooped up the change, crumpled bills and the coupon. When I opened the door Mazal was standing there holding my pizza box with a grin.

"I intercepted the delivery guy. Pizza's on me."

My best friend grabbed a slice, kicked back on my sofa, making himself at home. I grabbed the last remaining beer and handed it to him. He commandeered the TV clicker and put on the Dodgers. We ate pizza, drank beers, listened to Vin Scully and swapped commentary on the game. My best buddy had no way of knowing that I was down to seventeen bucks in my checking account. Because he'd bought the pizza, I could put gas in my car for the weekend.

I tried to sink into our Dodger conversation and let it wash away the anxiety I was hiding. I was physically there but mentally nowhere near Mazal or the seventh inning. All I could think about was my meeting with Ken...and Buzz's subsequent warning. I couldn't shake the notion that I'd just met someone who could change my life.

I stared blankly at the TV, wolfed down the last slice of pie and made my decision. I would take the ride with Ken Richman. I'd call Rex and Ken on Monday and tell them I was, "IN." What better option did I have?

4

Winter 1983

There were unwritten rules. I learned about them soon after joining the business. Before Rex Logan and I even knew what they were, we were told they shouldn't be broken.

I was issued a few uniforms. One was a nylon tracksuit; the other was a pinstriped business suit and a few red and yellow power ties. Wearing the trendy tracksuits in the middle of the week was supposed to convey we were living the dream. It was a persona Ken believed in and if Ken believed it, you believed it. Our Mafia inspired business suits were worn at night and had to fit well. Ken's tailor cost more than I made in a month. Rex was kind enough to cover me.

Rex and I had always enjoyed a good ribbing at the other's expense. He'd be the first to mock my hangovers and I never missed an opportunity to point out his eyes turning a vibrant shade of red after he'd smoked out. It was all in good fun but as with several aspects in my life, that too was about to change.

The business was alcohol and drug free. There was no wiggle room, no wiggling of any sort, actually. Even in the elaborate home of Ken Richman, the mahogany bar stood empty. Not a bottle of liquor in sight. Rex and I had an unspoken agreement. I wouldn't mention his hobbies and he wouldn't mention mine.

The business was squeaky clean and so were we as long as we were in view of our upline. There was a heavy Christian influence in the business that we figured we needed to respect. I was raised Roman Catholic, so I could fake it real good. Rex was a born again agnostic, so I wasn't quite sure what he was going to do. If you were married, then you built the business as a couple and you each had a role. If you were single, you were waiting for the right person, not test-driving multiple partners.

From the moment I told Ken I was, "in," I began to change. I shaved every day, my hair was brushed and my car was washed. I learned the products, knew the AmericanMade award levels by heart and followed the top distributors the way I idolized my sports heroes. I knew never to question, only to follow.

The seven months since I'd signed up as an AmericanMade distributor had moved quickly. I felt like I'd gone to sleep and woken up a different person. But I wasn't sleeping much. In fact, I'd learned that when you worked with Ken Richman, sleep would be in short supply. The business had become my life.

Ken was a big brother to me, and at times, my drill sergeant. He wouldn't let me off the hook and didn't allow me to slack off. The days of rolling into Starbridge at noon and leaving for three-hour doughnut sessions with Rex and Annie were a faded memory. He had us operating at factory capacity. We were living the Ken Richman doctrine: sleep when you're dead.

I'd been hosting two "show the plan" meetings a week at my house since I became a distributor and was drawing circles almost every other night. My body had gotten used to the amount of coffee my new lifestyle demanded. My car had gotten used to late nights on the L.A. freeway system and I swore my tongue was turning unhealthy shades of orange, pink or red from ingesting a substance called Power Punch.

Power Punch was a staple product of the business. It was the only beverage served at our meetings. I pounded down the powdered substance every chance I got. We each had to move a minimum of $100 of AmericanMade products each month. That was the commitment we made. Because we didn't sell door-to-door or do retail, I was trying to personally consume all I could from our AmericanMade catalog so that I could meet that commitment.

That was the sale we made to people coming in. They'd have their own business, their own catalog of products, but they wouldn't actually have to sell anything. In addition, we'd hype them on all the additional tax advantages they'd have as business owners. The typical family of four could easily consume one or two hundred dollars or more each month simply through personal use.

But I wasn't a family of four, so I was living off Power Punch and Muscle Bars. There were days that I didn't eat regular food till dinner. I was also dousing myself with the odorous Bora Bora men's cologne. I figured I could eat, drink and stench my way to a hundred dollars each month. I could easily have spent the money each month to launder my tracksuits. Ken didn't care what I did with the growing stack of AmericanMade product boxes in my garage. He told me to "bury them in the backyard" if I couldn't move them.

After my initial meeting with Ken, I didn't think too long or hard about what he was offering. I called Rex the next Monday morning. Rex was technically my sponsor, but Ken made it clear that he'd be mentoring me personally. Rex didn't take umbrage to this arrangement. The way he figured it, Ken would be doing some of his work for him. That concept appealed to his hippie nature.

My MLM business with AmericanMade was growing steadily as were my life insurance commissions at Starbridge. Fred Cohen gave me a big smile when I was in the office. He seemed proud of my turnaround. For the first time I even had a little cushion in my checking account. The Richman boot camp was grueling, but paying off.

As soon as I signed up, I drafted a list of everyone I knew on a first name basis, as Ken had directed. I phoned each of them and used what we called the "curiosity approach." I'd entice them to attend a house meeting where we'd show them "the plan." A few of the people on my list agreed to attend, but most didn't. Some were polite when they turned me down. Others weren't so cordial.

A few prospects laughed at me, accusing me of being part of an illegal pyramid scheme. I tried to explain that it was all very legitimate and AmericanMade was an established company. The rebuttals didn't seem to make much of a difference. People had preconceived notions about our industry. Their minds were closed. The tapes called this condition "stinkin' thinkin.'"

I learned a valuable axiom one evening from one of Ken's personally sponsored guys, Stan Schultz. Stan was an aerospace engineer, like my dad had been. He was reserved, but very warm once you got to know him. He was in his early sixties and in pretty good shape for his age except for a slight limp from what he described as an old college football injury. With his wire-rimmed glasses, short sleeve shirts and pocket protector, he could have been mistaken as a nerd, but my guess was he'd be the last person to back down from a fight.

Stan's wife, Katy, was quiet, but strongly supportive of her husband and what they were trying to build to supplement their retirement. She was a beautiful woman with a grandmother's smile. Her weeks were filled with volunteer work and church meetings.

Stan cornered me after a house meeting at Ken's one night. I guess my frustration was evident. I'd grown tired of people no-showing my meetings, and I was over being laughed at. He knew I needed a talking to.

"Tony, you won't last long unless you develop a thick skin. The way I see it, some will, some won't, so what!" He took out his yellow pad and wrote out the letters, *SWSWSW*. He tore off the page and handed it to me.

"Tattoo these letters on your brain and you'll do fine," he said.

Stan's sage wisdom and humor was just what I needed that night. He was a calming influence and a voice of reason. From that point forward he and Katy were my surrogate parents in the business. They reminded me of my own parents in many ways.

Stan and Katy were plodders. They weren't building the business fast,

but were convinced they'd get what they wanted if they continued drawing circles, listening to the tapes and attending the meetings. They were
typical of many of the distributors I'd met. Many were in their late forties, fifties or even their early sixties. They'd realized that their companies
didn't give a shit about them and their stupid jobs had a glass ceiling. Sitting home clipping coupons, and worrying about the money lasting after
retirement wasn't their kind of American dream.

For Stan and Katy, supplementing their retirement was first and pursuing their dream of buying a new top-of-the-line RV was a close second.
Like good members of the congregation, they followed instructions. This
meant plastering a picture of their dream vessel on their refrigerator beside
family photos and grocery lists: Implanting dreams as if they were obligations, as if they were as obvious as the need to buy milk and eggs.

I had much larger goals and a different timeline than Stan and Katy
Schultz. To build the business as fast as I wanted, I had to show the plan to
anyone who would stand still. As a result, I'd started to look at people dif-
ferently. If I were standing in line at the store, I'd devise a reason to begin
a conversation with the person next to me. At first it was awkward and my
approach was pathetic, but soon it became second nature for me to stalk a
stranger and get a phone number.

AmericanMade had achievement levels related to the amount of product you moved monthly and the number of "personal legs" it moved
through. Ken and Nancy had just qualified at the Emerald level and entered Diamond qualification. AmericanMade used gemstones or precious
metals to signify their levels of recognition. The company awarded you a
small lapel pin imbedded with the corresponding jewel when you hit that
level. People killed themselves to get to the "next pin level."

The Richmans were six months away from hitting Diamond, the big
prize. They would become one of the fastest couples to ever reach the Diamond pin level in AmericanMade's history.

The pin levels started at 1,500. They called this the "believer's pin." It
was suggested that upon joining the business you focused on the first three
levels within your initial twelve months. I was wearing my 1,500 pin and

rapidly on my way to 4,000. The funny thing was, I wasn't necessarily looking forward to hitting the Silver level, which was 7,500. When people attained that pin level they were asked to make a quick speech on stage at our monthly event. The idea of public speaking made me nauseous.

Ken had been pushing me to focus on the Diamond level from the second I signed up.

"It's the big prize, Tony. This is where you need to be in the business," he told me over and over. "This is the only level you need to focus on in the business."

Everybody on the inside simply referred to AmericanMade as "the business." If you were talking to someone about *the business* you could have an entire conversation in code.

Understanding the business meant knowing every cog in the machine. I learned the pitch, how Ken romanced me under his wing. I'd been taught to draw circles—perfect, enticing circles—with my red felt marker on my yellow pad. I was learning to push the tapes, the ones that filled Ken's Cadillac trunk and soon filled my Oldsmobile trunk.

Beau Willis, the man behind the cassettes, was an independent distributor a few levels upline from Ken. Willis formed a private corporation, Willis Enterprises, many years earlier. It was his entity, separate from AmericanMade. Willis mass-produced and supplied his downline with training and motivational materials. This included tapes, books, and a full calendar of seminars held each month around the country.

AmericanMade's home office did a great job producing and shipping household products; however, they didn't have the infrastructure to train or support their distributors' sales and recruiting efforts. Beau Willis refined a system to support his downline. It worked well and American-Made was fine with the arrangement. There were other systems like Willis Enterprises dotted across the US, but his training and motivational system was the envy of all others.

The Willis Enterprises training catalog had more than four hundred cassette tapes from which to choose. We were trained to place each new distributor on a "standing order." This meant that each distributor automatically received and paid for the newly produced tape of the week. We were masters at persuading our downline to purchase additional tapes and books each week to build their educational libraries.

Ken impressed the importance of upline support referring to it as "plugging into the system." He often told us the organization was bigger and more powerful than any one person. Ken believed if we plugged people into the Willis machine, they couldn't fail. He knew the lessons on the tapes and he knew how effective they could be on someone in the business. I'd seen the fruits of his labor and had no problem selling tapes in exchange for that opportunity.

Rex and I weren't completely gullible. We did the math. The tapes were sold to us at four dollars. Although we knew there were hard costs in the production, packaging and handling of the tapes, we knew there had to be some profit. Ken turned giddy when we inquired. He'd dangle the answer in front of us with a line like, "Profit sharing comes with the bigger pins. Get there and find out."

Rex and I had just returned from our first major Willis Enterprises motivational event. It was in Eugene, Oregon. They called it "Go Diamond Weekend." I originally wanted to skip the event. My twenty-two year old mind couldn't fathom a weekend with a bunch of married couples in their forties, but Ken, Rex and even Stan and Katy talked me into attending.

I didn't want to spend money on a plane flight, so I wound up hitching a ride to Oregon with Stan and Katy in their vintage Winnebago. It wasn't a big RV, but somehow they'd jammed eight bodies into the tin can for the journey. I was squeezed into the dinette with a few of their distributors. Of course, there was no beer or alcohol of any kind on board, just Power Punch and a deck of cards. It was the longest road trip of my life.

I'd never been to a motivational event. I had no idea what to expect when I arrived in Eugene, but the moment we rolled into the arena parking lot I was in awe. People swarmed the venue from all directions, thousands of them, all dressed in business attire. We paid our fees, passed through the turnstile and into the lobby. The atmosphere felt like a rock concert. The arena held seven thousand and was near capacity. I took my seat, my pulse racing to the beat of the crowd, and soaked in the surroundings.

The crowd rose to their feet, clapping in unison to the beat of the song *Eye of the Tiger*. The silhouette of a couple appeared on stage behind the curtain. A booming voice bellowed out of the public address system:

"Ladies and gentlemen, please welcome to the stage your upline Triple Diamonds, Beau and Rhonda Willis!"

The applause grew in intensity as Beau and his wife emerged into view. The roar was deafening as they stood on stage, working each side of the venue, waving and blowing kisses. They were royalty.

As an audience, we were a sea of color-coded clones. Men were all wearing the official AmeicanMade business uniform—dark suits and red or yellow ties. Ladies were all conservatively dressed, skirts below the knees and high necklines.

The Willis' opening statements were powerful messages of the real possibilities of personal and financial freedom. Beau's chubby pink cheeks bounced with each word, Rhonda nodding along hypnotically to his sermon. They spoke of the stature and wealth they'd built due to the business. I closed my eyes and mentally transported myself to the front seat of my car seven months earlier, when I first heard him on tape. I opened my eyes realizing how far I'd come. Beau and Rhonda Willis painted a picture of where I could go.

Each speaker that afternoon and evening, one after another, offered similar messages. Rex and I listened closely as each couple gave witness to how AmericanMade offered them opportunities and how Beau Willis changed their lives. Katy grasped Stan's hand with a squeeze of a promising future. We basked in the afterglow of each speaker's success.

The over-the-top event culminated with a quasi-optional Sunday morning non-denominational Christian service. Ken suggested we attend. The worship service concluded with an alter call. Beau came to the stage and asked if there was anyone who had "not yet committed his or her life to Jesus Christ."

Rex lived a secular lifestyle. His comments over the years led me to believe he didn't subscribe to any particular god, but wasn't completely willing to cast out the idea either. Because of my force-fed catholic up-bringing, I was religious on holidays, when I was in trouble or when my mom insisted. My mother instructed me to pray to the saints based on my specific needs—not that I ever prayed.

While the altar call was unfolding, Rex and I quietly slipped out to the lobby passing Stan and Katy Schultz. I couldn't tell if they were in their religious element or simply more willing to play the game than I was. They'd never come off as zealously religious yet they were the biggest believers I'd ever met. The business to Stan and Katy was a chance at the future of their dreams.

Our walk back to the hotel was too quiet. After a while Rex said, "That was a trip." I laughed, a little concerned about what kind of business I'd gotten myself into. I smiled at him, nodded my head and muttered, "Amen."

Even with the unexpected religious dogma on display we couldn't help but be absorbed by it all. While on stage, Willis instructed us how to dress for success and how men should groom themselves. Willis had a disdain for long hair and beards. As a result, I cut my hair even shorter when I got back from the event. Rex trimmed off the beard he'd worn since college at Kent State. The purpose of the function was obvious. The power of it was ominous. We saw how our new distributors responded to the event. The look of hope on their faces said it all. We all wanted to be up on that stage one day, living that lifestyle, earning what they earned.

As my MLM business grew, I spent less time at Starbridge. I was avoiding Fred. He'd tried to corner me at one point, asking me about Rex and Ken—where they were. It was all I could do to escape out the back door. It was starting to feel awkward. The office started to look small to me, and my stupid cubicle seemed even smaller.

5

March 1983

My mornings had become a ritual of reminding myself where I'd been and how far I'd come. This morning was no different than any other until the doorbell rang. I threw on a bathrobe and looked through the peephole. There, on my porch in the chilly morning air, dressed in tracksuits, stood Ken and Rex.

I unlatched the door and they walked in, barely mumbling hellos. I was ready to close the door behind them when Annie Wu came around the corner. She rolled a dolly of file boxes toward the front door. The boxes were stacked over her head. Annie gave me a charming smile as she passed, juggling to steady the leaning tower of boxes, almost tripping over her high heels.

"Sorry for the early morning wake up call. Nice bathrobe!" she jabbed.

Annie doing heavy lifting for Ken was occurring more often in their relationship. She'd attached herself to Ken just after Rex and I had joined forces with him. She wasn't alone; Ken had recruited other lackeys, but in this case the connection was stronger than that. She was becoming his overworked shadow, keeping the same hours—but not aggressively build-ing her MLM business like the rest of us. I assumed she was more inter-ested in being his unofficial executive assistant.

Ken and Rex helped themselves to some coffee while Annie wheeled a second load of boxes into my living room. I wasn't sure what was going down, but wasn't wide-awake enough to put up too much of a fight.

"What's with the file boxes?" I asked through a yawn.

Ken didn't blink as he dumped milk into his coffee cup. He stirred it with the handle of a dirty spoon he'd fished out of my sink.

"We used my keys to open the Starbridge office last night. We cleaned out all our files...yours too."

He nonchalantly dropped the tidbit on me as though it was no big deal. He sat down at my dining room table with his cup of coffee, making himself at home.

"Sit. Let's talk," he said. "I know you like Fred. I like him too. He's a good guy but it is time for us to walk."

"Walk? What do you mean?"

"Our time at Starbridge is over," he calmly replied. "We've recruited everyone we want out of there. Fred's asking too many questions—trying to micro-manage us."

I searched Rex's face for some sort of acknowledgement. I expected to see his calming smile or hear his familiar chuckle, the one that always gave away a practical joke. But instead, Rex stoically bobbed his head in agree-ment, deferring to Ken, not saying a word.

"Fred doesn't dig our MLM business," Ken said. "He figured out how large it's grown. It would be toxic for us to stay. Since we need to continue selling insurance for a while, we need a more controlled environment."

It hit me. Ken had made a career decision for me without my consent. My mind was reeling. I was irritated and confused as I watched the file boxes reproduce like bunnies in my living room.

"What the fuck is with all these boxes?"

"Look, we have this all figured out. We need a place to set up shop for a few weeks. We can't do it at my house." He pointed at Rex. "I'm allergic to his cats. You live alone and this was the most logical place until we find office space here in the Valley. This is all temporary."

Before I could ask another question, he launched into his plan.

"Our new insurance agency is named Richman Financial. Rex and I met with a few life insurance carriers last week and secured some juicy contracts. We'll have some additional phone lines installed here. Rex is the V.P. of marketing; you're the V.P. of sales. Annie will be the executive administrator and office manager."

Ken motioned to Annie. She subserviently retrieved four sets of business cards. Ken passed them out. For a moment, seeing the "V.P." title beside my name trumped my irritation. Annie was busy unpacking a box that was marked "facsimile machine."

"Where can I plug this in?" she asked.

My eyes left the stack of business cards. I stared at Annie as she lifted the machine out of the box and balanced it on her thighs.

"Shit, Annie. I really don't know," I said, unnerved by the sudden remodeling of my home.

"Buddy, trust me," Ken said. "This is temporary. Annie and I are working with a commercial leasing agent to find a suitable office on Ventura Boulevard. This is just for a few weeks."

I took a deep breath and tried to understand their proposal. It wasn't as if Ken was going to set up shop in his pristine home. Ken and Nancy had to keep their lives picturesque.

Rex's north Valley apartment was obviously not an appealing option to Ken due to his allergy to cats. It was just as well. Rex and his wife Linda did all of their meetings at other people's homes, because their pad often smelled like a combination of kitty litter and pot smoke. As Ken stoically popped open and poured out the last three Pabst Blue Ribbons I had left in my fridge, I realized Rex's survival in the business depended on his private life staying private.

Annie lived all the way out in Culver City, but I'm sure that wasn't the only reservation about using her place as a temporary office. Her household was lively with two growing boys, after-school activities, and pet hamsters that had the run of the house. Annie's home was full of life. Mine was full of space.

On his way out the door, Ken flashed his trademark shit-eating grin.

"We'll talk later today, buddy...your life's about to change. You're a vice president now."

Vice president of what? My living room?

Ken backed his El Dorado out of the driveway. I stood frozen on my porch, dazed, with my bathrobe flapping in the breeze. All I could think about was how Fred was going to feel when he arrived at his office and realized two-thirds of his business had been wiped out in the middle of the night. I doubt in Fred's wildest dreams he'd ever think the vice president he hired to help build his agency would be the one to clean him out.

I couldn't delude myself. I knew Ken would eventually betray Fred and we'd have to break away. I'd shoved the thoughts of that likely outcome down below the consideration of my potential income. Guilty feelings bubbled up to the surface as I closed the front door and walked back into my living room.

I gazed at the stacks of boxes and sank into my couch, mind racing. Had Ken planned to clean out Fred and Starbridge from the start, or did the split become essential as Ken grew more powerful and Fred more paranoid? I quickly reached the conclusion that either scenario was plausible, but the truth wouldn't change Ken's plans.

It wasn't the time for me to worry about Fred Cohen. After all, he drove a Rolls Royce and lived in a mansion in Beverly Hills. Why should I spend time worrying about him? Ken was my mentor and friend. He'd changed my way of thinking completely, helped me reinvent myself and he lifted me out of the financial hole I was wallowing in. I was making decent money for the first time in my life.

My home had just become Ken's property. Fueled by the promise of riches and sandwiched between file boxes, I poured myself another glass of Power Punch and washed down my guilt.

6

Spring Break

Another six weeks of sixteen-hour workdays had worn me thin. The cool winter air had disappeared and it was spring break, college break, which meant my high school buddies were back in town looking for a good time, as was I. Some old school Saturday night depravity seemed a fitting reward for the hours I was putting in.

I owned the only crash pad not inhabited by parents, so naturally the shindig materialized at my home. Mazal got on the phone and made the calls. He conjured up an instant house party complete with an ex-girlfriend of mine. The drunken festivities that occurred the night before left me in a thick fog that morning. I stumbled into the kitchen, careful to avoid the broken bottles and discarded clothing scattered across the floor. Beer cans and liquor empties formed a trail into the backyard.

I looked around my living room. Even in my hung-over state I knew I had more furniture before I passed out than I did at that moment. Poking my head outside I found a circular arrangement of random pieces forming a makeshift living room in the dirt. The *coup de grace* was a carefully stacked pyramid of beer cans. Minor details of the evening crept back into my soggy brain.

I dropped down onto my new outdoor seating arrangement and fished around for whatever was sticking out between the cushions. I unearthed an empty beer can and a pair of red panties. Stretching out across the love seat I closed my eyes and allowed the night to replay in my mind.

My ex and I got right into reacquainting ourselves the minute she arrived. We got real busy with each other after everyone else stumbled home. She could have left with the rest, but she stayed. It started in the kitchen. She playfully pushed me against the sink. I'd forgotten how much fun she was, or maybe I'd forgotten what fun felt like. She tasted like cherry lipgloss. We christened places in my house I didn't know possible and gave anyone with a view of my backyard a good show.

I don't recall when she left. It was better that way. I couldn't take the look on her face when she realized our relationship was still not happening. That night I clearly recognized a slight shift in everyone I once knew. They were having awesome college experiences while I was earning my degree in MLM.

When my ex-girlfriend, Kathy, originally went off to a small private college in the Midwest a few years earlier she'd sent me letters about how much she missed me and loved me. I never knew how to tell her those feelings were hers and hers alone. I was too immature and self-absorbed to even respond properly. The letters eventually stopped. I assumed they stopped when she realized I didn't feel about her the way she felt about me. A giggle in her tone while rehashing those days made me think it wasn't that she realized I lacked feelings for her, it was that she realized the silliness of her own feelings.

Yet she was familiar. Her sexy smile made me feel like a teenager again, taking me back to our senior year in high school—taking me back to lifeguard station number 11 on our stretch of beach in Santa Monica. Every time she was home we forgot how far we'd grown apart. Every time she came by we'd revisit those good vibrations. Every time she left I was relieved.

I needed to tidy up the house. It would be business as usual the next morning with Rex, Annie and the agents arriving at 8:00 AM. Ken's promise of using my home as an office for "a few weeks" had turned into a few months, but I'd gotten used to it.

I moved my furniture back into place and shoved the empties into garbage bags. I destroyed all evidence that I still occasionally lost control and partied like Mick and the Stones. Ken may have suspected I backslid once in a while, but I certainly didn't want to rub it in his face.

I crashed on the love seat, exhausted from cleaning and in dire need of a nap. The ringing of my phone spoiled my plans. I found the cordless phone handset wedged beneath a cushion and reluctantly answered it. It was Ken.

"I need you to meet me tomorrow morning."

He gave me an address on Ventura Boulevard and hung up.

Tony DiBona, the slacker, was long gone. You didn't screw-off around Ken. When we first started working together he said, "You either have a full calendar or a fool's calendar." He said a lot of cute shit like that.

Other changes in my life were subtler. The previous night's carnival seemed like a good idea when Mazal suggested it, but halfway into the evening's drunk-fest I was already regretting it. I found myself trying to tidy up the house in the midst of the festivities. I was relieved when the party broke up and all of them went home. The banging headache was a temporary reminder of the lifestyle I didn't completely identify with anymore, but still occasionally craved.

I'd somehow remembered the address Ken reeled off to me. It was one of the most exclusive buildings in the Valley, right across the street from the iconic Sherman Oaks Galleria. Ken introduced me to the leasing agent. She was a boisterous lady with an east coast brogue that suggested she was from the Bronx. She snapped her gum loudly and ushered us to the vacant offices on the eleventh floor. The space was five thousand square feet and featured an ornate, marble reception area. She began the tour, squawking in my left ear while Ken babbled into my right.

"What do you think of this space," Ken asked, not waiting for an answer. He walked me down the main corridor pointing out private offices where key personnel would be stationed. Annie was already unpacking in her private office. She gave me a little wave as we passed but the smile on her face made me giddy. Annie had her own private office. I knew what that meant to her.

We continued down the hallway. There was an office for our Certified Financial Planner, a spot for the photocopy machine, then Rex's cushy spot. We neared the end of the hallway. Ken led me into an enormous corner office. It had spectacular views of Ventura and Sepulveda boulevards. I assumed it would be his office. "This is your office," Ken said. "The phone lines will be in tomorrow and the furniture delivered on Friday."

I was dumbfounded as I stared out the massive windows facing the Boulevard. The real estate agent began reviewing points of the lease with Annie as Ken draped his muscular arm around me. "I'm counting on you. I need you to step up big time. Make sure this agency makes money and keep your MLM business exploding. No guts, no glory, right?"

Annie entered, approached Ken and whispered into his ear. She appeared very much in charge. I'd originally thought Annie had become Ken's lackey, but she was crafty enough to leverage into the promise of equity in the new agency. She suddenly wasn't a struggling insurance agent any longer; she was a partner in an insurance agency.

Ken and Annie fled with the leasing agent in tow telling me to lock up on my way out. I was alone in the cavernous corner office. I leaned against the wall, then slid down to the newly laid carpet and gazed out the big window. I ran my hands back and forth over the taupe colored floor covering allowing the fibers to tickle my fingers. From that perspective I could see the top half of the nearby foothills and the massive homes perched on the hillside.

It had only been nine months since Rex introduced me to Ken. In a few days I'd be moving into a large corner office in the swankiest building in the Valley. I went from barely holding a job in a small cubicle to being vice president of a growing insurance agency, while my MLM business was thriving.

A wave of panic swallowed me. The part of me that feared failure was looming, ready to pounce. My father's words played in my mind. "All that glitters is not gold," he told me. "Be careful what you chase."

I continued to gaze out at the expensive homes floating in the foothills. Ken had built me up quickly. There was an immense opportunity ahead of me. I wasn't sure if it was real gold but I knew I was growing accustomed to the glitter.

7

June 1983

Nancy was seven months preggers with their first child together and she was unable to handle the duties of hosting any sort of social occasion, let alone a major surprise party for Ken. He doted on her every move—if he let her move. Ken's reaction to her pregnancy was as if he'd forgotten he had two kids from his previous marriage. He was a thrilled first time father-to-be for the third time.

They wanted to know the gender and Ken was ecstatic to learn the child would be a boy; he would be able to pass his empire on to this fortunate son. Ken had already selected a name: Chandler. Their child was due in late August.

Nancy enlisted my help. It would be a month until the next major organizational event, but she didn't want to wait that long to celebrate the big occasion. None of us wanted to wait. It was as if we all had qualified as Diamonds.

The party was a success. I arrived at 6:30 PM and the Richman house was already packed. Ken and Nancy's downline spilled into the backyard enjoying the warm Valley evening.

When Nancy reached out to me for help, I quickly reached out to Annie. It was an easy fix. I was better at the schmooze than the planning, plus Annie was a workhorse. Who better to pull off a surprise party than her? Annie had been meticulous, planning every detail from parking instructions and floral arrangements to who would give the speeches. She scheduled a late afternoon meeting for Ken giving her enough time to get everyone stashed in the house.

The energy was palpable. Stan and Katy Schultz arrived a bit early, hoping to show their devotion by helping to set up chairs and shower Nancy with comments about her glow. The Logans strolled in right on time; Rex smelling like he'd had a puff or two on the ride over. They never fully embraced the ass kissing involved in the business but were respectful and Rex's hippie upbringing wouldn't allow him to turn down a party with free food.

Ken walked in the front door right on time at 7:05 PM and was truly surprised. Everyone immediately started chanting, "Go! Go! Go!" Ken took his cue and stood on a chair. He pumped his fist three times as the crowd yelled, "Diamond! Diamond! Diamond!" It was one of many cult-like behaviors that I had come to find normal. Ken gave a quick speech and finished it with a big "Ain't it great!" for emphasis.

I'd been in the business for nearly a year. It had been a good year filled with good people, and I acted good around them. How much trouble could I get into when surrounded by Christian couples ten to twenty years older. Nancy had recently approached me, worried I wasn't having enough fun, concerned that I connect with some single people in the business, closer to my own age.

During the weeks leading up to the surprise party she began hyping me about spending time with her younger brother who was moving down to L.A. from Idaho. He was twenty-one, a year younger than me.

Apparently, Nancy's kid brother, Ted, had packed a lot of uncontrolled living into those twenty-one years. There were suggestions voiced about excessive partying. There were whispers about alcohol being the least of his problems. As a result, Ted had worn out his welcome at his parent's house. Ken and Nancy were stepping in, making sure he "straightened his act out."

The plan to keep Ted on the straight and narrow included Ken setting up a business for him. They'd make sure he had some responsibility and a steady income, while surrounding him with people who'd keep him out of trouble. Ken bought him a used Chevy van and set him up cleaning pools and tennis courts in his upscale neighborhood. Nancy enlisted me as a sort of babysitter. Originally, I wasn't too keen on the whole thing, but did find it ironic that they thought of me as a good influence. I hadn't lost my partying ways—I'd simply become better at hiding everything. Nancy told me he'd be moving in to their home the day prior to the big surprise party. Before I could talk my way out of it, Nancy spotted Ted and waved him over.

"I want my baby brother to meet one of my favorite young guys! I thought you two could hang out and have some fun—but not too much fun," she said. "Don't corrupt him, Teddy."

Ted smirked and held up his hand; evidently he was waiting for me to give him a high five. My first impression of the tall, thin simpleton with the popped Polo collar, moussed hair, tight jeans and cowboy boots was that he'd probably have to drop his pants to count to eleven. I slapped him an obligatory high five anyway. "Good to meet you, dude," he said. "Heard all about you."

Ted spun his head around, scanning the room with his beady blue eyes; then he nudged me out of earshot from Nancy. "You ready for an adult beverage?" he asked.

I stammered a quick, "Yeah." He motioned me over to the stairs. With Nancy distracted, we snuck up to his room. He'd stashed a bottle of rum in a planter box on his outside deck.

"Hey man, let's gas up that fuckin' punch of yours," he laughed.

Ted had given a name to the drink he was mixing: he called it a "Coo-pa Loopa." The concoction consisted of AmericanMade Tropical Flavor Power Punch and a stiff pour of Bacardi 151. I asked him what the name of the drink meant, but he didn't respond. He went off on a tangent explaining the many beverages you could mix with rum. This was my first experience in not getting a straight answer from Ted—but it wouldn't be my last.

The moment I set the drink to my lips, I wondered if I was being set up. Could this all be a chance for them to see if I'd been following the rules? My pulse quickened. I gazed out the window pretending to take in the scenery and prolonged ingesting the drink. I tried to think of a way out. I turned back to Ted and caught sight of him taking a small bump of the white stuff off his little finger. I realized not only was this not a set up, but any secret of mine would be minor compared to his problems.

He gestured to me, holding out the small vile of blow in my direction. I shook my head and he stashed it into his jeans pocket. We made some small talk about life in Boise compared to the speed of life in L.A. while we hurriedly polished off our drinks. As we did, I realized that Ted might be a useful addition to my world. First, he was on the inside of the business; he'd be able to tell me what was going on behind closed doors. Plus, I could use him as an additional escape valve without judgment. Lastly, he seemed to be an amusing guy. It had been awhile since my laugh wasn't fake and aimed toward a forty-year-old telling me a stale joke at a house meeting.

Most of my old high school golf buddies were hanging around less and less, even when college was out. They didn't understand the business; Mazal was busy getting his master's degree in Arizona. We were moving in different directions.

Ted and I each slammed down a second cocktail and headed back downstairs. Two black limos had arrived and six couples emerged from them. The couples were crossline from Ken. Crossline meant that they weren't directly upline, but they were peers in the organization. These couples would all soon be qualified Diamonds.

Stewart Moore was top dog in this next wave. He had an air of sophistication to his self-righteous persona and stank of upper crust. He and Ken were of like mind on most things and had formed a significant alliance. Moore was a high-level corporate guy with a large utility company in San

Jose. He'd climbed their corporate ladder as far as he planned to go. He had the kind of chiseled features and slicked-back dark hair that could easily get him cast onto a soap opera as the polished executive with a dark side. Moore was very steady, almost reserved in his manner, and a lot more conservative than Ken, but they seemed to collaborate well. In this case, opposites attracted.

There was another surprise in store for Ken. Moore blindfolded him and led him to the driveway where Nancy was waiting. When Moore removed Ken's blindfold he discovered his new custom built Auburn, a car like no other I'd ever seen. Nancy hid the vehicle in a neighbor's garage all week.

She was a beauty, a throwback to the pre-World War II era when cars were custom-made and only owned by the wealthy. The pearlescent white paint job and chrome bumpers reflected the lights while the burgundy leather interior gave off that unmistakable new car smell. The custom vehicle was one of only two hundred of its kind made that year. It was an ostentatious ride.

The car was adorned with a big silver bow and a banner that read, what else, "Ain't it great!" The faithful downline swarmed the car, snapping photos, draping themselves on the hood and climbing inside. Nancy had shown me a picture of the car earlier in the week, but eyeing the Auburn itself was an awesome experience.

I liked that I knew about the car ahead of time. It felt good to know the color choices of the paint and interior. Stewart Moore might have waltzed Ken to the car but that was all for show. I was the right-hand man. I'd be the first trusted by Ken to drive it other than himself.

Ken looked like Jay Gatsby posing beside it as the myriad of camera flashes blinded him. He looked good posing with an air of modesty, blushing a bit with every snap of the shutter. It was all well-orchestrated. Sometimes I wonder if it all would have disgusted me if I weren't on the inside, yet I was. The whole scenario had the stink of wealth and I wanted to bathe in it.

I glanced over at the bigger pins. They were standing together near

Moore and it was hard not to notice the symbols of unity. They had similar gold chains around their necks featuring eagles holding gemstones in their claws. The stones signified their pin levels: Pearl, Emerald or Diamond. They were all outspoken Christians, often leading a house meeting like a sermon. I wasn't all that outwardly religious but I prayed at the church of that Auburn in the driveway. My faith dangled in the form of gold chains around their necks. They stood together, arms draped over each other posing for photos. Envious of their bond and their cash flows, I soaked in the sight.

After everyone got their chance to fondle the new car, Moore waved the group back inside and called us to order. He handed Ken a small jewelry box, its contents courtesy of Beau Willis and the other Diamonds in the Willis organization. The ring was comprised of six gaudy diamonds surrounding one huge diamond—the significance being that you had to have six Gold distributors underneath you to qualify as a Diamond. I instantly wanted one for my hand.

Ken placed the ring on his finger and thrust his fist in the air. The crowd immediately went wild, again chanting, "Go! Go! Go!" as Ken stepped up on the stairs and pumped his fist in the air again, we all yelled, "Diamond! Diamond! Diamond!" I had a definite buzz from Ted's concoctions and was also swept up in the moment. I yelled along with the throng of sober partygoers. We were basking in Ken and Nancy's success. It was mind-altering to be part of a venture that was so successful. I'd never felt a rush like that before.

The last official act of the evening was a short speech by Ken. He commanded silence in the room by calmly waving his hand in the air.

"I want to express how much I love Nancy," he gushed. "Don't mistake it, she's the reason we've made it this far. She hung with me when we lost it all—when I was lying in the hospital with a broken neck. When our friends from Boise had the guts to show us the business, it was Nancy who saw it first. She said, 'Baby, we need to do this. This is our vehicle, this will make our dreams come true.'"

Ken fumbled in his pocket for a moment.

"I was planning on doing this in private, but..."

Ken's voice cracked as he pulled out a small box and looked at Nancy. "We didn't have a ton of money when we got married, sweetie. I bought you the nicest wedding ring I could afford. You've been my rock. Now you deserve a bigger rock of your own."

There was an audible gasp when Nancy opened the box. It was a monster solitaire diamond, the biggest stone I'd ever seen. Nancy clasped her hands to her mouth and burst into tears. She grabbed Ken and hugged him. She was speechless as he removed her old ring, and placed the new one on her finger.

I made my way to the top of the stairs overlooking the festivities. I soaked it in as the crowd cheered Ken and Nancy. The high provided by Ted's potent cocktails had fully kicked in as I scanned the living room. Annie lingered on the outskirts of the party below, inching closer and closer to the backyard clinging to an unlit Virginia Slim. She looked worn. She had an "always the planner, never the man of the hour" look to her. While her grin oozed with pride, her chain smoking and hidden yawns made me think Annie was anxious to leave.

Ted reappeared and motioned me to his room. We quickly slammed down another drink and he nonchalantly tossed the empty Bacardi bottle over the fence into the next-door neighbor's hedge. I gave him my phone number, threw a half dozen Tic Tacs in my mouth and slipped back downstairs.

I spotted Rex and his wife, Linda, heading out the door. I quickly fell into step with them and asked for a ride home. I was plenty loaded and didn't want to test my luck with the California Highway Patrol. I may have fooled Ken and some of the others, but I wasn't fooling Rex. He didn't ask any questions. He knew who I was and he smelled the liquor. Our time working together in the cubical world gave him a front row seat to all my drunken stages.

I was slumped down in the backseat as his wife, Linda, rambled on about how "wonderful" the surprise party was, how "cool" it was being around all the "big pins and the Auburn, and the jewelry." We were all feeling a sense of rapture. The business was more real to us now that Ken was a Diamond.

I shut my eyes to keep from getting carsick; I imagined what it would be like for me as images of Cadillacs and big houses in the hills rolled through my mind. I wanted to join their club and reap the money, recognition and freedom that came with the package. For me, it couldn't come fast enough. My life was spinning as fast as my head.

8

July 1983

The dinner break was over. I herded my group back to the high school auditorium in Manhattan Beach for the evening session of our monthly event. The Willis support system held a training and motivational event the last Saturday of each month in every city with enough distributors to fill a venue. My downline continued to expand along with the other legs of Ken and Nancy's organization. We were attracting attention in a big way.

The juggernaut that surrounded Ken spilled over on me, placing me more prominently in the spotlight. What made this particular evening so unique was that three new Silver pins in Ken's downline would be recognized on the same night. This would send out a signal to the Willis line of sponsorship that Richman's new Diamond organization was for real.

I was backstage with the Logans and the Steenbergs. Ken personally sponsored Steve Steenberg and his wife Samantha about the same time Rex and I signed up in the business. He was a local real estate agent and she was a homemaker. They were in their early thirties, originally from

South Africa. Their growth curve had tracked alongside the Logans and mine. We were the three new Silver pins being recognized.

Each event had an official host, usually a Pearl pin. The events also featured an Emerald or Diamond couple who would serve as the keynote speakers. The speakers for this event were an Emerald couple from Fresno. The husband, Cal, was a dentist that had built a huge downline and recently retired. The host approached me and asked if I could help collect money at the door, which was considered an honor at the events. As the faithful started pouring in, forking over their four bucks, I became conscious that the word was out. My Silver pin was a done deal and my Gold pin was right around the corner. People I didn't know were congratulating me. There were no other young, single Silver or Gold pins in Southern California.

I scooted to the front of the venue as our host brought the evening to order. The evening assembly was referred to as a rally—a motivational event—centered on recognition and testimonials. The host would recognize all new pin winners and then bring on the keynote speakers. Our host lined up the smaller pins near the stage. The 1,500 pin level award was given out first, then 2,500, then 4,000, and so on. We would be the last new pins to be recognized prior to the keynote speakers taking the stage.

I joined the Logans and Steenbergs on the steps to the left of the stage. The energy in the high school auditorium was an electric current. The buzz was audible. I was moments away from being handed a microphone and pushed into the middle of a stage in front of eight hundred people. I'd have to string a few coherent sentences together. The pulsating atmosphere wasn't making me feel any less nervous.

I lined up in front of the couples. I wanted to go first and get it over with. Just then, the event host's wife inched over and whispered to me, "They want you to go last, Tony."

I nodded submissively and moved to the end of the line.

The Logans spoke first. They didn't have a great handle on public speaking. They were homespun. Their lack of polish took a little pressure off me. The Steenbergs were next. The crowd seemed to like Samantha's cutesy Johannesburg accent and all of her cultural idioms. They earned a nice reaction from the crowd.

It was my turn. I stood on the verge of hyperventilating; telling myself it was no big deal. I made the mistake of glancing toward the audience. My eyes traveled directly to the second row. I'd recently sponsored my sister, Regina, and she'd convinced our parents and my aunt Jean to come to the event. Seeing them sitting there, beaming at me with proud smiles stirred emotions.

I scanned the crowd. There wasn't an empty seat in the house. Each wall was lined two-deep with men in dark suits and power ties. It looked like a Young Republicans convention. After eyeing family faces, familiar faces and random distributors, I caught sight of Stan and Katy. I felt a tinge of guilt by outperforming them. They applauded proudly. I'm not sure if that made it better or worse but they looked at me as the son they'd never had. It was something I fed off in moments like those.

As the Steenbergs walked off to a polite round of applause our host signaled me to center stage. My mind went blank and time moved in slow motion. I can recall the aroma of the varnished wood stage in the high school auditorium. It engulfed me with each step. I'd never been on a stage in front of hundreds of people before. That was for achievers, top athletes, and scholars.

The collective ovation became a roar. The crowd slowly began to stand. Before I could sputter a word, the raucous multitude started chanting my name. The host handed me the microphone, shrugged his shoulders and said, "For the next two minutes, Tony, it's your show."

I walked to center stage and felt an immediate calm wash over me. A smile broke out across my face. It was like a switch had been flipped inside of me. For the first time in my life, I was significant.

I don't know what I said. I do remember I ended my short address with, "Ain't it great!" and handed the microphone back to the host. The crowd was still on their feet and started chanting.

"Go! Go! Go!"

The host waved me back to finish the job. I strutted to center stage. Letting the energy build, I cupped my hand over my ear in a playful "I can't hear you" kind of way. They got louder as I wound up like I was preparing to hurl a fastball. I threw my fist in the air three times as the crowd yelled.

"Diamond! Diamond! Diamond!"

I disappeared into the wings.

The keynote speaker, Cal, grabbed me as I wandered into the darkness backstage. "Great job. You have awesome stage presence," Cal told me. "What an inspiration you've become to the singles on the west coast. We need a young guy like you to carry the torch," his wife said.

Our host was well into his introduction of Cal and his wife as they continued showering me with praise. I stammered a "thank you" as they hurried onto the stage to give their keynote address. I sat down on a metal folding chair backstage next to Rex and drew a deep breath. He was puffing on a Marlboro with a wide grin on his face. The smile was half-proud and half-mocking.

"I guess you're the new rock star," he said. "Good job. You knocked them dead."

I smiled politely and nodded, not sure how to respond. Cal and his wife wrapped up at 9:45. As was customary, many in the crowd approached the stage and formed an orderly meet-and-greet line. They'd pay homage to their heroes, shake hands and take photos. The Emeralds and Diamonds who would come to speak at these events were proof that you could make serious money, retire early and become financially free. Having human contact with someone who'd actually "done it" made it all seem real.

I left the backstage area and bumped into my family. Mom and Dad were swelling with pride. They were as overwhelmed as I was with the spectacle. We hugged and they said their goodbyes, told me they were heading home.

I turned to discover that an attractive young redhead had approached me. "You are an inspiration to the young, single distributors trying to build the business."

Her words were as flushed as her cheeks.

At some point she said her name was Stacy and followed it with a flutter of her eyelashes and a lingering handshake. She continued piling on the compliments as I caught Rex's grin over her shoulder. He gave that "eat it up while you can" nod. Married men loved giving me that nod.

I blushed and thanked Stacy, who was soon joined by a few other young women. She and her friends threw me more accolades. They were desperately trying to build the business so they also peppered me with a ton of questions. I was focused on them and didn't notice what happened around me. A line—more than twenty deep—had formed. The line was for me.

Over the next forty-five minutes I shook hands, posed for photos and accepted praise. I acted like I knew what I was doing. As it approached 11:00 PM, there was still a group of ten or fifteen singles hanging around, soaking up the afterglow. I looked up and saw Nancy's little brother. Ted was leaning against the side door taking in the whole scene.

Since the surprise party and those Coopa Loopa 151 cocktails, Teddy boy and I had become inseparable. My first impression was that he wasn't too bright. I was wrong; the guy was extremely clever, and great at working a room.

Unbeknownst to Ken and Nancy, Ted and I had been regularly trolling the Valley's finest nighttime establishments. He was more than simply an additional party escape valve for me; he had become another mentor of sorts. He was shark-like in a bar. If he saw a girl he liked, he'd circle. The girls rarely turned him down.

Glancing toward the exit to the high school's parking lot, I saw the Logans and Steenbergs as well as a few others in Ken's group. There'd been no meet-and-greet lines for them. Stacy grabbed me by the arm.

"Can we go grab some coffee? I know this great place near the beach."

I eagerly agreed and solicited Ted to herd the rest of the good-looking entourage off to coffee. I had to laugh. I'd never rounded up girls in a high school auditorium to get coffee before, not even when I was in high school. Ushering women into a bar was more my style.

I tried to imagine Mazal and me hitting on girls while chugging a hot beverage with foam moustaches. Yet you couldn't draw circles intoxicated and these girls didn't need a few drinks to think I was something special.

When we arrived at the coffee shop parking lot I took stock. Ted had convinced quite a few single, female AmericanMade distributors to join us. He jogged over to me with his hand in the air for his trademark high-five.

"Groupies! These are the perks of your stupid fucking business, dude."

I'd never cataloged people's vices before. Rex enjoyed a toke of some good pot, a Zeppelin album and his couch. Mazal and I caught our stride with a full kegger. Annie loved to suck down a Tequila Sunrise or two. Ted's drugs of choice included all of the above in addition to the blow he purchased in risky apartment complexes with his brother-in-law's money.

Although I was no altar boy, my drug of choice had suddenly become the applause of an adoring crowd. I felt it hum through my veins. This was a buzz I didn't want to lose.

9

Monday, August 1st, 1983

The spiritual influence Beau Willis and the Bible-thumping Diamonds exerted over their flock was becoming harder and harder to disregard. I swear if you were quiet enough you could hear the hymns. The subtle pressure caused the Richmans to act in even a more pious fashion than before. Bible verses crept their way into our conversations, the occasional swear words had evaporated and Ken's hearty pats on the shoulder became gentle hands guiding me in the direction he wanted me, usually in a pew in his Presbyterian church in Bel Air. I found myself nodding off in the Sunday services, usually recovering from a rough Saturday night. I didn't want to be there—yet I did it for the business.

Sometimes he'd ask me if I still "partied" with my old friends. He stopped short of telling me not to hang out with them, but I knew where his questions were headed. In truth, I was partying harder with his brother-in-law than I ever did with Mazal and my old crew, but Ken seemed oblivious to our barhopping activities. Teddy was my new partner in crime, allowing me to satisfy my craving for depravity.

The event in Manhattan Beach the previous month served as my coming out party. I was the next big success story for our upline organization to herald. I was their prototypical young, single, clean-living, successful distributor. The platoon of new Diamonds flaunted my rapid growth in their downline groups. They had as much to gain from my advancement as Ken.

I wasn't fighting off the lush recognition that was being thrown in my direction. There were definite advantages to being a minor celebrity in the business. Stacy, the pretty redhead, and a steady stream of enthusiastic single ladies began attending my house meetings and coffee shop gatherings. The increased female attention didn't elude Ken. He felt the need to give me the standard speech about "messing around" with girls in my downline and crossline. Whenever Ken preached to me, I simply nodded my head. I played the game the best way I knew how; trying so damned hard to be compliant.

The game kept me on my toes. I never knew if a crossline single woman was a test, interested in seeing if I was really as golden as I'd been described. Ken trusted me because Ken created me. Stewart Moore trusted me because he tested me. I was too close to getting what I wanted to screw it up by jumping in the sack with someone who would talk.

Basking in my newfound popularity, but yearning some old school normalcy, I accepted an invitation from Mazal. I joined him and his college newspaper cronies for a Dodger game. I'd just finished my first beer when I noticed her. She was settled in a few rows ahead. She was plenty cute with a contagious laugh. I found myself counting the seconds until she'd turn to toss a comment at her friend, giving me a passing glance. I started working Mazal for some info on her. She was a fellow college journalist and also a photographer. Mazal told me that her name was Gail and that she was from a "nice Jewish family." Most importantly, by the seventh inning stretch I had learned that she didn't have a steady boyfriend. That was all I needed to know to abandon Mazal and move two rows down into the empty seat next to her.

I began talking her up, using all my sales skills and those other skills that I had learned from watching Ted. She had a carnal look in her tiger brown eyes, and a dangerous lip-gloss enhanced smirk. As we exited Dodger Stadium, I suggested we keep the party going at my house. Nobody in the group disagreed.

I no sooner put my key in the door when Mazal located and cracked open the first bottle of booze. It was a handle of cheap clear tequila. Gail poured a double shot into a red cup and drank it before I could locate a shot glass or lime. She'd been trained well by her Tri Delta sorority sisters. Her drinking prowess wasn't the only trait we shared. The conversation was blurry, but the ease of it was amazing. Gail was smart and had a "one of the guys" personality tied up in a sexy package.

As the night rolled on, our impromptu after-party slowed down. There was an exodus of participants and Gail reluctantly followed her college crew out the door. I don't think she really wanted to leave, but also didn't think she wanted to look like the naughty girl who stayed behind in front of her college friends. She thanked me for hosting and gave me a soft kiss on the cheek. Her lips lingered, inviting me to make the next move. I thought about asking her to stay, but didn't.

I took a quick shower, regretting my decision. As I turned off the water I heard the doorbell. A smile broke out on my face. I knew who it was. I threw on a towel and hurried to the front door. I unfastened the deadbolt and she stepped in. Her kiss penetrated me. She kicked off her heels as we collapsed onto the living room couch. She wasn't the mindless old school normalcy I was expecting that night, but she was the physical release I needed.

Weeks passed and I didn't tell anyone about my ongoing liaison with Gail. I wanted an element in my life I could call my own. I didn't want my relationship to be scrutinized by Ken or the organization. I was taking precautions. Gail lived alone in a one-bedroom condo in Reseda so we'd meet there, or she'd come to my place, late at night, after I was done drawing circles. We'd have marathon sessions, then crash, and she'd leave before the sun rose.

Gail was more than just an experiment in sexual stamina. I loved our conversations. She worked at a local bank after classes but aspired to work in sales or marketing. She was extremely persuasive and never afraid to challenge me. I was constantly impressed by her mind as she discussed the success of a specific ad compared to the failure of another, or her opinion on art or politics. Gail was the type of person I wasn't used to and I couldn't get enough of her.

Our relationship had been perfect until a month into our tryst when she amped up her questions about the business. I knew it was coming. I gave her a little rap on how it worked but she wanted more. For a moment I thought I shouldn't go further. I loved the separation of my work and my play, yet I knew the potential in a woman like Gail: the stronger my downline, the faster my climb.

With my yellow pad and pen I did what I did best. I drew circles. She was enthralled. I watched her eyes grow wider. I could see the numbers crunching in her head. Within an hour we'd gone through the entire AmericanMade marketing plan and she'd started a list of which acquaintances she'd approach first. Gail signed up, became part of my downline and it was soon obvious that she was in it for more than just the discounts on soap and vitamins.

* * *

My evolving relationship with Gail was heavy on my mind as I wound my way up Beverly Glen Boulevard, high into the foothills on that warm summer morning. The big house in the hills was all Ken and Nancy had spoken of, fixated on the lifestyle upgrade. Nancy had given birth to their son, Chandler, two weeks prior. Chandler would never know a middle class lifestyle. He'd also never truly know hands-on parents and would be the cause of much anxiety for Nancy as she struggled silently for her lack of a mothering gene. Yet at the time he was the jewel of their new estate.

Their new house was a six-thousand-square-foot mansion originally built for a B-movie actress in the mid-1960s and renovated several times. As I pulled to the curb I saw a moving truck in the driveway. I bypassed the movers and entered the house. Roaming the grounds, I found Ken floating on a raft in the pool. Ted's voice echoed throughout the property as he chewed out the movers.

"That doesn't fuckin' go there," he huffed.

The power of being in charge of Ken and Nancy's move had apparently gone to his head. Ted was also moving. He was relocating to a studio apartment down the hill off the Boulevard. Ken and Nancy had suffered their fill of his late night stumble-ins. It was their plan to reform him, but all they'd done was pluck him from Boise and introduce him to a privileged life in L.A. with a pot or blow connection waiting outside every video rental shop.

I looked around. There were windows everywhere. From the entry, the view included the living room, massive pool, and a stunning panorama of the Valley. The kitchen and dining area also featured views of the Valley floor. I wandered out the side door past a basketball court and fire pit that led to the manicured lawn. From there I saw deer gazing in the ravine below. I had never seen a deer in Los Angeles before. The place was unimaginable, the embodiment of my dream home. My spell was broken as Ken called to me from the pool.

"Grab a raft," he hollered.

It was only ten in the morning, but it was shaping up to be a suffocating, triple-digit day. I didn't bother with the raft. I removed my T-shirt and flip-flops and dove in.

"I wonder what the poor people are doing this morning," he laughed. "Nice dump, huh?"

"This place is amazing," I said. "Can I ask what you paid for it?"

I wanted to swallow the question the moment I released it. I knew it was a classless question but I also knew I needed to know what the possibilities were. Ken smiled.

"It's valued at a million, but we're leasing it," he said nonchalantly.

I dog-paddled toward the deep end of the pool, taking in the view, wondering if I'd ever live in a home like it. Ken, the mind reader, interrupted my trance.

"You'll have a home like this some day," he said. "Better if you want. Hell, you can have this one after we're done with it. The lease is year-to-year so we can upgrade to a nicer place when we hit the next American-Made pin level."

Ken was an alien to me. I couldn't imagine wanting more than what he and Nancy already had, but he was already visualizing their next home. After a few minutes of luxuriating in Ken's life, he asked if I wanted a soda, which was code for, "Get off your ass and fetch me a Diet Coke."

I made my way to the fridge and found the cans. They were lukewarm. Even the massive stainless steel fridge was new. Ted barked at the movers from a back bedroom as I made my way back to the pool. He intercepted me and poked his finger in my chest.

"Time for our first road trip, Tony. What're you doin' this weekend?"

"I don't have any plans, yet" I replied. "Where we headed?"

"Vegas," he whispered. "I only have a couple of pools to clean on Friday. I'll pick you up, one o'clock sharp."

He held up his hand for the unavoidable high-five, I slapped it. He immediately continued his verbal assault on the movers.

"Jesus, you guys are morons! Where does the king mattress go? You have to ask me that? You guys ever do this before?"

I jumped back into the pool cannon ball style and handed one of the shaken-up Diet Cokes to Ken.

"Going on a road trip with your brother in-law this weekend," I told him.

Ken laughed in a nervous sort of way.

"Don't try to keep up with him," he warned.

I wasn't worried about keeping up, but I did wonder what was in store based on Ken's caveat. I leaned back on the steps in the shallow end of the pool. I gazed at the Valley floor for a moment then closed my eyes tightly. The sun warmed my face as I imagined that Ken's home and lifestyle were mine.

10

Friday, August 5ᵗʰ, 1983

It was 1:30 PM and Ted was nowhere in sight. As I leaned against my garage door in the shade I decided I'd need to add "always late" to the growing list of his bad habits.

I told Gail I'd be in Vegas with an "old buddy" for the weekend.

Gail had yet to meet Ted. That was a sensible choice on my part. Ted represented a dark side I didn't want Gail to recognize in me. Gail needed to know as little about Ted as possible. I wasn't ready to curb my compulsion to the fun he offered. I needed the kind of poor choices he presented. I needed that release. I simply needed to keep it from Gail.

It had grown complicated.

While I had to keep the shenanigans that Ted and I got into private from the business, I also wanted to keep my relationship with Gail on the down low. So I had at least two private lives to keep underground. But it didn't take long for Mazal to figure out Gail and I were a couple.

The time I previously spent hanging out with him was now seriously compromised. Between building the business, rocking it hard with Ted and seeing Gail, there was little time left over. I loved Mazal, but the shiny objects in my life were more exciting. Our friendship was falling to the side.

Ted's Chevy van careened around the corner, skidding to a stop half in my driveway, half in the street. His stereo blasted AC/DC's *Highway to Hell* as I motioned for him to turn it down and spare my neighbors, but he ignored me and tossed my duffle bag in the back as I slipped into the front seat.

* * *

The van was a classic. It was furnished with a red velvet couch and yellow beanbag chair. Ted gunned the van and reached under the driver's seat. He produced a zip lock baggie and flashed a devilish smile. He was waiving the bag of contraband for my inspection. I spotted the pot, but there were other, more ominous substances in the clear bag. I pushed his hand down below the radar of the front windshield and laughed uneasily.

"We have what we need for the long weekend bro," he said, waving the baggie around again. He stowed the stuff under his driver's seat and bellowed, "Are you pumped for the fuckin' weekend? Got some girls lined up who wanna' have some fun. Got a buddy with a ski boat on Lake Mead."

I settled into the front seat. Ted was a handful but it was the kind of handful I needed. He took me away from the business even if just for a long weekend. And it was going to be a very long weekend.

The van rolled to a stop back in front of my house just after 7:00 AM. Ted was still raging with energy. I was in a state of semi-sleep, sprawled on the velvet couch in the back. I only netted about four hours of actual sleep since we'd left on Friday. It was now Monday. Ted swung open the rear doors and pulled me out by my ankles.

"Wake the fuck up, little buddy. You got a breakfast meeting with the big guy in fifteen minutes. Get your shit together."

He tossed my duffle bag on the lawn, jumped in the van and peeled out.

I'd just experienced the weekend from hell. I wasn't sure if I'd lost money or won. I wasn't sure if I'd even gambled. The lost weekend was a blur of stimulants, loose women and high fives. Yet sitting on my lawn still damp with morning dew, I quickly snapped back to reality.

I dragged myself into the house and into the shower. I prayed the hot water would wash away the odors of pharmaceuticals and women that lingered on me. The fifteen minutes felt like fifteen seconds but I was able to make my way to the restaurant for my meeting with Ken. He'd left a message on my home answering machine over the weekend. I'm lucky I checked it on Sunday night. It seemed urgent.

I walked in, hair still wet, nylon tracksuit attached to my damp skin and fearing I still smelled of liquor and pot. Ken waved me over from the back corner. Sitting behind a plate stacked high with pancakes, he got right down to business.

"Sit down. Got a challenge you need to be aware of."

In the jargon of the business there were never any "problems," only "challenges". When Ken uttered that word, it was all I needed to hear to know we had a problem.

"A couple of cassette tapes got back to AmericanMade's legal department. They were recorded at our house meetings and late night sessions."

Up to that juncture, I hadn't questioned the proposition we offered. Ken taught us how to draw circles, what words and phrases to use, and that's how we did it. Period.

"So what?" I said in a rather cavalier manner.

"Our organization is growing faster than others around us," he said. "We've attracted their attention."

My eyes glazed over as I tried to keep my food down. I was still semi-nauseous from Mr. Ted's Wild Ride through the high desert.

"When you outgrow people, they get insecure. I'm not certain who sent the tapes to AmericanMade's home office or who's out to get us, but Beau Willis himself may even be unnerved."

He devoured his breakfast, speaking with food shoveled in his cheeks.

"Our upline is run like the flipping Mafia."

I was quite surprised by his curt comment.

"Stewart Moore did some research. In the past, Willis has employed a recurring strategy to maintain control of his downline. He aligns himself with AmericanMade's corporate compliance people when it is convenient for him. Moore thinks he may be talking to the compliance department of AmericanMade about us right now."

Ken was bleeding all over me and breaking one of our cardinal rules, never dump negative stuff downline. When Ken confided in me it made me feel important. Even in my hung-over state I could rally a smug feeling deep inside that he had chosen me. There was a pride that came with being his number one. Rex must have felt it before I came along. I wondered if Annie felt it or if she simply felt like a slave to the man. I was more than that. I was his confidant.

On the other hand, I wasn't sure I wanted to know about the junk going on behind the curtain. The curtain was lovely, thick and regal. The curtain was normally drawn leaving me in its shelter. I just wanted to sell some soap and vitamins and make some money.

"They want to nail us," he said. "Document that we aren't following the distributor rules of conduct then they'll crucify us. They'll censor us so we can't take a crap without their approval. That's how AmericanMade controls independent contractors like us."

I chewed on my rubbery bacon, questioning why the AmericanMade corporate guys, or Willis, wanted to sabotage our growth.

"I still don't get it. Who's sending the tapes to them?"

Ken leaned back in the booth. He knew I didn't understand the forces at work.

"Well, it's complicated," he replied. "We just need to focus on how we're going to respond."

Ken laid out the new rules, telling me: "Don't use the tax savings angle when you are recruiting, don't tell people we don't have to sell door to door, discourage the taping of meetings." He went on and on.

"Tony, this is just a yellow warning light," he said. "We need to be more careful of what we say and do. We need to be more aware of who's attending our meetings."

I had a hunch we'd been dancing on the sidelines with the tax savings angle. Plus, we'd downplayed the need to do any actual retail sales—just buying the products ourselves for personal use. Ken and Nancy were the most Bible-fearing people I'd ever met. Stan and Katy were the gentle voice of reason, always understanding my youth while putting a fatherly hand on my back to usher me toward a better direction. We weren't doing anything that couldn't be repaired with an earnest apology.

I was exhausted. It had been a weird morning tacked onto the end of a fuzzy weekend. As we walked to the cash register, Ken asked about Vegas. I told him we had a blast and left it at that. I sure as hell wasn't going to give him specifics. I wasn't even sure I could recall any of the details.

Ken mumbled "goodbye" and jumped into his new red Porsche, 911. He pulled onto Ventura Boulevard and blew through the intersection. He sailed through a stale yellow light and was quickly out of view.

So much for the warning lights.

11

Halloween 1983

My downline had doubled since summer and I'd qualified as a full-fledged Gold pin. Gail was immersed in the business and growing her downline as well. It had become obvious to everyone watching that we were in a relationship. I stopped trying to dodge it. Ken and the other Diamonds weren't thrilled, considering they wanted to leverage my single status. Ken hadn't spoken with me directly, but he didn't have to. I was happy to avoid the subject.

Gail and I attended a major Willis event together in Long Beach called, Free Enterprise Weekend. She loved photography and fired off her Nikon like a pro. She took pictures of everything, took notes and also tape recorded most of the speakers. She had evolved into a serious student of the business. It was enjoyable attending an event with her on my arm. We were a power couple of sorts.

It was a Friday evening, Halloween weekend, and I was on my way to conduct a house meeting in one of my fastest growing distributor legs. I was enjoying my commute. I'd taken over the lease payments on Ken's Cadillac El Dorado a month after he picked up his new Porsche. It felt good to be surrounded by my new-used Caddy.

Since the bizarre breakfast with Ken months earlier, I'd started looking at everyone with a suspicious eye. I was guarded. Ken and I began trying to flush out the "Mole." We were both curious who had bothered to send the bootleg tapes to AmericanMade's compliance department. I also started asking more questions about the Willis system: the tapes, books and events; the way the profits worked, and how the money was shared. Ken wasn't giving up detailed information. He kept saying he'd tell me about the extra benefits of the system when it was the right time. The timing seemed fine to me but I also understood Ken's need to keep me out of the loop so I continued to respect his wishes and draw circles like a good little grasshopper.

Ken's paranoia had become even heavier. He encouraged me to screen everyone who came into my house meetings and late-night training sessions. AmericanMade sent him a certified letter requesting he fly back to the Midwest to discuss the matter. He'd just dropped that news on me earlier in the week.

The house meeting was overflowing with bodies when I arrived. Bob and Laura Zelano were two of my first personally-sponsored distributors and, by far, my most loyal. Bobby Z., as everyone called him, ushered people to the metal folding chairs in his living room while Laura handed out cups of Power Punch. There had been a lot of growth in their downline, so much so that I didn't recognize many of the people in attendance. The recruiting machine was working so well that I wasn't sure which of them were already signed up in the business and which were seeing the plan for the first time.

I examined the people filling the cheap folding chairs. Gail was perched in the second row with a new prospect in tow. She was bubbling with enthusiasm. I hunted for familiar faces. People I didn't recognize fumbled with their cassette recorders. My own brand of paranoia began to take hold. I zeroed in on Stan who had joined the meeting with a handful of his new recruits. I continued scanning the crowd. Other than Stan, Gail and a few other regulars, the attendees were largely unfamiliar to me.

As Bobby Z. introduced me, I heard the clicking sound of twenty-some cassette recorders. The sound reverberated in my head like machine gun fire. A myriad of microphones were suddenly pointing in my direction. I broke into a cold sweat. I took a deep breath, shut off my brain, and simply started drawing circles.

It was all I knew how to do.

12

New Year's Eve 1983

The notes were meticulous. They were jotted down on yellow lined sheets of paper with a red felt tipped pen. The cassette tapes were painstakingly catalogued with dates and other pertinent content. The envelopes were addressed by hand.

The large manila envelopes were sealed with clear tape. There were three copies of each set of materials. One was kept for file purposes. The other two would be deposited in the mailbox on the curb outside the local post office. One was addressed to AmericanMade in Champaign, Illinois; the other was addressed to Willis Enterprises in Augusta, Georgia. Both organizations believed the information was exclusive to them at this juncture.

The return address used was the same for each parcel. It was a post office box in the Valley that bore a fictitious business name. Both parties received their packages from *TSV Associates*. The recipients were so consumed with the details inside the big envelopes that the sender's name and identity went largely unexamined.

It was also to the attention of TSV Associates that the recipients were instructed to send their money orders—made payable to cash. This beautiful tax-free income stream and the routine that created it were becoming instinctive to the Mole. The informant opened the blue steel receptacle and dropped the two packets inside.

It was the very last Friday of 1983. The snitch was looking forward to a New Year's weekend spent evaluating this cagey side venture and its extraordinary profitability.

13

February 1984

The meeting was mandatory. Everyone in Ken's downline at the Silver pin level and above were present. It was held on a crisp Saturday morning in February. There were even a few crossline Diamonds in attendance at the request of AmericanMade's home office.

It was official: our organization had been placed under formal *censorship*. It was Ken's staunch opinion that we'd been oppressed and unfairly singled out by AmericanMade's corporate office. But Ken used obstacles such as these as motivation. Our machine fed off the news of this roadblock. In fact, our growth had accelerated since the formal letter arrived. We'd become more intense and focused as a result of the unwanted scrutiny. Ken had grown even closer to Stewart Moore and the other new Diamonds. He was building his own private army.

AmericanMade executives took issue with many of the recruiting methods that Ken taught us. They'd labeled them "bait and switch" tactics. Ken felt they were defensible and he'd flown back to Champaign to argue his point. He'd lost that battle and as a result we were paraded into the swanky Bonaventure Hotel to receive our lashings. They had a long list of "corrections" they wanted us to make.

They passed around innumerable pages of transcribed audiotapes, notes from house meetings and late-night leadership sessions. Their message was clear: They were watching us. I sat between Rex and Stan. There was a edgy air in the room as though we'd been informed of a pop quiz for which none of us were prepared. Rex never showed remorse. He took his lashings and moved on. Stan wasn't as cool and calm. It was the first time I realized Stan was the type of guy whose nerves were on display as a cop issued him a parking ticket.

I was indifferent to a degree, although I'd never been one to enjoy a lecture. I knew we had behaved ourselves—more or less. Had we bent the rules? Sure. Ken rewrote the rules in a way—a very successful way—and I knew he would take good care of us. He needed us to sit there, pay attention and nod along in agreement. I'd grown very practiced at nodding.

The reprimand began. They prohibited us from securing potential downline members by using the small business tax savings angle. Inasmuch as none of us were CPAs, they strongly opposed us offering tax advice to new distributors.

They also told us that saying "nobody has to sell...all the volume comes from personal use" was forbidden. By telling new recruits that we didn't actually sell we were inadvertently creating a wholesale buying club, or what the Federal Trade Commission deems an illegal pyramid scheme. From that point forward we'd have to document that each of us ran a small retail business with customers buying AmericanMade products. The final indignation was a letter that was piously read to us at the very end of the meeting.

Dear Sirs:

I want to make it perfectly clear that the leadership of Willis Enterprises Inc. takes no responsibility for the alleged falsehoods, mistruths or misleading statements made by Kenneth Richman, his downline distributor group, or any of the other related distributors now under formal censorship. We disavow involvement in any training that would result in misleading recruiting tactics.

Sincerely,

Beau Willis

The curt missive from Augusta was damning. One objective American-Made corporate clearly had was for our organization to know that Willis no longer took responsibility for us. They read the letter to produce a chasm in our loyalty to the support system. It was a classic divide and conquer technique.

While the note was read, the California Diamonds fumed. Ken and Stewart Moore maintained solid eye contact. When the AmericanMade executives adjourned the meeting Ken, Moore, and the rest of them bolted from the room without looking back. They had a meeting of their own to conduct, down the hall, behind the closed doors.

14

Spring 1984

B^{eep.}

"Your life's about to change. Give me a call."

Oddly, I'd grown used to the life altering answering machine messages from Ken. I had no choice but to embrace them. After all, wasn't a life altering experience what I'd signed up for?

We'd just returned from the first Richman Leadership event held in Phoenix. It was Ken and Nancy's first Diamond event. It was their show. I was recognized as a new Ruby pin and Ken hyped the fact that I was in Pearl qualification.

On the last night, Ken and Nancy asked me to be the keynote speaker on the agenda. My speech was capped off with a standing ovation from the eleven hundred attendees. I didn't need a pat on the back from Ken; the look on his face as I came off the stage said it all.

The certified letter from AmericanMade acknowledging I'd qualified as a Ruby arrived March 5. Ken hinted that when I hit the Ruby level it would be time for me to give up selling insurance. I wasn't in complete agreement, but he asked me to meet him in the Richman Financial offices so we could talk it over.

I'd only been going into the offices a few days a week, selling a few policies here and there, banking the commissions, but not living off of them. Selling insurance was far from my passion and I was totally consumed by my MLM business. The tired insurance gig was quickly becoming an afterthought.

I stopped at the receptionist. I expected our normal banter but she barely glanced at me.

"Ken's waiting for you in the conference room," she said, eyes averted.

The door to the conference room was closed, the blinds drawn. I wasn't sure what awaited me but I allowed my hand to linger on the doorknob for a moment. I opened it with trepidation.

"SURPRISE!"

Everyone from the Richman agency as well as a few others were in attendance. They were all there to celebrate my big day—the big day I was not aware of until then. Annie put together the early morning surprise party. She stood in the corner, head cocked with the bittersweet expression of a mother watching her child grow.

Rex was my first embrace. He mocked my shocked expression, tousled my hair like a brother and tossed me into the masses. Bill Franklin was the first to call me a "lucky dog." Franklin held court as our token Certified Financial Planner. He'd followed us over from Starbridge, yet hadn't built an MLM business. He had little interest in the business.

All the perks the business offered us was rubbed in his face on a daily basis. I believed it was fair punishment for him not having the balls to join our MLM world. I let him shower me with praises. Beyond the balloons and confetti there was a banner taped to the window: Freedom Isn't Free... Congrats on your retirement, Tony!

I stared at the banner. I was no longer in control. Ken's plans for me were in motion: I was now a bystander in my own life. I smiled, enduring the slaps on the back and watched the doughnuts disappear. Ken asked me to join him in his office. Like a good little lemming, I did.

I didn't think I was making quite enough money from the business yet, but he had a plan for me. I trusted him, but I just wasn't prepared for the decision to be made for me. Ken kicked back in his chair and threw his feet onto his desk.

"Let's talk about the tape profits," he said, rocking back and forth slightly in his chair, wearing a smug expression. "You'll be a qualified Pearl in a month. That means you'll buy your tapes from me directly and you'll purchase them at a buck-fifty break—instead of four dollars per tape, you'll now pay two-fifty per tape."

At that juncture I was running two hundred tapes a month through my organization, so my cut on the tapes represented an additional three thousand a month of net income. Ken went on to tell me that I'd purchase books at 25 percent off cover price. That would be another thousand dollars of net profit per month. I'd just been handed a monthly raise of four thousand dollars.

"You'll also go on the Willis speaking circuit as a regular, doing opportunity meetings, seminars and rallies," he advised. "You'll get paid starting next month and you're already booked in four states"

Ken handed me a schedule with my name on it. Why had I assumed that the bigger pins spoke for free? I sat numbed by my own stupidity.

"You get $1,200 per rally and another $600 for an open opportunity meeting," he said. "You're scheduled to do twelve opens a year."

My mental calculator went back to work. That would be another $20,000 a year. My yearly income had just increased by more than $70,000. My head was spinning.

I had estimated that during 1984 I would make $45,000 by moving AmericanMade products through my MLM business. However, my total annual income would now balloon to more than $120,000 as the Willis system profits kicked in. That's when it hit me: At the higher levels, two-thirds of the income—maybe more—came from the Willis support system. Only a third of a Diamond's income was generated by sales of AmericanMade products. I felt foolish.

"You got this so far, buddy?" he asked.

I laughed, nodding uncomfortably. I was torn between hugging him and flipping him off for having kept me in the dark.

"You okay?" he asked again.

"I gotta tell ya," my humiliation came masked in a chuckle, "I've been looking at the lifestyles—the homes, cars, jewelry—the math never added up. I had no idea I thought the money collected at the door went to cover the expense of the meeting rooms."

Ken howled with laughter, barely able to contain himself. My palms were drenched; my mouth turned dry. Within a half-hour's time I'd involuntarily retired and been told my income would almost triple. I'd been given a peek behind the curtain and saw more than I expected. Ken composed himself while I sat there humiliated, looking for a place to hide.

"That's why we use high school auditoriums. They're dirt-cheap. We cram a thousand people in the seats and take in eight to ten grand per event. Those meetings are going on all over the country, hundreds of them. Plus, the tapes only cost twenty-eight cents to produce. Between the tapes, books and events Willis makes a fortune. He can afford to pay us for speaking."

Ken basked in my naivety. I doubt he would have liked me so much if I wasn't the little brother who needed guidance. Nobody reaches greatness without someone bowing down before them. Ken just handed me a six-figure income. I bowed.

"I told you that I'd tell you about all this when the time was right," Ken said. "I'm telling you more than I'm comfortable telling others. I trust you like a brother. You should know how it works."

"A UPS guy in the business picks up tons of tapes each week at a duplicator here in the Valley. The shipments go to a company named W.E., Inc. in Georgia. That's Willis Enterprises. I get the name of the duplicator. Annie calls anonymously—she makes up a name, telling them she wants to place a large order. She negotiates with them and tells her their lowest price point is twenty-eight cents. There you go! They're making a bloody fortune on our backs and then they piss all over us."

Ken leaned back.

"This tape business is easy...too easy," he said. "They record all of our events and the master tape reels are sent to Willis. They do a little bit of review and editing and then ship the masters to the duplicator. The duplication company does the rest, from mass production to packaging. The monthly events are simple. The distributors fork over their four bucks at the door. The gate is collected by the host and overnighted to Augusta. Willis' staff cuts the checks for the speaking fees and mails em' out. Oh, and when you hit Diamond your speaking honorariums are triple."

With that last little nugget he stood and grabbed his sport coat. I remained seated, still in a stupor.

Rex popped his head in the door and asked if I wanted to go down the street, grab a doughnut and play some Ms. Pac Man at our old hangout. I studied his face for a smile, assuming he was kidding. At that moment I found myself feeling sorry for him. He wasn't riding the business with the strength that I was. I politely turned him down.

Ken smiled and motioned towards the door. "We're going to the Jaguar dealership so you can buy yourself a retirement present," he said.

During what Ken referred to as a "dream building session" a year earlier, he asked what my dream car was. I wanted to drive a Cadillac, El Dorado Biarritz. He told me I should dream bigger. I let myself drift into a fantasy where money was no object. There I was, perched behind the wheels of a midnight blue S-Type Jaguar. My mind stroked the supple white leather interior; my eyes squinted from the reflection off the rims. I was there, behind the wheel of a car I rarely allowed myself to fantasize about.

Ken instructed me to fill my life with photographs of that car. He wanted me to paste a picture everywhere from my bathroom to my bedroom, refrigerator to washing machine. He'd warned me to be specific and get a photo of the exact vehicle I wanted. I tore a photo of a black S-Type out of a magazine.

Black—close enough.

That picture hung on my fridge for a year. I drooled over it daily. I took it down and placed it in my wallet a week earlier and began calling local dealerships. With my Pearl qualification in the bag, I thought it would be the right time. I mentioned to Ken that I'd located a midnight blue XJS in stock at the local dealership. On our way over Ken filled my head with other fantasies.

"You gotta get one of those car phones installed. There is a guy in my downline who can do it. You gotta add fog lights, you gotta add chrome racing wheels, you gotta..."

Walking onto the showroom floor I was overwhelmed by the vision of several incredible vehicles. They were machines of beauty, dripping of money and prestige. I felt out of place yet as the sales manager bounded over I found myself barking orders.

"The midnight blue metallic S-Type," I said. "I was told you had one on the lot."

"We had one," he said apologetically. "We sold it last evening. I'm so sorry. Can we interest you in another color scheme?"

I was crushed. I had my heart set on that midnight blue Jag. I looked at Ken and he shrugged his shoulders.

"Why don't you order one," Ken suggested.

The sales manager smiled broadly. "We can have one here in eight weeks, made to order!"

There was no way in hell I was going to wait two months. I'd let it leak to a few people in my downline that I was going to get the Jag soon. Letting it leak is an understatement. I'd already spoken to Rex about it being a no smoking vehicle and Ted called permanent shotgun. Gail was so excited about it she made me promise her that she'd get the first ride.

I sure as hell wasn't going to admit I'd screwed up and didn't order one in advance. I had the check for the down payment tucked into my shirt pocket. I had to drive a Jag home that day. That's when it happened.

The glass windowpanes of the showroom floor peeled open and another new S-Type Jag was rolled onto the showroom floor. The car had just been detailed and the black paint job reflected the lights like a mirror. I walked around it. It had gray leather interior, fog lights and the chrome racing wheels Ken had harped on during our drive over.

I removed the magazine clipping from my wallet, the one that had been taped to my fridge for a year, and unfolded it. The car that I had drooled over daily was the exact car that had just been rolled to my feet, exact, to every last detail.

"This S-Type is available," the sales manager said.

I looked at the magazine photo. It was mocking me. Ken shrugged his shoulders, already knowing which car I'd be driving home.

"I told you, your dreams have to be specific," he said. I politely ignored Ken's words. I locked eyes with my new car, while addressing the sales manager.

"I'll take it."

15

September 1984

I woke up as the Aloha Airlines DC10 banked into a turn and settled into its final approach to Maui Airport in Kahului. I'd fallen asleep just after lunch. It was the first sound sleep I'd had in a while.

Nineteen Eighty-Four was flying by. It was already September, six months since my forced retirement. I jumped onto the Willis speaking circuit just after the compulsory departure from selling insurance. I was on the road a week-and-a-half each month addressing open meetings, seminars and rallies. My star power in the Willis organization was rising even faster on the broader speaking platform. I enjoyed the enhanced recognition as well as some of the perks of life on the road.

The speaking circuit wasn't a bad gig. A person they'd assign as a host greeted me at baggage claim. He'd carry my luggage and give me a comfortable ride to the hotel. There was usually a surf and turf dinner at the best steakhouse in town and then it was off to the speaking engagement. After the event, I'd be whisked away by appreciative distributors wanting a little bit of my time over coffee and pie. Then I'd be delivered back to my hotel. I'd graciously wave goodbye, push the elevator button and pretend to turn in for the night—but I wouldn't take the elevator to my room.

There were always a few stray single women hanging out at the hotel bar. The women I went for were easy to spot; our mutual need for a good time was magnetic. Some were flight attendants, some in sales. It didn't matter if it was the Marriott in San Diego or the San Jose Hilton, I could always find them and they were always ready to party. The temptation was immense.

Whenever I could, I'd slip one of the willing party girls back to my room. I longed for those moments of temporary release. They felt real to me in an existence that slowly became a steady diet of gratuitous bullshit.

I would pull off the late-night indiscretions and then sleep in the next morning. I never booked early flights home. I'd become nocturnal. It was difficult for me to wind down after an appearance on stage. The applause, accolades and attention were potent and those synthetic highs lingered.

Gail and I were still together, yet sometimes that fact eluded me when I was on the road. Between the demands of the business when I was home and the time spent on the speaking circuit, I had very little left for our relationship. When we did steal time together it was spent discussing her downline rather than discussing us.

One of the many facets of Gail's personality that I liked was her carefree side. The deeper she became involved in the business the more that lighthearted part of her complexion faded. I liked the fact that she'd come from Mazal's college world—a connection to the uncomplicated life and person I once was. Yet all of that was slipping away.

I wasn't traveling alone on this trip. As the plane touched down in Maui, I turned and smiled at my parents, my sister and my aunt Jean. None of us had ever been to Hawaii before. The Maui Pearl Club was a Willis recognition outing for new Pearls. When I mentioned to my parents that I wanted them to join me, mom cried and Buzz started planning a golf outing.

I'd finally get to meet many of my heroes. The people in attendance were the voices to whom I'd been listening on tape since day one. They always ended their speeches with "come join us on the beaches of the world." I'd shaken hands with a few of them at the major functions but never had the chance to talk with them one-on-one. They were rock stars to us. I'd get to join them on the sands of Maui as an equal.

While I was focused on the thrill of connecting with the big pins in Maui, Ted was all over me to score him some weed—some *Maui Wowie*. He went as far as telling me I could pick up a bag on the streets of Lahaina. I could just imagine the drug-sniffing dogs at the airport as I departed, discovering the stash as Willis and the other Diamonds looked on. I was smart enough to take a pass on his request.

I was interested to see how each side postured themselves in Maui. The dark side of our political climate in the business had become evident after Ken explained the system profits. There were millions of dollars at stake. The tension between the new California Diamonds and the Willis camp was unmistakable.

The censorship meeting earlier that year was not accepted well by Ken and the others. Ken wanted the other California Diamonds to bolt from the Willis organization immediately. He wanted them to establish their own tape, book and speaking system. They voted as a group. He was overruled almost unanimously.

Ken had only one other person on his side. That vote came from Stewart Moore. Moore was the only one with business savvy and a righteous set of balls. The others felt safe within the cocoon of the Willis support system. My distant hope was that the two factions could somehow make peace.

The Maui trip was an opportunity for the kingpins of our organization to take a careful look at the new crop of Pearls. The Willis Family Reunion in Portland was fast approaching. People at my level were expected to speak. There'd be more than ten thousand people in attendance. Rex and I were already writing our speeches. Maui was their opportunity to decide who should get that kind of exposure. Hence, Ken and Nancy had the talk with me. Ken warned me, "Be on your best behavior in Maui."

As we touched down I could see the look in my Dad's eyes. There was a twinkle—one I'd rarely seen during the last five years. We made our way to baggage claim. There was a fleet of white limos waiting to take us to the Royal Lahaina Resort. The rides were courtesy of Beau Willis. I had heard we'd be catered to but actually experiencing it was different. As we got into one of the limos and prepared to depart, my father grabbed me and pulled me in tight.

"I'm proud of you, buddy," he said. The look on his face said even more.

Fruity drinks and warm face towels smelling of coconut awaited us at check-in. The views from our rooms were stunning. You could step out on the balcony and see three of the other islands. Native music played down by the pool and the smell of wild orchids and ginger wafted up from the edge of the beach walk. My family was in awe. There was a large fruit basket in each room, courtesy of Beau Willis. Each had a card that said—what else—"Ain't It Great!" I didn't have much time to enjoy my complimentary fruit basket. I was due downstairs in the Kona Meeting Room in thirty minutes.

As I walked into the meeting room the first person I saw was Bucky Rivington from Tennessee. He looked just like he did in the photo on his tapes. I'd listened to him over and over again. I felt as though I knew him. He was a legend and one of the few people in the country to make it to the Diamond level as a single man. There was a time or two that I wanted to give up. It was Bucky's tape, *Never, Never Quit,* that kept me going. He'd married immediately after he achieved Diamond qualification. I assumed the lady draped on his arm was his wife. Bucky was an average looking guy, shorter than I imagined, so seeing his beautiful and statuesque wife made me think she must have married him for other reasons.

I nervously approached Bucky and stuck out my hand.

"Mr. Rivington, my name is Tony DiBona."

"You can call me Bucky, Tony!"

He couldn't have been a nicer guy. I told him how much I admired him, chatted him up for a moment, then he passed me off to another Diamond from the East Coast. That went on for forty-five minutes. I met a dozen more of my personal heroes. My head was spinning. I posed for pictures with each of them while they slapped me on the back, congratulating me on my Pearl qualification. Each asked me when I planned to go into Diamond qualification and they all echoed the same message: "You need to join the club, we're waiting for you. We want you on the beaches of the world with us!"

The "club," yeah, I wanted to join it. Each of the guys wore the ring: The diamond cluster ring, the same ring that Moore handed to Ken at his surprise party. They also all wore eighteen-karat gold chains around their necks. Eagles with fat diamond chips in their claws dangled from the chains. The rings and chains were iconic of their membership to this exclusive club. Lesser pins had smaller eagles with a pearl or emerald affixed to its claws.

Rex, his wife, Linda, and I made small talk, pretended the rooms weren't extravagant, telling one another we'd seen better, trying to act as cool as possible. Then the talking quelled and the laughter suddenly stopped. Polite applause broke out. Beau and Rhonda Willis had entered the room, sucking all the air out of it.

I got it. They'd built the largest multi-level marketing downline organization for AmericanMade—or any MLM in the free world for that matter. He'd pioneered the concept of an upline support system, a model that everyone either plugged into or tried to copy. He was reportedly worth more than twenty five million dollars. The Willis clan owned a palatial mansion in Augusta and vacation homes across the US. They traveled in a Lear jet and had a fleet of luxury vehicles in their ten-car garage at the family's main estate. The cars and homes were fully maintained by a staff of employees. Beau and Rhonda Willis were royalty. We approached them reverently.

Willis wore a pinstriped suit and tie while most of us wore our requisite tracksuits. I was told that Willis was all business, all the time. I was instructed to have a coat and tie for a formal dinner we were to have with him. Willis required business or formal attire for dining in his company. I dutifully waited in line to greet him and his wife.

"Hello Mr. and Mrs. Willis. It's an honor to meet you both," I said.

She just smiled, and he responded in his southern twang.

"What's your name, son?"

"Tony DiBona, sir."

Willis cocked his head sideways as though he was trying to make a connection. "You're that young hotshot downline from Richman, right? You're the single kid who's tearing it up out there in LA-LA Land—the land of fruits and nuts."

I shook his hand deferentially. I was shocked; Beau Willis knew me by name.

* * *

Our Hawaiian Airlines 727 reached ten thousand feet on our return flight to LAX. I reclined my seat as far as it would go and jammed the cheap little plastic headset into my ears in an attempt to block out the engine drone. The California organization did have our private audience with Willis in Maui. It was held in the hotel's Presidential Suite. The tone of the gathering was polite, but strained. Beau spoke about "edifying the upline" and "following the system." At one point he said, "We've seen many organizations grow up fast and think they were better or smarter than the system. Well they weren't and they're gone today." I noted that he placed special emphasis on the words, WEREN'T and GONE.

On the third day of the trip, Ken and Stewart Moore corralled me by the pool for a meeting. They were well aware that the impact I was having within the organization was becoming even greater since I'd joined the speaking circuit. They wanted to make sure I was, as Moore put it, "on board for the long haul."

"We're not disclosing our plans to all other Emeralds or Pearls just yet," Moore said. "Because of your higher profile it's important we have your support and confidence."

They explained there would be an eventual split between our organization and Willis Enterprises. They went into detail, rationalizing the whys, but I had a hunch it was more about the money than any other factor. Near the end of this little pow wow Ken ran off to the beckoning call of Nancy. They'd brought young Chandler along on the trip allowing Ken to play the family man angle while Nancy ordered around the nanny.

Moore wasn't finished with our talk. I instantly wished Nancy called my name instead of Ken's. He put his arm around me in a fatherly nature and we wandered out to the beachfront walk.

"It's critical you make the right judgments in your personal life," he warned. "It's important to select the right partner at the right time. It's up to you to carry the torch for the young, single crowd. Don't you agree that it would probably be better if you were truly single right now?" he asked as he shook his melon up and down like a bobble head.

The conversation took me by surprise. I was lost as to how I should respond. So I didn't.

"Ken tells me you are a believer in Christ."

I was, kind of, but I didn't want to have any sort of spiritual conversation with him at that point. I was so mind-screwed from the load of stuff they'd just dumped on me that all I wanted to do was sneak off to a quiet island bar and drain a few beers. I'd been raised a Catholic but didn't really know what I firmly believed. I wasn't sure how to explain to a Bible thumper like him that I was simply interested in making some good money and getting laid once in a while.

"I know you want to live a Christian life, walk with God," he said. "That also means that when you select a mate we need to make sure she's also a believer. You understand what I'm saying, right?"

I nodded knowing that my current relationship with Gail—a person of Jewish faith—was now under his and their scrutiny.

"We're concerned that you may be going down a road that isn't right for you in the long term. Taking a life partner and getting married is a serious choice."

Moore was a bit ahead of where my moral compass was pointed. I was dating Gail and getting some tail on the down low whenever I could. He was talking "walk with God" and "life partner" and generally creeping me out. After he finished his pious-ass little sermon I told him that I'd put some thought into it. I wanted the conversation to be over.

"Good talk," he said. "Let's make good choices."

He hugged me and left.

I sat on a bench looking at the surf. Yeah, good fucking talk. Moore's dissertation—dripping in Christianity—sounded well rehearsed. He was the chosen messenger to counsel me on the cold, hard fact that the organization didn't want me in a committed relationship at that juncture, certainly not with a Jewish girl. I was disgusted that Gail's religious beliefs would be an issue with them at all. The more I thought about it, the angrier I grew. What right did they have in passing judgment on Gail or her faith or tell me what to do with my personal life?

I stared out at the vast Pacific Ocean and watched the sun sink. It was a free night on our agenda, yet I didn't feel very free. And I didn't feel like being around anyone. I called my room, leaving a bullshit message for my family stating that I had "some plans."

I needed a stiff drink, or two, so I began bar hopping, slowly working my way north along the Kanapali strand. I knew I wouldn't be running into anyone I knew inside those bars. I was on the hunt. I found her at the third bar. She was an attractive blonde from British Columbia. We had a few cocktails and wound up stumbling to her hotel room. We drained her mini bar and had as much fun as we could have until we both passed out. I slipped back into my room at the Royal Lahaina just before sunrise, undetected, with a slight headache and a smile on my face. I wondered what Moore would have thought about my wholesome evening's activities.

We had our formal group dinner with king and queen Willis on the last night of the event. It was courteous but artificial. The California contingent was seated at separate tables from the other Willis Diamonds and located in the back corner of the banquet room. It was as if the big pins in the California organization were lepers, however, even those of us seated in the leper colony were expected to approach Beau Willis to pay our respects and pose for photos with him. When I crouched next to them for my picture Willis told me, "Tony, you're going to be a big part of the Willis Enterprises family for many years to come. We'll walk the beaches of the world together."

I smiled and nodded my head in mock agreement as he gave me the thumbs up and the photo was snapped. Willis might have been wearing an expensive pinstriped suit, but I knew the more cunning California Diamonds would eventually strip him naked. The poor bastard had no idea what was coming.

While waiting to board the plane, Buzz draped his arm around me. It was comforting, a completely different sensation than when Stewart Moore had done so. Moore's hug felt insincere at best; his prejudice toward Gail left a bitter taste in my mouth, but one I'd have to swallow for the moment.

The pilot announced we'd reached cruising altitude and I reclined in the seat. I wanted to fall asleep, but couldn't. I stared out my window at the blue Pacific. The Maui Pearl Club trip was an eye-opening experience. I wasn't flying blind anymore.

16

Thanksgiving Week 1984

If it were possible to find a sixth gear, I'd found it. It was the weekend before the Thanksgiving holiday and most people were slowing down, filling themselves with holiday spirit. That is, everyone except me.

There was our family's traditional turkey dinner at my uncle Mike's house, but I'd barely be there. The cousins always came early to watch the Detroit game, and then we'd toss around the football in the street until the huge dinner was served. The food fest would be followed by a short communal nap on the old couch by the fireplace, then the pumpkin pie and other desserts would be brought out along with a second run at the turkey and stuffing.

I came late, left early and missed most all of it. I was home working the phone, getting my downline pumped for an upcoming event.

Mazal wanted to get together for a beer Thanksgiving night and play some golf the next day, but I blew him off on both offers. We hadn't seen each other much during the year. He was living back at home, having completed his graduate degree in journalism that summer. I was aware that he went on a few interviews, but apparently, it only took a few months for Mazal's plans to be a professional journalist to get derailed. He was now running the extremely profitable family flower business along with his older brother. I wasn't sure whether the gig was temporary or permanent, but it looked like it was rather eternal to me.

Based on my intended schedule and their busiest season in the flower business, I doubted I'd see him very much during the balance of the holidays.

I wasn't interested in the conventional holidays. The next holiday on my calendar would be the day I qualified as an Emerald. I was completely focused on achieving my next pin level.

Friday morning unfolded and I hit the road. The call from Bill Franklin took me by surprise. Franklin never joined the MLM business. He'd grown comfortable in his status as a Certified Financial Planner—but now he was expendable. "I'm no longer with Richman Financial," Franklin told me. "Yesterday, Annie Wu stormed into the office and told us to find another agency to hang our licenses. Ken is getting out of the insurance business. He needs the office space. She wouldn't tell us any more than that."

I had to ask him to slow down. He caught me off guard and my thoughts on the subject were louder than his explanation. "Annie told us we needed to be out by Friday because they're hiring staff for Ken's new business."

"Hiring for what new business?" I asked.

"I don't have the details. I heard he's hiring for some real estate stuff. I asked Annie, but she shut me out. Bottom line, he's wiping out the insurance operation."

I ended the conversation and pulled off the freeway to find a cup of coffee. Between Franklin's call and my constant state of exhaustion, I couldn't even contemplate the conversation until I took care of my caffeine problem. I jumped back in the car and called Ted.

Ted confessed that Ken had been talking and working with Johnny Gergin for a while behind the scenes. I knew this guy, Johnny. He was deep in Ken's downline. Gergin was a man of many talents. He'd mostly floated between selling homes and arranging various types of loans. He acquired the nickname "Dr. Johnny" because, allegedly, he could doctor up any loan application and get his client approved. His reputation around the Valley as a raconteur and blatant self-promoter preceded him.

Some thought he was a sleazebag, but I just saw him as edgy—a dude that bent the rules in his favor when needed. He was Irish-bred, a hard living, hard drinking guy with flushed cheeks, a full beard and a red, bulbous nose. Dr. Johnny was the life of the party for damn sure.

Ted acknowledged that Dr. Johnny convinced Ken to acquire a large parcel of land in the northeast Valley. Dr. Johnny told Ken the area was short on affordable apartments and he could get the parcel re-zoned. In other words, Johnny could pay off a city zoning clerk and get a ton of doors approved. Ted mentioned that Dr. Johnny told Ken, "Trust me, ditch the stupid life insurance gig, clean out the office, we'll need the space and let's keep this on the down low...you'll make a killing on the deals I bring you."

Instantly, I recalled my breakfast with Ken after my lost weekend in Vegas, listening to Ken and chewing on the rubbery bacon at Denny's. The concept drilled into my brain during our breakfast meeting was trust. Ken made a point of letting me know I was part of the inner circle. If he trusted me enough then why didn't I know of his new plans? My paranoia set in. I'd grown accustomed to being the hotshot in Ken's pocket, yet I was out of the loop on a major move.

I numbed my pride while getting back on the freeway. It wasn't that long ago that Ken, Rex and Annie landed on my doorstep the morning after they'd cleaned out Fred Cohen's office. I'd seen Ken make impulsive moves before.

* * *

The chartered yacht was at full throttle as we made our way into open water. There were thirty couples on the Saturday outing to Catalina Island. It was an incentive trip for top distributors in the Richman MLM downline.

The vibe on the boat was electric. The attendees were handpicked. They were either hard-core devotees, like me, or brand new hot shots whom we were grooming to join the fold. Nancy hobnobbed, enjoying her virgin Pina Colada like it was a Long Island ice tea and playing hostess with verve. Annie did her best to socialize, although her eye rolls at the ladies' conversations were difficult to miss. A girl that tough rarely fit in with the "my nanny was running late" conversations. I hunted down Ken and stalked him until he gave me a minute of his time.

"Let's go up top. I want to talk with you alone. Some exciting stuff," he said.

We made our way two levels up, to the very top of the boat.

"I'm making some changes with Richman Financial. Going to convert the corporation into a real estate development firm."

"I wish you would've warned me before I got blindsided by Franklin." I said. "The guy called me yesterday. He was real pissed off about the way it was handled."

"We had to move fast," he said. "I was planning on meeting with everyone personally, but Nancy and I were out of town. Annie did what had to be done."

I looked at Ken, searching for any sign of regret I could find, but there was none. This was somehow comforting. Ken never regretted cleaning out Fred and look where that got us. If Ken felt strongly about it I could as well.

"Life insurance is small-time stuff and all we had left in the agency was a bunch of washed up insurance guys—losers."

"So, real estate?" I asked.

"You know Johnny Gergin, right? Dr. Johnny?"

Before I could respond, Ken was already in the thick of it.

"Johnny found us a large piece of dirt. It can be re-zoned. We picked up the land on the cheap. We can have apartment units built and rented out inside of ten months. We can either keep it or flip it. If we keep it, the money will roll in. If we flip it we can make over an eighty percent return on our money."

"I'm raising capital. It will mostly come from our downline. We'll be able to offer investors a guaranteed return—eighteen to twenty percent. Got all the legal work done. We're ready to rock and roll."

Ken saw my stunned gaze.

"Your father wants to retire, right? Buzz takes cash he has in his retirement account or the equity in his home, and we turn that dead money into cash flow. Let's say your parents invest two hundred thousand. We'll pay them twenty five percent. That's fifty thousand a year in interest. Your dad can quit his job and relax. I'm taking all the risk."

"But, what if the project takes longer or building costs run over?" I asked.

Ken wasn't going to spend a lot of time with me on the details.

"Look, let the pros I'm hiring worry about all of the minutiae," he said. "The project will return a grand total of eighty percent, so if I'm paying out twenty-five to an investor I still have a big cushion to work with. We're going to do two deals at a time once we get going. I'm bringing Dr. Johnny on board full time to oversee acquisitions and loan negotiations. You are going to be a big part of this, trust me."

I listened closely. The potential to make a million rang in my ears. I knew what that income could mean on top of the business. Then he hit me with a stinger.

"Hey, need to let you know, you and Rex aren't speaking at the big Willis event in Portland. Willis made the decision. He thinks you both qualified as Pearls too fast and aren't solid. He doesn't believe you earned the right to speak at a major event."

It was a punch in the gut. My shock leapt into anger.

"Fuck Beau Willis," I snarled. I stood up and paced around the empty boat deck a bit, trying to compose myself. Ken gave me a moment before approaching me.

"You okay buddy?"

"I'm fine," I replied through deep, calming breaths. "What difference does it make? Who gives a shit about those assholes—we're bolting soon anyway, right—like you guys told me in Maui, right?"

"Yeah buddy, we are," he said. "Willis is just using you guys to try to get to me—try to coax me into doing or saying something ill-mannered. Then he'd slam me."

"We don't need to give him any ammunition. I need you to go up to Portland and be positive, respectful. I need you to be a team player. We're near the end of having to kiss his ass. Hey, we'll catch up on the island. I gotta' get back downstairs and socialize."

The boat was well out into the channel and the air felt heavier. I had written and rehearsed a speech for the event. I'd rewritten it over and over again, ironed out every line, and perfected the tone. It would have been a huge opportunity for exposure. Willis, however, had really stung me with his shun.

My old feelings of unworthiness resurfaced. The feelings I thought were gone slowly crept in again. Was I really just a pawn? Had we grown too fast?

I didn't have all the answers, but I sure as hell knew Ken had changed my life. That was real. That was obvious. For that I believed Ken was right. I forced myself to see no truth in Willis' hesitations about me. It was an attack on Ken, using Rex and me as fodder.

The new Diamonds in California weren't going to eat the shit Willis was serving them with his big southern grin much longer. Eventually the humiliations would become intolerable to even the weakest of the bunch. Splitting from the Willis system was logical. There were several million reasons it would be profitable.

The split was coming.

It was inevitable.

It was festering, itching, and bubbling over. Soon, we would be an island.

17

January 1985

I woke suddenly to the sound of a ringing phone.

My cordless handset was on the couch in the spare room that doubled as my office. It took me a while to find it. It was buried under AmericanMade product brochures. The caller continued to redial, hanging up after a few rings, before the machine clicked on. It had to be Ken.

"Wake up," Ken's voice thundered out of the receiver.

"It's FIVE AM," I said in a woozy, but loud voice.

"Sleep when you're dead. Meeting at our house at ten tonight. Have your Gold and Silver pins there. Make the calls. It's time for the break. Happy New Year."

Click.

After two years in the business these strange, abrupt calls, the ones that would change my life again, weren't that strange to me anymore. They were a way of life and a sign of my importance in Ken's eyes.

I made the familiar drive that evening into the foothills en route to the big house on Beverly Glen. This would be where the California Diamonds intended to announce their revolution, taking control of their tape, book and speaking businesses. Ken and Stewart Moore had finally convinced 100% of the California Diamonds to make the split from Willis. The corporate executives at AmericanMade had seen it before. As long as trifling distributor politics didn't negatively affect their brand, they'd shrug their shoulders and continue pushing products out the door.

Since my confidential chat with Ken and Moore in Maui, I'd become aware of signs foreshadowing the break-up. Our local Diamonds slowly stopped mentioning Beau Willis from stage. They began edifying each other instead. They methodically stopped pushing tapes that featured Willis and instead, hyped the tapes that their voices could be heard on. When the Diamonds and Emeralds in the California organization spoke at events they made sure that there was a second set of master tapes being recorded. Ken and Moore stored those masters and were quietly building a library of tapes in vigilant preparation for the split.

I pulled up to Ken's home. Rex was outside smoking a cigarette.

"What do you think Ken has on his mind tonight?"

His question confirmed he didn't know what was unfolding. I wasn't sure how to answer Rex. Sometimes when I looked at Rex I saw the man who handed me my future on a scrap piece of notepaper. The pompous golden boy inside of me felt unabashed pride at how I'd surpassed his popularity. I hated that part of me—the competitor whose ego grew stronger with every pin level. Rex was steady. He worked hard but never too hard. He kissed only the asses he had to kiss and made it home for dinner at least three nights a week. For those reasons I often thought of him as weak.

"Not sure," I replied softly, as I scooted into the house. I felt good knowing privileged information, but felt horrible knowing Rex sparked a feeling of supremacy in me. I'd never been that type of guy.

There were neat rows of folding chairs set up facing the fireplace with an aisle down the middle. The prearranged configuration of seats reminded me of Ken and Nancy's church. The loyal members of our congregation filed into the home, yellow notepads in hand.

Stan and Katy sat front row center, just like always. I didn't have to waste time contemplating how Stan would react to the news of the break from Willis. He would be ALL in.

Ken shot me a furtive wink as I sat down. Nancy ushered the smokers in from outside, signaling the meeting was ready to begin. Ken moved to the front of the room and checked his watch. The front door opened and a throng of California Diamonds strutted into the room. The heavy artillery had been called in. It was an obvious show of unity.

I felt a hand on my shoulder.

"Hi, stranger."

It was Annie. The meeting was for Silvers and above but it wouldn't be a function at Ken's if she hadn't set up the chairs and written his agenda. She sat beside me and whispered into my ear. She told me she needed to "see" me after the meeting. There were "some papers" I needed to sign. I nodded as Ken called the meeting to order.

"Hi everyone. We have some visiting dignitaries here tonight and we need to get started on time so they can get home before their Cadillacs turn into pumpkins."

A few of us chuckled at the subtle jab. Most of the other Diamonds hadn't yet graduated to Porsches or custom Auburns. Ken was clearly winning the race for the most toys and the biggest home. He waited for the laughter to subside and continued his address in a more sober tone.

"You are all aware that over the last two years the California Diamonds have provided most of the growth for the Willis organization. You also know AmericanMade placed us on probation at one point. We believe Willis triggered the censorship as a way to control us. We also know Willis has no respect for us and no intention of giving us the recognition we rightly deserve. You saw how Willis snubbed two of our new Pearls at his event in Portland. Which one of you will be next if we remain a part of his tyrannical system?"

I looked around the room curious to see if the attendees were keeping up with Ken's weighty message. Ken reached over and pulled down a white sheet covering a banner behind him. He dramatically allowed the sheet to fall to the ground.

"Welcome to Professional Executive Network—PEN for short: Your new home for training, recognition and support."

Ken stood beaming in front of the banner. Most attendees sat motionless, unable to grasp what they'd just seen. I understood their silence. We'd spent years enthralled with Beau Willis; now, we were slamming him as "tyrannical" and deserting him.

I stood and began clapping. Willis had singled Rex and I out. It was personal for me. My hands stung from my violent show of approval for the man who revealed success to me. I believed in this. I believed in Ken.

The applause was infectious. Rex stood and then one by one the others followed. They applauded genuinely. Ken's eyes welled with tears. Moore joined Ken at the head of the room followed by the other Diamonds. Each added their brief testimonial of support. When they were done Ken offered a few final words.

"I can't tell you how much your support means to me. PEN will be the biggest MLM support system in the world one day and you can say you were there for its birth. Nancy and I love each and every one of you because you have guts. No guts, no glory!"

Ken's voice cracked as he turned and walked out of the house with the other Diamonds in tow. Apparently, they were on a major road show, up and down the state over the next forty-eight hours. All seven California Diamonds would announce the split from Willis to their leaders within two days.

Annie slid over towards me and handed me a few documents as the Diamonds slipped out the door.

"You're still an officer of the old insurance agency; we're changing the name and need you off the books. You don't want to have liability for the new real estate projects. Here's a pen," she said, not taking a breath.

"Makes sense," I said, taking the pen and signing.

An unlit Virginia Slim dangled from her lips as she shoved the papers into her folio. Annie was distant. I was sure Ken had her working some long-ass days in preparation for his new real estate venture.

"How've you been?" I asked, trying to muster up some small talk.

"Good. This new role with Ken is better for me. I'm in charge of all operations for the new real estate venture. He's going to make me an equity partner."

She made the proclamation in a rather flat tone. She was either tired or not completely convinced of what she just said.

"I'm glad. You deserve it."

She smiled feebly and glanced at her watch.

"I'm sorry. I'd love to catch up Tony. Maybe a cocktail some time, but I have to go."

She gave me a smooch on the cheek. She didn't say goodbye to anyone as she slid out and lit her cigarette. Annie was probably anxious to get back home. There were two reasons she worked as hard as she did and they were waiting for her at home.

My team took the news well. Most of them had already left. I said goodnight to Nancy and slipped out the kitchen door. Rex stood in the side yard, smoking in the shadows.

I approached him. "Some night, huh?"

"Yeah," he replied, coldly.

We stood in silence. I could feel his eyes burrowing through me but I never broke eye contact with the ground.

"How long have you known about the split?" he asked.

I had to think fast. I didn't want to lie, but I didn't want to hurt his feelings either. Ken had obviously not included him in the inside track of information. A little fibbing was best.

"I figured it out in Maui last year."

A grin crossed his face as he drew on his cigarette.

"You figured it out in Maui, huh? And you didn't bother bringing me into the loop?"

I immediately reminded myself Rex Logan was my friend; I would have never been in the business if it had not been for him. I owed him a better explanation. But I was given privileged information for a reason and was asked not to divulge it. I'd never been a teacher's pet before and I was wearing it well and justifying it. "After I learned about the possibility of a split I was asked to keep my mouth shut. I had no choice," I said.

"You went up to Portland knowing this was going to go down. I get it.

I just wish I was trusted enough by Ken to be brought inside on this one, but I guess I'm not."

He was stung. Rex tossed his cigarette into the wet grass and walked away. I felt like shit. That washed over me a lot in those days. But I learned to ignore the feeling, get my mind off it fast.

I thought about calling Gail, seeing if she'd let me come over. Mazal popped into my mind. Maybe I could meet him for a beer. Maybe he could bring me back down to earth. I wasn't sure if I needed to feel like myself again or if I simply needed to not feel at all.

"How did the sheep handle the news?" Ted asked, startling me as he emerged from the shadows.

"Slow on the uptake, then they got into it. I need a drink. You game?"

"Got some tequila and a full bong at the apartment. Let's go celebrate the jailbreak!"

I didn't argue with Ted's plan. I quickly erased the other options of hooking up with Gail or hunting down Mazal.

When Ken and Nancy moved to the big house on Beverly Glen, they kicked Ted out and he rented a place down the hill. His new crib was a studio apartment over some couple's garage. It was furnished much like his Chevy van: a shag rug, an old futon and two beanbag chairs.

Ted flipped on his thirteen-inch TV. The tiny television was wired for cable, but not legally so. He'd climbed onto his landlord's roof and neatly spliced into the existing cable. He traded some weed for a black box. The pirate component was programmed to de-scramble the pay stations, including, *Spice*, the porn channel. I formed a mental picture of Ted sitting in front of his TV, watching bad porn and eating Cheetos until his dick turned orange. The image amused me.

"Okay, Tony. What are we celebrating?"

"A mutiny in the Valley," I replied.

* * *

I woke up—body on the shag rug, face pasted to the yellow beanbag. After I quietly peeled myself off the sticky carpet and vinyl blob, I staggered to the bathroom. Holding onto the sink to steady myself, I checked the mirror. It revealed an impression of stitches on my cheek from the seam of the beanbag chair. It was a temporary battle scar from another night with Ted.

I softly tottered toward the front door. I spotted the half-gallon bottle of tequila that was sealed when we began our celebration. It was lying on its side, cap off, empty. I couldn't recall whether we drank it all, or if we spilled some of it on the carpet, but the bottle was sure as shit empty.

I glanced at my Timex. It was 8:20 AM, I could still get home and shower by 9:00 AM, ready to draw circles. The only problem was that my head and liver would be lagging a few hours behind my willing spirit.

There was no need to say goodbye to Ted. He was comatose on the futon, snoring like a lumberjack. If I woke him, he'd want to do a "morning shot," a "bonus bong," or worse, a "wake up line."

I drove home. I had to sober up enough to field the barrage of answering machine messages awaiting me. Not all of my downline were present for the big event, yet career-altering news traveled fast.

I'd do what I was supposed to do, assure them that splitting from Willis and forming PEN was the right move for our organization. I'd tell them the new organization was going to be just fine. I'd say all that because I was programmed to say all that. Hung-over or not, I was the best at what I did.

18

Winter 1985

Our transition from the Willis organization to Professional Executive Network went smoothly. We'd just returned from a PEN event called Go Diamond Weekend in San Diego. There were more than four thousand distributors in attendance. It was PEN's first major event and it was flawless. The flock was more motivated than ever and if the distributors missed being part of the Willis support system, it didn't show a bit.

At this point I had more than two hundred and fifty active distributors in my downline and they were mostly all in attendance for the event. The chatter about my impending Emerald pin qualification was palpable. I'd just earned over eight thousand dollars in January, by far the most I had ever earned in one month. Life was good.

There was another phenomenon taking place around me, the second coming of the California Gold Rush.

Ken had casually let people know about his real estate development plans and the investment capital immediately began to pour in. It was as if someone had turned on a spigot of cash. Ken wiped out anything connected with the old insurance entity and had renamed the corporation, Richman Properties. The new entity had already raised more than a million dollars for its first deal, the "Allegheny" project. The Allegheny deal would be a 32-unit apartment complex jammed onto the first piece of raw land that Dr. Johnny convinced Ken to purchase.

Stan and Katy were first in line to invest. Although Stan had many years on me, I offered some advice. I told him conservative investments should be his main objectives nearing retirement, but I knew by the look on his face he'd already made his decision. They invested $150,000 in the first project. Stan sat back, feet up, awaiting their fat monthly interest check.

Meanwhile, Ken somehow talked his way out of the lease at the old building in Sherman Oaks. He moved his new enterprise into the newest and most expensive square footage in the Valley. It was a swanky building in Warner Center, mostly inhabited by powerful legal firms, CPAs and investment operations. Ted had described it to me over the phone. "We have the top floor of the building," he bragged. "Ken dropped a boatload on the place, top of the line furniture, a conference room with custom mahogany build-outs. The place is radical."

Teddy boy had rapidly and predictably become involved in the new venture; apparently he'd graduated from fishing leaves out of swimming pools. However, as many times as I had asked him what his title was, or what work he'd actually be doing, I never quite got a straight answer.

It was just past midnight on a cold Thursday in February. I was driving home from a house meeting in Orange County followed by a late night training session. I was working deep in Gail's downline. Her group was growing and that was a good thing; however, spending time in her organization had grown awkward.

I stalled the break-up as long as I could, but I finally yielded to the pressure that began in Maui. Ken and Nancy had grown more overt in their aversion to my relationship with "the Jewish girl." Ken would throw snarky comments in my direction about "upgrading" while Nancy suggested that there were "more suitable" single women "out there." Nancy would casually mention that she'd bumped into a "great girl at church" whom I "just had to meet." She'd even alluded to the new string of Swed-ish *au pairs* who circulated among the families in the business.

They wanted me with anyone but Gail.

The weight of it all wore me down. Ken and Nancy always led me in the right direction. I had to believe they knew what they were doing. That belief resulted in the talk I had with Gail over coffee. She remained silent for a few seconds, then her eyes started to glisten. Gail wasn't what they wanted me to end up with and I was weary of fighting the battle.

So I didn't.

I sat across from her and watched her cry. I listened as she hurled insults; I wondered how many of them were true. I convinced myself that she was bet-ter off without me, using every logical justification I could dream up. I wasn't the person she'd originally chosen to be with anyway. That guy was mostly gone. She wasn't the one they'd chosen me to be with, and she couldn't change that. I surrendered to Ken and Nancy and in return I broke Gail's heart.

But she wasn't going to stop building the business. She made that clear.

I was bushed as I made my way home on the freeway that night. I pulled into the emergency lane twice. I'd learned the trick from Rex. If you got out and ran around your car five times you could work up enough adrena-line to go another ten miles without dozing off again. The cold air did its job. I jumped back in my car as the phone rang. It was Ken.

"Hey Ken," I answered. "Had a killer house meeting tonight. Spon-sored three new bodies and got fourteen people to hang out for the late-night training session..."

"Good stuff," Ken said cutting me off. "I picked up a plane this after-noon. It's a pressurized cabin Piper Malibu, seats eight including the pilot. We flew back to Santa Barbara to test it out. I hired the pilot full-time. Oh...and I also leased a Lincoln stretch limo yesterday. They just delivered it and we decided to hire a full time driver."

I was well aware that Ken enjoyed the toys that accompanied his wealth, but these toys—a private plane, a full time pilot, a new stretch limo and a driver for it? This all represented a new level of conspicuous consumption, even for him.

"Oh...cool," I muttered, not knowing what else to say. "What kind of plane again?"

"It's a turbo-prop. Seats up to eight including the pilot and depending on ski gear," he said. "Reason I'm calling is our new driver will pick you up in the limo tomorrow at 4:45 AM. We are going skiing, so be ready with all your gear. Ted's gonna' join us. Great job tonight buddy."

Click.

*   *   *

My internal alarm went off before dawn. How long had I slept? Three whole hours? I hadn't gone skiing in years and wasn't sure I could easily locate all of my gear. I threw on a nylon warm-up suit, grabbed my skis, poles and gloves and jammed what other gear I could find into my boot bag. Ken's limo rolled up in front of the house. The driver threw my stuff in the trunk and opened the back door. Ken was kicked back on the oversized leather seats, drinking his signature Diet Coke. He grinned.

"Ain't it great!"

"Shit yeah, it's great," I said.

I glanced toward the front. Ted was passed out, snoring, drool seeping from the corner of his mouth. Ken and I snickered at the pathetic sight as he handed me a soda and we banged cans. The bar had been raised. There was beauty in that smooth ride to the Van Nuys Airport down Roscoe Blvd. Roscoe was a street that constantly reminded me of what I used to be. The moment the limo driver turned into the private entrance to the airport and paused to enter a code, I felt it. It was no longer simply wealth: it was status.

Rolling onto the tarmac, we woke Ted up. He was unable to exit the limo unassisted so Ken and I pulled his tall frame out of the back. We boarded the plane and I settled into a leather seat as Ken and the limo driver helped Ted aboard. Within seconds we were all strapped in and a deck of cards materialized along with iced down Diet Cokes. Ken took out his bulging money clip and began to deal a hand of Acey Deucy.

And just like that, we were airborne.

"Where are we skiing?" I asked, pushing back from the table and taking in the sight of the harvest moon sinking behind the Valley foothills.

"Aspen," Ken replied. "We'll ski for a while before our lunch, take a mid-day Jacuzzi and then ski-out of the place whenever we want this afternoon."

"The place?" I asked, knowing the logistics of getting to and from a typical resort hotel wouldn't make that kind of ski schedule possible. My eyes met Ken's and his characteristic smirk broke out across his face.

"Oh, I forgot to mention, I bought a ski-in, ski-out condo with access to all the trails. Bought it last week. Told ya this was gonna get good."

* * *

We touched back down at Van Nuys Airport later that evening. The limo driver was waiting for us on the tarmac. I was delivered back to my house less than twenty minutes later. I thanked Ken for the experience even before it had completely sunk in. That day I learned it was possible to leave your house in the morning, ski Colorado powder and be home in time to watch Johnny Carson.

We spent forty-five days on the ski slopes that season; each time I was picked up in a limo, flew private and stayed in Ken's ski-in, ski-out condo. Each night I laid my head on the pillow, slipping off to sleep with images of where I'd come from dominating my dreams.

Only a few years back I had seventeen bucks to my name and was wondering if I could hold onto my shitty job selling life insurance. Now I owned a business that was exploding, was a popular keynote speaker, riding around in limos and flying private to exclusive ski destinations.

My standard of living was rising daily. I could barely remember the commission paycheck-to-paycheck life. All of Ken's promises were becoming a reality.

It all felt so authentic.

19

Memorial Day Weekend 1985

The home was out of place in the otherwise architecturally bland community of Granada Hills. Steve and Samantha Steenberg's house featured an ostentatious faux Grecian design that stuck out in the beige, stucco jungle of the north Valley. Inside and out, the home reflected Samantha: Loud.

Ken and Nancy adored Steve and Samantha, and as time passed, so did I. They were about ten years older than me and the parents of two small children. On the surface it would seem we didn't have much in common, but we were experiencing the same growing pains in the business. It was reassuring to be able to hang out with peers who were also in the thick of it.

Steve and Samantha were religious yet never pressing about it. She'd be the first to fudge a prayer under her breath to make me smile or to explain away a religious question from her children as "because God says so," with a shrug and a smile. As there were levels of our MLM, there were levels of religious zeal. It was comforting to find people who leaned more in my watered down direction.

Steve was good for me. He had Ken's business drive but knew when his workday ended. His children made him smile. He and Samantha had a marriage that always projected they'd just said their vows, no matter how many years had passed. Plus, they threw a mean barbeque.

I made my way into the backyard to find a lively pool party unfolding on that warm May afternoon. Samantha stepped in front of me, blocking my path. She quizzed me in her cute South African inflection.

"What's shakin' Tony? Are you going to spend time with our newbies today? Pump 'em up a little, or is this party a hit and run for you?" Without waiting for an answer she turned in the direction of the sun-drenched contingent and shouted in her shrill voice: "Hey everybody! Tony's here!"

There was a small smattering of sarcastic applause mixed with catcalls. I knew why I'd been invited. As a twenty-something, in a sea of couples in their thirties and forties, my job was rather clear. I'd been summoned to mingle with their younger new recruits. Not a bad job—warm day, good barbeque, not to mention the lavish and complimentary attention to which I'd grown accustomed.

Rex and his wife were also on hand for the free food. Rex would kid around and mock me throughout the afternoon. His eye rolls were legendary. He was never the golden boy but found it hilarious that I had risen to such status in the organization. He found a comfy lounge chair in the shade, parked his body there and got up only when there were ribs and chicken coming off the grill. I, however, had to sing for my supper. I tackled the chore of motivating the eager young hopefuls on hand.

My first introduction was to Alex Josephs. He was a professional contact of the Steenbergs. He owned a small, but growing residential real estate office in the Valley and thought I was a person worth meeting. He listened closely to what I had to say. Guys like Alex were quick and painless. Yet I didn't plan on spending my afternoon with a lot of dudes. I'd be on the look out for some better scenery.

Breaking up with Gail meant one thing for sure, my favorite wingman, Ted, would be glued to my hip again. And he was. I'd slid right back into the gutter with him. We were trying to reincarnate the kind of late night depravity that only he and I could conjure, away from Ken's watchful eye, of course. But it wasn't quite the same as it was before; there were parts of my steady relationship with Gail that I missed. In addition, Ted's party habits were more out of control than ever and I was even more conscious of getting caught. But late nights with Ted were a familiar scene and a way to cancel out some of the pressure of the business.

My original plan that afternoon was to work my way around the pool, shake a few hands, motivate a few hopeful new distributors, and then I'd get home for a nap and shower just in time for my date that night with a new girl I'd just met.

My plans quickly derailed when I spotted Ken and Nancy's new *au pair*, Catarina. I'd met her a few months prior, just after they'd summoned her from Sweden to care for Chandler. The little guy was almost two years old, but already a handful of trouble.

Ted predicted the Scandinavian invasion. Ken and Nancy wanted the status of having an *au pair* as soon as Stewart Moore and his wife hired one. It was only a matter of time before it became standard practice within the business. Ted was right: The *au pairs* had invaded the Valley. I wasn't complaining. They were all very pretty, very sexy and ready to have some fun in the L.A. sun.

Catarina waved me over. She was platinum blonde with classic Scandinavian features. As enticing as I found her, my eyes landed on the tanned bikini-clad girl sitting beside her, dangling her feet in the Jacuzzi.

The Steenbergs had figured out how to budget for an *au pair* as well. They had to keep up with the *Joneses*. They decided to employ Catarina's best friend from Sweden, Annika. She had me as soon as she uttered a simple, "Hello". My eyes were instantly fixed on hers. Maybe I stared too long, I'm sure I did. I couldn't take my eyes off her. They traveled from her face down to her bikini tan lines.

Her English was very good. She said my name in a way that barely hinted her background but had an effort to it that was intoxicating. She was different than Gail.

I watched as she tended to the Steenberg flock, magically healing skinned knees with a kiss, clearing the tears from one child while the other rested comfortably on her hip. I found myself watching her every move, waiting for an opportunity to talk to her again.

The distributors at the pool party quickly figured out my attention would be dominated by Annika for the remainder of my visit. As such, they circulated over with their newbies in tow for introductions. I don't remember a single new person to whom I was introduced that day. For the entire afternoon it was just Annika and me. Nobody else existed.

The afternoon flew by. I had been looking forward to my date that evening, but now I was full of dread. I barely knew the girl I had a date with, but knew she wasn't Annika.

"Is it okay if I call you?" I asked.

"What are you doing tonight?" she inquired.

Before I knew what I was doing, plans were being made to meet up with her and Catarina later that night after the Steenberg's kids went to bed. That moment plays back like a blur. I remember my heart racing, the feeling I had when she asked what I was doing that night. I had no idea how I was going to dispose of my dinner date. I snuck out of the party offering polite goodbyes from afar to the people I'd ignored for three hours.

During the appetizer course with my date, my mind replayed Annika flipping her hair in the glistening sun. During the main course I made a mental checklist of what I'd need to learn about Sweden to make conversation easy. By dessert, my thoughts were focused on what Annika may look like underneath that bikini. By the time the check came all I was fixated on was how I was going to get my date deposited back home. I needed to get over to the dance club I told Annika and Catarina I'd meet them at.

The Universe cooperated with my twisted plan that night. Shaking my date was easier than I imagined. My date's entrée didn't agree with her. With a ten-minute drive and a peck on the cheek she was history and I was off to the dance club.

Problem solved!

The rest of the evening was both fuzzy and magical and it included a stop over at Mazal's parent's pad. They were out of town and we had the place to ourselves for a midnight swim and Jacuzzi. It was just after 2:00 AM when we called it a night at the Mazal estate. We agreed it would be best if we took ourselves back to my house rather than to have the girls do early morning buzzed stumble-ins. When we arrived at my pad I gathered blankets and pillows from the closet for the impromptu slumber party. I tossed the stuff on the two couches. Catarina was already putting herself to sleep when I realized Annika was missing.

I walked towards my master bedroom. It was dark as I neared, except for the lights emanating from my stereo. She'd hit the button on my cassette deck. Roxy Music's *Avalon* played. Her clothing items were strewn on the shag carpet, forming a trail that led to my bed. The sheets only partially covered her suntanned body that was reflecting the red and green lights of the tape deck.

There was no conversation. There was none needed.

She'd come out of nowhere.

It was all coming out of nowhere.

20

May 1986

My life was a big rush. A race-around-the-track, no-hands-on-the-wheel, max-out-the-speedometer kind of rush. I wasn't scared. I wasn't smart enough to be scared. The combined effects of money, recognition and the euphoria of being in love had taken over. I was Teflon—invincible again, just like when Mazal and I were seventeen years old. The eleven months since I'd met Annika flew by like an incredible fantasy. I didn't want to be single anymore. I wanted to be with her.

Our relationship was sweet. I'd never described any relationships I ever had as "sweet" until I met Annika. She was caring, wise beyond her years and supportive. If you could have molded the perfect, young MLM wife she was it. If Gail was the World Series, Annika was the tickertape parade after the 7th game. She wasn't as challenging as Gail. She was more of a cheering section. She cooed at my jokes, flirted with every word she uttered and she adored being on my arm. I never thought I wanted or needed the stay-at-home wife who'd have dinner waiting, but that was before I met her.

My tape and book business continued to expand and the speaking income was easy cash. They were assigning me the best PEN gigs. Everyone wanted me to come to their town and fire up their crop of young, single AmericanMade distributors. I qualified at Emerald pin level a few months earlier and was counseling with Ken closely on when to actually begin my Diamond qualification and then how to announce it to my group and the world.

Dr. Johnny rang up my car phone. I was expecting his call. He was going to hype me on a house that I supposedly needed to buy. Richman Properties picked it up at an auction. Ken casually mentioned the home to me a few days earlier and he told me to take Dr. Johnny's call.

"It's a steal. It's in Woodland Hills," Dr. Johnny said. "Big lot. Killer neighborhood. It was seized in a drug raid—was on the news. Drug dealer was shot in the house or some shit like that. Richman Properties got it real cheap and we'll make you a smokin' deal. Ken will remodel it for you—do whatever you want. You need to buy this place. We'll make a little on top, of course, but you'll get a killer deal and I'll get you the loan too. Ken said you need a bigger home anyway."

I didn't balk. I figured Dr. Johnny and Ken knew a good real estate deal when they saw one. Dr. Johnny's excitement was infectious. If he thought I needed this house, and Ken thought I needed this house, then I needed this house.

"What's the address?" I asked Dr. Johnny.

He reeled it off and hung up. I took the next exit off the Ventura freeway and headed for Woodland Hills. The words Dr. Johnny relayed, "Ken said you need a bigger home," echoed in my head. I reached the address. The home was beautiful, a sprawling ranch-style property with tall palm trees framing the entrance. I liked it. Annika would love it.

I jumped onto the Boulevard. It was getting late and I was buried. I had a house meeting scheduled that night and ten other things to do beforehand. Ken had been pushing me to upgrade my lifestyle, and the money was getting good, but I sensed the place in Woodland Hills would be a stretch. Part of me wanted to play it safe, wait until I was a full-fledged

Diamond before buying a bigger home, but Ken wanted me to step up. He always seemed to know what was best for me.

The paperwork had just been completed for my parent's second round of investment money with Ken. Their fist round was working out well and had enabled my father to step away from his job and retire a few years early. The second round seemed like a no brainer. I had also given Richman Properties a little money along with my aunt and uncle. In total, our family had invested $470,000. With the monthly interest coming in from Richman Properties, my father and mother were able to live more comfortably. It was just another reason to thank my lucky stars that I had met Ken Richman.

Stan and Katy had also invested an additional round of capital with Ken. Although Stan hadn't retired just yet, he was close to pulling the plug on his engineering job. They were even starting to visit motorhome dealerships to test-drive some of the big expensive units, like the ones pictured on their refrigerator.

I rolled to a stop in my driveway and looked around. Suddenly, my house in Canoga Park seemed tiny, humiliating and uninhabitable. I'd never noticed the shabbiness of my blue-collar neighborhood. I couldn't believe I was parking my dream car in that driveway. It felt wrong. It was wrong. I'd surpassed that address.

My hand glided to my car phone. With no hesitation I dialed Dr. Johnny. "Johnny...tell Ken I want the home."

* * *

Catarina told us the Richmans' new pad was "humongous." When I reached their new address I couldn't believe it. I immediately found her description modest. The mansion was magnificent. It sat high in the foothills, a much higher elevation than even their place on Beverly Glen. It was protected with ornate iron gates and several security cameras. I hit the buzzer and the gates slowly opened.

I drove up the winding driveway to a circular motor court. It displayed the Richmans' toy collection. From sports cars to limos, even a trailered twenty-four-foot tricked-out ski boat named, *No Guts, No Glory*. Nancy popped her head out the front door.

"What're you doing standing out here?" she asked.

I was actually counting up all of the cars and toys adjacent to his tennis court.

"Hi, Nancy. Congrats on the new house," I said.

"Thanks! Catch up, Ken's giving Stewart the grand tour."

Obviously, Stewart Moore was paying a visit and surveying the new property. Nancy ushered me into the living room. I didn't recognize the furniture. It was all new. Their previous decor was barely broken in, but apparently it was already dated. Ken turned the corner with Moore behind him.

"Quite a dump, huh Tony?"

"What can I say, Ken?" I shrugged. "I'm not sure I'm gonna be able to describe this place to my downline."

"You better figure that out," Ken said. "I didn't buy this place to keep it a secret."

Ken continued his tour. There were views of the Valley from every part of the house. They even had vistas that provided an ocean view on a clear day. We passed Chandler's bedroom suite. It was a series of three rooms adjoined to his private bath. His actual bedroom was much larger than mine. There was a dedicated room for his toys and books and yet another that they had turned into a two hundred square foot walk-in closet. Their maid was hanging up the boy's clothes and I watched, numb at the thought that young Chandler Richman's wardrobe was at least five times the size of mine.

Moore paused and interrupted Ken's diatribe as we moved past Chandler's room and made our way back to the guest bedrooms.

"I'm not sure how you pulled this purchase off," Moore said, in the way of a question.

Moore was walking slow, making small talk, but I saw through his sham. The maid was not bad looking at all. As I studied the furniture and wall hangings I couldn't help but catch Moore studying the maid's ass.

Ken chuckled, never planning on answering Moore's earlier question. He changed the subject.

"Hey Stewart, Tony agreed to buy a home from us. We picked it up at an auction. We're remodeling the place and it'll show like a custom home when we're finished."

"That's great," Moore said. Then he turned his attention to my personal life. He was good at that. He was blunt, very businesslike, and rarely beat around the bush, unlike Nancy who had been circling our house tour like a shark.

"Ken tells me you're hot and heavy with this Swedish girl. Is that right?"

I immediately wished the conversation was back on Ken's new home. Hearing a man twice my age make references to my love life, referring to my relationship as, "hot and heavy," made me queasy. I had no interest in discussing my sex life with Moore. "We're fairly serious," I simply replied.

"Cut the crap," he said.

If I knew I was going to walk into an ambush I would have skipped the Richman home tour. I didn't answer him. I looked away. Moore rubbed the eagle that hung on the thick gold chain around his neck, massaging it with his fingers.

"Ken and Nancy are very high on this girl—Annika is her name, right?"

He knew her name.

"I'll just ask one favor," he stated.

Of course he would.

"Hold off your nuptials until you're safely into Diamond qualification and we know you are going to qualify. Will you do that for us?"

Ken inserted himself into the conversation. I could tell by the look on his face that he even thought Moore had gone too far. Their side looks and eyebrow raises were pathetically obvious. I tried to zone them out imagining them rehearsing this like idiots before my arrival.

"Nancy and I love Annika," Ken declared. "This is the right one for you buddy. You need to marry her. It'll be good for you to settle down. We'll get you to my jeweler so you can buy a proper ring. But Stewart's right, let's wait till we know you are going to nail down your Diamond qualification and then we can plan a wedding. Make sense buddy?"

I knew what they had in mind. They wanted to elevate the first single Diamond on the West Coast—claim it as a big victory. However, there was another part of this equation. If I continued my single life after Diamond qualification, it wouldn't be a great bargain for them—especially if I continued bar-hopping with Ted. It would be ideal for them if I stayed single well into Diamond qualification, then came off the market.

I shrugged. "You can count on me."

Moore smiled, and then told Ken, "Have your driver take me to the Burbank Airport. I have to catch that flight to San Jose."

Moore hugged me and told me he wanted what was best for me. Ken decided to ride with him to the airport and they were gone.

Nancy and I watched them drive off through the kitchen window while Catarina chased Chandler around the house and then outside onto the tennis court.

"Would you like a drink?" she asked.

Nancy wandered over to the ornate, but empty bar that was positioned in the vast living room. Even in this friendly atmosphere, she still played her hostess role flawlessly. She located a well-hidden bottle and mixed us matching gin and tonics, never bothering to ask if I even wanted one.

"Let's have a drink—celebrate our new homes," she said, matter of factly.

She tended the bar with an attitude of, "I rarely do this, but what the hell." The pressures of moving into the big new house had worn her down.

"I know you're feeling stressed right now. Annika is a great girl and we want to see you together. But Ken and Stewart are right," she said as she stirred her drink. "You owe it to yourself to go into Diamond qualification as a single."

I nodded. I knew she was right but I was tired of being told what to do and how to live my life. I sipped my beverage, listened to the ice in my glass echo in the spacious kitchen and tried my best to go numb to the topic. Nancy looked smaller in this property, overwhelmed and swallowed up by the expectations of it all. I tried to humanize her while she continued her sermon.

"Counsel with Ken and he'll tell you when to pop the question. It's an important decision. God has brought you and Annika together for a reason—he's brought all of us together for a reason."

I nodded to be courteous, not really sure what I believed in my heart about God and the universe anymore. Yet I knew what I felt about the business and Annika. I finished my cocktail and left.

*   *   *

I was nervous as Annika and I clinked glasses, toasting to my entry into Diamond qualification. That was my deal with Ken. As long as I was in the Diamond qualification period, and all was solid, I had his blessing. I had Ken's blessing before I'd even mentioned it to my parents. I decided to tell my folks after Annika agreed to the marriage.

The ring was from Ken's jeweler in Encino. I arrived at the jewelry shop to find three pre-approved rings waiting for me. Each was out of my price range—yet that was before Ken started setting my price range on things. It took very little convincing from Ken before I wrote one of the biggest checks of my life.

I was uneasy. The expensive Italian restaurant was suggested, the wine pre-ordered and the candlelight excessive. I ordered for the both of us, having memorized Nancy's suggestions but I couldn't tell you what we ate. I was too nervous to recall the menu.

My "put the ring in the dessert" plan was vetoed. Instead I dropped to one knee after a short post-dinner drive and lovely stroll along the Pacific Coast Highway. When she said yes, I immediately felt overwhelmed with joy. Next, I felt confident Ken and Nancy would be proud. Finally, though, I felt a stab of regret that I hadn't done it my way.

21

Friday, August 1ˢᵗ, 1986

Annika and I squeezed our way into the packed Mexican restaurant. Ted waived us over to the table and timidly introduced us to his new "steady" girlfriend. It was a landmark that he was introducing us to a girl. She was cute, but didn't say much. She seemed content to sip on her Cadillac margarita and let Ted do all the talking.

The dinner was a pre-nuptial celebratory dinner for Annika and I, but I knew Ted wouldn't be picking up the check. Even though the dinner was in our honor the discussion was focused on Ted's newfound monogamous relationship. I refused to buy it.

Annika was doing me a favor; she didn't enjoy Ted's company and I understood why. She had a compliant nature. It was useful to me. It made moments like this easier to endure. I wanted to hang out with Ted so we hung out with Ted.

Finally, Ted strayed from raining compliments on himself to raining compliments on Ken. Between mouthfuls of chips and salsa, he told us what was going on at Richman Properties. I was glad to learn any information at all on the subject. Ken was so busy that all I'd gotten from him were sound bites, if even that.

Ken originally planned on only developing one or two projects at a time, but the investment money flowed so voraciously into Richman Properties that he had to do something with it. More than four million dollars had been invested, most of it emanating from Ken's downline and the crossline Diamonds' groups. As a result, he increased the number of projects to seven. "It's perfect, dude," Ted bragged. "Ken has total credibility from the business so he's cashing in on it. He puts the word out that he has another new project and the cash rains in. Bam! Who wouldn't want to invest with him? Right?"

At that point I interrupted Ted, mostly because I was weary of listening to his conceit. "Sounds like a lot more work than you guys imagined."

"You said it." Ted sighed, "I've been working sixteen-hour days all month, Tony."

The restaurant was so dark it could have been morning and we never would have known it, but a glance at my Timex was all I needed. I smiled at the workhorse impersonator. I knew Ted better.

I suspect Ted picked up on my skepticism. "Gotta make an exception every once in a while," he quickly added. "Annie wouldn't be happy if she wasn't doin' most of the work, anyway."

I wish I could have disagreed with him and stuck up for my old friend but he was right. I pictured her slumped over a desk trying to make the office hum. Annie believed in a good day's work and was relieved to have found a boss who leaned on her the way Ken did. To Annie, hard work was the catapult to more money, better titles and early retirement. Ted was allergic to work. He'd retired at birth. He motioned to the waiter.

"A Tequila Sunrise...and make it a strong one," he said. "I'll drink to Annie. Without her the place couldn't run."

Annie enjoyed Tequila Sunrises; Ted ordered the drink out of either guilt or obligation. He drank it faster than a proper toast could have been made and continued to ramble on about the "machine" that Ken was steering. Ted and Annie were two people from very different stations in life. She spent her career working tirelessly while he bypassed work all together.

I'd sat in that restaurant a hundred times before. It was a Valley gem named Casa Vega. I'd been there with Annie and Rex. The subject we were celebrating or the sorrows we were drowning were hard to remember, but the laughter and conversation were hard to forget. It had been Mazal and the golf team before that. We'd started drinking there just after we acquired fake IDs in 1978. Mazal and I sat at the bar, hoping our true age wasn't discovered.

I enjoyed the restaurant with different company, but this was the company I was keeping these days. The woman to my side, who was never a real fan of Mexican food, glowered at the man across from me, who was never really a fan of losing me to a wife because he knew it would ruin our good times. He continued rambling on as I tried to stay in the present and not flounder in the past.

"Dr. Johnny's the man," he said. "He finds the deals, structures the loans, and works his magic with the Zoning Department. It's beautiful."

I nodded, munched on the tortilla chips and listened to Ted's chatter. I had questions, but I knew not to doubt Ken's business acumen. He wasn't stupid. So I kept quiet and ate my carnitas.

I let Ted's voice drift off as my mind turned to the two weeks ahead of me. I'd be one of the keynote speakers at the upcoming PEN event at the Anaheim Convention Center. The event was PEN's most ambitious function to date with more than six thousand people expected to attend. We'd also be moving into the big new house. I needed to stay focused. My attention needed to be on the woman at my side, the jewel on her finger, and my imminent Diamond qualification.

* * *

I hurried out of the limo door to faint music emanating from the arena floor. It was a monsoonal August afternoon and I wanted to get into the air-conditioned building before the sweat showed on my custom Italian suit. I helped Annika out of the back. In the heat of the excitement, I'd almost forgotten she was sitting there. A small entourage waiting to direct us into position immediately surrounded us.

We walked down a backstage hallway passing several of the Emerald and Diamond couples who'd completed their speaking duties on the afternoon agenda. They were staying to hear me speak. I kissed Annika and she walked to her seat in the wings where she'd watch my keynote address.

Once Annika and I were legally married, she would join me on stage. It was a thought that hadn't hit me until then. I looked at my bride-to-be and she looked so pretty. Her dress, hair and make up were perfect, although she was so naturally beautiful that she looked great without being all made up. I wondered if she would enjoy the spotlight as much as I did: If she'd find her stride beside me. She flashed me a smile and wave, her engagement ring catching a sliver of light. She'd do just fine in the spotlight.

I was directed to the bottom of the staircase that led to the stage. In a moment Ken and Nancy would introduce me to the multitude of distributors who had come to pay homage to the rock stars of the business.

By this juncture I'd become a confident and polished speaker. My routine prior to a speaking event included writing what I'd say, editing my speech a dozen times, and then internalizing it. I paced back and forth in front of my bathroom mirror, drilling on the key lines and phrases, even pausing—waiting where I knew there'd be laughter or applause. I'd do this in the mirror until my speech and body language were in sync.

Ken and Nancy began the introduction. I peeked through the curtain, into the crowd. Stan and Katy were seated in the second row. Stan was on the edge of his seat, notepad in hand, hanging on every word, ever the dutiful distributor.

My emotions toward Stan and Katy were divided. Part of me pitied their slow growth, his age and optimism. I was sure Stan would never feel what I was about to feel. He'd never grow as fast or climb as high. Yet the other part of me admired what they had. There she was, her hand on his leg, just a resting reminder that she was always by his side.

The lengthy introduction by the Richmans and a thunderous ovation for me finally arrived. Peter Gabriel's *Big Time* blared from the studio monitors on stage and the house system, filling the arena with the booming base. I bounded up the stairs with summoned energy. My brooding expression transformed into a huge smile. My fist instinctively began pumping the air in time to the music as I leaped onto the stage from the last stair. Thousands of screaming AmericanMade distributors stood chanting my name. I gave big hugs to Ken and Nancy.

I grabbed the microphone. I took a deep breath and wailed into it.

"Who wants to be free?" I shouted.

The crowd went wild. They celebrated the first single distributor to enter Diamond qualification on the West Coast. It was the big time. I was in total control.

I didn't walk across the floorboards, I glided on them. I didn't motivate, I preached to the devoted members of our church, the parishioners who attended to hear my words. The stage was mine, the audience was mine and it was so much larger than my life had ever been that I was unrecognizable to myself.

22

Monday, August 11ᵗʰ, 1986

The privately-owned Learjet touched down at Montana's Gallatin Field. Beau and Rhonda Willis sauntered down the stairs while their luggage was loaded into a waiting limousine. Their lavish ranch property was located close by and would serve as the spot for the meeting.

Willis hadn't been heard from since the California Diamonds split from him. In his opinion, AmericanMade had merely slapped Ken on the wrist with the censorship two years earlier. Their compliance department wasn't stern enough with him. The outcome Willis desired didn't happen. Willis would have settled for a more obedient Ken Richman, but if that wasn't possible, he wanted a "terminated" Ken Richman.

He got neither.

Willis had grown up on a farm. He now knew what kind of animal he was dealing with. Ken Richman was both a strong and clever species. Instead of becoming docile when slapped with the censorship, Ken swiftly adapted to the new hostile environment, changed his tactics and created a pack to run with for protection. He also channeled the sting of the minor setback into focused perseverance and energy. It was the kind of drive that wounded animals often summoned to finish off their prey after being bloodied.

Willis had underestimated Ken Richman—saw him as a soft city boy, soaking up the sun by his oversized pool in L.A. But he now knew that Ken Richman was nothing of that sort. He was a cunning and dangerous animal that had staged the coup that cost him millions in tape, book and speaking revenues.

Beau Willis retrenched his position and remained patient. Like any skilled hunter, he knew that, if you wait long enough, your prey would eventually make a mistake and show their soft white underbelly in the open, then you can take your shot.

His prey had done that.

The first surreptitious letter appeared in his mailbox promising sensitive information about Ken Richman for a fee. If the offer "was of interest," he was to send a money order to an entity that identified itself as *TSV Associates*.

The offer very much appealed to Beau and the fee for services seemed reasonable to him. However, the Mole could have asked for anything, money was really of no object. Over the next several months Willis invested a great deal of it, collecting reams of information from the Mole. The last package received from TSV included information that he thought could be particularly damaging to Ken. Willis didn't care to share the information he had collected with AmericanMade's home office just yet. They seemed aloof to his vendetta against Ken.

Willis would share the damning information with a natural predator of his intended prey. As such, there was one more person due to join the party in Montana. The commercial commuter plane taxied toward the gate. The lanky federal inspector stepped off the flight that had originated in Los Angeles. His attire was far from the standard issue: He wore a gray suit and crocodile boots; his long hair tied into a ponytail. His thick handlebar mustache suggested a man with serious intentions.

Charles Boone was a veteran Chief Inspector for the Federal Bureau of Investigation. He specialized in consumer-based investment schemes. He worked closely with the Securities and Exchange Commission and the U.S. Postal Fraud Division to bring perpetrators to justice. Boone had seen it all in his thirty-two years on the job. He could smell an investment scam a mile away.

Brief pleasantries were shared before Willis motioned to the waiting limousine. Boone was anxious to learn about the investment practices of one Kenneth R. Richman. Willis was just as anxious to tell him all about it.

* * *

Halfway across the country another assembly on the same subject was underway. A parcel from TSV Associates had reached the Compliance Department of AmericanMade's home office in Champaign, Illinois.

Over the years, the Compliance attorneys there had seen many shoddy sales practices and abuses of the company's marketing plan. Some distributors resorted to any and all means, legal or not, to grow, or profit from their downline.

The package included extensive and detailed information. The compliance department dug into the volumes of photos, tapes, documents and handwritten notes, but puzzling questions remained. Fledgling distributors were usually the culprits who initiated the type of scam that may be unfolding in front of them. These unseasoned distributors would run a quick scam and swindle their downline or crossline. They'd pocket the money and vanish quickly. They usually had no substantial income or business at stake. Yet, Ken Richman was the subject of all of this incriminating information and he was far from a *fledgling* distributor.

Richman had one of the largest and most profitable distributorships on the West Coast. The attorneys in Compliance knew all about the *extra* profits in the business—the tapes, books and speaking fees. By their estimates, the Richmans were earning more than six hundred thousand dollars a year from ALL of the income sources. All they had to do was keep on cruising across the stage at big events yelling "Ain't it great!" like the rest of the Diamonds. If they simply did that, the cash would just keep pouring in.

What befuddled the compliance officers at AmericanMade was the size of the scam and who was steering it. Why would the fastest growing Diamond on the West Coast sabotage such a successful operation? It simply didn't add up. They had to be missing something.

By their estimates, just over eight million dollars had already been sucked from the pockets of AmericanMade distributors and deposited into the Richman Properties bank accounts as well as Ken's personal account. The internal investigation had slowly become formal; however, the compliance department still had a lot of work to do to make a solid case for termination. It wasn't yet time to alert the authorities.

Moreover, no information would be released to anyone until a solid containment strategy was in place. AmericanMade's chief compliance officers had a primary responsibility. Their job was to make sure American-Made remained squeaky-clean when any scandal surfaced. For the investigators and staff attorneys in the compliance department, the hard work was just beginning and they had to get it 100% right. They would take their time.

23

Saturday, August 30ᵗʰ, 1986

After walking off the stage in Anaheim, the crowd stayed on their feet and summoned me back for a curtain call. The place was still buzzing big time as Stewart Moore took the microphone and sent the crowd to dinner.

I was mobbed as I made my way to the arena floor. The meet-and-greet line was massive. Eventually, Ken rescued me and told me I had an "urgent message." Thankfully, my urgent message was that my soon-to-be wife was waiting in our hotel room and my job was over for the night.

I was sure that watching me on stage was a mild aphrodisiac to Annika. She still had a limited knowledge about our country and our culture, but the MLM world she saw unfolding around her made me a star. I was celebrated on stage, and also by her. Life was very good.

Annika and I rolled up to our new home with the movers right behind. I slid the key into the door and we entered our future.

We wandered through the empty rooms. Annika acted as tour guide, telling me where she planned to position the new furniture. She had been spending more time with Nancy, which helped enlarge her vocabulary to include designer labels I feared we couldn't afford, yet I'd never tell her no. She'd envisioned this house: It was more than just a home to her—it was status. I looked at Annika the way I'm sure Ken looked at me a year before. She was taking her steps toward becoming the MLM wife I couldn't wait to have beside me. She continued with her architectural prophecies.

I didn't listen too closely to her ideas; instead I listened to the echo. I'd never owned a home where the sound bounced so strongly. Before I could point out the enormity of it all, she disappeared.

I found Annika in the kitchen feverishly unpacking. She barely heard the doorbell ring, the florist come in, and the delivery made. She perked up, nose high like a bloodhound. She turned and caught sight of the massive floral arrangement that now sat in the center of our entry table. I read the card. "It's from Ken and Nancy."

Annika bounded toward me to read the words accompanying our first housewarming gift.

Dear Tony and Annika:

We are so happy for you and wish you all the best in your new home and in your new life together. You are very special people to us. We look forward to spending time with you guys on the beaches of the world.

Love,

Ken and Nancy

Annika shuffled boxes around like a woman on a mission. She'd already planned the first meal she'd cook in our new kitchen before she unpacked a single pot. She was nesting. I was relaxing, watching the house come together by the woman who made it a home.

Annika had worked in other people's homes. I don't think I understood the importance of a home of your own until I saw the joy in her eyes. She had folded someone else's linens and rocked their babies all without complaint.

I heard Annika calling me again. While I was in a back bedroom a courier delivered a small box. "Open it baby, open it," Annika begged. She was in pure bliss, like a kid unwrapping gifts on Christmas. I waited a moment. I wasn't sure what was inside and I didn't know how much more happiness I could handle. I opened the small box, revealing a smaller box with embossed gold leaf letters that read "Rolex." I flipped open the box and found the watch—a Presidential model, along with a card.

Dear Tony:

Please accept this gift as our congratulations for going into Diamond qualification. Nancy and I love you and Annika very much.

Ken

I gawked at the watch as it glistened in the light. Annika squealed, pleading for me to put it on. I took off my old Timex and tossed it onto the kitchen counter. I'd worn that old watch since I first started in the insurance business in 1979. My dad gave it to me for my eighteenth birthday. Buzz picked it up used and polished it up for me to wear when I first started selling insurance.

I slipped on the Rolex and instantly felt its weight.

"It looks great," Annika said.

"It's so different," I said, my eyes fixed on the diamond-encrusted bezel.

Annika took me by my shoulders. "You deserve this life," she whispered.

For a moment I wanted to laugh. Annika didn't know the Tony I was before the business. She had no idea what I did or didn't deserve. I wondered for a moment how Gail would have handled that moment in my life. Annika looked at me as though I was something special. Even the way she touched my shoulders had a 1950s, stand-by-my-man feel to it. I wasn't used to it yet. Changes were happening so quickly. I was overwhelmed with the perks raining down on me.

The phone rang. Annika answered. I could hear the voice; it was Mazal.

His distinctive base-drum sound boomed through the receiver. He wanted to come by and "see the new pad." Annika glanced at me then told him I wasn't home. She was protective of me in that way. I was relieved. I hadn't returned some of his recent calls.

"What do you want me to do with your old watch?" Annika asked.

"Just set it on my nightstand," I said. With that, I strolled outside through the screen door and plopped down on the old rusty lounge I'd dragged over from the house in Canoga Park. The old piece of crap was like a reminder. The sun beat down on me as Annika continued to speak to me from inside. She asked me questions about how I'd like to decorate the rooms, what I wanted and how I wanted it. She never waited for an answer. Her excitement had taken control.

She rambled on about the friendship of Ken and Nancy, what they had done for both our lives. She gushed over their lavish gifts, including what she found to be the most important—an invitation to attend their Presbyterian church with them as a couple.

I lay there and tuned her out while raising my wrist to the sky to obscure the blinding sun. I looked intently at the diamonds on the outer rim on my new watch and allowed her voice to fade into the background. There, beneath the shadow of my Rolex, I felt the weight of it all.

24

Saturday, September 6ᵗʰ, 1986

I'd be married in two weeks. Meanwhile, I was on target to finish Diamond qualification in the coming months. All vital signs of my business were healthy. My tape and book flow was exploding. My August earnings were my largest month of income ever—over eleven thousand.

I had spent the day at Ken and Nancy's. I played two sets of tennis with Ken and then we sat in the Jacuzzi. Ken mentioned they'd just reached the "nine million dollar mark." He was referring to the total monies invested in Richman Properties. He mentioned that they had twelve major projects in the works. His numbers were staggering.

"I'm pumped that your family's involved," he said. "We're getting ready to finish and flip our first project—the Allegheny deal. We're turning a huge profit on it, more than eighty-five percent. I want to get you involved as a general partner on a project or two—you'll pocket a half-million or more."

I couldn't comprehend the figures he was touting and I didn't know enough about real estate development to think my personal involvement would be warranted. His matters of fact statements were scary and exciting at the same time. I didn't know what my involvement as a formal partner meant, but the conversation shifted quickly, as it often did with Ken.

"I've tried to get a few of the Diamonds to come in with me on these deals. They tell me they're paying off homes and cars so they can be debt-free—as though that makes sense from a tax standpoint. Some of these guys are flipping idiots."

I nodded my head like a good little sheep, but I wasn't sure I completely agreed with his philosophy. It was also odd to me that he was dressing down his peers. I'd never heard him disrespect any of his fellow Diamonds before.

"If they don't have the balls to jump in," he added. "We'll just keep raising money with the people underneath them."

Ken stared out at his awe-inspiring view of the Valley.

"Outside of Stewart, most of the Diamonds are weak. The PEN board fights me on every point. I get the impression that some of them would have been happy to stay with Beau Willis and keep sucking his dick."

He stepped out of the Jacuzzi, dried off and continued his tirade. "When my net worth is ten times theirs, then maybe I'll get the respect I deserve."

Ken finished his rant, leaving me sitting in the hot tub, stupefied by his stance. But I couldn't stew on what he was saying—or stew in the hot tub—any longer. I'd promised Annika a quiet night at home and that's what I was going to deliver. The wedding plans had started to overwhelm her and the business was continuously smothering. Annika and I needed a tranquil night together and alone. I dried off and headed home.

I tried to dismiss Ken's ranting and complaints about his peers from my mind. My focus for the night had to be Annika. As I entered the house, I heard the phone ringing. I answered to hear words from my mother I'll never forget:

"Honey, come home right away. Something has happened to your father."

*   *   *

The news on my dad wasn't good.

Buzz suffered a stroke the day of my mom's call. When I arrived at their house, he was slumped down in his favorite chair, an unlit Camel cigarette dangling from his lips. One side of his body was paralyzed. He wouldn't allow Mom to call an ambulance. I approached him and knelt down. He looked at me and smiled weakly. I removed the cigarette from his mouth.

He said, "I'm not doin' so good."

His words were labored and his eyes cloudy. I'd never seen a stroke victim, but I knew instantly. The right side of his face was sagging and limp, as was the right side of his body. I asked him to squeeze my hand but he couldn't. I fought back tears, trying to remain calm. I signaled to Mom to call an ambulance. Buzz took notice.

"Buddy, I don't want to go," he mumbled, his words hard to understand.

"Dad, we gotta get you to a hospital. You've had a stroke or heart attack. We need a doctor to see you. Understand?"

He didn't answer. Instead he moved his head slightly and gazed downward.

Weakness was foreign to my father. Buzz may not have made millions or built companies, but he had a great deal of pride, pride that was slipping away as he struggled to blink. Finally, he moved his eyes back to mine and spoke. "Do what you need to do," he whispered.

The agonizing days that passed brought a blur of bad news. Prior to his stroke, Buzz had been complaining about a sore shoulder. It turned out he had lung cancer: a tumor was hidden behind his shoulder blade. The doctor was treating the stroke when the tests came back and we learned the tumor had metastasized to his brain. It was inoperable. When the doctor used that word, "inoperable," I didn't fully understand the weight of it. I thought it meant other treatments would be used to help him recover. A few days later the truth sank in. I was hoping for a miracle...any kind of miracle. The oncologist ordered linear radiation treatments immediately to prolong his life.

Buzz would be hospitalized on the date of our wedding, but Mom arranged for a one-day pass so that he could be with us.

He told her he "Wouldn't miss it for the world."

25

Saturday, September 20ᵗʰ, 1986

I crept out of bed and tiptoed outside. I tossed myself down on a lounge chair aimed toward the orange glow emerging in the sky. The sun was rising on my wedding day.

Annika's family and friends from Sweden were asleep throughout our house, having traveled to Los Angeles for our nuptials. Some of them were in guest rooms; some were sleeping on couches. Between their luggage and the mess of pizza boxes, beer cans and folding chairs from the previous night, my home resembled a college frat house.

The human litter was Annika's; the other untidiness was mine, leftover from a halfhearted attempt at a bachelor party that didn't seem like one.

Annika's bachelorette party was held the previous week. She knew nothing of it until her friends arrived and swept her away. AmericanMade distributors with children were stuck with parental duties that weekend as the mass of Swedish nannies flocked to celebrate with my bride-to-be. She arrived home having been showered in drinks and gifts of lingerie.

I was distracted by my father's poor health and, basically had to throw a party for myself. My best man was Ken. He was charged with sending me out of single life with a bang. He'd reached out to me the week before to discuss it.

"The bachelor party...what do you want to do?"

"What can I get away with?" I asked.

"I'm asking what we can do that won't get too crazy," he said.

What's the point? I immediately felt I'd blown it and should have selected Mazal or Ted to organize the party. With Ted I would have most likely wound up in a Vegas hotel room with three hookers, some blow and a donkey. With Mazal I would have at least been treated to a cold keg of beer and a few of the Valley's finest strippers over at Bob's Classy Lady.

"I appreciate anything you wanna' plan," I told Ken, trying to sound grateful.

"Good. How 'bout a poker game at your place?"

I assumed he'd take care of everything, but I didn't hear from him until I called him the Thursday afternoon, the day before the poker party.

"What are the final plans for tomorrow night?" I asked.

I could tell by his tone that he hadn't made much headway, but I was taken aback when he asked me whom I'd invited. At the end of the day I made the calls myself.

Except for Mazal, my old friends hadn't been invited to the wedding so the calls quickly became awkward. When I phoned Mazal he gave me a bullshit excuse. When I hung up I realized my oldest friend wasn't involved in the most important day of my life, except for delivering the flowers.

Two years after he'd begun working there "part-time," Mazal was still part of his family's thriving flower business. In fact, he was firmly ensconced in it. After completing six years in college and earning a master's degree in journalism, he simply fell into the trap. Who could really blame him? He was pulling down six figures and he didn't have to take any shit from a boss, other than his older brother. Still, there was a part of me that wanted to see him pursue his dream. He was a gifted writer, but the allure of the cushy job in the secure family nest took its hold on him. Like I said...who could blame him?

Mazal and his workers would be setting up the room for my wedding, but the guy whom I'd always thought would be my best man wasn't even in the wedding party. How the hell did I let that happen?

My bachelor party wound up consisting of two cases of beer and some take-out pizzas. Most of the small gathering arrived at 7:00 PM and were gone by 10:00 PM. Ted showed his face at 10:15 PM, locked himself in my master bathroom and engaged in his own party. He emerged with a coke-stained nose and plans to "meet some bitches over at the Red Onion." Apparently, his steady girlfriend was out of town.

And with that my bachelor party was over.

So there I was, eyes closed, lying on that lounge chair in my backyard, watching the orangey morning sunrise, trying to imagine what the day would be like...for Buzz...for Mom...for all of us.

I drove alone to the banquet hall in the hills of Burbank. I handed the valet my keys, grabbed my garment bag and found my way to the dressing room. I kicked off my jeans and dressed in the tuxedo. I fiddled with my bowtie finding it hard to look at myself in the full-length mirror. I wasn't sure who was looking back at me.

There'd be just over three hundred people in attendance. When we started making the list and adding key people that were part of our downline it was difficult to draw the line. Then, we had to add all of our good friends crossline, as well as all of the PEN Diamonds and Emeralds. Four years earlier I could have barely filled my living room with friends, but at least they were genuine. I could fill a ballroom now, but who were they and why were they there?

The image of an insolvent Tony DiBona walking into Ken and Nancy's house four years earlier popped into my mind for a second. Even though I only had seventeen bucks to my name, I might have been a happier person back then. I might have even been living a richer life in some ways. My existence was certainly less complicated back in the day. My thoughts traveled back to those long rounds on the public golf course with Mazal and those long nights on that beach in Santa Monica.

Noise leaked in from the ballroom. I cracked open the door that led to the banquet hall. It was Mazal and his employees hauling in the flowers that would cost me more than my first car did. I watched them work. He was good with his crew, gentle with the centerpiece flowers and although it wasn't his dream job, he looked content.

I couldn't remember the last time I'd called him and asked him to hang out, have a beer, or hit some golf balls. That would have been unproductive. I'd chosen the fast-paced lifestyle of the business. I wasn't sure if I neglected him because I was embarrassed of who I was back then or whom I'd become. I'd abandoned him, but he'd never abandoned me. He'd been right there all along. I closed the door and sat in front of the mirror again, dozing. I hadn't slept well in weeks.

Ken walked into the room and startled me.

"It's show time buddy. Time to become an honest man."

"Did my sister show up yet?" I asked.

I don't remember if Ken answered me. All I remember is he entered the room and jolted me back to the reality that this day wasn't only big for me. It was big for my family and I owed that to Buzz. I needed to be there when he arrived.

I walked outside and directly into Mazal, the closest person I'd had to a brother my whole life. I couldn't recall if I had even called Mazal to tell him about my Dad. Before I could ask he pulled me in for a hug. "Sorry about not being able to make it last night—three weddings to set up to-day—had to get up early."

"You didn't miss much," I said.

The seats were filling up. I shook a few hands then saw my sister's car arrive. I rushed over. Buzz needed help getting out of the car. He was weak from the stroke and the radiation treatments. He was a shell of his former self.

I glanced over at Mazal and saw the look of shock on his face. That confirmed I hadn't bothered to tell him what was going on with Buzz. I instantly felt like shit.

I embraced my father.

He smiled.

"I made it, buddy!" he said. "They couldn't keep me down for this."

The words tumbled out of his mouth. And then he broke down sobbing. Then I broke down—but stifled it back.

Buzz covered his face with his hands. I held his weakened body to mine as tightly as I could and shielded him from the view of others until he was composed.

"I'm going to get through this," he said through small tears. "I'm going to fight this—beat this."

"I know Dad. I know."

I was so preoccupied with my father that the actual reason I was at the event—for my own wedding—had completely slipped away from me. I helped support my father as we slowly made it into the seats in the front row. And then I took my place at the end of the aisle. For the first time that day my thoughts turned to Annika.

* * *

To say I was mentally exhausted would have been a gross understatement. Thank God the freeway was mostly empty for the drive to our makeshift San Diego honeymoon. I was barely keeping it between the lines. Our postnuptial celebration would be short. We'd be home from Carlsbad in a couple of days so I could be with my parents for some additional testing at the local cancer center.

The spectacle I'd been part of that day was more like a showcase for the business than a sacred wedding day. Since most of the PEN Diamonds were in attendance, a lot of the attention was directed at them.

And then there were the comments they made.

Stewart Moore said it was about time I made an "honest woman" of Annika. He smugly ignored the fact that my delayed proposal was partially his doing. Ken quipped about not having to apologize for my "backsliding behavior" anymore. Parts of my wedding felt like a roast.

Doesn't anyone say congratulations anymore?

The Diamonds were relieved that I was formally OFF the dating market. In their eyes, I couldn't do any damage to the organization as a happily married man. They'd successfully directed my attention away from Gail, or any other temptation, keeping me single and out of trouble until I'd entered Diamond qualification.

It was a masterful ploy.

But I played my part too. I'm sure they already had their eye on the next young, single hotshot. I didn't envy that person.

I was told wedding days are exhausting but I had no idea how draining all the congratulations and back-slapping could be. The steady train of people seemed endless. Stan and Katy couldn't applaud Annika and me enough. I have never blushed that much in my life.

Rex embraced me for a hug, slipping a joint into my pocket. "For the honeymoon," he whispered. I suppose it was his wedding present. I chuckled and thanked him, and then I searched quickly for a trashcan to dump the spliff in. Annika didn't know all that much about my partying days and I wasn't about to spend my wedding night stoned.

Annie and the Logans sat at a table on the outskirts of the action. The Diamonds had preferred seating; a perk for them I hadn't noticed at the time. Annie made her way to the head table and gave me a peck on the cheek. She spent a minute warning Annika what she was getting into. "I knew this kid when his bank balance was less than his age," she snarled.

That she did. She was probably my oldest acquaintance at the reception after Mazal finished arranging the flowers and left.

As the cake was being cut, I glanced at the DiBona family table. I hadn't said two words to my cousins, aunts or uncles all day. Sadly, they were out of place amongst the "elite" of our business—the ones talking in code. My two uncles Lou and Mike approached me to pay their respects.

When we turned sixteen it was Mike DiBona that made sure me and my sister, Regina, had cars to drive. He had no children of his own and would give us the shirt off his back. When I was a little kid it was Lou DiBona who bought me my first set of boxing gloves and enough baseball gear to break a few windows. I had special bonds with both uncles, but uncle Lou and I had an even more unique bond. As I got older everyone said he and I were a lot alike. We had eerily similar sensibilities.

Uncle Mike gave me a hug and went back to the family table. Uncle Lou placed his hands on my shoulders and said, "We're very happy for you and Annika. You are my favorite guy and you deserve the best." His eyes were glistening. He'd been holding back tears most of the day because he was so broken up about my dad's condition. They were as close as two men could be.

"You sure have a lot of friends. I didn't know the wedding was going to be this big," he said, in awe of the crowd that had assembled.

Yeah. I didn't either.

Near the end of the afternoon, each Diamond in attendance took the floor to offer a toast, but there were no humorous old stories. How could there be? My four-year involvement in the business had successfully erased most of my past. The toasts never traveled to Stan or Annie. They were simply too low on the totem pole to get the microphone. Rex was also in Diamond qualification but he opted to stand down and not make a toast, probably in light of the fact that each Diamond's toast contained New Testament references.

I hoped the microphone would somehow reach Ted. He could have made a joke; one I would have visibly regretted and secretly loved. Wedding days were supposed to be exhausting but not isolating.

On this day, at this event, the Tony DiBona sitting at the head table in his thousand-dollar tuxedo had completed the successful conversion prescribed by his organization. At my core I struggled. The task of playing a role wore me down, but I justified it as a small price to pay for what I was getting in return. There had to be some trade-off, right?

Stan approached.

"Say cheese," he coaxed waving his Polaroid camera. Annika and I smiled and accepted the little picture.

"Make sure you let it dry," he warned.

Katy chatted about having never seen a bride as beautiful as my wife and I heartily agreed. I glanced at Annika and couldn't believe how absolutely stunning she looked, from head to toe, and in every way. I looked back down at the reincarnated Tony slowly emerging in the rectangular

Polaroid picture. As the tuxedoed ghost materialized, I realized the guy smiling back at me was of my own design and of my own free will. Nobody held a gun to my head. At any point along the four-year journey I could have said "No, thank you" to the whole world I had joined. I could have refused to compromise my values and principles. But I didn't.

My dad was ready to leave. I hugged my sister, Regina, tightly. I hadn't thanked her for her help with him since he'd become ill. I also hadn't included her in much of the wedding stuff. I held her tighter as the regrets piled up in my mind. I kissed my dad. His eyes glistened again. The look of love and pride on his face was unmistakable.

I knew at that moment I'd been way too harsh in judging his level of success in life. He had unwavering principles and values.

He knew what true success was.

Despite the wealth and status represented by my wedding list, it was he who was far richer than any man in attendance that day.

26

October 1986

Chief Inspector Charles Boone smiled broadly on his flight back to Los Angeles after his trip in Montana had concluded. In fact, he and his team were almost three full months into the investigation and it was still hard for him to wipe the smile off his face. He knew the amount of work ahead of him, but this case had the potential to make some headlines.

Beau and Rhonda Willis had been gracious hosts. Their ranch home was no average log cabin. The mansion in Montana was exquisitely adorned with antiques on all three of its floors. The outdoor fountains were dotted with sculpted Cupids and their pool was Olympic-sized, and was bordered on the far end with a two-bedroom casita equipped with a cabana boy for every need. Boone counted four people on duty at the Willis "ranch house," providing round-the-clock chef and maid service for the king and queen and their guests.

The six-car garage was loaded with motorized toys for every season. There were numerous ATVs along with a set of snowmobiles for good measure. Willis' lifestyle was unimaginable to Boone. He called home the first night and told his wife all about the splendid estate. He knew there was money to be made in multi-level marketing deals, but he'd never imagined the level of conspicuous consumption that was on display in front of him.

Willis got right down to business after a quick meal that day. He fed Boone inside information on Ken Richman and his real estate activities. The information was provided by an informant Willis either couldn't or wouldn't identify. He told Boone that he mailed cashiers checks to a post office box located in Reseda, California. He advised Boone that he sent the checks to the attention of an entity named "TSV." All he desired in return for providing the information, he told Boone, was a "federal indictment against Richman for investment fraud."

Boone described the extensive investigation and adjudication process to Willis, explaining in detail the laws defining fraud. Boone outlined the elements of a Ponzi scheme. The "burden of proof," Boone said, fell on the prosecuting attorney. Willis showed indifference to Boone's lecture. He wasn't looking for lessons on the legal system.

He was looking for something else.

Willis normally radiated poise. His skin was the color bronze, thanks to a never-ending string of tropical vacations and endless days spent on his yacht, docked in Florida. He'd made a living by keeping up the appearance of being calm, cool and in charge. Yet talking about Ken Richman brought out a different side of him. When Ken Richman was the subject of discussion, the hue of Willis's square face grew bright, flushed in shades of red. His voice hit a childish octave and he lost a measure of his composure.

This amused Boone. His opinion of Willis quickly took shape during their meeting. Boone figured out what he was dealing with. Willis and his wife acted sophisticated, but he knew they were plain old hicks under a thin veneer of polish. During his stay in Montana, Willis made the message abundantly clear: He wanted to see Ken Richman convicted of fraud and sentenced to a lengthy prison term.

Boone and his staff were doing their best to verify all of the incriminating information they'd been handed. His team was busy scrutinizing the information piece-by-piece. The still anonymous Mole, TSV Associates, had provided Willis with photocopies of bank and escrow documents with the signatures of Ken Richman on them. The other officer's signatures that regularly appeared on other documents were that of Annie Wu and a Mr. Johnson Gergin, who they had learned went by the nickname, "Dr. Johnny."

Boone speculated that the informant could be on the inside of Richman Properties, but that defied logic based on what they were learning. Ken's elite employees were enjoying six-figure salaries, hefty bonuses and company paid luxury vehicles. There would be little motivation for any of them to leak information about Richman—and, in turn, screw up that kind of wet dream by incriminating themselves.

While keenly curious about TSV's underlying identity, Boone was more fervently absorbed with Richman and the information in hand. He would eventually figure out who was supplying all of this juicy stuff. When he met with his team, Boone stressed that their top priority was proving Ken Richman intentionally orchestrated a Ponzi scheme and defrauded investors.

Their strategy was clear. The F.B.I. team headed up by Charles Boone planned to pinpoint a high-level Richman Properties executive and then motivate that person to cooperate with the investigation. That person would be expected to testify against Richman in return for immunity from prosecution.

Boone and his team had already profiled the Richman Properties executives. Initially, they thought Dr. Johnny would be a promising candidate. He'd already served jail time in the early 1970s for marijuana trafficking, albeit small time. They thought he might be less than enthused about a return visit to prison. However, as Boone's investigators followed Johnny, they found themselves less anxious to approach him with an offer. He appeared to be drinking his weight in whisky and be using a heavy amount of street cocaine. They photographed Dr. Johnny with Ken's brother-in-law, Ted, purchasing an eight ball outside of a strip club in North Hollywood. They also followed Dr. Johnny to several of the most notorious massage parlors in the Valley. They finally concluded that these bad habits would make him a far less credible witness than others when put on the stand.

The brother-in-law, Ted, had made the initial candidate list, but they quickly lost interest in him after Boone learned he didn't have officer status in the corporation and had no access to critical documents. He was a flunky at best and wasn't worth pursuing.

After weeks of digging, Boone's team focused on the candidate they wanted. Now it was Boone's job to convince his target that turning state's evidence and cooperating with the F.B.I.'s investigation would be a much better strategy than going it alone and spending a four to six year stretch in some federal prison.

Boone didn't think this particular target would be hard to convince.

27

Friday, November 21ˢᵗ, 1986

B^{eep!}
"When you have a few minutes I need to speak with you. It's kind of important. Don't want to leave a long message. Just call me."

It was Rex. His voice on my answering machine seemed alien. I was puzzled. Usually, his messages sounded as though he was speaking from the depths of a hammock with a joint in his hand. This was not one of those messages. I called him back; he wanted to meet face to face. We agreed to meet for a drink.

My wedding day was only four months removed, but it seemed like four lifetimes. Shortly after we returned from our abbreviated honeymoon, we learned my father's linear radiation treatments had failed to produce anything positive. Buzz's lung cancer had spread. His doctors exhausted all healing possibilities and there was little we could do except admit him to hospice care and give him morphine for the pain.

I was well into Diamond qualification, pushing forward. Our income was growing; yet, the money and the next level had lost most of its significance to me.

I parked next to Rex's Cadillac and strolled into one of our old hang-outs in Sherman Oaks. The Pineapple Hill was a semi-dark dive bar where nobody in the business would ever go. I guessed that's why Rex chose it, or did he just want to recall the old days as much as I did. I spotted him bellied up, jawing at the bartender. "Come on," he said. "Where's the Jack in this Coke?" The bartender laughed as he took the bottle and added a generous dose of Jack Daniels to Rex's drink.

I laughed. "You're pissing off the bartender before I even get a drink."

"Ya have to keep this guy honest," Rex snorted.

I ordered a beer.

"I played tennis with Ken yesterday," he said.

Whom did he think he was kidding? Rex didn't play tennis. Rex didn't play any sport. I think I saw him toss a Frisbee once. What was he doing at Ken's house and why wasn't I invited? "When did you become Ken's tennis buddy?" I asked. "Did he run your flabby ass all over the court?"

"He invited me up to play tennis and talk about my Diamond qualifica-tion. What was I supposed to do? I put some sneakers on and showed up, he handed me a racket and started rocketing tennis balls at my face. But that's not my point," he said, in a rather abrupt tone. "I overheard some twisted shit. That's why I called you."

He paused to take a long drink from his cocktail. I looked at his cleanly shaven face and focused eyeballs, behind his conservative wire-rimmed glasses. He'd changed his appearance to accommodate the business. It made me flash back on what he used to look like.

I'd met Annie first, in the new agent license class in the summer of 1979. She told me about a guy she knew. I assume she'd tired of nudging me awake during class and thought if she introduced me to Rex he could babysit me for a while. Rex was a different person back then. He wore a full thick beard, dark prescription aviator shades and he chain-smoked like a Turkish prison guard. It was hard to find the man behind the smoke, facial hair and dark shades but during that lunch he enlightened me. Rex taught Annie and me how to survive in commission sales.

Eventually, the business even twisted Rex's strong sense of identity. He and I had both adapted to the game so we could reap the benefits. Even with the façade he was regretfully maintaining, he hadn't lost his bullshit meter. His deep-rooted need to rebel against authority and mistruth had not been completely squashed.

"Ken was on the phone with Annie when I got there. I heard only his side of the conversation, but it was tense. Ken said to her, 'It's your job to get the investors paid this month. Figure it out.' Then he slammed down the phone. I asked him if there was a problem and he said, 'Well, some days are better than others, but we have a chance of pulling it out.' I asked him, 'Pull what out?' but he blew me off and said, 'Let's play some tennis.'"

Rex waved the bartender over and slid his empty glass toward him. "After two sets he picked up the conversation again, complaining that he may be able to keep the investment firm together but he'll have to place a moratorium on interest payments. He called it an 'uphill battle.'"

I gripped my beer bottle tightly. I felt dizzy as Rex chewed on the ice from his drink and continued. "I asked Ken what he meant by a 'moratorium' and he said, 'Stop paying interest for a few months, get at least one project completed and sold, plug the leaks.'"

"What the fuck does he mean by leaks?"

"Not sure. We finish playing. We were sittin' there at the courtside table and Nancy came out. She was holding the cordless phone, her hand cupped over the receiver. She told Ken a prospective investor was on the line...a guy in the business in Santa Barbara. She handed the phone to Ken. I heard Ken's side of the conversation. He told the investor it sounded great and he asked if he could have Annie call him on Monday so they could draw up notes and mail them out. I'm freakin' out figuring this guy dropped a pile of cash in Ken's lap. Ken hung up with a smirk on his face. He smiled and said, 'How 'bout that? Another hundred-seventy-five thousand.'"

I felt short of breath. Ken had admitted to Rex that there were serious challenges at Richman Properties, but he took new investor money, anyway. Ken was full of optimism the last time we spoke. I was silently panicking, but Rex had more to say.

"I asked Ken, 'Didn't you just tell me you're having a problem making interest payments to investors?' He nodded. And then I asked why he'd agreed to accept this guy's money if he couldn't pay current investors their monthly interest. Ken told me, 'With a little more cash, we can probably pay investors for another month or two—ya know...buy some time.'"

Rex finished his Jack and Coke and wrapped up the bad news. "I asked Ken if the money he just raised would make a difference long-term. He shrugged and said, 'Don't know, but if I can buy some time and finish and sell the Allegheny project nobody will know about our current shortfalls.'"

"I got ready to leave when Steenberg pulled up," Rex said. "Ken told me Steenberg has a potential new AmericanMade distributor: a doctor who also has some investment money. Ken said, 'I'm going to show this guy around the house, sponsor him in the business and then convince him to invest.'"

I felt numb, confused, and stupid. We were talking about Ken—my best friend, the best man at my wedding. Rex's version of their exchange had to be either poorly recollected, or induced by an afternoon bong hit.

The thoughts that shot through my mind were conflicting. I'd known Rex for years. He'd never lied to me, but we'd grown apart. He was no longer my primary mentor, Ken was. I paid for the drinks and we left the bar. Rex took me by the shoulders.

"I'm sorry to dump all this crap on you when your father is in hospice, but I know you and your family have a lot of money invested with Ken. You know I haven't been a big fan of Ken's real estate venture—never believed he should be surrounding himself with people like Dr. Johnny. If you can possibly get your family's money out, get it out."

I nodded.

Rex grew wistful. He said, "Thanksgiving is gonna be hard for you guys. I know."

I drove home in a coma.

Ken insisted the real estate projects were solid; he even asked me again to be a general partner. Dr. Johnny was getting me a copy of the new offerings for my review. I had some reservations about the fast-paced growth, but since the day I'd met Ken in 1982 I developed the habit of ignoring transactions that hinted of unethical behavior. Ken had improved my life. My car phone rang.

"Tony? It's Stan."

I composed myself and tried to sound upbeat.

"Hey, haven't talked to you in awhile," I said. "How ya doin'?" My mind was so screwed up I wasn't even sure I should talk to Stan at that moment. Part of me knew he was a steady voice of reason and the other part of me knew I shouldn't spread a story I had yet to confirm. I didn't feel like making small talk but answering my phone by the second ring had become a reflex. Ken didn't like to wait. I'd now pay for that with a friendly chat with a heavy heart.

"We're doing real darn good," he said. "Katy and I might qualify as Gold pins next quarter. We're moving slowly, but we're moving. Some good news." Even Stan's bragging was weak. "We liquidated the rest of my retirement account and put it into one of Ken's new projects."

I shuddered. I couldn't get off the call fast enough. There were only two logical answers to this scenario. Either Rex had dreamed up the story, or Ken was telling two completely different stories. But I'd never known Rex Logan to lie.

I considered calling Ken but then placed the handset down. If Rex was right, then I didn't know Ken like I thought I did. What was the point in asking a liar if he was lying?

I needed to seek out a truly reliable source.

28

December 1986

I turned twenty-six a few days after Thanksgiving. Five days later Annika turned twenty-four. Then I fell into a pre-Christmas funk. I'd never enjoyed the holidays for reasons I'm sure a psychiatrist would have helped me understand. It was simply easier for me to be in a shitty mood for the twenty-three days following my birthday.

But, this holiday season was more depressing than usual. Visiting my father each day in hospice and trying to console my family was necessary but draining. It was especially depleting on Annika. This wasn't how she'd imagined the honeymoon phase of our life would be.

I could hear Annie's car stereo a block away, blaring Elvis. Annie and I shared a love for the King. She gunned her BMW up to the valet circle, got out, dropped her half-smoked cigarette on the asphalt and snatched the valet ticket. She was fifteen minutes late, as usual.

"Fuckin' Ken," she said. "I'm trying to leave and he gives me ten things to do on my way out the door."

"Good to see you, too, Annie."

"I'm sorry," she said. "I've been stressed. Good to see you too, sweetie."

She gave me a peck on the cheek and we walked into the discreet martini bar she'd picked for our late-afternoon cocktail. I initiated the rendezvous, wanting to isolate Annie and learn what was going on inside Richman Properties. She selected the out-of-the-way place for our rendezvous, wanting to distance herself from work.

"How's your father?" Annie asked.

"We're trying to keep him comfortable."

"Your parents are good people," Annie said. "Give your mother and your family my best." She ordered a Tequila Sunrise. Lately, a lot of people were asking me to relate their best wishes to my parents. Unlike the others, I was certain Annie was sincere.

Her drink arrived and she took a sip. "To what do I owe the honor of a private audience with the great Tony DiBona?" she asked. "I know you didn't call this meeting to chit-chat about old times."

I was hurt by the remark, an emotion that Annie read on my face. She looked out the window at the passing traffic, lit a cigarette and said, "Shit. How long has it been since you, Rex and I hung out? Remember how much fun we used to have?"

I couldn't recall the last time I'd seen Rex socially. I hadn't talked to him in more than a month before he called to tell me about his mind-blowing tennis game conversation with Ken. It had been years since I'd seen Annie socially. "It's been a while," I said. "We didn't have money back then, but we always had good times. We should get together, the three of us, take a night off and go out."

Annie looked at me blankly. She puffed on her cigarette and smiled.

"You walked into the Richman door the moment Ken needed someone like you," she told me. "You had star power and Rex didn't. I'm sure he's jealous, but who cares? It doesn't make much difference anyway."

"Aren't you getting what you want out of this?" I asked.

She tapped her cigarette on the table and pondered her answer.

"You sit with your people over coffee, ask them what their dreams are and then promise to make them rich. That's fine, but you know what bothers me? In all the time I've been with Ken, he's never asked me about my dreams. He barely spent any time with me on the MLM business after he and Rex sponsored me. I was invisible. I was never going to crack the boys' club."

Annie made me feel guilty. I watched her try not to sink into the humiliation her statement induced. Ken never took her seriously. I doubt he made the business a viable option for Annie. To be a superstar in Ken's world was nearly impossible if you were female and in your late thirties, unless you were someone's wife. And if that's who you were, your job was to stay home, stock the garage shelves with soap, vitamins and Power Punch.

"Let's do this," I suggested. "I'll tell you my dreams if you tell me yours."

Her face brightened. I saw a glimpse of the old Annie for a moment—the sardonic, but genuine person I'd first met.

"You first," she said.

I sat there for a moment. The little game was my idea but it was turning out much harder than I'd expected.

"What would make me happy probably doesn't look much like where I'm at right now," I said.

Annie looked at me, clearly puzzled.

"Don't get me wrong, it's great," I said. "The big house, the car...I don't know." I stopped talking; I couldn't find the right words.

"Not liking the game anymore?" she asked.

"I thought it was a team sport. I expected more widespread success. A few people in my group are making money, but most are just breaking even. It's hard to stomach sometimes."

Annie looked at me, sternly. "It doesn't bother you that you're getting rich making bullshit promises to people that probably can't or won't do what you did?" Yes, it bothered me. It bothered me a lot. Hearing Annie put it into those words made it hurt even more.

"The majority of your distributors aren't going to do nearly as well as you because you were willing to put in the 18 hour days and sell your soul. In addition, you had Ken's hype machine behind you," she continued. "This business is loaded up for the guys who have real recruiting talent and who're willing to do anything to make Diamond. The rest want to belong and hold on to a dream. You guys are selling hope, not soap."

I shrugged, offering no defense.

"You were an easy mark," she said. "How were Ken and the others going to tap into the young, single market if the only people succeeding were middle-aged couples? Ken needed you to recruit a demographic he didn't have before."

Annie took the last swallow of her Tequila Sunrise and held up the empty tumbler, signaling for a refill. As for me, I found myself swallowing the truth I'd rarely had the balls to look at.

"Okay, so you've been a pawn in their game," she said. "It hasn't hurt your wallet."

I wanted to tell her some stuff at that point—bare my soul. I wanted her to know that I was getting to the point where I no longer wanted to draw circles every night and I felt trapped. But I suspected Annie wouldn't believe me.

The barmaid delivered a fresh round of drinks. I drank my beer quickly. Annie could see my misery. Moreover, she could tell I knew the reason for my misery. She sensed the foolishness I was feeling. I broke the silence: "Buzz never needed all this shit to be happy. Hell, I never thought I needed it."

"You never think you need a sock in your jeans until you put one down there and see how much bigger it makes you look," Annie quipped.

Annie was on fire with her Tequila infused cynicism. But she was also making sense.

As for me, I knew that I'd allowed material possessions to mean too much to me. I loved the moment I bought the Jaguar—the feeling of power, the knowledge I drove a car few people could afford. I always felt a burst of pride whenever people gawked at me in that car, particularly guys driving beat-up Pintos who found themselves stopped next to me at traffic lights.

My Jag wasn't even the model in the picture hanging on my refrigerator door, but I didn't care. I was simply committed to driving a status symbol. That was all that mattered. When the hell did expensive toys become all that mattered? Lately, during those long drives on the crowded L.A. freeway system, I'd spend my time thinking about the lifestyle we sold to people and the distance between that and the truth.

Ken and Nancy were on the road constantly. Catarina rambled on incessantly about how "little Chandler missed his parents." Ken's lifestyle wasn't exactly what he made it out to be. What the hell happened to six Saturdays and a Sunday? My parents were never away—never absentee parents. My mom was home every night. Buzz never missed even one of my little league games.

I turned from Annie, concealing my tears.

"It's really okay," she said, averting her gaze; I don't think she wanted to embarrass me.

After a moment I composed myself. "Okay," I told Annie, "now it's your turn."

Annie talked about her first meeting with Ken. She saw in Ken a way out of Starbridge and gladly joined him when he walked out on Fred Cohen. Ken promised her more responsibility and an income to match what he promised would be a significant role in his organization. "I thought I was set when we established the insurance agency," she said, spinning the ice in her empty glass. "I'd have a permanent equity position, but then Ken rolled into the office one day and told me about the *new* plan."

"He'd been introduced to Dr. Johnny. That asshole convinced him that he had a captive audience of investors—his downline and the downline of his fellow Diamonds. Just like that, Richman Financial, the insurance gig, turned into Richman Properties, the real estate thing, and my supposed equity in the insurance agency vanished."

She sat back, and lit a cigarette. "You know how Ken is," she said. "He sold me on the new direction, told me I'd become a partner of Richman Properties after we built it to a certain point—I'd become the 'chief operating officer with stock ownership'"

I could see the frustration in her eyes. She mentioned the "trouble" that soon arrived.

"Dr. Johnny was supposed to be an external advisor, but Ken gave the bastard a corner office, fat salary and a company Mercedes. I told Ken we shouldn't be spending money on perks like that before we completed a project. He blew me off. He said, 'Trust me. We have heavy investor money coming in.' Obviously, Ken wasn't going to listen to me."

Even though it was the truth that I'd come to hear, I wasn't completely prepared for it. Annie continued her story.

"I read the Allegheny proposal," she said. "That was the first circular Ken started mailing out to everyone. The numbers in that offering didn't make sense to me. I gave it to a friend, a CPA in San Francisco with a background in private placements. He checked with a buddy in zoning and it turned out there was no way Ken could get 32 units jammed onto the building envelope of that lot. Dr. Johnny had guaranteed him we could. I told Ken the numbers were bogus, but Ken didn't want to hear it. He told me he'd hired "talented people" to handle "those types of details and problems." Then he stated that he planned to hire two more people to assist Dr. Johnny. Two days later there were new employees on staff, also with inflated salaries and company cars."

Annie was seething as she began to dump some of the information I so badly needed to know. It was very apparent that she despised Dr. Johnny and his tactics, but had nobody else to tell that to. Next, she stated that Ken asked Dr. Johnny to take one more look at it and make sure "Allegheny would fly." Johnny finally admitted that Annie was right about the zoning and there'd be fewer units, but they could project higher rents to alter the capitalization rates so they expected the income to be similar to what they originally projected.

"But it was all just a bullshit manipulation of numbers on paper," she snarled. "And Ken didn't want to know anything more about the numbers after that. 'It would all work out in the end,' he told me."

Annie was finished with her drink, but she wasn't finished firing down on Dr. Johnny.

"After that, Dr. Johnny avoided me as much as he could, but he basically told me that I should do my job and he'd do his. He essentially told me stay in my office and shut the fuck up."

As she told me that, I saw the muscles in her face tighten. I asked, "So Dr. Johnny spun the numbers on the Allegheny deal from the start?"

"Worse," she said. "That's just one part of what makes him a sleaze ball. I'm almost certain that he's been collecting kickbacks on each raw land purchase. I think he's colluding with the sellers on the purchase prices—padding the final price—getting some money back from the seller outside of escrow. I can't prove it, but how would any of us even know, let alone Ken, who's out on the road doing his MLM thing three weeks out of the month. I'm sure Johnny's also been getting kickbacks from the mortgage brokers we use. Shit...the escrow companies are probably paying him a referral fee too. He picks the escrow companies, not me. He collects from everyone!

"Does Ken know this? Have you told him?"

"Yeah, I told him," her fingers tapped the table uncontrollably. "He told me to look into it and make it stop, as though I had the power to do that."

If Annie was telling me the truth—and she had never lied to me—then I had no choice but to believe Rex's story as well.

"Ken is interviewing a potential new C.O.O., his name is Griffin Davis—a real high-priced gun, a turnaround guy." Annie barked. "He told me I'm not capable of running a company this size—and not to 'take it personally.' He told me to be a team player. Meanwhile, I have no stock, no equity—which he'd promised me."

Annie glanced at her watch. I realized that she probably needed to get home to her boys, but I still had questions I needed answers to.

"I heard a rumor about a moratorium on monthly interest payments. Any truth to this?"

She set her cocktail down and examined me through her thick prescription glasses. "Where'd you hear that?" she asked.

"Can't say."

She lit another cigarette. "It was suggested we consider that as a means of reorganization. I don't think we're gonna have to do it immediately because we still have new investor cash coming in, but by the middle of the first quarter, we may have a serious cash-flow problem."

We sank into an uncomfortable silence. She waved her credit card in the air. I took that as a signal that our conversation was near an end.

"Ken loves you," she said. "If he decides to downsize or close the business, I'm sure he'll take care of you. We're bleeding over there. A moratorium may help. There are too many projects underway and none of them have been completed—including the first project, Allegheny."

She rose abruptly. We left the bar and headed for the valet circle. "You think Ken walks on water," she said. "He doesn't."

Her car rolled up, then my Jag behind it. Her eyes locked onto mine as she sighed. "Hey, if I decide to go away for awhile and not say goodbye, don't think I'm snubbing you."

After dropping that weird statement on me she flung her purse in the car and tipped the valet. Then she retrieved a book from her passenger seat.

"I picked you up a belated birthday present," she said, handing it to me. "It's an Elvis biography."

I flipped through the pages. "Thanks."

"I thought you might like to read it someday...maybe it'll make you think of me."

As she jumped in her car, it hit me. Annie never told me what her dreams were.

"Hey, no fair!" I called as she crept passed me toward the street. "You never told me about your dreams."

She leaned her head out the window and smiled. "My kids—for them to go to the best schools. I'd like to have the money to do that for them. For me...maybe a home by the ocean—one that I own and not rent...with a veranda. I can sit, watch the sunset and have my favorite cocktail on my veranda."

I laughed. "Beats a rental with a kiddie pool in Culver City."

"Yeah," she smiled. "I want to sip a Tequila Sunrise on my veranda," she told me, "Someplace tropical, and watch the sunset. That's my dream."

"That's it?" I asked.

"Yeah, that's it." She smiled again. Her smile reminded me of our good times in the booth at the doughnut shop. It was a simple gesture, a girlish smile, but it was genuine. Annie tossed me a wink and sped away.

I headed west on Ventura Boulevard; joining rush hour traffic as I made the slow crawl home. I fixated on dreams and their power. I also recognized the emptiness that can occur when you get what you think you want and it isn't really what you need.

Wasn't this the life I dreamed about when I was scrounging up spare change to buy a pizza? If you told me back then that I'd be living in luxury, driving a prestigious car, making over six figures, but feeling empty inside, I would've called you, "nuts". When I was broke, it never occurred to me that I could be living large, earning big money and still be unhappy.

My objective for meeting with Annie was to obtain some truthful answers about what the hell was going on at Richman Properties. I'd accomplished that, but the meeting with Annie also facilitated me in arriving at some more personal, and painful, truths.

29

April 1ˢᵗ, 1987

I wasn't at my father's bedside for his last breath. The choice was conscious. The choice was selfish. It was probably the only one I could make from a standpoint of self-preservation.

I chose to remember him laughing as he tried in vain to hit his golf ball further than mine. He'd swing from the heels, a lit Camel dangling from his lips, his well-worn Magnum PI cap flying off his head at impact. He'd yell, "Shit!"—that was the worst swear word he cared to utter. Typically, he shanked his golf ball out of bounds. He'd stare at me, inhaling deeply from his cigarette. "That's a trick shot, Tony," he'd laugh. He used the same line every time he hit a bad shot, always called it a "trick shot."

That was the image I chose to hang onto, not the image of the sick man I stood over during the previous eight months. I did not want to remember the picture of my father wasting away in a hospice bed until he was barely recognizable. The lung cancer destroyed his body and eventually robbed him of his ability to speak. I refused to let those moments play in my head.

I ate a quiet breakfast with Annika. The dark cloud of my father's illness had enveloped us since we said, "I do." I was beginning to understand the toll it had taken. Annika was sympathetic, but there was a noticeable space between us: one that I badly wanted to close, but didn't have the ability to.

I had little opportunity to be alone with my thoughts. The calls, notes, flowers and meals dropped off by friends had all been very smothering. There'd been little time to grieve. I was too lost to be grateful.

The first day of April was a beautiful day. A warm Santa Ana breeze whipped through the San Fernando Mission Cemetery as we walked to the gravesite. Each step brought back memories of my sister, Regina, and me, when we were just little kids, at our grandmother's grave in the early 1960s. After completing our Catholic recitations, we would each take a small flower to the statue of the Virgin Mary and reverently place them at her feet.

I walked behind my father's casket; I did not cry. The gentle smiles, hugs and kisses from the people in attendance were sincere, but they didn't comfort me or help me understand why I felt so angry.

I looked at the people attending the funeral. Mourners included Rex and his wife, Stan and Katy and the Steenbergs. Virtually all of my organization was there. Mazal and most of my childhood friends also attended the funeral. Ted was there. Stewart Moore, and most of the California Diamonds were there as well. Everyone loved Buzz.

Ken and Nancy stood stoically in the back. Ken wore dark sunglasses and fidgeted uncomfortably. I knew he'd rather be someplace else. It suddenly occurred to me that when it came to throwing bachelor parties and attending funerals, Ken was unreliable.

Meanwhile, a cloud had gathered over Richman Properties. The interest payments had continued for the time being, but were late. Ken avoided giving me any details about the late interest payments. He assured me everything was "under control," but his words did little to ease my fears.

The priest read the compulsory Bible verses, some of them in English, some in Latin. An Army bugler played taps as another soldier, shouldering an M16, fired three rounds of blanks into the air. The military representatives folded an American flag and handed it to my mother.

The priest ushered us from Buzz's final resting place by saying, "Go in peace."

Go in peace, huh?

That would be great. How the hell do I do that? I walked hand in hand with mother and my Aunt Jean. They looked weary. Mom was at Dad's side every day until he died. She wanted to stay with him until the end and be his rock. Now, she hoped I would be her rock. In my heart, I knew she was asking too much of me.

* * *

Beep!

It was the answering machine on my home office desk. Before I could reach the phone a voice came over the speaker. It was mom. "Honey, we received a letter today from Richman Properties. They can't pay interest anymore," she said. "They're calling it a moratorium. I don't know what this all means. Honey, I'm worried. Please call me."

30

May 1987

A month passed since we'd buried my dad and the letter from Rich-man Properties hit our mailbox. The change in me affected Annika. I wasn't the same guy she'd fallen in love with. My mood was rarely good, and I smiled only when I was paid to do so. Deep down I was mostly dead-ened. My routine became that of sinking into the sofa with a beer, star-ing blankly at the television. Annika found excuses to escape when I was home. I couldn't blame her. Most of the time I didn't know if she'd left home to run an errand or was simply staying out of my way, using one of our spare bedrooms to read a book.

Our relationship was deteriorating. I was so wrapped up in making sure we made it through Diamond qualification that I simply wasn't conscious of the widening chasm in our lives. It had been weeks since we'd made love. Annika tried to seduce me by wearing sexy clothing and going to bed in lingerie. Sex was the farthest thing from my mind.

And then there was mom. She'd never driven a car; she depended on dad for that. She'd never been without someone to care for. Regina and I took turns handling her errands, keeping her company and trying to ease the blow of Buzz's death. It was also now my responsibility to take care of her financially.

That made the letter from Richman Properties even more distressing. I was at a loss of what to do. I felt removed from Ken. Why wasn't I privy to this information before everyone else? Why wasn't there a conversation similar to our talk on that trip to Catalina when he informed me of the split from Willis? Why wasn't Ken keeping me informed?

I phoned Ken immediately after receiving the letter, but two excruciating days passed before he returned my call. When we spoke, Ken tried to reassure me. "Things aren't perfect," he said. "We've gotten some bad counsel pertaining to zoning and construction costs. Some overhead issues are eating into profits, but don't worry about your family's money. You know I'll always take care of you guys."

Ken explained the moratorium would give them time to finish the Allegheny project and sell it off. They were also considering flipping some of the other pieces of raw land or deals in progress to larger developers. It was "simple," he told me; they just needed to "shrink down" to a size that was manageable. And then his voice turned a bit intimidating, barking at me that he didn't need his people "panicking" during what he called a "minor reorganization."

He stated, "We don't need people running on the bank. I hired a new C.O.O. and we're meeting with our CPAs and attorneys to decide on the moves that'll get us back on track. I need your help here, Tony—keep people calm."

And that was that. I was back on board, working hard for my mentor, resenting myself for having questioned him in the first place. I dutifully embarked on a public relations campaign on his behalf. There were a lot of investors looking to me for answers. A steady flow of calls came in from investors and I did what I could to address their concerns. I was slightly uncomfortable making assurances for Ken but I was diligent in my efforts to calm everyone down, just as Ken asked.

I even recruited Stan to help calm the investors. I relayed Ken's words to him: He believed in Ken but also believed in me. He found comfort in learning privileged information from me. We both wanted to believe.

Our survival depended on it.

31

June 1987

Stewart Moore's chartered flight from San Jose took just long enough for him to rewrite his notes one last time. It was going to be important for Moore to spell it out clearly to his fellow PEN Diamonds; they had all committed to be in Santa Barbara for the emergency board meeting. All Diamonds were expected to attend—except for Ken. He had not been invited.

Moore had asked several Diamonds to speak with Ken—to learn as much about what was really going on with Richman Properties. They compared notes and found Ken extraordinarily positive about the prospects of returning the company to profitability. However, Ken expressed concerns to them about the panicky depositors who were demanding their investments refunded. Ken complained to them that these "jumpy investors" could hamper his efforts to keep the company afloat. The PEN Diamonds were painfully aware of how many people in their downlines invested with Ken. His problems were now their problems. They knew the situation with Richman Properties was delicate yet action had to be taken. Suspicion about the viability of Richman Properties would create fear. Fear, fueled by rumors, would turn into panic. Panic injected into the sensitive scenario would create a run on the bank and possibly, alarming calls to the authorities. Nobody wanted to see that.

Stewart Moore had recently received an interesting package in the mail. It was a small amount of incriminating information—a few vital documents that suggested Richman Properties was not what it purported to be. The Mole was now working overtime, wanting to maximize the profit potential of their enigmatic side business. After all, if you could sell the exact same information to four different sources, collect thousands of dollars from each of them, have each believe the information is exclusive to them, and do it all in complete anonymity, why wouldn't you?

The documents and notations were mailed from an entity that identified themselves as, TSV Associates. At first, Moore thought it was some kind of cruel joke. Who the hell was TSV? He decided to send the cashier's check they requested for "additional documentation," and he then received the second package. Moore was stunned by its contents. It was then he realized that one of his closest friends—a guy he had trusted like a brother—might be operating an intentional investment scam.

The Diamonds slowly filled the meeting room. Some knew there were problems with Richman Properties; some were not aware at all. Ultimately, Ken was right to hold this bunch in contempt. The timid group included a dentist from Ventura who seemed afraid of his own shadow, as well as the contractor from Hermosa Beach who couldn't say his wife's name on stage without crying. Ken and Stewart had enjoyed mocking these guys behind their back, but now Moore needed them to grow some balls.

Moore shook hands, made small talk and mingled like the polished host he was. The resort conference room was full of nervous smiles. Nobody would be smiling after the meeting got underway. Moore planned to use the phrase "Ponzi scheme" then watch his audience's reactions. He'd made a career as a successful corporate executive, reading people's faces in boardrooms. He'd know immediately how many of them accepted "finders fees" when referring AmericanMade distributors to Ken.

"Gentlemen, thanks for coming on such short notice," he said. "You're aware that we did not invite Ken to this meeting. We're here to examine his extracurricular practices, some of which might be considered criminal under scrutiny."

"Simply described, a Ponzi scheme is a fraudulent operation that pays returns to existing investors using money from new investors coming in the door—rather than from any real profit."

Moore circled the room. The dentist bent his head, his hands covering his face. Ken's old friend from Boise, the guy who'd sponsored him into the business, Chad, was clearly dazed. Moore knew that Chad would feel an increased sense of guilt because he introduced Ken to the business.

"Ponzi schemes require a steady stream of new money, but they collapse quickly when new investors dry up," Moore continued. "They usually come to the attention of authorities through complaints—the type of complaints that will inevitably come in droves if Richman Properties doesn't resume paying its investors their monthly interest checks pretty quickly, which may or may not be possible.

"This has grown too big to ignore," Moore announced. "Ken has now raised more than fourteen million dollars, mostly from our downline distributors. I believe we've been negligent in not keeping closer watch on how Ken was operating."

Moore opened his briefcase, the snapping metal latches interrupting the quiet in the room. He carefully passed around copies of a massive report.

"This documentation is the result of many hours of research. The information is partially from a private investigator, and also from an anonymous informant, a Mole who surfaced and supplied me with some of this information."

Each Diamond accepted their copy. The retired dentist set it down but didn't open it. Instead, he continued to drink his coffee. The ex-contractor ripped it open and rifled through the pages, but Moore could tell he wasn't actually reading the information. He was skimming and probably wasn't sophisticated enough to know what he was looking at. Chad stared hard at the pages in front of him; he understood the gravity of the accusations. Moore could see the anger building in Chad's face.

The package included letters from Richman's bank showing the loans on each property. Most carried second and third mortgages, leaving no equity in the properties. There were invoices for expensive personal items such as a speedboat, a baby grand piano—all purchased with Richman Properties, Inc. corporate checks. The report also contained ample documentation suggesting embezzlement ran rampant inside the firm.

The most damning of all the information was a recent letter from Richman's primary bank. The bank set a date for an internal audit of Richman Properties' books. Moore told the board members to turn to page 111:

> ...Mr. Richman, Mr. Gergin, Ms. Wu and any other signing officers should consider having legal counsel present during this institutional audit...

The letter was a clear indication that Richman's bank believed unsavory actions were taking place. Moore scanned the room. He noted the expressions of concern on everyone's faces. Chad spoke first. He stood, voice cracking.

"He's using the money he raised from our distributors—people in our business—for his personal lifestyle. The cars, the vacation homes, the boat, the plane—rubbing our faces in his success...and he hasn't even completed one damn project!" Chad's face flushed, his veins protruded. "I say we turn him in right now and let the authorities sort this out."

Moore waited a moment to see if anyone else wished to speak. The balance of the Diamonds that made up the board sat in stunned silence.

"Assuming Richman Properties could be judged a Ponzi scheme under state or federal scrutiny, we have two choices," Moore told them. "Our first option would be to do as Chad suggested and immediately contact the authorities. We'd tell them what we know."

He wrote "CONTACT AUTHORITIES" on a white board in bold letters.

"Of course, if we do this, we'll also need to contact AmericanMade's corporate office. In addition, we'll have to be honest with our downlines, tell them exactly what we've learned. This decision and these declarations will have an immediate and definite impact on our income as the facts emerge. There will be the inevitable questions of just how much we knew and when each of us knew it."

Stewart continued pacing the room as he prepared to explain their second option.

"Also, I need to be clear. There are some around this table who solicited their downlines on Ken's behalf. Some of you accepted finder's fees from Ken. These actions could expose you to criminal charges, the degrees of which depend on the amount of fees or commissions you accepted. You were, in fact, soliciting securities without a license, which is an SEC violation. The Securities and Exchange Commission would quickly become involved."

"We have a second option available to us at this juncture," Moore proclaimed as he wrote "TAKE NO ACTION" on the white board.

"If we're able to calm the investors and prevent a run on the bank, Ken may be able to find a way to remain solvent. Even if he can't, remaining quiet for now gives us time to prepare for what may come next. We'll need a plan for dissolving ties with Ken and those of you who accepted referral fees would need to secure legal counsel."

Moore looked around the room as silence prevailed. "Feigning ignorance shouldn't be that tough," Moore said, adding a sarcastic tenor to his voice. "It's a skill we've perfected nicely since we all tied our futures to Ken."

There were a few nervous laughs, but most everyone remained quiet as Moore offered them time to reach a decision. Moore knew that going to the authorities was the most ethical option; however, he'd decided that he would yield to the quorum. He wondered how many of them would vote to contact the authorities and how many would take the more spineless course.

"Gentlemen, it's time to cast our votes."

Moore let the weight of his words sink in. "All in favor of contacting authorities say, 'Aye.'"

32

Monday, July 13ᵗʰ, 1987

Ken told Nancy to cancel the meeting with his newly hired C.O.O., Griffin Davis. It was a meeting to prepare for the looming bank audit. He told her to make it sound like his absence couldn't be avoided. Nancy gave Grif a believable story about a family emergency back home in Idaho and told him Ken would return "soon."

The limo traveled down the Boulevard with Ken and his large duffle bag tucked safely inside. Ken had ordered the plane to be fueled and waiting on the tarmac at Van Nuys. He told Nancy he was meeting a potential investor in Denver, but the flight plan said something else. He'd spend one day in Vegas, trying his luck, then he'd be off to the condo in Aspen. Ken would be making one last deposit to his well-hidden floor safe, the one only he knew the location of.

Grif Davis could wait. The bank audit could wait. The pissed off investors could wait. They weren't going anywhere. He'd clean those things up when he got back. One of Ken's bad habits was that of conceit.

As Ken left town, Nancy attended to the rituals of running their MLM business. She practiced her routine as usual, inventorying the products, tapes and books stacked in their four-car garage. When finished with inventory she looked over the incoming orders on her computer.

Nancy appreciated her time alone more and more as the years had passed. Lately, when Ken was out of town, she'd finish her tasks, ask Catarina to tend to Chandler and then she'd curl up in her favorite outside lounge chair. It was positioned near the end of the patio offering her an expansive view of the Valley below. She'd zone out and stare down at the humanity below as she floated high above it.

The contents of her glass helped her drift away to simpler times. Her cocktail of choice was gin and tonic. She poured her drinks from the well-hidden bottle of Beefeater, the one only she knew the location of.

In the stillness of her spacious backyard, Nancy happily exercised her most private vice. She waited for the moment the alcohol numbed her senses, washing away her troubles. They had been festering. Ken lamely explained his trip to Denver "a key investor meeting and some necessary banking transactions." He ordered her to stay home. For what was supposed to be a partnership, Nancy was growing weary of staying home while Ken gambled with their money and their lifestyle.

Nancy was relieved to hear that Ken had decided to hire a "real C.O.O." She had grown to not like or trust Dr. Johnny. She actually challenged Dr. Johnny once, tried to suggest they slow the growth within Richman Properties, but she was quickly shut down. Johnny was the first to point out that her current lifestyle wasn't solely based on the profits from "selling soap."

Nancy knew where some of the extravagant toys of their lifestyle came from, and she unapologetically embraced them. It was all well deserved in her mind. Every inch of that property was payoff for the constant commitments, obligations and maintenance of their image. Every upgrade cushioned a blow, from the private plane that allowed her husband to leave her behind, to the high thread count of the Egyptian cotton sheets under which she slept alone under most nights.

Even with the challenges at Richman Properties, Nancy was the last person to abandon Ken. She knew what they had built and she knew Ken's capabilities. She saw the difference in her life. She had been a receptionist when she met Ken at that singles church mixer. They'd even managed to transform Ted, converting the hapless idiot into a six-figure earner.

Gazing out, eyeing the orange glow cast on the foothills, she threw back the last of her gin and tonic. Nancy knew over the years she should have been more of an active partner to Ken, reining in his unscrupulous side.

But, one of Nancy's bad habits was that of select ignorance.

33

Thursday, July 16th, 1987

A new photo was taken. The Mole's passport needed to be renewed, just in case. It was also time to close down the post office box. The informant hoped the nice older man was there. He was such an easy mark. A little small talk went a long way. The Mole would give the old codger a bogus forwarding address. A dead end was the objective if someone came looking, and at this juncture, someone surely would. The forwarding address was once the home of an American idol, but that icon was long gone.

The Mole's various clients had sent hundreds of thousands of dollars to the P.O. box during the four plus years *TSV Associates* had been in business. AmericanMade, Beau Willis, Stewart Moore, they were all happy customers. They'd been more than delighted to employ the private services of TSV so that they could take a glimpse inside of the Ken Richman machine and confirm their worst suspicions. The Mole's favorite customer, however, was Stewart Moore. The Mole charged Moore double for the same information that was sold to Willis and AmericanMade. Moore had always been so condescending and dismissive—it gave the Mole pleasure to extract as much money as possible out of the creepy little prick's pocket.

Over the years the money orders had been carefully collected from the Reseda P.O. box and then deposited in small amounts into the bank across the street. The money was used for spot investments in the stock market. None of the capital had been at risk for too long. For an amateur investor, the Mole had compiled a stellar record despite the bear market. The money was at play in sectors that were growing. The informant used strategies learned from books written by Benjamin Graham, Warren Buffett and Peter Lynch, becoming a student of the masters. The original seed money had doubled, tripled and eventually quadrupled.

Profits were methodically taken off the table, then out of the account. The bundles of cash were stuffed into two safe deposit boxes in the same bank. The Mole planned to empty those safe deposit boxes out the following morning. Altogether, more than a half-million dollars had been accumulated.

The Mole's thoughts turned to what would come next. Whatever the future held, money would not be too much of a concern.

34

Mid July 1987

July was halfway over and the long period of Diamond qualification was nearing its close. If all went according to plan we'd be Diamonds in a few weeks and our income would rise substantially. It was 1987, a gallon of gas was 96 cents, and a dozen eggs cost seventy-eight cents. The median income in America was $26,000 and I'd be bringing in well over a quarter-million bucks a year.

My downline, and anyone else looking in from the outside, would expect me to be riding the biggest high of my life. The truth of the matter was that there were days I couldn't even leave my bed until noon. The pressure of Diamond qualification, the loss of my father and the uncertainty of my family's investment with Richman Properties had sent me into an eternally gloomy mood. Closing my eyes and going to sleep at night was becoming difficult.

There was still a moratorium on interest payments. The monthly interest checks for my family and myself were still not coming in. It was starting to get real tight for my mom, aunt and uncle. They had become dependent on those checks. The weight I was under grew heavier after a brief conversation with Ted a few days earlier.

He casually mentioned that Ken had taken a trip to Denver to meet with a key investor. I asked him when, checked the dates and realized that, during the time in question, I'd called Ken at his office for an update on things. An assistant then informed me that he was in a "closed-door, three-day meeting with advisors." I asked for Annie and she was "unavailable." That made it official: I was being lied to and blown off—I was officially on the outside.

I couldn't let it fester. I had no choice. I had to focus on my Diamond qualification. It was the reason I signed up in the business. Ken had worked hard to prepare me for Diamond qualification as well. If I was going to make my way back to his inner circle this was how I would do it.

I owed Ken. He brought me this far and I needed to show him I was worth the investment. I had to make sure each of my six distributor legs moved enough AmericanMade product to qualify me for Diamond by month's end. If I didn't, I'd have to start the Diamond qualification period all over again.

*   *   *

Stewart Moore dismissed the high-priced San Francisco lawyer from his home office and kicked his feet onto the desk. He casually flipped through the local newspaper, scanning the headlines. The meeting with his hired gun left him confident that he was clear of direct involvement in Richman Properties' activities, those that could be considered unlawful. He was confident in his defense.

At the recent secretive PEN meeting in Santa Barbara, Moore presented two options to the Diamonds. He asked the board members to make a choice. It turned out that only two of the Diamonds cared to admit knowledge of the incriminating information contained in the report. The others reasoned that running to the authorities would create widespread panic and the collapse of Richman Properties—which would have an immediate effect on their MLM income. A solid plan for damage control was what they wanted—and they needed some time to accomplish that.

The dentist from Ventura said, "I'll have to urge the board to table any communication to outsiders. Let's put a lid on this whole mess for now." He bent forward in his chair, rubbing his eyes of this bad dream as he made his plea. His comb-over fell to the side, vibrating with each word he uttered. He looked up for validation, trying in vain to reposition his uncontrollable hair. He nervously ran his tongue over his teeth.

He'd accepted ample finder's fees from Richman, but he wasn't alone. There were others in the room whose hands were just as dirty. Based on the consensus vote, they adjourned the meeting with briefcases full of communal silence.

Moore made careful notes of those who admitted accepting fees. He also noted that only himself and Ken's old buddy, Chad, were willing to contact authorities. They yielded to the wishes of the majority, however, and it was just as well. This mysterious *TSV* entity had sent one additional package of information to Moore since the meeting in Santa Barbara. It was even more damaging than the last batch of intelligence. He kept that information to himself.

As they exited the meeting that day in Santa Barbara, Moore collected back each copy of the report he'd handed out. He planned to personally shred them when he returned to his home in San Jose—except for one copy. He would keep that copy for his own security.

* * *

After months of investigation, Inspector Boone believed he had most of the individual elements he needed, but knew he was still short of delivering an airtight case to the prosecutors. He had yet to tie Ken directly to the specific knowledge of wrongdoing—and a clear intent to defraud.

Boone had enough on Dr. Johnny for a conviction and long prison term. He was just plain dirty. Griffin, 'Grif" Davis, the new C.O.O., could walk with little or no jail time. He'd arrived on the scene after the damage was done. He would be portrayed as the good guy who tried to return

Richman Properties to legal conduct—clean things up. He might make a good secondary candidate to turn state's evidence if their primary target had a change of heart.

Boone remained concerned about what kind of story a defense attorney would tell the jury. A skilled lawyer could argue that Ken didn't know what was going on at his own company. The defense would proffer that he may have been the C.E.O., but Richman Properties was merely a side business. It was a fact that Ken had little physical presence in the office for most of the scam. Ken's name was certainly on all the documents, but in many cases his name was signed by Annie or Dr. Johnny, or a rubber stamp was used.

Boone had to put himself in the mind of a juror. He had to question motive as they would. After all, Richman was grossing more than a half-million dollars a year through his MLM. With his loyal and growing downline he was set for life. Why ruin all that he had built by perpetrating a Ponzi scheme?

The defense attorney would surely suggest something like "Ken's dreams to develop real estate were grander than his capabilities, but there was no criminal intent. He was lead astray and taken advantage of by the people that he hired." Boone needed Richman to acknowledge the fraud in some way—admit that he was aware of it. The case was consuming Boone; he was neglecting his family and even his own health. He needed hard evidence incriminating Ken.

Boone had finally placed a call to AmericanMade and informed the compliance officer that Ken Richman and Richman Properties were under federal investigation. The compliance officer asked Boone to let him know when he expected to announce the indictments. AmericanMade wanted some advanced warning. Boone agreed.

When AmericanMade did receive that courtesy call from Boone, they'd immediately terminate Ken and Nancy. AmericanMade was willing to ignore some minor transgressions by their bigger pins, but the company feared one of their own being televised on the 11:00 PM news in handcuffs. They wanted to keep their skirts clean and be able to announce something like, "We terminated our relationship with this distributor as soon as all of this came to our attention."

Boone pulled into the restaurant parking lot. His final meeting with their primary target for state's evidence would take place in the back booth of the dark Chinese restaurant just off Topanga Canyon Blvd. From his extensive profiling, Boone knew that the staff of Richman Properties would never dine at this humble establishment. Boone and his target would have complete privacy.

Boone would discuss immunity and in exchange, the witness would have to provide testimony that would put a few people away for a while— Ken and Dr. Johnny among them. Also, there were several hundred investors who lost their life savings. It would be hard for their witness to stay in the community after the testimony of what they knew and when they knew it. As such, relocation would be discussed as well.

Boone's final objective was to convince the state's witness to wear a wire, meet with Ken and engage him in conversation. If Ken admitted that he knew that Richman Properties wasn't solvent, but took investor money anyway, Boone would have what he needed to hand the case off to prosecutors.

35

Thursday, July 23rd, 1987

Ken walked into the intimate steakhouse he liked to frequent and asked for a back booth. He was to meet Annie, at her request. Annie had been left almost completely out of the higher-level conversations after Ken hired his new C.O.O., Grif Davis. Grif was to be his savior. Ken assumed that Annie was anxious to know more of what was going on with the reorganization and was also probably going to gripe about not being given some of the control she wanted to have. That was the least of Ken's problems, but he would meet with her anyway and keep her in check.

Annie was a few minutes late, as always. She started off with small talk but soon peppered Ken with tough questions. Initially, Ken placated her by answering with broad generalizations. He told her a little bit about Grif's suggestions for the reorganization. Ken mentioned that they might place Richman Properties into bankruptcy to protect their remaining corporate assets and buy them some time. Ken told her that she'd need to help Grif get all the necessary paperwork together for the filing if they decided to "go that direction." Ken rambled on and on about Grif's great ideas.

All of the talk about the plan for reorganization—their feeble attempt to save the company—was all well and good, but Annie was looking to take the conversation somewhere else. Ken seemed very hyper-focused on solutions, he kept using the hopeful word, "re-org," and he uttered the phrase "right the ship," several times. She would try a different approach— she'd slowly guide the conversation to the problems they had created and question the genesis of those difficulties. Annie would show empathy. She hoped he might find comfort in her words and become revealing.

"We started out with the best intentions, Ken," Annie said. "You wanted to help so many people make money on these projects. Off the record, how did everything get so fucked up?"

Ken took a deep breath. "Look," he said, "I hired Dr. Johnny and then listened to everything he said. We went too big, too fast, and he was flipping reckless. I didn't manage the operation hands-on, now we need to clean up the mess. If we can buy some time, with a bankruptcy, finish Allegheny and then flip a few of the pieces of raw land we're taking a blood bath on, we can probably start paying interest to the investors again."

Annie concealed her need to yell, "Bullshit!" She knew Ken and she knew when he was lying. She also knew that this wasn't the information that would solve her problem. Annie decided to keep him talking.

"But the current properties," she said, "We have second and third mortgages on most of them. Even if we completed Allegheny or dumped a few pieces of raw land, there'd still be little cash to work with."

"I know, I know, you're right," Ken said, "But if we can buy some time with a continued moratorium or bankruptcy, I know I can convince some of the investors to accept lesser interest payments or I can liquidate their positions at a discount. These investors are friends, they're part of my downline. They'll work with me."

By now, Annie had concluded the sympathetic approach wasn't working. And so she changed her tactics. She knew enough about Ken to know that if she pressed, backed him against a wall, he would lash out, say things he wouldn't normally say.

"I get it. You have your loyalists, but what about people like Stan and Katy Schultz?" Annie asked. "They have their entire nest egg with us. I took an angry call from Stan last week. I had to lie to him—tell him his investment is safe. I fucking lied to the old man, Ken."

"I've got bigger problems than Stan and Katy," he barked at her. "There is more than fifteen million dollars at risk and two hundred investors who are going to be just as unhappy as Stan and Katy. I've got to figure out how to take care of my business and my family first!"

Ken slammed his Diet Coke on the table. Neither of them spoke for a moment. Annie picked at her Caesar salad as she thought hard about what to say next. She knew she was close to making him break. She kept pressing. She'd go to the thing she knew he was most worried about.

"The bank audit," she said. "They want to come in and look at the books. They want to see a lot of records, specific loan docs matched against deeds we supposedly hold, information and disclosures we gave investors, other details. Those loan docs have Dr. Johnny's handiwork all over them. Our circulars show land we don't own. When the bank sees those documents they'll go directly to the Securities and Exchange Commission first, and then the S.E.C. could easily dump all of this in the hands of the F.B.I., am I wrong on this?"

"No!" Ken shouted. "You're not WRONG!"

A moment of silence followed Ken's outburst. It was so quiet only breathing was audible. Annie remained silent, knowing Ken would have more to say.

"Look, there's no easy way out of this," he said. "If we cooperate with the bank—give them complete access to our books, they'll learn that we made inaccurate statements on the loan docs we submitted them. Then they'll immediately go to the Securities and Exchange Commission. The S.E.C. will put a microscope up our ass and will classify what we sold investors as, "unregistered securities", and then we're done."

"If we don't allow the bank to look at our books, we're screwed anyway. They'll suspect we have something to hide and probably go straight to the S.E.C. or some other federal agency—turn us in. Like I said, Grif is trying to stall this out. He thinks that if we can pay off a few of our bigger notes with them, maybe they'll back off."

Ken seemed spent, but he wanted to talk and Annie wasn't going to interrupt him.

"Everyone does this shit, you know; fake the financials, show phantom income. Ask Dr. Johnny. He'll tell you. The banks just want their interest payments on time."

Ken sipped his soda and rubbed his temples. He stared across the table at Annie. He leaned forward and confided in a woman who, for the past five years, had been the most loyal member of his organization.

"By the time I realized the numbers were bullshit and our overhead was out of control, all I could think to do was raise more money. We were months behind on Allegheny and the project's a mess. We had to pull second and third mortgages on some properties to keep current with our overhead. Shit, investors just keep throwing money at me. What the hell am I supposed to do? Curl up and die?"

Lunch was over.

As they stood to leave, Ken counseled Annie to find an attorney.

"You might need one," he said. "Your name is on a lot of stuff. This thing could get ugly."

Ken gave Annie a hug and walked out ahead of her.

Annie slipped into the ladies' room and locked herself in a stall. Her pulse raced as she unbuttoned her blouse and pushed the 'stop' button. She removed the small microphone clipped to her bra as well as the clear surgical tape that secured the microcassette and wires to her skin. Annie buttoned her blouse and tucked the recording apparatus into her purse.

Annie emerged into the afternoon sunlight. She noticed her hands trembling. She lit a cigarette to calm her nerves. Finally, she called for her car at the valet stand. While she was waiting for the valet, an unmarked car pulled up beside her. Boone's hand reached out the driver's side window. She dropped the microcassette unit into his open palm.

On her short drive back to the office, Annie recalled what her father told her: "Always take care of your own business. If you don't, nobody else will." Annie was promised a good deal from Boone: full immunity from prosecution and assistance in relocating her family after her testimony. She had secured a lawyer weeks earlier and her attorney assured her that the FBI's deal was a good one. She wanted to be far, far away from the nastiness that would arise when the indictments were handed down and the investors were left with empty pockets. She had followed her father's advice and taken care of business.

Annie cleared her face of tears with a laugh—unsure of why she'd even been crying. The opportunities Ken offered her dissolved, the promises never materialized. Her loyal work had been accepted but never appreciated. Maybe the tears were a sign of relief—or maybe regret. It didn't matter.

Annie drove forward knowing she could never look back.

36

Friday, July 24th, 1987

Boone had gathered a team that included deputies from the Los Angeles Sheriff's Department. The lead deputy sheriff convened his squad in the parking lot across the street from Richman Properties. The deputies rode the elevator up at 11:50 and quietly stood outside the office door. Boone and his team of federal agents stationed themselves at the lobby entrance, waiting for their cue.

Boone knew the patterns of the Richman personnel well. On Fridays, shortly before noon, all work stopped. The Richman Properties employees would then break up into small cliques for their two martini lunches. This meant that 11:55 AM would be the most opportune time to stage the raid. At exactly that time the lead deputy sheriff posted and affixed the search warrant on the door and opened it. The uniformed deputies flooded in and Boone rushed in behind them. He made the announcement to the stunned staff: "Attention please. This is a Federal raid. Put your hands in the air and slowly move toward the wall."

Boone's men quickly identified Johnny Gergin, Annie Wu and Griffin

Davis. They were escorted into Ken's rarely used corner office and shown the official arrest warrants. Annie watched the deputies and F.B.I. agents scramble, searching for Ken. He wasn't there. He was in Orange County drawing circles. She overheard them dispatch a deputy sheriff to Ken's home. For the time being, Ken Richman was a fugitive.

Annie, Dr. Johnny and Grif Davis were read their Miranda rights. The arrestees would be cuffed and taken into temporary custody. The clerical workers would be searched, identified, and sent home.

Two of the deputy sheriffs would stay behind to guard evidence until Boone returned with a forensic accounting team and a moving van. They'd begin the tedious job of removing computer hard drives and paper files the next day. Within a half-hour, Ted and the other rank and file employees were questioned and escorted out. Ted was released with them. When the suite of offices was devoid of all human beings, a deputy sheriff placed yellow police tape across the front door, barring anyone from entering.

Three cars holding the arrestees sat in the asphalt parking lot waiting for their orders to depart. Two were sheriff cruisers, one holding Johnny Gergin and the other holding Griffin Davis. Annie Wu wasn't in a black and white. She was placed in the back seat of a dark blue air-conditioned Chevy sedan. The windows of the other two cars were rolled down on the hot Valley afternoon. It was obvious that Grif Davis had been crying. His face knotted in disbelief. Dr. Johnny was far less expressive. Annie looked his way and noticed the smirk on his ruddy, bearded face.

Annie wouldn't be joining the others on their ride to the Sherriff's station. She would be taken to the 17th floor of the Wilshire Federal Building. She'd already arranged to meet her attorney at that F.B.I. field office. Final details of the immunity deal and the relocation assistance would be worked out and then she would be taken to a temporary residence where her two boys would be delivered to her.

*　*　*

His meetings in Orange County had been therapeutic. He still enjoyed drawing circles and getting people hyped about the business. Ken loved the game. MLM was an integral part of his makeup. Even with all the pressures caused by the impending failure of Richman Properties he continued growing one of the largest organizations in the business. Ken Richman had the incredible ability to completely segment things in his head and focus on the business at hand. He never let one thing deter him from another. Ken and Nancy were almost qualified for the next level: Double Diamond.

Ken cruised north on the 405 in his Porsche. The 911 still looked as shiny as the day he'd picked it up. Ken had owned quite a few expensive cars, boats, and toys over the years, but this vehicle was special. He had taped a photo of this car to his refrigerator door.

Still, as he drove, he thought hard about saving Richman Properties. He'd reorganize, maybe file for bankruptcy. Grif could buy him some time. All he needed was more time and he could fix this. He planned to jettison some of the big salaries and cut overhead. He could talk to the investors—get them to agree to accept negotiated settlements. If he could manage all of that he could save his company.

Ken's mind churned with plans, as it always did. His car phone chirped and he answered with a carefree gusto.

It was Nancy. "Are you on your way home?" she asked. Her voice seemed to tremble.

"On the freeway. Had some great meetings with the new leg in Orange County..."

"Ken, there are people here for you. A County Sheriff and two investigators...F.B.I. I think. They have a warrant for your arrest."

Arrest?

The word echoed through the phone. Had it come to this? Ken's mind raced in a dozen directions. Ken was no fool. He knew Richman Properties had been breaking numerous laws for months. But he still found himself shocked when Nancy used that word: Arrest. How had he made himself believe he would escape prosecution?

Ken quickly cleared his mind. Now was not the time to panic. He must remain in control of his thinking. Whatever evidence that might have been gathered, Ken knew he would hurt his defense if he took rash and illogical steps.

"Call our lawyer," he sternly ordered. "Tell him to get to the house—and tell him to rush. And don't answer questions."

A few seconds of silence followed. Ken was about to hang up when Nancy said, "They closed Richman Properties, made arrests there too." Her words were barely audible to Ken.

Ken felt wounded. He wondered who had been arrested. Annie? Dr. Johnny? Ted? Who else?

"Don't' say a word," he said, finally. "I'll be home soon"

The deputy sheriff took the phone from Nancy's trembling hand and placed it back on the receiver. He guided her to the couch. She was home alone. Catarina had taken Chandler to the Steenbergs' house for a play date. The security gate buzzer sounded.

"Postal," the voice announced. "Certified letter.

Her trip to the door to sign for the envelope was a blur. The message was from the Compliance and Legal Departments of AmericanMade. She read the letter to herself, and then let it fall to the coffee table. It signaled an abrupt end to the way of life she had known during years of devotion to AmericanMade.

Nancy returned from the kitchen with her favorite Tweety Bird coffee mug in hand. It disguised the potent contents inside. She politely asked the uniformed officers if they would wait for Ken in their cars. As they left the home, Nancy walked into the backyard, collapsing onto her lounge chair. She curled up and drank from her special cup. She suddenly felt vulnerable—it was a strange and foreign feeling to her.

37

Tuesday, September 15ʰ, 1987

The ringing jarred me awake. I slid over Annika and grabbed the phone. It was a blaring dial tone. I rolled back and squinted to see the clock: 3:10 AM.

"Shit," I mumbled. I couldn't remember the last time I'd slept through the night. Annika was awake and glaring at me, a glare I'd recently become familiar with.

"Who the hell was that?"

"How am I supposed to know?"

I collapsed onto my pillow just as the ringing started again. I lunged for the phone and picked it up on the second ring.

It was Ken. "I need a favor," he said.

"Can it wait until morning?"

"I don't have time to explain," he answered. "I need you to come over and stay with Nancy and Chandler."

The line went dead. I got out of bed and looked for my jeans.

"Where are you going?" Annika asked, the tone of her voice telling me she was somewhere between hurt and anger. I think in those days she was always somewhere between feeling hurt and feeling angry.

I tried to think of what I could say to her that would sound the least bit logical given Ken's outlandish request.

"Ken needs me to stay with Nancy and Chandler," I said. "It seems like he's going someplace."

She looked at me as though I were insane. I wanted her to tell me I was an asshole for still being Ken's lackey, but she had exhausted all of her wife-like concerns. Her emotional gas tank was becoming as empty as mine.

Several months had elapsed since all the terrible crap came down. Word of Ken's criminal arrest and AmericanMade's termination of him and Nancy spread like a California wildfire. The Daily News had reported that Ken's mess would shake out to be the largest Ponzi scheme ever perpetrated in the San Fernando Valley. I had no answers for my downline and the others who called me. Ken's company had been raided. Ken had been arrested and criminally charged. His bail was set at one million dollars. American-Made had terminated the Richmans for "cause." What spin could I possibly put on all of this that would convince anyone of Ken's innocence?

As a result of this negative heap of shit, my Diamond qualification came apart at the seams. Every single ounce of momentum in my business stopped when the news broke. There was no possibility for me to qualify as a Diamond when all my volume shut down. I had been within a few weeks of Diamond qualification. I was that close.

I could've started the lengthy Diamond qualification period all over again if I had a solid downline. But I didn't. Most distributors lost faith in everything we'd ever told them as the facts unfolded. Most distributors in my downline stopped ordering products immediately. My tape and book orders slowed to a trickle. Many of them stopped going to meetings. Those who didn't fall away quietly did so rather loudly. It was as if a cancer was now eating away at my precious business just like it had my father, leaving an empty shell.

Predictably, PEN acted swiftly. Stewart Moore was now controlling the Diamonds and acting more piously than ever. PEN shifted into damage control and sent out letters to the congregation. Their communications, authored by Moore, were carefully peppered with New Testament scripture. The missives offered a well-placed mirage. One line from a letter read:

> *We offer our prayers for Mr. and Mrs. Richman and trust they decide to reject Satan, and again, recognize Jesus as their Lord and savior.*

My communication with Ken had been spotty. He continued to assure me that he had a plan and that my family would be "taken care of." He couldn't tell me too much about the plans. His attorney had asked him to lay low while he worked with the prosecutor. Rumor had it that Annie and her two sons were staying with her sister in San Francisco for the time being. Dr. Johnny was just plain missing. He was a ghost.

I was halfway to Ken's home before I was fully awake. As I drove up into the hills I realized that, once again, I had become one of Ken's closest allies: Despite the chaos in Ken's life and the financial ruin, I still found myself holding on tightly.

I reached the driveway and pushed the security buzzer. As the gate opened I heard the faint barks of Ken's newly-acquired guard dogs. As I reached the top of the driveway, I caught a glimpse of the dogs running free. In seconds, the vicious Akitas were all over the car as I rolled to a stop.

I heard Ken's voice before I saw him. The dogs were trained to respond to their commands in the German language. Akitas were a breed known for the love of one master. It was that kind of loyalty Ken sought after his arrest. He appeared in the shadows, giving commands to the dogs. The Akitas slowly backed away from my car. Ken leashed the dogs to a nearby lamppost then pulled me in for a hug. From the driver's seat, Ken was just a figure in the dark, but standing in his embrace I saw that he was holding a gun.

The hair on my arms stood on edge when I saw the weapon. Ken gestured, using the gun, to follow him inside. He dead-bolted the door behind us and slumped down on the couch, feigning a smile.

"Thanks for coming," he said.

I swallowed hard and as he laid the gun on the table, asked, "What the fuck's going on?" Ken rubbed his forehead. His words came quickly.

"I don't have a lot of time to explain. My driver will be here in a minute. I'm headed to Van Nuys Airport, then onto Vegas in the Piper Malibu. Can't tell you why. Don't ask. And...don't mention to anyone I'm getting on a plane. It's a violation of my bail. Ted will relieve you in the morning."

He drew a deep breath and continued his vague instructions.

"There's been a threat. The whole property is going to stay locked down. All the doors and windows are locked and all the drapes closed. The dogs will have the run of the exterior grounds after I leave."

He grabbed the gun from the coffee table and slapped it into my hand. It was a .45 automatic. He said, "If anyone steps on this property, they're here to hurt my family. Shoot 'em."

My eyes focused on the gun resting in my hand, then quickly away. I couldn't look directly at the weapon. Instead, I looked at Ken and felt its coldness in my hand. My job was to sit on the couch and wait for an intruder. I was to use the weapon in my hand. This was my mission from Ken. I'd yet to ever say, "NO" to Ken. I was like the Akitas in the yard. I was given commands and expected to obey.

Ken showed me where the safety on the gun was located then jogged upstairs as I gripped the gun tightly. I heard one ring of the house phone and saw the headlights of the limo as it cruised by the front window. Ken bounded down the stairs with a large duffle bag slung over his shoulder.

"You know how much your friendship means to me," he said to me pausing. "Follow me to the door and set the dead-bolt."

Ken stepped through the ornate front door and into the waiting limo. I watched through a break in the curtains as the limo disappeared down the driveway, the Akitas following in close pursuit.

I walked to the rear of the home and parted the thick velvet drapes facing the backyard. All I could see was the heavy, gray blanket of fog that covered the Valley floor. It had thickened since I'd arrived. Despite the fog, I imagined there'd be no delays on his trip to McCarran Airport—his trip to do whatever the hell he was doing, which apparently included the contents of the duffle bag he carried with him.

I reclined on the couch. All of my movements were slow with the gun in my hand. There was a chill in the expansive living room. I found a blanket and pillow he'd left for me. I pulled the blanket up to my chin and adjusted the pillow. The house offered a multitude of guest rooms yet I was not a guest.

I was an unpaid bodyguard.

My eyes traveled to the large eagle painting that had haunted me since my first meeting with Ken five years earlier. It had hung in each of his subsequent homes. Eagles signified freedom. None of this felt free. The clock on the mantelpiece said 3:45 AM. I listened for sounds, but could hear none except the pattern of my own breathing, which I tried to slow. The house was silent.

I drifted off to sleep.

* * *

The phone rang twice, jerking me to attention. I heard the security buzzer. I struggled to clear my thoughts. I saw Ted's car cruise by the front entrance; his company vehicle had been upgraded to a Mercedes a few months prior to the raid and the asshole was still driving it. He mentioned to me that nobody from the F.B.I. or the court had asked him to turn it in yet. The Akitas were barking but wagging their tails and sitting in perfect formation, waiting for Ted to step out of his car. He made his way to the back office door and I met him there.

"You get any sleep?" he asked.

I didn't answer. I knew I stared at the painting for a while, looking at it so closely the eagle was no longer a bird but a compilation of brush strokes. I knew I tried not to stare at the gun although feeling it in my hand was sufficient to keep it on my mind. Yet I didn't know if I slept.

Ted looked down at my right hand. I was still clutching the .45. He slowly took it from my grip.

It was at this point I realized I hadn't let go of the gun since Ken slapped it in my hand six hours earlier. I peppered Ted with questions about what Ken was doing in Vegas and who'd threatened him. He was tight-lipped;

he'd obviously been coached. What was I thinking? That I'd get a straight answer out of Ted?

At this point in my life, I didn't know who the hell I even was. I'd been summoned out of a deep sleep and handed a loaded gun. That kind of stuff just didn't happen to me. I wanted to go home, take a shower and a long nap. Maybe I'd wake up and my long nightmare would be over.

I was dangling from the words Ken told me during our sound-bite conversations. He told me they were "cooperating" with the prosecutors and a plea bargain looked favorable. He made repeated assurances that my family would get the majority of their principal back.

For now, I would hang on to those words.

As my car rolled onto the street, I glanced in the rearview mirror. The big security gates shut slowly. The clanging sound of the gates reverberated down my spine.

38

Thursday, September 24th, 1987

Ken found the pressure of the case relentless; each day he became more reclusive. Rumors and theories about where the missing money was hidden ran rampant through the MLM organization. The collateral fallout crushed whatever opportunity we may have had of salvaging our business.

My once thriving business was just plain dead. October would mark the first month Annika and I couldn't pay some of our bills. With the big mortgage, luxury cars and cavalier spending, we were buried. We were simply out of cash.

We'd been programmed to increase our lifestyle, whether it made sense or not. I'd saved no money. I enjoyed showing off, which I did with a self-serving attitude although flamboyant displays of wealth were good for business. I'd convinced myself that the money, the cars and the mansion were permanent, even though Buzz warned me to be prepared for the day when it all came to an end.

The only members of my downline who stayed active were Bob and

Laura Zelano. They were loyal but they were also heavily disillusioned and in debt themselves. I knew the only reason they were still showing up was for me. I told them it was okay if they wanted to quit.

After Ken's termination, his original sponsor and old friend from Boise, Chad, assumed control of his downline. Neither Chad nor anyone else at PEN contacted me. I was a cast-off. Annika started searching the classified ads for a job. She didn't tell me she was job-hunting until she took a job with a travel agency. She worried that my pride would be wounded. It was, but we needed her paycheck.

Mazal called me repeatedly but I didn't return his calls. He knew I was broke. His messages included witty mentions of seeing my face on the side of a milk carton but his tone was clearly one of hurt. Sadly, at that point I had a lot more that needed my attention than his bruised feelings.

Stan and Katy stayed in close contact. Stan was one of the few people from the business I felt I could still trust. Everyone connected with Richman Properties had disappeared. I'd placed several calls to Annie. There was no response. Dr. Johnny's phone and pager were disconnected. Since that night as a bodyguard, I'd spoken to Ken once; he assured me his highest priority was to make certain the assets were conserved so investors could be repaid. For the first time, I found his words less than comforting.

Few were talking. The only guy I could pry information out of was Ted. I convinced him to meet me for drinks. He was already on his second beer when I entered the bar.

"What's the occasion?" he laughed.

"I just want to catch up a little," I said.

"We haven't had a drink together in six months and you wanna catch up? Cut the shit."

He gulped down his remaining beer and leaned against the wall, arms crossed, staring at me.

"The real estate company gets raided by the cops and then American-Made terminates Ken's distributorship. Then I'm called by Ken—in the middle of the night—to come over and guard his home and his family with a gun! What the fuck?"

"What do you want me to say?" he responded.

"Tell me who's after Ken. At least I deserve to know that much."

A long pause followed my question. Ted stopped staring at me and let his eyes fall to the floor. I could tell he was carrying a tremendous weight of information and was uncomfortable bearing the responsibility—which was, of course, typical of Ted. When he started talking, revealing what he knew, I couldn't say I was surprised. Ted was a coward and needed someone to dump on.

"One of the investors is connected," he said, his voice falling into a whisper.

"Connected to what?"

"Connected," he said slowly, making a juvenile show of rolling his eyes. "A made man. A mobster. Organized crime. Don't you get it?"

My head suddenly filled with memories from my recent night at Ken's house, shivering under a blanket, gun clenched in my hand. "I was on Ken's couch waiting for a visit from a Mafia hit man?"

"Shit. You're thick as a brick, dude."

"Who was it? Which investor is connected?"

"Can't tell ya."

"Can't? Or won't?"

"Listen, the threat passed...at least that one has. Ken took care of it," Ted said. He appeared to be backpedaling, perhaps wondering now if telling me what he knew about the mob's involvement was a good idea, after all.

Still, I pressed him for answers. "How did Ken take care of it?"

Ted shrugged in the most bullshit noncommittal way possible. His eyes darted around the room, locking onto a beautiful girl at the far end of the bar.

"He took care of it," he repeated. "What the fuck was he supposed to do?"

"I don't know what he was supposed to do, but what about all the other investors?"

He looked at me as though I was insane.

"He isn't sitting on piles of cash if that's what you're asking. Hell no! He had to scrape up all he could to take care of that fuckin' problem. He and my sis are tapped as far as I know."

They were tapped yet they were able to pay someone off—it just wasn't my family and me. My stomach churned, acid bubbling in my throat. If Ken could scrape together some money, then why couldn't he pay me back? Why was I stuck protecting his family from a threat when he never protected mine?

Finally, I asked, "Why won't anyone talk to me?"

The childish feeling of having been left out was building in me. I felt everyone else was in on the joke but me. If Ted felt a need to share the weight of what he knew with someone, that need passed. He reverted back to the old Ted, flippant as ever.

"What, you think you're gonna' hear from Dr. Johnny...that asshole? You won't hear from him again. Ken thinks he's gonna' run. But if you do hear from Annie, you tell us. She's a ghost right now, either holed up in her pad in Culver City or maybe back home in San Francisco. She's not answering calls."

Ted leaned in close, and again dropped his voice to a whisper. "Shit's weird," he said. "Ken's lawyers think Annie might have cut a deal with the Feds, might take the stand against him if the case goes to trial."

I shook my head emphatically. It couldn't be true. Annie was too loyal to Ken. It was hard to imagine her cutting a deal with the Feds and testifying against him—hurting him.

Ted smiled. "You find that shocking? My sister tells me that 'covering your ass' is the name of the game now."

Ted leaned in again. "I got one more little fucking nugget for you. Ken says that there is some kind of Mole, some kind of informant? Somehow the Feds got their hands on internal documents and bank stuff...a lot of stuff that shouldn't have ever been floating around. And they had all this stuff well before they raided the office. It was leaked out."

"Who the hell did that?" I blurted out.

"Could be anyone," Ted shrugged. "Ken and I have a few ideas. Your old girlfriend, Gail, comes to mind. She worked at one of our primary banks. She had access to a lot of loan documents and credit statements. Ken never trusted Gail."

While I was still trying to get my head wrapped around the shit about Annie possibly testifying against Ken, it was even more far fetched to believe Gail could be some kind of Mole. But Gail did work at Ken's bank, she taped all the MLM meetings, took notes and photographs. I hadn't talked to her in a long time, lost touch with her after my marriage to Annika. She quit the business. At some point I heard she was planning to move out of the Valley.

My mind was just plain spinning.

"I don't know what happens now," Ted said, "but it sure as shit ain't gonna involve me. I dumped the company Mercedes at the old office this morning—left the keys on the floor. Those fucking dumbshits still didn't know I was driving it."

Ted chuckled, then fell silent. He was someplace else, his eyes working the room again. He smiled at the girl sitting at the end of the bar. She smiled back.

"What are you gonna do?" I asked.

"I bought an old Ford pickup yesterday. I'm packed up. I'm not staying around for this shit."

"When are you leaving?"

"Right now," he answered. "This is my last stop before bolting."

Leave it to Ted to bail on his sister at a time like this. Sure he didn't create their mess but he profited off them for years. His desire to cut and run didn't surprise me. It was Ted. Even so, I would miss him. Even with all his faults, he was my friend.

I decided we needed to drink to our friendship. I ordered two shots of gold tequila. After I ordered the drinks, Ted asked, "Don't they have any Power Punch behind the bar?"

I found the joke funny and laughed. Despite all that happened during the past few months—the raid, the arrest, the suspicion that someone on the inside was providing the Feds with information—Ted hadn't lost his sense of humor. And neither had I.

The bartender delivered the shots.

"These'll be our adios shots," Ted said, raising his glass.

It would be the last round we drank together. Ted drank the tequila in one gulp. I drank mine slowly. We walked to the parking lot. As we reached his truck I asked Ted one last question.

"Does Ken or the court have access to enough assets to make this right?"

Ted sat on his driver's seat sideways, feet dangling out of the pickup. He said, "I'd look out for my own ass at this point if I were you." He put his keys in the ignition and glanced at me a final time. "Give Annika and your family my best." He drove off. I waved my hand once and said, "Adios."

*   *   *

When I arrived home I found Annika peering at a letter.

"Stan and Katy dropped this off. They wanted to make sure you saw it. It's from PEN. They're holding a meeting for anyone who invested with Ken. It's at the Burbank Hilton on Monday night." She handed me the letter.

I read the contents. "It's signed by Moore," I pointed out. "I guess he's taking the lead on this mess. I'm sure I'll get one in the mail."

The letter had been copied to an attorney in San Jose. It read, in part:

It is our intention to help provide guidance to all Richman Properties Inc. investors who are also AmericanMade distributors and part of the PEN downline. We are deeply concerned about injuries you may have suffered through the activities of AmericanMade Diamond Ken Richman. As PEN had no affiliation with, or knowledge of the alleged illegal actions of Mr. Richman, we are anxious to better understand what you were promised by him or his employees. We are dedicated to helping each investor recover their principle to the extent we can. You are our top priority.

I wasn't fooled. PEN was far more interested in absolving itself of guilt and responsibility than helping injured investors. The meeting would be a public declaration of divorce from Ken Richman. The remaining Diamonds weren't going to admit what they knew or when they may have known it. It was all about damage control.

* * *

I arrived at the Burbank Hilton alone. I didn't want Annika there. When I asked her to marry me, I envisioned that we would build our business together. I saw her standing on the stage at my side. I saw us walking hand in hand on exotic beaches. I never expected to be attending a meeting where all my dreams would be crushed. There was no reason for her to be a witness.

I'd been to the Burbank Hilton many times as a keynote speaker at recruiting meetings, seminars and rallies. Arriving at the hotel should have helped me conjure up happy memories, but they were far from my mind. The fact was, I had never actually received an invitation from PEN to attend the meeting.

I saw Rex's car as I neared the entrance of the hotel. I hadn't spoken to him since the raid and arrests. He had quietly qualified as a Diamond and then took his seat on the PEN board. We'd grown apart. He was never comfortable with Ken's real estate scheme. He tried to warn me about it when he told me about the tennis game with Ken, but I ignored him. I should have immediately demanded answers, but I presumed Rex was jealous of him. If I had listened to Rex I may have rescued our $470,000 investment. I felt like an asshole.

I saw the Steenbergs in the parking lot. I hadn't realized how nervous I was. I approached them to say hello. They stared at me with disdain. "I'm surprised you had the balls to come here," Steve said. Samantha quickly added, "I don't know how you can show your face. You know where the money is. I'm sure your family is going to be well taken care of."

Steve put his arm around his wife and ushered her away from me. I was stunned. These people had been my friends. It had been years since I'd walked into a hotel conference room and not been met with applause. I suddenly realized that overnight, the feelings of people I'd known for years turned from love to hate. Just as I felt myself fall into the depths of self-pity, I felt a hand on my shoulder.

"Young man, how's your mother doing?" It was Stan. His voice was exactly what I needed: fatherly and reassuring. He recognized my sad expression.

"You okay?" he asked.

"No," I said. "People are pissed at me. They hate me. They think I have the money." I found myself spitting out the words like an immature teenager. I avoided making eye contact with Stan or Katy for fear they would turn against me as well.

"You're here," said Stan. "That's a start. We've all heard the rumors. Perhaps this meeting will put the gossip to rest. Catch your breath, we'll see you inside."

I gathered myself, thankful for Stan's counsel. I needed to clear my name. I approached the door, finding a security guard standing duty. He immediately motioned to someone inside. I heard Stewart Moore's voice, calling the meeting to order. One of the two doors swung shut and the security guard blocked the other with his wide frame.

"This is a private meeting, sir."

"I'm here for information and answers, same as every other investor."

"This is a private meeting, sir," he repeated more firmly.

I took the copy of the letter out of my pocket. I read from it verbatim.

"It is our intention to help provide answers and guidance to all Richman Properties investors who are also part..."

"Sir!" he said sharply, "I have been instructed to ask you to leave. Time for you to go."

I looked past him and into the meeting room one last time. I heard Moore on the microphone, launching into his discourse. I glared at the back of the heads of people I'd brought into the business; I'd drawn circles for them, made money for them.

There was stillness to that moment. Suddenly, I realized I had no interest in hearing the lies Moore intended to peddle. The security guard was right. It was time for me to go.

Adios.

39

October 1987

U sually, the big wrought iron gates to Ken's mansion were kept closed, but when I arrived I found them wide open, which I found odd. When I got to the top of the driveway there were no sign of Ken's cars and toys in the motor court. In fact, the only car I saw parked there was a dark blue Chevy.

The front door of the home was open. I stuck my head in.

"Hello?" I called out, the sound echoing back at me.

I stepped into the sunken living room. It was empty. I moved towards the family room. Empty. Not a stich of furniture. I made my way into the kitchen. Some of the cupboards were open. Empty. No dishes or cups.

The house was empty.

A man walked in and startled me. He carried a note pad and a camera. He was a rather tall man and oddly dressed, in my opinion, at least for southern California. He wore a plaid shirt fastened with a Bolo tie. He had faded jeans on and a wrinkled sport coat. But what stood out was his crocodile boots. Nobody sported croc boots in Los Angeles. His hair was long, secured in a ponytail. His mustache...it was the biggest handlebar mustache I'd seen in a long time.

"Can I help you?" he asked.

"I'm a friend of the Richmans. I didn't know they moved," I stammered.

"Yeah. A bit sudden, don't you agree?"

He studied me. "How are you associated with them?"

It was then I noticed his badge clipped to his belt. I instantly wondered whether I should be talking to him. Before I could answer, he said, "My name is Charles Boone. I'm with the F.B.I."

He handed me a business card. As I took it from his hand he asked again, "How are you associated with the Richmans?"

"We worked together," I weakly responded.

"Were you in his downline—AmericanMade—or were you an investor?"

"Both," I said.

"Can I ask your name, son?"

"Tony DiBona," I answered.

He opened and glanced at a small spiral bound notebook that he'd retrieved from his coat pocket. He put it away and stood for a moment, his right hand cupping his left elbow, his left hand scratching his chin. Finally, he said, "We'd like to talk with you. You and your family lost a lot of money investing with Ken Richman, is that right?"

I nodded.

How much?

"My family and I invested four hundred and seventy thousand."

"I'm sorry," he said.

It was an awkward moment. I don't think he truly felt empathy for me but, instead, believed I knew a lot about Ken and the way he did business. Perhaps he believed I was an accomplice. I wondered if Boone had approached Rex and Stan as well.

"I just came to talk to Ken," I said. "I had no idea they were moving."

"Very well. Yeah, they moved on in a hurry. Yup, I don't guess they said goodbye to many people. Ken petitioned the judge to allow them to stay in their home in Aspen, Colorado. I think that's where they were headed, son."

I didn't want to talk to this guy and I was a little nauseous. I decided to leave. I smiled at Charles Boone half-heartedly and walked towards the front door. I could sense he was following me out as I reached into my pocket for the keys. I heard his voice over my shoulder.

"Mr. DiBona, we'll be in touch, all right?"

Beautiful. That's all I need. Now I have the F.B.I. wanting to talk with me. God only knows what they've been told by the assholes at PEN and other scorned investors. The whisper rumors suggested I was hiding money for Ken. Those rumors coupled with me showing up at Ken's home while an F.B.I. investigator was poking around the place was perfect timing on my part.

What else could go wrong?

I glanced back. I saw Boone standing in front of the home's entryway. Behind him were the doors to a home that once symbolized wealth, security and friendship to me. As I started the engine of a car I could no longer afford, I realized how wrong I'd been about some things. I thought I was building a business, a future and lasting friendships. But good friends don't move out of town in the middle of the night without telling you. I realized then just how much Ken lied to me, and how much I lied to myself. It was the emptiest feeling I'd ever felt in my life.

40

Wednesday, December 2nd, 1987

After my visit to the vacant Richman house I drove to the top of Topanga Canyon and sat there in my car. I stared out at the Valley, staggered by the reckoning of what I'd done: The reckoning of whom and
what I'd invited into my life. I sat there calculating what my actions cost
my family and me and how helpless I'd become. My tears that afternoon
were over my stupidity—a stupidity that resulted in a huge cost to my
family. In my mother's case, it was most of the money she and my dad had
saved for their golden years. In my uncle Mike's case, it was ALL of his
retirement savings. I was directly responsible for them losing it. I was the
person that introduced them to Ken.

I spent the next two months searching for answers but finding few av-
enues open. The court appointed a U.S. trustee to handle the jumble of
supposed assets left behind by Richman Financial. Their role would be to
conserve assets and create liquidity for the investor's eventual benefit. I
called them and even sent several letters to them asking pointed questions.
My calls weren't returned and my letters were not answered. Stan pursued

answers from the trustee also, receiving a similar silent treatment. I quickly determined that they were an unresponsive level bureaucracy that had been added to an already messy situation.

Ted had been spot on about Dr. Johnny. I learned through the grapevine that he was missing. He wasn't checking in with authorities as required. He'd skipped bail. I guess he'd decided that he couldn't do federal jail time. So, Johnny Gergin was gone and Ken and Nancy were hiding in Aspen. Ken was only talking to his attorney and the U.S. Trustee was too busy to answer questions. That left my old friend Annie.

I decided to locate Annie. I wanted to talk to her face to face. She was the one person who would tell me the truth and might also be one of the few people who didn't believe I was hiding money for Ken.

I drove to her rented home in Culver City. When I arrived, I discovered an overgrown lawn and the walkway cluttered with newspapers. Junk mail overflowed the small metal mailbox. I rang the doorbell. No answer. The drapes were split slightly, enabling me to see into her living room. It was empty except for a phone sitting on the floor still plugged into the jack.

I lifted the dead potted plant that hid her spare key. I thought of the times I used that key. When I was somewhere on the west side, too drunk to drive back over the hill to the Valley, I slept on her couch. When Annie took her boys on summer vacation I fed her cat and watered her plants. When Annie celebrated a birthday quietly, with the hopes we wouldn't catch on, that key helped me fill her place with balloons from ceiling to floor.

"Hello?" I called as I let myself in.

I heard my voice echo as I slipped into the hallway of the dark house. I called out one more time, just to make sure the place was unoccupied. After a quick check of the bedrooms I stepped into the small kitchen. I opened the blinds to let in the little light left in the day. A few paper plates and plastic forks littered the sink. An empty box of cereal and a soda can sat on the kitchen counter.

I walked across the living room and lingered on a creaky floorboard, caught by an amusing memory. Back in our Penn Life days, Rex complained a lot about that floorboard. He would never volunteer to fix it but he never shut up about it, either.

Annie never upgraded her lifestyle. She was a saver. She considered stepping up to a bigger home right when Ken opened Richman Properties but instead saved her money, marking it for college educations and a future filled with tropical drinks with silly umbrellas. There were so many times we teased her about it but now it didn't seem funny.

Suddenly, my thoughts were interrupted by a woman's voice.

"Can I help you?"

I snapped my head around as an older woman entered the doorway.

"Hello," she said sweetly, "are you looking for Ms. Wu? I live next door."

"Yes. I'm an old friend," I answered. "Do you know where she went?"

"I know when she left," she replied. "The movers were here two weeks ago. Her company transferred her to San Francisco, back to her hometown. To keep her job she had to move right away, she told me. She was in a real hurry—drove away and the movers picked up her furniture the next day."

She inspected the leftover trash on the floor, shaking her head.

"I was chatting with one of the moving men. The man in charge said they were hauling her furniture to Phoenix. That confused me based on my conversation with Ms. Wu. I sure hope her belongings arrived in San Francisco."

I escorted the meddlesome neighbor out with a thank you and a steady arm as she feebly descended the front step. I watched her walk slowly to her house through the overgrown lawn then I wandered back inside for one last look. I closed the blinds and locked the back door.

As I walked through the kitchen I discovered what I overlooked. There, on the door of the refrigerator, was a small memento Annie left behind. It was a postcard, held to the refrigerator door with a magnet shaped like a guitar—the name *Elvis* displayed on the neck of the guitar. It was a souvenir from Annie's trip to Graceland years earlier. I removed the postcard. It had a soft sepia tone image of a house overlooking a tropical beach. The home featured a large wooden veranda with a single unoccupied lounge chair on it. The words "Greetings from Maui, Hawaii" were splashed across the top of the postcard. Like the rest of us, Annie had her dreams stuck to her fridge with a magnet.

I placed the postcard and magnet in my pocket. I locked the front door, returning the key beneath the potted plant.

No matter where she was, San Francisco or Phoenix, I doubted she'd be there forever. She had a dream and I hoped she'd cut a good deal for herself with the Feds and could somehow rebuild her life and realize those dreams. Maybe she would look me up when she came back in town to testify against the others. Or maybe she wouldn't. I wasn't sure I even cared that much. I just had the hunch she'd land on her feet.

I'd never thought Annie would turn on Ken but I never thought Ken would do what he did, either. I guess I learned people could surprise you.

I never realized how much I relied on Annie until she was gone. I understood her motivation—Ken took advantage of her, just like he took advantage of me. I guess it was time I listened to the advice of her father: It was time for me to take care of my own business. Still looking for answers, I had one more stop to make.

41

Late Afternoon, December 2ⁿᵈ, 1987

I marched toward the door of his real estate office. It was located in the corner of a sleepy, north Valley strip mall. Alex Josephs and I met on the same day I met Annika. We developed a nice friendship over the next few years as he tried to build up his MLM business. Even though he wasn't in my downline I had counseled him and helped him build his business.

Alex was in his mid-thirties and already quite successful in real estate when he decided to dive into the business headfirst after he was exposed to Ken Richman. He built it to the Gold level, and then he stalled. As he began to slow down I recalled he mentioned that he was "burning the candle at both ends" and needed to "put one end out." Finding less and less time for his family, Alex elected to stop drawing circles so he could save his marriage and continue to grow his flourishing real estate business.

I needed to ask him to call his title company and run some title searches looking for Richman Properties, Inc., Ken Richman and a few of the other corporate aliases he used. I was aware that Alex's father had invested with

Ken. I felt those of us who brought this destruction on ourselves and our loved ones shared an odd bond. Driving away from Annie's, I needed to see if that bond was real. I was blasting through my shrinking list of people who could help me that I'd also assisted over the years. It was time to ask those people to return a favor.

"Good to see you. How have you been holding up?" Alex asked with a nod for me to help myself to a seat.

"Getting by," I told him. "My downline is decimated."

There was no need for pleasantries.

"Most of my distributors quit," I said. "The business was my only source of income so I'm pretty much screwed."

"You don't deserve this crap," he said.

"I need some help," I told him. I hated the way the words sounded the moment they left my lips but they were true. "My family and I put almost a half million in Ken's deals. I want to know if the equity in the properties is still there so that when Ken is sentenced, we'll have some chance to see our money returned."

"I need to give my family and friends some answers. Can you run some title searches for me?"

He didn't immediately answer. He opened his desk drawer, removed a red file folder and tossed it on his desk.

"I don't have to run any new searches."

He nudged the file over to me. I opened it and removed a three-page report prepared by his local title company. It was dated August 21, 1987. There were a dozen or so pieces of land listed on the report. At first glance it could appear that there were ample assets to repay Ken's investors—but if you looked closer, you could see that this wasn't the case.

Many of the properties had first, second and even third deeds of trust recorded on them. Most of the property groupings were crossed out with a big red X. There were two assets that weren't. They only had first mortgages. They were the final two pieces of land purchased by Richman Properties. The report confirmed Ken had systematically sucked the equity out of each property. He used a myriad of different commercial banks and private lenders, most likely supplying them with inaccurate information.

"These last two—the ones that only have a first mortgage—why'd you circle them?" I asked Alex.

"I told my father about the Richman Properties federal raid the day after it happened. He immediately called Ken, left him several messages, but Ken didn't return his calls. My father is not the kind of guy you want to ignore. He asked me to investigate. When I contacted Ken he told me he and his attorney were cooperating with authorities. He told me that there would be a plea deal and he promised that there'd be enough assets to take care of investors. He told me to tell my father to "calm down" and that he'd get "most of his principle back.""

"My father isn't a guy you say 'calm down', to. He's not a patient man. A few weeks went by and my father grew skeptical and irritated. I ran these reports", Alex said, nodding toward the file folder. "I had to tell my father most of the properties were worthless. I advised him that the last two pieces of land might have some equity in them, but we couldn't count on that either. We couldn't be certain Ken hadn't already drained those two with non traditional hard-money loans—deeds that just hadn't been recorded yet."

Alex took the folder from my hands and tucked it back into his bottom drawer.

"When my father saw this report he realized Ken was operating a Ponzi scheme. He sent an associate from Vegas to visit Ken and they reached some sort of understanding. I don't know what they worked out, and I don't wanna know."

My spiny senses instantly lit up. What the hell did he mean by some sort of understanding and what line of work was his father into to have "associates from Vegas?"

"Your father, what business is he in?" I asked.

"He helped build a few of the big hotels in Vegas back in the day, before they went corporate—the Golden Nugget, the Riviera, and a few others. He was responsible for the funding and worked as a liaison between the union and his employers. He did well. He's retired now."

"Whom did he work for?"

Alex's demeanor suddenly changed. Clearly, he did not want to answer the question. "He worked for the groups that built the hotels on the strip," he said.

A few awkward seconds passed as I put a few more pieces of the puzzle together in my head.

"The bottom line is what?" I asked. "No money left for the U.S. Trustees to work with except for maybe the last two properties?"

Alex nodded. His demeanor changed again, this time to one of sympathy. "Tony, this is heartbreaking for you, I know. I feel horrible for you and your family. I don't know where the courts, the U.S. Trustee or whoever the hell has to clean up this mess is going to find assets. My father thinks that Ken's hiding some money. He thinks Richman was smart enough to have 'stashed some cash for a rainy day.' There's even some rumors out there that you're hiding cash for him, but, I know you...I've been telling people that's bullshit."

Did he feel horrible? He didn't feel horrible that his father apparently used some sort of muscle to retrieve what he was owed.

Alex stood, signaling an end to our meeting.

"I gotta do a walk-through on a listing, Tony. We're closing a big escrow tomorrow. Let's have lunch soon."

I agreed to the lunch I knew would never happen and left. I walked to the parking lot with my heart racing and hands trembling. I paused there for a moment. I had stood in the Richmans' living room, clutching a gun, protecting his family from Alex's father's "associates." Alex attended my father's funeral and his father almost brought on mine. It all still felt like a dream, a very bad dream.

A part of me wanted to tell the authorities about the favored pay-off—bust out Alex's father and Ken for cutting a deal outside of the proper channels. That little revelation would exonerate me in the eyes of the assholes that thought I was hiding money for Ken. It would set the record straight that my family and me weren't receiving any preferential treatment. But that wouldn't be too fucking bright. I didn't feel like pissing off members of an organized crime syndicate and I knew Ken owned a gun and would do anything to protect his family.

It seemed like everyone was taking care of their own business, with their own layers of defense. All I had was the truth and it didn't offer much protection or solace.

* * *

My relationship with Annika had grown strained. For some misguided reason, I expected a miracle would occur and our cares would vanish.

It was the evening of my twenty-seventh birthday. The night before, Annika asked me how I wanted to celebrate, but I never answered her. That day, I received a letter from PEN and wasn't in the mood to celebrate:

> ...We regret to inform you that your services on our speaking circuit are no longer needed at this time. Your upcoming events have been reassigned to other qualified Emerald-level pins, which are in good standing with our PEN support organization.

The rebuke was humiliating. The loss of the speaking gigs would kill what remained of our income. Annika was shaken. She knew this would finally break me. I stumbled into the kitchen, crumpled the letter and jammed it into the trashcan.

I felt indignation. For the first time in this situation I allowed myself to feel rage. It was real: It was the early morning wake-up call in '83, discovering my home would be turned into an office. It was the subsequent retirement party for a retirement I never agreed to. Even with my beautiful wife standing before me it was the awesome connection I had with Gail, the one that I misused and mishandled. All of those things were boiling inside of me. All I had worked so hard for, all I embodied, and all I had become was crumpled and trashed.

I grabbed the toaster, ripped its cord from the socket and heaved it against the wall. It shattered into pieces. I peered at my wife. I knew from the expression on her face there was no coming back from that moment. She slipped on her coat and went for a walk. I knew she'd be returning to the house even more of a stranger.

I'd hoped beyond reason that everyone's suspicion of me would pass. It didn't. The business was done with me. I called Rex. He was now installed on the PEN board as a qualified Diamond. He didn't take my call. He quickly aligned himself with Stewart Moore and the others after he qualified Diamond. Rex had quietly, and without fanfare, accomplished what I couldn't.

As I sat on my couch draining a beer, my mind became remarkably resolute. I retreated to my home office desk and composed two letters: The first to be sent to Stewart Moore and the Diamonds of PEN. I would not choose my words carefully for them. The second letter would be more respectful and would be sent to AmericanMade. It would be a formal termination of my distributorship. I asked them to liquidate my deferred bonus account and send me the money. I needed it badly.

Annika returned from her walk, cleaned the remnants of our shattered toaster and sat on the couch with a glass of wine. I walked through our living room, ignoring her, stamped letters in hand. I was in a hurry. I wanted to drop the letters in the mail before I had second thoughts.

Reaching the mailbox on the corner, I pulled on the handle, then stopped. I choked back the lump in my throat, stifling a sob, but my eyes welled with tears. Paralyzed for the moment, I tried to find a reason I shouldn't do what I was about to do—severing the last five and a half years of my life.

I shoved the letters into the mailbox, felt my fingers release them and allowed the handle to snap back with a clang. The barely audible sound of the two letters as they slid into darkness was louder than I'd ever known. With that single act I'd removed myself from AmericanMade, PEN and my prior life.

Still, I found a measure of satisfaction in knowing I'd regained control of my life. Approaching my house I felt unburdened yet with every step closer I discovered I had no idea what to do next.

On the evening of my twenty-seventh birthday I recognized and accepted what a deluded, unrecognizable asshole I'd allowed myself to become. I was initially a lemming and then, later in the game, a more knowing participant, dabbling in the art of deceiving one's self. I could barely remember the principled person my mother and father had raised me to be.

For the first time in more than five years, I was being truthful with myself. For that I was glad.

42

Monday, March 14th, 1988

Annika and I were sleepwalking through our marriage. Our life existed in stark contrast to the magical times we shared early in our relationship. I'd held onto the belief I could support us financially, yet Annika knew otherwise. Her job at the travel agency provided us with an income—certainly not enough to maintain the standard of living we'd known while living the sweet life, but enough to put food on the table. As for me, I started selling insurance again.

I figured that I could convince myself to like the commission-only insurance game again, enough so that we could begin to solve our money troubles. I didn't have any other attractive options. I had to do something. It had been months since we made timely car or credit card payments; finally, we simply stopped making those payments altogether.

Meanwhile, the calls from finance companies and credit card companies came daily. We let the answering machine handle them. Eventually, the repo men arrived. They hooked Annika's car first, then the Jag. I handed them the keys, walked back to my kitchen chair, and watched my dream car disappear around the corner. After the cars were repossessed we sold all of our jewelry, except for our wedding rings. We cancelled our health and life insurance. Somehow, we survived, but I'm not sure how.

The financial challenges continued for my mom, aunt and uncle. I can't explain the level of guilt I felt about their losses. I brought Ken into their lives and Ken sucked out their money. It was bad enough knowing I wasn't the man Annika thought I was, that I couldn't provide the life she expected me to provide. Yet the feeling of failing my family, placing them in the position they were in, was worse.

I called Mazal the week before. He was happy to hear from me; we drained a few beers together. I finally told him everything that had happened, but I didn't have to. He had heard the stories. He knew. He didn't pass judgment on my poor decisions or say, "I told you so." He just listened and made a few jokes about what Ken's boyfriend in jail would look like. We laughed a lot that night. It was the first time I'd laughed in months.

That next morning I showered, shaved and dressed for a day of work—cold calling on insurance leads. Annika was already long gone to her job at the travel agency. As I knotted up my tie I heard the doorbell. As I approached the door I saw the silhouette of a man through the frosted glass. I took a deep breath and opened the door.

I recognized him from our encounter at the Richmans' abandoned home months earlier. It was only a matter of time before the trail of rumors and innuendos led to my door. I invited Charles Boone into my home and pointed to the kitchen table.

"Am I a target?" I asked.

Boone settled into a kitchen chair. "Should I be looking at you as a target?"

At this point in my life I was a thoroughly defeated man. My money was gone. My marriage was falling apart. I had ruined the lives of my mother and other family members. People I trusted were likely to be going to jail soon. Friends abandoned me. I suspected Boone was well aware of my condition. Certainly, he may have guessed the quality of my life when he parked in front of my house and saw my mode of transportation. It was an old, dented station wagon I had borrowed from my uncle.

"Do I need to call an attorney?"

He smiled. "You're certainly welcome to, Tony, but for now I'm here to ask questions about Ken Richman. At this juncture, I don't believe you've done anything criminal. This is all about Richman and his staff."

"Okay," I said, "Ask your questions."

Boone took out a notebook. Glancing down, he flipped through some pages. "You and your family invested $470,000, is that correct?"

"Yes."

"You and Ken were close?"

I nodded.

"How close?"

"He was my mentor in the business. He was the best man at my wedding. We were close—like a big brother." The words sounded curious as they came out of my own mouth. I'd been asking myself how close Ken and I really had been over and over again. How could someone I considered a close friend do all this shit to my family and me?

"As we piece together the case against Richman, your name keeps coming up," Boone said. "Now, son, I have no reason to believe that you're sitting on a pile of cash for Richman—unless you want to admit to it—but we did learn that he transported a large sum of cash to Las Vegas and gave it to one of his investors on a certain date...when was that..."

Boone was consulting his notebook, head down, while I was trying to process what he just told me, and what he knew. The F.B.I. had obviously been tailing Ken 24/7...that means he had to also know Alex's father was mob-connected.

"So, yeah...In Mid September of last year, I believe Richman transported over a quarter-million dollars on his private plane, which has since been repossessed, to Nevada so he could repay a single investor. That proves he had some cash stashed away."

Boone leaned back, fingering his well-manicured handlebar mustache.

"Tony, we're wrapping up this case for the prosecutors. We are looking for assets. Trying to tie up some loose ends and at the same time give them everything they need. Don't misunderstand me...our criminal case against Richman and the corporate officers is already airtight," he continued. "Some people are going to do some time. But I do want to follow the trail of money and find any assets that Ken may be hiding."

He leaned his lanky torso back in the chair and crossed his arms.

"If you or your family received a payout...if you are concealing money for Ken it would be a felony and you could do prison time also."

And there it was. I sensed he would have to sniff around at me—take his shot.

Since the raid at Richman Properties and Ken's arrest, I had been wounded—I lost my money, my status, my friends and my marriage was crumbling. But it had never occurred to me that I could also lose my freedom. I knew I hadn't committed any crimes for Ken; now, I wondered whether I would have to convince a jury of my innocence.

I suspected Boone knew I was innocent, but he wanted to play games. I decided to test him with what I already knew, that he didn't know I knew.

"So Ken cashed out someone and that investor accepted the money, knowing they shouldn't have? Which may also be a state or federal crime since Ken's assets are frozen and that money, technically, would belong to all investors equally. Right?"

Boone nodded.

"So, I assume you recovered that money and that investor is facing some level of scrutiny or even charges?"

I knew the answer was a big fat, "NO". It would have been all over the Daily News if Alex's mob connected father had been pinched by the F.B.I. in connection with Ken's case.

Boone folded his arms and looked away. He hummed a low tune as he evaluated the sad state of my current existence. When his eyes finally found mine again, he softened a bit and leaned toward me.

"It's not that simple, Tony. Ken's apparent preferential payoff wasn't made directly to any investor on our list. We believe a bag of money was dropped to an associate of an investor. The trail of Ken's cash led us to a person of interest who's attached to another ongoing investigation, a case that's being handled by our RICO team in our Nevada bureau."

Boone then started to explain what "RICO" meant, but I stopped him. I knew a little about the Racketeer Influenced and Corrupt Organizations Act. I had watched all of the mafia movies. RICO was a 1970 law that allowed the Feds to bring charges against organized crime leaders even if they, themselves, didn't commit the actual crime.

My mind trailed off to visions of casinos and mobsters. I doubted Fred Cohen at Starbridge ever dealt with mobsters. I doubted my father would have ever kept such company. I let a smile spread across my face.

"I'm not hiding any money," I said. "I wish Ken had slipped me some cash, but he didn't." I stood up, approached my sink and tossed what was left of my coffee down the drain. I was sure Boone and I would talk again, but for now I simply needed to be by myself. Feelings of betrayal bubbled inside me. PEN had shunned me, Ken and the others vanished, and here I was answering questions from an F.B.I. agent.

Suddenly, my anger welled up. I slammed the mug on the kitchen tile, shattering it to pieces and cutting my hand. I took a deep breath, found a kitchen towel to wrap around my hand, and sat back down, wanting to do some of my own questioning.

"Can I ask you a few questions?"

Boone nodded.

"Where's Ken now?"

"The Richmans are in Aspen, Colorado. The judge on this case gave them special permission to move their family there. Ken and his attorney have been very cooperative and the judge saw fit to allow them to relocate temporarily."

"Annie Wu?"

"She turned state's evidence," Boone said, matter of factly. "We convinced her it was her best option if she wanted to stay out of jail. She's been most helpful. We can't discuss her whereabouts or other details."

"Dr. Johnny?"

"He's a fugitive. He surfaced last month at the MGM casino in Reno. Casino security caught him ripping off a few people at the slots. The Reno cops put him in jail, but they didn't recognize the federal warrants against him, and he easily made bail. He was back on the street in less than a day."

It was too bad that Dr. Johnny got away, but I respected Boone for telling me the cops had botched their one good chance to nail him. Finally, I asked Boone the question that had been nagging at me for months, but I thought I already knew the answer to. "How much of the fifteen million dollars of investor money still exists? I wanna know what the hell to tell my family and whatever few friends I have left."

"We're chasing down some leads. As you may be aware, the U.S. placed Ken Richman and Richman Properties into involuntary bankruptcy. They did this to ensure that he couldn't liquidate or divest assets before they had a chance to conserve them for investors. However, from what we can see, there's nowhere close to fifteen million dollars of value left in the corporation, the properties or Ken and Nancy's personal accounts."

I knew the money was gone, but hearing Boone provide confirmation made my stomach churn. At least I could stop fixating on where and when all the money would be found. Boone interrupted my daydream with another question.

"We're trying to identify a certain anonymous informant," Boone said. "This person provided sensitive information regarding Ken, bank documents and other financial information. The snitch sold the information to certain parties. The informer goes by the name, TSV Associates. We want to know whom that person or entity is. They have little to do with our criminal case against Richman, as we have ample evidence that he knew he was operating a Ponzi scheme—actually admitted to it. But, we think this Mole could help locate other assets. Whoever they are, they seem to know where the bodies are buried."

It had been months since I'd thought about the erroneous Mole.

"They sent information to AmericanMade," Boone said. "They also sold information to Beau Willis. The informant also had communication with Stewart Moore toward the end."

"Do I understand you correctly?" I asked. "The informant provided dirt on Ken to AmericanMade, Beau Willis and Stewart Moore—and was gettin' paid for it?"

Boone nodded. He added that AmericanMade possessed information suggesting wrongdoing well before the company terminated Ken and Nancy. I asked Boone when AmericanMade originally contacted authorities. His answer surprised me.

"AmericanMade didn't contact us. Beau Willis did."

AmericanMade's legal division sat on this information and didn't bother to call anyone? Infuckingcredible. Boone explained that when he originally contacted AmericanMade's compliance officer, the guy admitted they received packages from an anonymous informant using the name, actually the acronym, *TSV*. They disregarded the information because they frequently received invalid tips from disgruntled distributors.

Boone added, "It wasn't AmericanMade's practice to accuse distributors of wrongdoing on unproven, anonymous tips. They said the information was hard to interpret. When pressed, they told us they were in the process of an internal investigation and they planned to notify authorities when the investigation and review was completed."

It made sense for Willis to tip off the Feds. He had a giant hard-on and wanted to see Ken burn just as much as the Diamonds of the PEN organization did.

"Did any of the PEN Diamonds contact you?" I asked.

"Nope," he said firmly. "We contacted Moore and several others. They emphatically denied having any advanced knowledge of wrongdoing. I didn't believe them for a minute. So I pressed Stewart Moore—got a sit down with him in the presence of his attorney up in San Jose. This time he told a slightly different story."

Boone told me that, shielded by his attorney, Moore admitted that some "cryptic information" had been sent to him anonymously—but he claimed to have shredded it. He told them he still believed Ken to be a fine Christian man and that the information must have been part of a vicious attack on his close friend.

"I didn't believe it," Boone said. "I'm certain that what TSV sent PEN was a duplicate of what they also sent Willis."

Boone produced a large envelope from his briefcase. He let the contents spill out on the kitchen table. "The informant had access to banking information," he said. Boone sifted through some documents. He showed me some pages. "Do you recognize the handwriting?"

I studied the samples. The handwriting didn't look familiar to me. I wondered who would have access and motive. Gail? Could it be? Ted and Ken had suspected her. Ken never fully trusted her. Ken did degrade her, yet I found it difficult to believe she could have done something like this... she wasn't a vindictive person. But, then again, what did I know? I'd proven to be a poor judge of character recently.

"If the Mole got paid, there is a money trail. Can't you follow it?" I asked.

"Give this TSV person some credit," he said. "TSV instructed each client to send them multiple money orders in modest amounts. The money orders were payable to "cash." The address of the informant was a post office box in Reseda."

I glanced down at the handwriting samples again. Gail lived in Reseda.

"TSV doesn't exist." Boone said. "The entity isn't filed as a corporation, and our DBA searches proved fruitless. When I visited the Reseda post office and reviewed the microfilm, I learned the box was opened under the guise that it was for an out-of-state employer. The informant talked their way out of having to give identification. It's frustrating as hell. The employee who handled the P.O. boxes there was an older man who recently retired and has since died. The boxes were closed in July of last year. The post office requires a forwarding address when you close a box. The address given by the informer was on Monovale Drive in Holmby Hills, a real swanky neighborhood. One of our agents called on the owner. He was a high-powered business executive. He'd never heard of "TSV" and had no connection with the P.O. box. It was a big, giant dead end."

"I'm curious...the Mole, did this person break any laws?" I asked.

"It's not illegal to sell information for remuneration as long as there's no evidence of extortion or theft," Boone said. "I'm just interested in what the informer can tell us about hidden assets. I think we can eliminate the officers and key employees of Richman Properties since they wouldn't be foolish enough to impeach themselves. We know this much, this TSV is damned good at staying under the radar."

Boone jammed the contents of the envelope back into his briefcase as he rose to leave. I decided to ask, one last time, whether he thought I should find a lawyer.

"Not if what you've said is true," he replied. "There is a small window of time if you recall more information. I'll leave my card as well as this." Boone slid a few copies of the handwriting samples across the table to me. "If you think of information that may be important to us, please call."

I walked Boone to the front door. Before leaving, he turned and said, "Can I ask you one last question—a question off the subject?"

"I guess, sure," I answered.

"How do people get sucked into these MLMs so blindly that they'll follow guys like Richman without asking the right questions? You made good money, so maybe it's understandable in your case, but what about the couples who hang on forever and never really make any money?"

It was a good question and a logical one. I'm sure an outsider like Boone found it all very foolish.

"Maybe you've got to be there," I said. "But there's a common theme we pushed. Most people wake up one day and realize they're in a dead-end job, a career that ain't going to get them what they want. What's worse, they are working for a company that usually doesn't give a rat's ass about them. Their dreams are simmering just under the surface, and then they just had to take a ration of shit from their boss."

"Then someone like Ken Richman shows up. He's got this unbelievable life and lifestyle. He shows it to you, gives you a taste of it. Then he tells you he sees talent in you. And for the first time in your life you are connected to someone that has actually made a lot of money and has offered to show you and help you do the same thing. All of a sudden, your dreams aren't just pipe-dreams anymore, they seem real and attainable. And then you latch on for the ride because...what better option do you have?"

Boone smiled. "I guess selling hope is easier than I thought it was," he said.

I knew by his wry smile that he was judging me. I could tell by his swagger that he didn't need to buy any hope from a man like Ken Richman.

"Ken was the first guy who persuaded me I could be great," I added.

We walked to the curb in silence.

"That's why this is so hard for me to understand," I said. "It's hard for me to believe that being a conman was his original intent; but regardless, there's a trail of bodies out there and I'm one of them."

"You'll bounce back." Boone said, trying to sound sincere. "You have my card."

I shook his hand and watched him drive away. Returning to the house, I took solace on the couch. I was that needy person I'd just described to Boone. I believed I was better than that, but who the hell was I kidding?

43

Evening, March 14ᵗʰ, 1988

I glided into the driveway. I never realized how materialistic I'd become until I lost it all. Parking the borrowed station wagon in the driveway was out of the question. It had to stay hidden in the garage. I'm not sure if it was how our neighbors looked at us or how I regarded our situation. They saw our cars towed away. I didn't need to leave my eyesore of a car sitting in plain view, giving the neighbors excuses to gawk at us.

Turned out, having a nice car was less important to me than I could have imagined. I didn't buy the Jag because it was known to be a reliable, sturdy piece of machinery. I didn't buy it for the gas mileage. I simply liked the way the word sounded as I forced it into as many conversations as I could. Now that my Jag was gone, the station wagon was hidden behind a garage door.

Annika wasn't home. It was just as well. She left a note that she and Catarina were meeting for a cocktail. I was thankful for the solitude. I found a beer and some leftover meatloaf and headed for my office. Between bites, I sorted the notes and business cards from my day of cold-calling insurance prospects.

I opened the folder of papers Boone left behind that morning, studying the photocopied pages inside. I was fascinated someone pulled off the Mole scam with complete anonymity. I went through a mental Rolodex of people I knew who could have possibly gained access to Ken's financial records.

I thought about Catarina for a moment. She obtained a work visa and found a new job before Ken and Nancy disappeared. She'd been their nanny for quite a while. She certainly had the access, but I simply couldn't imagine her understanding the complexities of Richman Properties' financial records. Also, I didn't believe it was in Catarina's character to turn on Ken and Nancy—I always found her honest and good-hearted.

What about Gail? I retrieved a photo album she made for our second anniversary and paged through the contents. Five-and-a-half years passed since our breakup. The photos depicted the shaggy haircut I wore as a twenty-two-year-old as well as a slimmer waistline and smile that reflected my naivety. The album overflowed with photographs as well as little red hearts and sticky notes inscribed with silly citations.

There was the picture of her and I at Go Diamond Weekend in San Diego. She had scribbled a cute little note underneath it:

"Upline Pearl...hey didn't Billy Joel write a song about that...oh, never mind, that was 'Uptown Girl.'"

My eye fell on a photo from the 1984 Free Enterprise event in Long Beach. It was of Gail standing beside Rex and his wife, notepad in hand, camera hanging from her neck. She was always taking notes and photos and taping the meetings. Under her photo, she had scrawled:

"As a world famous college journalist, I'm always looking for a good story to investigate"

Was Gail TSV? I just couldn't rule her out. Indeed, she had worked at Ken's primary bank. Starting as a teller, she eventually worked her way up into operations. Lifting documents from the bank, copying them and then replacing them—it was possible.

On the last page of the album I found a photo I didn't ever recall seeing before. I removed it from the album. The photo showed Annie, Rex and me, the three musketeers. On the back, I found it had been dated October 1984, and taken during a Halloween party at Ken's house. I was dressed as Elvis that year. I wore dark sunglasses and leaned against Annie's shoulder. I assume I pre-partied with Ted and my eyes were probably bloodshot— hidden by the dark shades.

I remembered the night, but not posing for the picture. It felt good to see the images of Annie and Rex, the two people who knew me before I discovered greed. The memory of good times with Annie and Rex helped ease my blues.

I returned the photo album to the shelf but kept the picture in my hand. I located the Elvis biography, the one Annie had given me for my birthday the previous year. She was thoughtful. I tried to recall the gifts I had given her over the years. In truth, beyond a handful of gag gifts and buying her drinks, I don't think I'd ever given her anything meaningful. I opened the biography and placed the photo inside the front cover.

My smile faded as I sat down and faced the rest of my cold meatloaf and colder insurance leads. I sifted through Boone's notes on the Mole again. None of it made sense, and I was too damned tired to figure it out. I placed the notes back into the folder and jammed it in my drawer.

I found a cigar in a cluttered desk drawer. It was the last of a dozen Cubans Ken had given me in anticipation of my Diamond qualification. I couldn't throw the cigars away. They were Cubans—too expensive. I had smoked them one by one. Maybe I wanted to torture myself. It seemed as good a night as any to smoke the last one before it turned stale.

I left the house, stepped into the cool March air and sat down on the curb. My eyes wandered from the expensive cars owned by my neighbors to the front windows of their homes, behind which I knew I could find happy marriages. I didn't feel a part of that world or even my neighborhood anymore. I reached into my pocket for a match, also finding Boone's card. I lit the match, then ignited Boone's card and used it to light my cigar.

I didn't need Boone's card. I didn't have any information for him that he didn't already know.

I sat peacefully on the curb puffing on the cigar and finding my thoughts drawn back to the photo. My mind focused on Annie. In turn for her testimony against Ken, she wouldn't be serving any jail time. She and her boys were probably living in a tract home in Phoenix, starting a new life. I tried to imagine what story she'd tell her neighbors about herself.

44

Tuesday, September 20th, 1988

In September I closed the small insurance office I'd rented and let go of the few agents I'd recruited. I didn't have enough energy or strength to lead people. I found an inside sales job with a local bank selling annuities and mutual funds. I was the guy who dealt with depositors who complained about the rate of return on their passbook accounts. Annika didn't understand why I came home most nights clenching my teeth. I was earning a steady paycheck. With my pay and Annika's, we had enough to keep the mortgage current, but we still had little or no money to spare.

Our existence was depressing—working all week while dodging creditor's phone calls. On evenings and weekends we watched TV and drank, not engaging much with each other. I was lost and I wasn't sure how to find my way back home. I didn't know if that place even existed anymore but I desperately wanted to find it.

It was our anniversary and I wanted it to be romantic. An expensive restaurant wasn't an option so I decided to leave work a few minutes early and make dinner. I decorated the table with candles and an anniversary card I'd made by hand.

As I prepared dinner it occurred to me how little energy I'd actually put into our marriage. When we originally met, money and fame was my focus—even my god. I was so absorbed with the additional cash flow and celebrity that Diamond qualification would bring that I forgot I had a wife. Then, when all of the shit came down, my focus became survival.

The realization that I ignored Annika during our first two years of my marriage put more pressure on this dinner. I saw the dinner as an opportunity for us to reconnect and make a new start. I expected her home at her usual time, 5:45 PM.

By 6:15, the appetizers and first course were getting cold. By 7:00, I opened the champagne and started drinking it by myself. By 8:00, I threw some of the dinner on a plate and ate it on the couch. I dumped the leftovers in Tupperware and jammed them into the fridge. I hadn't bothered to tell her that I was making the special dinner. I wanted it to be a surprise when she walked in. Why had I thought she would come home after work, excited to spend our anniversary together?

It was 9:30; I was stretched out on the couch, watching a rerun of *Jake and the Fatman* when I heard her car. I turned toward the front door as she walked in. I looked at her but didn't say anything. She glanced at the kitchen table. She saw the remnants of my romantic dinner.

We hadn't acknowledged our anniversary in any way that morning. We had barely spoken to each other. Annika probably met Catarina, or her friends from work, for a drink. It was silly of me to assume she would hurry home. Why should she? To celebrate what?

Annika was embarrassed. I wasn't sure if she was embarrassed for herself or embarrassed for me. She said, "I'm sorry," and hurried into the guest bedroom closing the door behind her. I didn't pursue her. I didn't want to.

What would I even say to her? How could I apologize for a relationship that was failing? The person she fell in love with was the charming, confident person everyone cheered. We met and fell in love in a manufactured utopia. We were a product of the business. When our dream world crumbled it exposed the fact that we barely knew each other. In truth, we had damned little in common. The business began our relationship and would end it.

I reclined on the couch wishing I had enough guts to end the charade. I should have walked into the guest bedroom and announced it was over, but I didn't even have the courage to do that. I fell asleep on the couch. When I woke the next morning I didn't mention the dinner to Annika. She didn't bring it up to me.

*   *   *

I stopped caring about who saw the old station wagon I was driving. I didn't put it in the garage to hide it anymore. I just parked the old wagon alongside the beat up Chevy Citation we bought for Annika to drive. The week had worn me down. I never needed a Friday the way I needed that one.

As I exited the car I watched Annika's silhouette pass the window a handful of times with the phone in her ear. I'm sure she placed phone calls at my usual time of arrival home to avoid conversation. I was, actually, grateful for her habit. I watched her hang up the phone.

I'm not sure why, but I glanced at the clutter on the passenger seat of her Chevy. I saw the classified pages from the newspaper, folded to apartment listings with several one-bedrooms circled. I used my spare key to open her door. I entered the house with the newspaper in my hand. I sat at the kitchen table. Annika walked in and saw the paper. She sat across from me. For the first time in a long time we locked eyes. Annika put her hands gently over mine.

*   *   *

Katy Schultz bid goodbye to the final two distributors who stopped by her house to pick up their weekly AmericanMade product orders. She finished her bookkeeping, poured an iced tea and retired to the porch.

The old house in Encino was a traditional ranch style home built in the early 1950s. Stan and Katy purchased it in 1960 when Katy was pregnant with their daughter. They were proud to own their first home. They spent all their spare money and spare time to furnish and decorate the home.

It had been close to a year since formal charges had been brought against Ken Richman. Ken's attorneys had worked overtime delaying every aspect of his case. The U.S. Trustee that had been appointed to assist with liquidation and distribution of assets were less than communicative about the state of things.

Stan had dug into the case. He was following it much closer than I was. At first he believed Ken was only partially responsible for the fiasco. He'd spoken with Ken briefly before Ken took off for Aspen. During that last conversation, Ken convinced Stan that he was a victim of duplicity by PEN, but Stan looked into the case on his own and came to believe Ken was no victim.

Stan's obsession grew. He visited the Encino library several times a week, sitting for hours at a time. He studied case law concerning investment fraud, involuntary bankruptcy and federal restitution orders. He was becoming relentless in his quest to learn how he and the other wronged investors could recover any part of their lost nest eggs.

Even though their precious retirement savings was gone, Katy did not support Stan's vigilance. His research wasn't therapeutic. It was creating incredible bouts of anger and depression and he was beginning to drink during the day. The events of the previous year were straining their marriage. In addition, their MLM business was now costing them more to operate than it earned each month. She couldn't pretend any longer. Their lives were falling apart.

Katy intended to demand that she and Stan resign from the business. Their retirement dreams of travel and leisure were crushed. Katy had removed the picture of their dream RV from the refrigerator. They were another sad statistic of the MLM industry, but Katy had more bad news for Stan.

As the bookkeeper of the family, Katy knew exactly where they stood financially. Their home was free and clear when they met Ken. Now they had two loans on the home and little equity in it. Of course their retirement savings was used for the two investments with Ken. As Christmas approached Katy knew that they'd be unable to make their first and second mortgage payments. Based on their lack of liquid savings and their limited fixed income they would need to sell the home—and quickly.

Letting go of the business would hurt, but losing their home was devastating. Stan and Katy held solid values. The house, the neighborhood, the family bond—that was what drove them as a couple. They didn't need private jets—they dreamed instead of little getaways in their new RV. They didn't want to upgrade yearly, they wanted to plant roots. They worked hard on their dreams. Yet those dreams were quickly vanishing.

Katy sat on the porch swing, staring out at her picturesque neighborhood. She knew they'd made their own choices. She also knew they'd lost sight of what was important, and in return were losing it all. What Katy didn't know was how it all would end; yet she knew it had to.

45

Saturday, October 15th, 1988

Annika and I separated. Ultimately, she just wanted to escape the nightmare that had become our life—her life by default. She took a small apartment in low rent Van Nuys. I helped her move. The final load of her belongings included two mismatched lamps and a wicker chair I knew she liked.

I also placed a framed picture into one of the boxes. It was taken when we first started dating. We were photographed sitting on the hood of my Jaguar outside our favorite Italian restaurant in Palm Springs. I wanted Annika to have it—a reminder of what had been our good times together. I guessed she'd hide it away somewhere, but I couldn't look at it, but also couldn't throw it away. My visit was short. After I delivered the boxes, Annika thanked me, gave me a peck on the cheek and I was ushered out the door.

Our brief encounter pierced my ego. I still wanted her to need me. Maybe my self-image simply didn't want her to seem so comfortable without me. As she gave me a small wave and closed the door to her one-bedroom apartment I knew she would start over again. I knew she was free of me.

It would be my first night alone in the home that was supposed to bring us so much happiness. All that was left in the house was the couch, an end table and the TV. At least the TV was worth watching—my beloved Dodgers managed to make it into the World Series against the Oakland As.

I was draining my last beer as the game reached the bottom of the ninth. The Dodgers trailed 4-3 as Tommy Lasorda motioned Kirk Gibson into the on-deck circle as a pinch hitter. Gibson hadn't started the game due to a nagging injury. He limped to the batter's box and managed to run up a full count. The Dodgers needed a miracle but it didn't seem as though Gibson had the strength to provide it. I held my breath as Oakland bullpen ace, Dennis Eckersley, delivered the 3-2 pitch. It was probably ball four, low and outside, but Gibson swung hard. I knew it was a homerun as soon as he hit it. So did Vin Scully as he shouted, "She... IS...Gone!"

I jumped up off the couch, spilling what was left of my warm beer. I cheered in my empty living room as Gibson limped around the bases, pumping his arm. It was a solid minute before Vin Scully said anything: "In a year that has been so improbable...the impossible has happened!"

I calmed myself down and then turned off the television. I wasn't quite sure what to do with myself. I placed a record on the turntable and started a fire in the fireplace. It was a cool evening and I wasn't using the heater much in an attempt to save money. I had forty dollars in my wallet and eleven dollars in my checking account. All of that money had to last until my next paycheck.

I grabbed the open half-gallon jug of white zinfandel. It had been sitting in the refrigerator since our anniversary. I walked to my home office drinking straight from the bottle. My office walls had once been covered with awards, plaques and eagles, but I took them all down months prior and jammed them into two cardboard boxes. Only faded rectangles and bare nails remained on the walls.

I spotted the boxes sitting in the corner and slid them into the living room with my foot. I took another long drink of the Rose. I took the plaques, one by one, and methodically tossed them into the flickering flames. They were just symbols of what I'd fallen for and what I had lost. The action was instinctive and unconscious. The alcohol and bitterness served to fortify my destructive behavior.

I emptied the first box of awards into the waiting flames. The roaring fire was intense and danced out of the hearth, teasing the oak mantle above it. The mantle held a number of photos validating my botched attempt at a counterfeit life, a life supposedly filled with success. I turned my back and stumbled back to my couch, not caring it they too went up in flames.

*   *   *

I woke up on the couch, the disc on the turntable was still spinning, skipping and clicking. The vinyl was Roxy Music's *Siren* album. I hadn't chosen it purposely; it was simply on top of the stack of records. The irony was not lost on me. In Greek mythology, Sirens were dangerous yet beautiful creatures that lured their targets with hypnotizing voices. Eventually, their prey would become shipwrecked on the rocky coast of their island.

While the smoke alarm squealed I surveyed the wreckage that sat in my fireplace. Every honor I'd ever received in the business was gone. I had reduced them to a pile of ash. A layer of black soot covered the carpet in front of the fireplace. Embers burnt the rug giving off streams of smoke. What had I done?

I stood on a chair and ripped the battery out of the smoke alarm. The thick oak mantle over my fireplace was half burned, a part of it still smoldering. Some of the picture frames had burned or were molten. I surveyed the rubble.

Most of the photos depicting the business were obliterated. The photos of my family and friends outside of the business were mostly unscathed. The family portrait from my parent's twenty-fifth wedding anniversary was untouched by the flames. The framed photo of Mazal and me from our first Vegas trip when I was sixteen was intact. We were wearing suits in an effort to look older. A photo of me with Stan and Katy was still standing. It was taken during that stupid road trip to Portland in their old Winnebago. Somehow, the fire knew what pictures to burn out of my life and what photos to leave intact. For that I was thankful.

In the stillness and silence of my living room that morning, I realized I tried to kill myself. Of course I was blacked out, drunk, but perhaps I wanted to send a message to anyone who cared that I was a pretender, never deserving of the recognition heaped on me. It was all make-believe: the money, lifestyle, praise, friendships. I'd let down the only people in my life who truly mattered. Buzz told me, "Remember, all that glitters is not gold." The fire spared the images of the only people I could trust.

I had made a royal fucking mess of my life. I didn't want to remember my father's words since I hadn't listened to them in the first place. My life no longer glittered. I no longer felt golden. I stood before the gray ash and smoldering remains. That's what my life consisted of. I stood up, took as deep a breath as I could in the smoke-filled room and began cleaning the mess I'd created.

With my life burnt to ashes I had only one choice, rise from them. I would start again.

46

Spring 1989

The little shack was so darn perfect. It served as my six-by-four sanctuary. It was made of stone with a shake roof and an old air conditioner unit bolted into the window. The structure was situated on the first tee of the West Course at Braemar Country Club. Nobody bothered me there.

After struggling through my straight job at the bank, I simply gave up. Twenty-eight was a bit late to begin a career as a golf pro but my golf skills were still good enough for me to talk my way into the job at Braemar. The assistant golf pro job enabled me to escape the real world for a while. I was able to earn a steady paycheck giving lessons to members. I played in some local mini-tour events, had a few laughs. I wasn't sure how long my vacation from reality would last. My future wasn't planned beyond my next round and my next cold beer.

The job was a godsend, providing me with the type of mindless asylum I needed. The starter shack duty wasn't an assignment enjoyed by the other assistant pros but it was fine with me. After the rush of morning tee times I found many peaceful moments in the little hut. I volunteered to take shifts from the other pros, any time of the day. I appreciated the quietness I found in the shack.

My impromptu plaque-burning ceremony six months earlier was a wake up call. I could have burned down my house while I was in a drunken stupor on my couch. That outcome was only a few stray sparks away. I could have easily died from smoke inhalation in my sleep. Someone was watching over me.

A higher power—I'd like to think, God—decided to save me. For what reason or purpose I wasn't sure. I cleaned up the mess, reset my priorities and rounded up a few roommates to share the rent. For now, I was able to pay my bills and stay in the house.

Annika made an effort to stay in touch. She called occasionally and we met for cocktails a few times, but it was becoming increasingly difficult for me to see her. She represented a life I was trying to put behind me. The last time she called I made up an excuse.

Stan and Katy stayed in contact; however, Stan grew harder to talk to. There was a part of him that had been lost when the business dissolved. He fixated on it, suctioning himself to the topic of Ken and the revenge he'd take. While Stan and Katy stayed in contact with me, I rarely returned the favor. I felt guilty about that. Stan had been a father figure to me, someone I could always talk to, especially after Buzz passed away.

I was kicking back in the starter shack, eyes closed, listening to a fuzzy radio station that was playing the Milli Vanilli song when I was jarred back to consciousness by a loud voice.

"Tony...my man!"

I looked up to see a face from my past, one of the insurance guys from the old days. It was Bill Franklin. I hadn't seen him since Ken abruptly closed down the insurance operation, kicked him and everyone else out, and started Richman Properties. I hadn't thought about Franklin in years. We branded him a loser because he never entered the MLM business. But he wasn't a loser; he prospered in the insurance and financial planning business. Now he was able to relax, working a few days a week and playing a lot of golf.

"Somebody told me you were working up here," he said. "I didn't believe it."

"What can I say? I'm hiding out," I said. "Picking up a steady paycheck, trying to put my life back together."

"I've heard all the stories," he said. "I know what happened." He stepped back and regarded my condition. "Man, you have to get back on the horse," he said. "You don't belong here. You belong back in the insurance game. You're wasting your talents."

I didn't know what to say. I couldn't tell if he was simply being supportive or if he meant it. When Ken entered my life, I was an underachiever, but Ken showed me how to apply myself. At this point, I knew how to fix a slice or a hook. Other than that, I didn't know what else I had to offer.

"Bill, it's not that easy," I said. "I've been through hell."

"Don't take too long to get back in the hunt," he said. "Fred Cohen brought up your name the other day; he asked me if I ever ran into you. He said you were one of the most talented young men he ever knew."

It had been years since I thought of Fred Cohen or Starbridge. He hadn't entered my mind since Ken cleaned out his agency in the middle of the night back in 1982. And yet, Fred survived and evidently had prospered as well.

"I don't need to tell you that Richman was full of shit," Franklin told me. "I'm not sure why he did what he did and I'm sure you have the same questions. You were conned by one of the best. You know that."

"I also don't have to tell you that you were trying to chase something that wasn't real. There aren't any short cuts, young man. They don't exist."

Franklin grabbed a few balls out of his bag and pointed toward the first fairway.

"Is the tee box open?"

"All yours," I told him.

He smiled at me sheepishly as I stepped out of the shack into the mid-afternoon sun. Franklin sliced his tee shot into the tennis courts. He shrugged and teed up another ball. This time, his shot hit the middle of the fairway. He waved at me as he drove off.

Franklin's words that day served up a poignant reminder, a notice that I was wasting my capabilities, sitting in the little starter shack. I didn't know how long I could hide out at Braemar with a seven iron in one hand and a cocktail glued to the other. I wasn't certain of much.

But I was sure of one thing. In seven months the 80s would be over. I had seven months to end the shitty decade on a positive note. I had seven months until the plastic decade that built me up and crashed me down faded away. I had seven months to stop playing the victim and restart my life.

47

June 1990

We finished our self-guided tour of Volcanoes National Park, slid our rental jeep into the valet circle and walked hand in hand into the resort lobby. It had been a perfect day on the black sands of the big island of Hawaii.

I was on vacation with my live-in girlfriend. Stacy was one of the beautiful young ladies from the business who always seemed to be in the background, available for late-night coffees and occasional lunches—all purely platonic. Back then we were simply friends. She was the attractive redhead that I always thought would make a great girlfriend.

Stacy called me out of the blue and we reconnected when I was working up at Braemar. We were both older, and if we could be honest, both a little damaged from our recent, short-lived marriages. We were both rebounding, but more than that, we were having a great time together and it didn't take long for us to move in together.

The job as an assistant golf pro didn't last long. I'd quickly grown tired of folding sweaters and I badly missed commission sales. I re-entered the insurance industry as a regional sales manager for a company named, Great Pacific Life.

I didn't find the new position—it found me. One of my former AmericanMade distributors gave my name to the newly appointed state sales manager for Great Pacific in California. As coincidence would have it, this sales manager, Jimmy, was a former AmericanMade distributor in Virginia. He was downline from Beau Willis, but had quit the business. I told Jimmy a little about what had happened to me and he offered me a management position on the spot. We formed an instant connection and had many laughs about what an asshole Beau Willis was. He knew what I had gone through. He was a guardian angel who appeared in my life when I needed one most. I felt re-invigorated selling insurance again; I began to hire some talented people and make some pretty good money. It felt like old times.

It was also my good fortune that the real estate market bounced back. That enabled me to sell the big house in Woodland Hills and move back into the family house in Van Nuys. That's when Stacy and I decided to move in together. One of the reasons Stacy and I worked is that she understood the wounds inflicted on me by Ken. I didn't have to explain everything to her.

We saved up for the Hawaiian vacation. It was the first real vacation I'd had in a long, long time. As we entered the lobby, the concierge motioned me over. "Sir, you've received an urgent fax message. Also, a man called multiple times looking for you. He asked that I give this to you immediately."

I wasn't expecting any communication from my office. I hadn't told anyone at work where I'd be staying.

"Thanks," I said, taking the envelope from him. I opened it in the elevator. The two-page fax document was partially handwritten. At the end of page two I saw a familiar signature. It was Ken's. How did he find me and what did he want from me? What did I even have left to give him that he hadn't already taken?

Stan had continued to update me monthly on the case, whether I wanted to hear about it or not. After all of the delays, all of the posturing and the entire discovery, Ken pleads guilty. Annie's deposition was damning. Many of the investors were deposed and would surely testify in court, if the case did go to trial. Their testimonies would tear at the heartstrings of any juror. Ken's attorney had no choice but to convince him that a guilty plea—and some sort of favorable sentence—was the only plan that made sense.

Ken's attorney had also found a way to delay sentencing. They apparently wanted to go to the hoop strong on sentencing day. That was the nature of my two-page fax. What I was holding in my hands represented Ken's last chance at freedom. It was his prayer—his appeal to former friends and loyalists.

The first page was Ken's plea—a request for me to solicit the judge handling his criminal case, asking him to consider probation instead of incarceration so that Ken could work and pay restitution to the investors faster. The wording suggested that I also ask the judge to impose the minimum sentence under the federal guidelines, if probation wasn't possible. The second page of Ken's fax was a sample of what Ken wanted us to send to the federal judge. It listed Ken's assertions why the court should reduce his sentence. Ken hoped others would fight for him, a habit to which he'd grown accustomed. It all sounded like a Hail Mary to me.

Stan told me that Ken and Nancy were living in a small rented place outside of Boise. The bank foreclosed on the place in Aspen and they had petitioned the judge to allow them to move back to Ken's hometown. Ken borrowed money from Nancy's parents to keep their lawyer on the job. If they were hiding any money at this juncture, it wasn't evident.

I'd had no contact with Ken or Nancy since they fled the Valley. I didn't want any. I was no longer the slightest bit delusional about them. Their hands were dirty. Stan and Katy were among Ken's most unfortunate victims. Stan and Katy lost their savings as well as their home—the bank foreclosed before they were able to sell it. They now lived in a one-bedroom apartment.

Meanwhile, Stan told me that he'd gotten a tip that Ken was working on a deal with Oren Larsen, a former AmericanMade distributor. Oren lived in Seattle and bounced around from one MLM to the next, as a lot of MLM junkies do. The plan centered on Nancy's ability to earn money—income that would be shielded from the court's reach. After all, Nancy had not been convicted of anything. She could earn an unlimited amount of money and the investors could never attach it. The chosen venture was a new Japanese-based MLM company. I had no idea where Stan was getting the dirt on Ken and Nancy, but it seemed reliable and always panned out.

Stan was pissed. He was sure Ken would find some way to circumvent the system. Even though I had a morbid curiosity, I still cringed whenever Stan called to give me the latest news. I wanted to move on. I wasn't the Tony they remembered and I wasn't the Tony portrayed as a villain in the fallout following Ken's arrest. I had a solid job. I was dating a nice girl. I was looking forward, not backward.

I could feel my blood pressure rising as I sat on the edge of the bed in our hotel room, holding the fax from Ken. He was trying to leverage the scenario—trying to convince his victims that the quickest way for them to recover their losses was to urge the judge to give him probation instead of jail time. He was dangling the promise that he'd be able to make restitution much faster as a free man.

I felt insulted by his request. After all the damage he'd done, he was asking for our help? I reached for the phone with the intention of calling Ken to tell him where he could shove his faxed request, but I stopped. This wasn't about my wounds. If the judge gave probation then my mom, my aunt and my uncle could possibly get their money back sooner. They weren't getting any younger, all closing in on seventy.

I pulled a piece of blank stationary out of the desk drawer. I wrote a letter to the judge asking for leniency for Ken Richman. I would send the letter: Then, I'd be done with Ken for good and I could move on.

I dropped the handwritten letter at the front desk with instructions to fax it to the number supplied by Ken. I walked across the road in front of the hotel, onto a strand of beach. The black volcanic sand crunched beneath my flip-flops. The late afternoon sun sank, growing orange as it inched toward the horizon.

Unwelcomed scenes from the previous eight years played in my head. They were ghostly. I saw myself sitting in a cubical at Starbridge nursing a hangover. Then, there I was, storming across stage to thunderous applause with my fist punctuating the air. I was standing at my father's grave as the pallbearers approached, bearing his coffin. Eight years flooded my mind too quickly for me to rise with the tide.

For the first time in years I allowed myself to cry. I needed a release before I returned to my hotel room. My hotel room was for a man who had moved on from all of this. My hotel room contained a beautiful girl waiting for me. Stacy would greet me with a warm smile and dinner reservations. She was vacationing with a man who needed to be over his baggage. I needed to unpack it all right there.

Standing on the black sand I observed the tide. It withdrew—only to build up strength and return. I thought my guilt, along with my feelings of loss and self-loathing had left with the tide. I wasn't prepared for all of that debris to wash ashore again.

48

September 1990

Ken's last hope to avoid jail time ended when the judge handed down his sentence. The letters written by me and the other investors had no bearing on the judge's decision. Ken was headed for a stint in federal prison.

On a late summer day, Ken entered a minimum-security facility in Littleton, Colorado—his home for the next four years. The man who once seemed ten feet tall was pitifully tiny that day.

Nancy rolled the car into the gravel parking lot just before noon. They sat quietly for a moment. The only sound audible was a horn in the distance. It would become a familiar sound for inmate 94998-011. That horn would tell Ken it was time to wake, eat, go outside and sleep. The man who preached that personal freedom was the most fundamental of rights would soon have none.

He rehearsed what he planned to say to Nancy. As they left the car, Ken took Nancy's hand and drew her close to him. His eyes filled. None of the rehearsed words came out. They locked in a tight embrace. "I need you to be strong and get through this. I need you to be there," Ken said.

They hugged and kissed one more time and then Ken walked to the prison gate. He stopped as he reached the door of the red brick building. He shouted back: "Hey baby...the plan is rock solid."

Nancy smiled and shook her head in affirmation. Ken entered the facility. The metal door shut behind him.

49

Friday, October 7ᵗʰ, 1994

Ken picked at the dry meatloaf and powdery mashed potatoes as he combed the headlines in the *Denver Post*, his attention drawn to a story about the winner of a sixty million dollar lottery. Even there in the federal prison, keeping his head down during meals, as he'd done since his arrival, Ken felt he'd won the lottery.

Normally, if someone goes to prison after orchestrating a Ponzi scheme, his or her earning power ceases. Ken wasn't the usual inmate and he didn't plan on living a normal parolee life. Ken believed his prison sentence represented an unfortunate speed bump in his quest to earn back the wealth he desired. To Ken, maintaining his belief in his own abilities was a survival tactic. Soon, his prison years would be behind him.

Ken dumped his trash and returned to his cell. He gathered up the books and tapes he collected during his four years in prison along with the reams of notes he compiled during his incarceration. He sat on his bunk, waiting in silence for the guard to come.

The years of incarceration represented an opportunity for Ken to sharpen the vision of how he intended to spend the rest of his life. Ken kept very busy while in prison. His protégé, Oren Larsen, visited him weekly, providing updates on their joint venture. Even while serving a prison term, Ken was able to put together a profitable MLM downline with the Japanese water filtration company.

The plan was brilliant in its simplicity. Six months prior to Ken's incarceration he and Nancy enlisted the services of Oren, a clean-cut ex-AmericanMade distributor. He turned out to be a loyal partner. Convinced by Ken that he was railroaded, and the Richman Properties collapse could have been avoided, Oren had no reservations about signing on with Ken. Oren believed the story Ken and Nancy concocted about the other Diamonds. They painted them as jealous, conniving and ruthless. Oren became an instant devotee.

Ken identified traits in Oren he knew were important. He was a family man along with fierce dedication and complete focus on business. Oren was a member of the Mormon Church, which convinced Ken and Nancy that Oren would stay committed to the mission.

Nancy formed a new corporation, which partnered with another company created by Oren. An attorney in Boise whom Ken had known for years, drew up the incorporation papers for both companies. The legal loyalist tied both corporations together to make certain that 50% of all profits would always flow to Nancy's legal entity. He also made certain that all codicils of dissolution would benefit Nancy, if that time should come.

During his term of imprisonment, Ken taught Oren all he knew about drawing circles. The master guided his young follower, teaching him how to identify prime targets. He also taught Oren how to insert himself into unsuspecting lives in a way few could.

Ken programmed Oren what to say, when to say it and how to say it. Ken supplied him with a script of questions to trigger the responses in which to lock people. Oren was transformed into an MLM superstar, generating significant cash flow into Nancy's corporation. The plan worked flawlessly.

The guard arrived at Ken's cell, and escorted him into the corridor and through the cellblock. He was taken to processing and given his belongings. Ken studied the clock on the wall as it ticked down the seconds. Inmate 94998-011 scribbled his signature on the last form he was required to sign and was escorted to the exit.

The buzzer blared and the door swung open. Ken Richman had, in his opinion, paid his full debt to society. He walked out of prison with a clean conscience. Despite the lingering federal restitution order, Ken believed his responsibilities to the investors were over.

Ken squinted as he walked into the light of the Indian summer day. He looked beyond the flagpoles that framed the parking lot and spotted Nancy. She had been waiting for him, standing next to a new convertible.

Ken and Nancy embraced. They would save their true moments of reconciliation for later, after arriving at the attractive home in the upscale suburban Portland neighborhood. Nancy had leased the place with their MLM cash flow and profits. Ken took the driver's seat, and then opened the glove compartment to the car he'd never driven. He removed his Rolex watch and wedding ring from where he had instructed Nancy to stow them. He slipped them back on.

During Ken's time in jail, Nancy rebuilt their lives. She never allowed herself to show weakness. Speeding down the highway with her husband by her side she knew she no longer had to bear all the weight and responsibility.

By midnight Ken was in his own bed beside his wife. They drove the sixteen hours from the prison to their new home straight through. The next morning, he reunited with Chandler. After breakfast, Ken refocused on business. He planned to meet soon with their corporate attorney and also meet with Oren. It was time to dissolve their partnership. It wouldn't be necessary any longer.

50

Winter 1995

Katy Schultz enjoyed her temporary solitude. Stan was meeting with a Richman Properties investor and wouldn't be home for a while. She strolled down to the row of mailboxes in front of their apartment complex and retrieved a stack of mail. One envelope was marked with a federal seal, which offered Katy a tinge of hope. She hurried back upstairs, clutching the piece of mail from the court, holding it close to her body.

Since Ken's release from prison, Stan's fixation had grown. He'd researched the case to death, especially the aspect of restitution. Stan was telling every investor that would listen that Ken and Nancy had "gamed the system"—figured out a way to funnel income through a shell corporation that Nancy controlled. Ken wasn't connected to that corporate entity, so he hadn't technically earned any income from that venture. In fact, since his release from prison, Ken had earned little or no income, hence, there was little or no restitution to be collected and dispersed to wounded investors.

The Richman's were now living in Oregon. Ken's attorney had been successful in getting his supervised release transferred to a U.S. Probation officer in Portland. The problem that worried Stan the most was cloaked in the fact that the term of supervised release would eventually expire and upon the expiration of the supervised release, the District Court would no longer have jurisdiction to enforce the restitution order as a part of the criminal case. All investors would be on their own, only having civil action as a possible tactic to collect their money.

Stan spent hours on the phone keeping others rallied around the cause. When he wasn't immersed in the case, his days were spent on a brown vinyl recliner. He would stare blankly at the television, lost in a bottle of Old Harpers hard stuff.

Stan and Katy existed like roommates; their marriage was devoid of meaningful conversation. It was difficult for Katy to smile. Many of their closest friends were keeping a distance as their union disintegrated.

Perhaps the letter with the federal seal she held in her hands represented good news. Maybe it was from the U.S. Trustee. Possibly additional assets of Richman Properties had been found and liquidated. Maybe the U.S. Probation officer was dispersing a substantial amount of restitution to each investor. Katy prayed. She didn't even care about the money as much as she worried about what was becoming of her husband.

Katy slowly slit open the envelope; it contained a cover letter with a purple seal and a check. The check was marked "partial restitution." The amount was $115.

* * *

My decision to re-enter the insurance industry a few years earlier had been prudent. We were growing the team rapidly and I was awarded several promotions. I was the now a state sales coordinator for Great Pacific Life, and life was great.

Not only had my career taken off, but things couldn't be better in my personal life. I had met the one I was going to marry.

But it wasn't Stacy.

I was crazy about the redhead, and I think she loved me, but we crashed and burned anyway. It wasn't her fault, and it wasn't mine. There was something missing in our relationship and I don't think either of us could quite figure out what it was. It ended respectfully and disappointingly.

The one that I would marry was a girl named, Beth. I met her at a Phoenix Suns game, and by halftime I knew that she was someone I wanted to be with. It was that powerful and that immediate. But it wasn't at all like the Annika thing. There weren't love songs playing in my brain and doves circling overhead.

It was just real and comfortable and we were engaged.

I was on my way to conduct a training session of newly hired agents at a local hotel. I turned down the Pearl Jam song that was pouring out of my speakers and picked up the ringing flip phone from my passenger seat.

It was Stan.

"Can you believe this shit?" he said. "Did you get the Richman Financial restitution check?"

It had been a while since I'd heard Stan's voice. I don't think I ever recalled hearing him so angry. "No I didn't," I said. "Been real busy. Haven't sorted through my mail in a few days. How much was it?"

"It was one hundred and fifteen bucks. A hundred fifteen friggin' bucks."

It was 8:00 AM and I had a mild hangover from a little too much red wine consumed the night before. It wasn't like the severe drink-fests I used to engineer for myself, but all the same, I didn't need someone screaming shit at me so early in the morning. I'd successfully put Ken Richman, the business and the Richman Properties meltdown behind me—or at least I thought I had.

"I haven't seen the check and haven't spoken to my family," I said. "I'll call my mother tonight. You gonna be okay, buddy?"

"Am I gonna be okay? No I'm not going to be okay," he shouted. "Goddamned Richman got away with murder. Have you kept up on him? Do you know how much money he and Nancy are makin' now? He gamed the system, built a huge MLM downline while he was in fucking jail, and now he and his high-priced lawyer are figuring out how to worm their way out of restitution."

As Stan raged on I realized I wasn't focused on what he was saying. I had to break in.

"Stan, stop talking for a second. I don't know what they're doing. As I said, I've been kind of busy and..."

"Nancy's banking more than fifty thousand dollars a month in their Japanese water filtration deal. We're out our life savings, our home, and they live like a king and queen again?"

His voice was terrifying. I couldn't hate Ken the way he did. Part of me wanted to, but I couldn't. I might have at sometime, but I didn't any longer. What I learned from Ken changed me completely. I couldn't hate him for awakening in me a desire to succeed. I still had burning questions of what his original intentions were and why he went to the dark side. But, even though I knew he was a little dirty, I couldn't hate him like Stan did.

A lot of time—and a slightly different place than Stan—had allowed me the luxury to reframe the AmericanMade and Ken Richman experience; I held on to the positive messages from the business: the work ethic and sales skills I learned were not immoral. Lessons from the business stuck with me, both good and bad. I came away from the experience with valuable lessons and applied them to make myself a success. I was also providing income to my family each month, helping my aging mother, aunt and uncle. I had a little extra; I was making sure they were okay.

Stan, however, was in a very different place. Investors like him were well into what was supposed to be a comfortable retirement. They didn't have the time to rebuild. Stan had rallied a group of Richman investors. They were meeting on a regular basis and he updated me regularly on their discussions.

Stan continued his tirade. "His term of supervised release is over in a few months. I have some case law I want you to see," he said. "Civil court will be our only option after his supervision ends. We've got an attorney who might take the case on contingency. We need to meet, talk about all this."

Stan and his fellow investors were working overtime—strategizing hard to head Ken off at the pass. But I knew Ken Richman and the way he thought. He was two chess moves ahead. If there was a way to head off, stall out or avoid civil liability in his case, he and his shrewd criminal attorney were already on it. Any case like the one Stan was proposing would be years in the making and very expensive. Stan and the other investors would be hard pressed to get an attorney to work on contingency. Most of the investors didn't have time in their favor, let alone expendable funds to compensate an attorney.

Stan continued. His words blended into nonsensical jargon as I tuned him out. I felt guilty as hell for feeling the way I did, but I couldn't wallow in the past. I was creating the life I wanted to live and for the first time I was doing it on my own terms.

"Tony, you there?"

"Call me later this week buddy. We'll try to get together," I said, hoping Stan would forget to call.

"How 'bout Thursday?" he pressed. "You got some time on Thursday?"

He wasn't going to let it go. I agreed to meet him on Thursday, but knew I would leave him a message the day before and postpone—blow him off. I hung up my mobile phone feeling like shit.

I couldn't save Stan and it wasn't my responsibility to do so. Stan was headed down a road with no end. I'd write a letter to him—let him know that I'd need to move on from personal involvement. I didn't want to add to his pain but I didn't want to resurrect mine, either.

I was driving as if on human cruise control, my mind wandering to better memories than what Stan evoked. I passed one of the old municipal golf courses—the one on Balboa Boulevard—the one Mazal and I had played a thousand times in high school. My mind took me back to that day—the high school match when I rolled the putt in on the ninth hole, breaking 40 for 9 holes in competition for the first time. And then my brain flashed on Mazal's ugly three-putt on the eighteenth green at Griffith Park during his senior year. He was in the last group so there was a sizable gallery around the green. He three-jacked and then helicoptered his putter into the bordering L.A. Zoo. He pulled off this little stunt in front of all the players and both coaches. We buried our faces in our hands, half crying—half laughing, knowing he was automatically disqualified from the match. It was classic.

Those magical moments were almost twenty years removed; they felt prehistoric, as did the saga with AmericanMade, Ken Richman and all of the losses financial and emotional.

I pulled the car into the hotel parking lot and waited for the valet. I composed myself and rid my mind of Stan's call. It was time to wear a smile and project my motivational sales manager persona for the hopeful new salespeople anticipating my arrival in the hotel meeting room.

I chose to survive. I needed to.

We'd never see another dime of restitution—not Stan, not me, not my family. I knew that.

Too much time had passed and Ken would slip through the cracks. The judge, the U.S. Trustee, the U.S. Probation office, they'd all dropped the ball on this one and the investors would be out in the cold. I knew that.

Stan and I wouldn't speak again. I knew that as well.

51

Spring 1996

Katy waited until Stan left. She thought about walking out of the marriage for some time but had only recently started making her plans to do so. She intended to move to Northern California and live with their daughter, Diane. Katy knew Stan would call his daughter after he read the note she'd leave. Diane would explain to him that her mother needed the time apart and that he should consider a twelve-step program.

Katy arrived at the bank, took stock of the assets they had left, and wrote a check to "cash" for half their savings. Then she removed her name from the account.

Katy saw the branch manager, Terry. They'd been close friends at one time. Terry had even been in their AmericanMade downline for a short time before growing disillusioned. She bore witness to the collapse of the Schultzs' lives. Stan hadn't been to the church they all attended in years, and his recent DUI arrest helped spark rumors that the Schultzs' marriage was falling apart.

"I need to get into our safe deposit box," Katy asked. "Can you buzz me in?"

Terry fully expected Katy to clean out the box. She buzzed Katy into the secure area and offered her a plastic bag with the bank's logo on it. "Oh," Katy said, "I won't need that, dear."

Katy entered the small room and pulled the rectangular container out of its chamber. She opened the box, and then slowly twisted off her wedding ring. The gold band once belonged to Stan's mother. Katy knew she couldn't keep it. She placed it in the box next to Stan's Purple Heart and Medal of Honor from World War II. She slid the box back into its metal receptacle. She dabbed the tears from her eyes as she pushed the exit buzzer.

As the door reopened Katy's old friend, Terry, strolled with her toward the bank's front door. "Are we going to see you at church this Sunday?" she asked.

Katy stopped and turned toward her. "Please give my best to everyone, Terry," Katy said with a brave smile. "I'm going up north to visit my daughter. I may not be back down for a while."

Katy pulled into her assigned parking space at the apartment building and climbed the stairs. She had about two hours before Stan was expected to return home. She had gone to their storage unit and marked a few boxes with her letters, photos and keepsakes. She stacked them by the door so the movers could transfer them to her daughter's garage in Menlo Park. She planned to travel light. She took the garment bags down to the car, placing them in the trunk. From the trunk she removed a white cardboard file box and carried it back upstairs.

Inside were copious notes, a list of monthly bills, the checkbook, and the key to the safe deposit box with an inventory of its contents. Stan's half of their net worth amounted to less than nine thousand dollars. She left the name, address and phone number of the attorney she'd be using to file for divorce. She also left a lengthy note. Finally, Katy put on her sweater and left the apartment, locking the door behind her.

She planned to travel up the 5 through the San Joaquin Valley to her daughter's home. It wasn't a scenic drive and it smelled like livestock most of the way, but it was the fastest way to get to her daughter's home.

Katy thought about the places she and Stan hoped to visit but never did. They intended to buy a motor home. A picture of a shiny, new Win-nebago hung on their fridge for years. They wanted to tour wine coun-try, starting in Santa Barbara and working their way north to Big Sur, Monterey and Napa. Her eyes welled as she thought about those broken dreams. Then, suddenly, a new thought entered her mind.

She could do whatever she pleased. For the first time in more than forty years she didn't have to check with anyone. Instead of driving up the 5 she could head to the vineyards, take a room at a bed-and-breakfast and spend Friday sipping wine. She would call her daughter in the morning and let her know of the change in plans. Her tears dried up and a smile crossed her face.

As she negotiated traffic, her mind drifted to another time. It was 1960, the year they moved to Southern California from Wisconsin. They drove the old Route 66 across country and reached a dead end at the Santa Mon-ica Pier. They held hands, talked about starting a family and watched the sun set.

They arranged to rent a small home in the Valley. They jumped in the station wagon and crested the Sepulveda Pass. Dusk fell. It felt like home to her immediately.

Katy's thoughts returned to present as her car made the slow climb out of the Valley toward Ventura. She glanced in the mirror. It was dusk. She was leaving the Valley pretty much the way she found it.

For a time, their version of the American dream had materialized. Stan's career as an engineer helped them afford a quaint family home in Encino. They had a beautiful daughter, wonderful friends and money in the bank.

Stan blamed Ken and the MLM business for all that had been taken from them, but Katy understood the harsher reality. She knew she shared the blame with Stan. They made their own choices.

Katy put the past in her rear view mirror. A change of scenery would serve her well. She had a life to live and a daughter to love. She had a few unpretentious dreams to fulfill and nobody could steal them from her. Not Stan. Not Ken Richman. Nobody.

52

July 2001

My career with Great Pacific Life flourished but the pace had become frenetic. The company launched a massive advertising campaign in early 2000 sparking even more interest on Wall Street. As such, demands on domestic sales numbers became more pronounced. Executive management was asking more and more of those of us in the field. We were asked to build a more "compliant" sales model, a Chinese Red Army of sorts. As a result, the entrepreneurial nature of our business was beginning to vanish.

We were grinding through the last day of a sales meeting in Las Vegas. I wasn't running the way I could in my early twenties. The days of ten hour meetings followed by all-nighters were a thing of the past for me. During an afternoon break, I reluctantly followed a handful of coworkers to the pool bar, despite my desire to go up to my room for a quick nap.

After one beer with the guys, I started making excuses to leave when I heard her voice. I glanced up to see her sitting across the pool. It was Annika.

I considered walking around the pool to say hello. The thought of buying her a drink, hearing about her new life on the East Coast crossed my mind. I watched her for a moment. She was beaming, chatting with her friends, and sipping her drink. I rose, took one last look at her over my shoulder and walked back into the hotel and up to my room.

We had both moved on after the whirlwind marriage and even quicker divorce. We were both okay. That was the best either of us could have hoped for after what we endured at such a young age. I was content to leave it there.

After the meeting that day I drove the four hours home to the Valley with the past on my mind. Nobody was home, so I opened a beer, sifted through my mail and sat down to sort it all out. If seeing Annika had brought some of my past to the surface, the newsletter sitting on my kitchen table did the rest of the job.

They'd started coming in the mail the previous year from a group named *Victims of Fraud Association*, or *VOFA*. Stan was the founder. The membership was composed of the swindled Richman Properties investors who were still seeking restitution and revenge. I had not asked to receive the quarterly newsletters, but they continued to arrive on schedule.

The federal restitution order had been set in stone at Ken's sentencing, way back when, but federal supervision over him had long since expired. The court system would no longer attempt to collect or distribute money to the investors. Way too much time had passed. Ken and Nancy had clearly won the war of attrition.

It had been more than five years since I'd spoken to Stan or Katy. In the winter of 1995, I sent them a letter. I begged Stan to understand that it wasn't healthy for me to be involved in the civil restitution battle. The stinging futility of chasing something so hopeless was nothing I cared to experience. Stan never responded to my letter, yet he never removed me from the newsletter mailing list.

Katy, however, did respond to me. She sent me a personal note, telling me that she "understood my pain" and my position. Katy cared about me, even said she "admired" me. She ended her note stating, "We all need to make our own choices".

After reading Katy's letter I couldn't help but feel I had abandoned them. Months after I received her letter, I'd learned that Katy walked out on Stan. She felt she had to—for her own sanity. Then I bumped into a former AmericanMade distributor who spotted Stan at a grocery store buying cans of soup and generic whiskey. He told me Stan insisted he would, "even the score with Richman." For the first time I thought about what a man in his mental state could be capable of doing. I was aware that he owned several guns and had been a marksman in World War II.

Stan's quarterly newsletter contained a timeline of past events—as if any of the investors could forget what occurred. He often included extra pieces of information in my packages, usually articles about Ken and the other Diamonds he'd clipped from the newspapers.

Truthfully, the extra tidbits of information were the only reason I opened the VOFA envelopes at all. One clipping that Stan sent was a story about how Steven Steenberg's license to sell homes was revoked by the California Department of Real Estate. Stewart Moore used the otherwise unrelated offense as a convenient excuse to cut him completely out of the PEN support system. Some things never changed, Moore was still pulling all of the strings. Steenberg quit the AmericanMade business and moved to Florida. Stan's handwritten notes indicated Steenberg was selling time-shares in Boca.

Another piece of Stan's documentation related to Rex Logan. My old buddy was smart enough to see that Moore was a deceitful prick so he took preemptive action and moved most of his downline to a competing MLM. He then exposed a cover-up that shook the PEN organization. Rex discovered that cash collected at the door at the monthly events had been pocketed. Someone "anonymously" tipped off the IRS. This triggered an audit and several Diamonds were charged with tax evasion. Moore, however, was not charged or otherwise implicated in the scandal. He had good luck and a great criminal attorney.

Moore's luck didn't last for long, however. His other unsavory behaviors eventually caught up with him. Stewart Moore lusted after some of the young women in his AmericanMade downline. His run of surreptitious affairs came to an abrupt end when the husband of one of those women came home unexpectedly. The poor husband was drawing circles six nights a week, completely committed to the business only to return home and find Moore and his young, beautiful wife banging it out on the kitchen counter.

After that story broke, other women came forward, saying Moore used his position of power to force them into sexual liaisons. After the affairs were exposed, Stewart's wife—a good Christian spouse—forgave him publicly. She then insisted he attend church-sanctioned sexual addiction therapy treatments until he was "cured of his disease and the demons that possessed him." He also had to apologize to his church and downline. In his address to his downline, he evoked the evils of Satan and its temporary hold on him.

Moore's wife removed herself from the responsibility of the business. Instead of working on the business, she traveled the world in style and spent his money liberally.

I didn't miss duplicitous bastards like Stewart Moore, but I did miss Rex. There were times I wanted to look up his phone number and catch up with him. I never did. There was a part of me that just needed to leave the door closed on my former life.

Stan never sent a package that didn't include an update on Ken. His newsletters were full of facts, but also chuck full of rampant speculations.

The facts were fairly clear. Ken did hatch a plan before entering jail. He created phantom income using a myriad of corporate shells in Nancy's name. Their silent partner, Oren Larsen, built a network of distributors for them while Ken served his time in jail. Oren worshipped Ken so it was easy for them to persuade him to split all the profits of the water filtration MLM with Nancy, using the shell corporations.

After Ken was paroled, Nancy formed another corporate shell. That entity became a stand-alone distributorship with the Japanese company. They unemotionally dumped Oren, and then persuaded most of Oren's downline to join their new group. Whatever relationship Oren Larsen thought he had with Ken and Nancy was only a mirage in the long history of Richman illusions.

Ken built the new downline in Nancy's corporate name, but did all the work behind the scenes. He and his attorney knew that all Ken needed to do was wait out the expiration of his federal supervision. After it expired there'd be nobody to oversee the restitution order and he'd be free to start earning money in his own name again.

The courts couldn't legally attach any income Nancy earned separate from Ken, as she'd never been charged or convicted of anything. The courts were asleep at the wheel on the real nature of the corporate shells. Stan and the other investors had tried in vain to advise U.S. Probation what was really going on, but it was as if Stan and the rest were talking to a brick wall.

The transfer of venue that Ken and his attorney engineered was brilliant. Moving his case from the original U.S. Probation office in L.A. to the one in Oregon made most of the fine details unfamiliar to the new probation officer in Portland. After Ken's federal supervision was over, that was it. U.S. Probation in Oregon closed the files and washed their hands of the case.

Stan was kind enough to even update me on my old running mate, Ted.

I heard Ted married and then signed up with Ken and Nancy in their new MLM business. Nancy (wink, wink) had built the largest downline in the United States for the Japanese water filtration company. Ken suggested they maximize her profits so he invited Ted into the business to help him launch a support system, complete with CDs, books, digital training materials and large-scale motivational events.

In Stan's latest handwritten note, he updated me on the twists and turns of the Ken saga. Apparently, Ken did not enjoy a good rapport with the Japanese executives who controlled the MLM company. They threatened to audit some of his business practices. Ken pre-emptively moved most of his downline to another MLM that had been courting him.

It never seemed to end with this guy.

I placed all of the stuff back inside Stan's envelope and thumbed through the rest of my mail. Something caught my eye. It was a glossy postcard picture of Elvis's home with the title, *Graceland–Memphis, Ten-*

nessee. I snatched it out of the stack. I flipped it over, but already knew whom it was from.

The note was short, congratulating me on my success. Annie also told me she was "taking care of business" just as her father taught her. She wished me her best, hoping I was living my dreams. She ended it with postscript, noting that she "thought of me every time she sipped a Tequila Sunrise on her veranda." I wasn't sure how she found my new address but I was happy she did.

I didn't allow myself to become too nostalgic for that part of my life, but in that moment I would have liked to have spoken with her. I knew she turned state's evidence and was quietly relocated. Because Ken and the others plead guilty she never had to give testimony. The Feds took care of her.

As for me, no matter what I heard from other investors, no matter what details came to light about the players who finally got what they deserved, I was still nagged by many questions. I wanted to ask Ken some questions face to face. I needed to know how he could stand beside me on my wedding day, yet squander all of my family's money and leave me to be considered complicit in his scheme? I needed to know whether it was his intent to steal fifteen million dollars and ruin all those lives, or was his objective to build a legitimate real estate investment firm only to have fallen victim to the type of greed promoted by Dr. Johnny?

These questioned still bothered me so.

I wanted answers to questions I'd never be able to ask.

53

Summer 2004

Stan muttered to himself and banged his fist on the top of his Dell computer, but that didn't make the dial-up Internet connection run faster. Stan lived alone and talked to himself a lot. He hadn't spoken with Katy in years, and wasn't very good at keeping in touch with his daughter. Most of his so-called close friends had abandoned him.

His financial existence was paltry, Social Security his only source of income. He owned an old Dodge pick-up truck and he rented a one-bedroom apartment in a depressed Valley neighborhood.

Stan looked at the website for the newly formed network marketing company. The organization hawked nutritional products. The name of the company was NutriWell and Ken Richman was their new superstar kingpin distributor.

For Stan, there was little else to life other than surfing the Internet in his hunt for Ken. The investor group had dwindled down to just a handful of stalwarts—older people like Stan that had nothing else to occupy their time. Some of the aging investors had either died, were living in nursing homes, or just simply gave up the chase.

Stan quickly memorized the scheduled NutriWell events. He let the dates and times run through his head on a loop. That was how Stan's mind worked—a daily rerun of the events that ruined his life.

* * *

He entered the hotel and observed the bustling lobby. He saw people in suits, wearing eager smiles, holding notebooks—they had been going in and out of meeting rooms all day. It was a familiar scene, making him recall his days in the downline—although it felt like a lifetime ago. And then he saw a sign pointing toward a corridor. The sign read:

NutriWell
Founder's Legacy Dinner
Invited Guests Only

He followed the sign to a conference room. Slipping past the registration table he peered into the large ballroom. A banquet staff was setting tables, building the stage and vacuuming carpets. An audio-visual crew tested equipment. Large images of Ken and Nancy were displayed on video screens on each side of the stage. Captioned under the photos was the text:

Congratulations Kenneth and Nancy Richman
Winners of the prestigious
NutriWell Founder's Legacy Award for 2004
Thanks for your contribution to our company's growth
And twenty-five years of helping people realize their dreams

Stan stared at the image of Ken and Nancy, lost in thought. Suddenly, he heard a voice. "Sir, can I assist you?" It was the banquet captain.

"No. No," said Stan. "I just wanted to see what the room was going to look like for tonight. Thanks."

He left the room, but while he walked by the registration table he discreetly picked up a nametag, first hiding it in his palm then placing it in his shirt pocket without breaking stride. As he drove off he glanced in the rear view mirror and saw the top level of the hotel. Stan imagined Ken and Nancy enjoying the presidential suite and its view. They might be in his rear view mirror for the moment, he mused, but in a few hours they would be face to face.

Stan's suit smelled of mothballs. Katy used to hang his suits alongside their wool clothing in a closet in the house in Encino. Stan hadn't worn the suit in many years. He tied and re-tied his necktie unsure if it was nerves or simply an action to keep his hands occupied. He picked up the package he'd carefully prepared and placed it in the breast pocket of his suit jacket.

* * *

Nancy dropped three ice cubes into a tall glass she found at the wet bar. She removed two airline-sized bottles of Tanqueray from the minibar and poured them over the ice. She didn't bother to add tonic. Outside their suite, the sun set over the ocean, turning the Los Angeles sky a radiant orange while purple rays of light shot through the partial cloud cover. Nancy drained her cocktail, and then brushed her teeth. Ken had been in the bathroom, pacing, looking in the mirror and rehearsing lines he planned to deliver to the doting crowd.

Ken and Nancy left their suite for the main ballroom, entering an elevator. They made small talk as they descended to the lobby. The doors opened. An executive from NutriWell guided them to a service door that led backstage. He ushered them to the head table and they took their place next to the president of the company.

Stan entered the hotel lobby and headed for the ballroom. The nametag he swiped from the table earlier that day was pinned to his lapel. Stan ambled down the corridor, eyes focused on the ballroom doors ahead. He smiled to the woman sitting behind the registration and found an empty seat.

By now, dessert had been served. Ken Richman rose and launched into the speech the NutriWell distributors came to see.

At first, Ken recapped a long list of his achievements dating back to the early 1980s. Ken's jokes and stories were familiar ones—ones he had heard many times—but now Ken faced a fresh and zealous audience. Ken entertained the crowd as Nancy stood beside him smiling, nodding and laughing at all her husband's rehearsed lines.

Stan felt his jaw tighten as Ken continued his keynote address. The rage within Stan had been building for nearly two decades. Finally, he pushed his chair back, stood and made his way to the middle of the ballroom floor. At the time, Ken was recounting the first time he and Nancy walked into a Porsche dealership and paid for his dream car in cash. Stan reached the center of the room, where he stopped and glared at Ken.

"Do these people know who you two really are?" Stan yelled at the stage. "Do they know about the trail of bodies you've left behind?"

Ken abruptly stopped speaking. He didn't immediately recognize Stan. Nancy nervously crept up to her husband. Stan trembled as he continued his rant.

"You tell people they shouldn't let anybody steal their dreams, but you stole mine."

Murmurs rose from the crowd. Some members of the audience rose from their seats.

"You and Nancy ripped my life apart with your deceit. And you ruined the lives of two hundred others."

Signs of recognition crossed Ken's face. Before he could respond, Stan spoke again. "I want to show these people something tonight." Stan yelled, reaching into his coat pocket. "I'm going to end this travesty of justice tonight."

Ken acted quickly, yanking Nancy to the floor behind the podium. By now, dozens of men in the audience had left their seats to rush the man standing in the middle of the room threatening Ken. The banquet captain reached Stan first; he twisted him arm from behind, then rode Stan to the ground as three other men piled on and helped hold Stan down. Shortly after that, the hotel security guards entered the room and applied zip-tie handcuffs to Stan. They stood him up and searched him but found no gun.

Instead, in the breast pocket of his suit jacket, they found a ream of papers consisting of court documents and newspaper clippings dating back to 1987. The smoking gun was not a gun. Stan was escorted to the parking lot.

Back in the main ballroom, Ken, who was initially speechless, gathered himself quickly. He made a joke about people not being able to "handle their buzz" when the drinks are free. Peering into the crowd, which was just beginning to settle down, he tried to offer words of reassurance.

"Losers," he said, "always have to take shots at winners."

54

Sunday, January 8th, 2006

I was in the family room, stretched across the big couch, paperwork across my legs, eyes growing heavy. I needed to knock out one more report for my early morning meeting. Beth and I recently completed an extensive remodeling of our home. I didn't marry Beth because she was good for business, I didn't marry Beth because someone suggested I should. I married Beth because she was the most amazing woman I'd ever met. The choice was my own.

The purchase and remodel of our property wasn't meant to impress anyone. We bought the house because we liked it and it felt like home the moment we walked in. It was an older house, the type a real estate agent would say has "great bones," and it did.

The lot was big by Southern California standards, almost an acre, traversing a corner. It was situated in one of the oldest and most well-established areas of the Valley. It was a rustic neighborhood with no curbs or sidewalks to formally define the serpentine streets. The properties, including ours, featured mature black walnut and ash trees that made me feel I was anywhere but in the asphalt jungle of Southern California.

The place was so much more than simply a property to us. It served as home: the place for our daughter's birthday parties as she grew from toddler to the sweet curly-haired seven-year-old. It was where we hosted Thanksgiving, Christmas, and Easter gatherings. It was where family convened, red sauce was stirred, and our child's height noted on a doorframe as she grew.

We'd just settled in after the long renovation. I was involved in every aspect of it. I remembered moving into the big house in Woodland Hills with Annika, watching her nest. I never felt at home there, but this time was different. This was my home. This was the collaboration of who I was, who my wife was and where we wanted to be together. I remembered the weight I felt at that time in my life and the freedom I felt in that moment.

Beth had retired for the night; I would join her once I finished my work. I had a life I rarely questioned. If my timeline was correct it would have been right after I peeked into my daughter Alyssa's room to make sure she slept soundly. As I drifted away on the sofa—paperwork sliding off my lap—it might have been that moment when Stan reached into the glove compartment of his old Dodge pick up.

I wondered if it was around the time I climbed into bed beside my wife. Was it as I fell into a deep sleep with my arm across Beth? Was that the same moment Stan curled his hand around the .38-caliber pistol, put it to his head and squeezed the trigger?

A piece of me—the same piece of me that woke in a cold sweat in fear of being an underachiever, the same part of me that couldn't help but still question why Ken didn't look out for me when Richman Properties collapsed—that was the piece of me that would forever wonder what I could have done to help Stan.

It had been more than ten years since I had personally spoken to Stan. In a way, it had been a hell of a lot longer than that since Stan existed in my life. That tore me up as well. How could the actions of a man I admired so much destroy the life of a man who always treated me as family?

I wouldn't find out about Stan's death until a few days later. Katy called me. Truthfully, I lost Stan long before that call, yet I never grieved in the way I should have until that phone call. My wife asked me about him. I didn't dwell on the Stan he was when he decided to take his own life. Instead, I told her about the man he was when we first met. He was the guy who encouraged me, my biggest cheerleader outside of my family. Stan always had a smile and a wink for me back then.

That's how I would remember him.

55

Spring 2006

Stan's memorial, three months earlier, was a crushing experience. Katy was devastated. The lack of attendance was even more distressing. Stan was a good man. He deserved more.

It was there I learned he'd been awarded the Medal of Honor for his bravery during World War II as well as a Purple Heart, sustaining extensive injuries to his right leg. It humored me to remember his stories about the football injury, what he'd tell people caused his limp. All bullshit. Stan never wanted anyone to know. He didn't want to be called a hero, because some of his platoon mates didn't come back at all. Stan was just a good man. He was truly of the greatest generation, just like my father.

I felt guilty again that I shut him out. He was a man on a mission, wanting revenge or justice. He made poor choices for a man with so much wisdom and courage.

The choices Stan made were devastating for him. He never reached a point of absolution for anyone, including himself. He was never able to place the past behind him and appreciate what he had in the present. He allowed the experiences to eat away at him like a cancer and destroy all that was precious in his life.

A handful of older AmericanMade distributors attended Stan's service and updated me on the people I'd left behind. They told me that the great Beau Willis had lost more than ten million dollars in an investment scam, causing a falling out with his wife. Rhonda eventually left him, taking half his vast fortune.

Rex Logan and his wife, Linda, had moved to Northern California. He invested in a chain of medicinal marijuana dispensaries. His investment was very profitable; my guess was that he was smoking a lot of the inventory.

One of the guys invoked the name of Johnny Gergin. They never found Dr. Johnny after he slipped bail in Reno. He never served a day of time and never paid a penny in restitution. In my imagination, Dr. Johnny was on a beach somewhere in Belize. I visualized him living under an assumed name, running the local pot and blow distribution chain, covered up by his boogie board rental business.

It was good to hear about Rex's success in the newly emerging and quasi-legal cannabis business. It was also oddly enjoyable to hear about Beau Willis' losses. I would take it as a sign that karma still existed for most people, except for maybe, Ken and Nancy.

Everyone made his or her choices.

The path Ken and Nancy took was the most curious of all. They absolved their own sins, moving forward as if they had no guilt to bear. Their choices were worse to me than those made by Stan. At least Stan chased a cause he found honorable.

My father gave me great advice during my upbringing, yet I didn't follow it until it was too late. In my naiveté, I judged my parents based on the size of their bank account instead of the size of their hearts and the values they lived by. I was still annoyed at myself for that.

I had left work early that April afternoon. It was getting harder and harder for me to put in a full day and comply with all the corporate minutiae we were being asked to facilitate. It was easier to ask my administrative assistants to complete the endless reports required from us. "Just plug in whatever numbers look good and sign my name to it," I'd tell them.

I motored down Ventura Boulevard, taking a small detour on my way home. I slowly cruised past where Starbridge Financial Planning used to be. Starbridge was long gone—an immigration attorney was situated in the old suite. The building looked shabby and worn down to me. The entire Valley looked that way to me. Our old stomping grounds downstairs, The Valley Donut Palace, was gone. In its place was a medicinal marijuana dispensary with a large, green cross hand-painted on the blacked-out windows.

The insurance industry changed, but Fred Cohen failed to change with it. He was out of touch. His Starbridge agency shrunk until he had a skeleton staff. He responded by encouraging friends to invest in a stock market arbitrage scheme he'd manage for them. It was a colossal failure and everyone, including Fred, lost all their money.

I arrived at my house that spring afternoon to find it unoccupied. My wife and daughter were shopping. At this juncture in my life, I could arrive at an empty home but not feel lonesome. Beth and our daughter made our home warm and full even in their absence. I grabbed the mail and sat down to sort through it. I was no longer the same man who could ignore my wife the way I had before. It wasn't only that I'd learned a lesson, it's also that I was in the right relationship.

When Beth and Alyssa entered a room, I found it hard not to give them my full attention. I'd been glued to Beth since the day she agreed to be my wife. I'd been glued to my daughter since the day she barreled into this world. It was easy for me to get my priorities straight when the right people were my priorities.

I sifted through the mail—I almost flipped right past it. The postcard displayed a tropical scene on the front, along with a small message written on the back. I thought it was simply a postcard from a real estate company, lawn care service or a timeshare company. Taking a closer look, the message made me feel twenty-one again.

Tony,

I'm finally enjoying that Tequila Sunrise on my veranda. If you're ever in Maui...

Annie

It had been years since I'd heard from Annie. She made it. Her dream came true. Considering how hard she worked and how little she received from her experience with Ken, I couldn't think of anyone who deserved it more. My face broke into a broad grin.

I walked into my office and tossed her postcard on my desk. Beth and I had been going through the garage, doing some spring-cleaning of sorts. I walked over to the stack of clear plastic tubs that housed old correspondence. I opened the tub that held AmericanMade papers. The tub included mementos starting from the time I first met Ken until the collapse of everything. There were magazines with my picture and certificates of achievement. There was even the glossy program from the big event at the Anaheim Convention Center. The tub contained an envelope jammed full of photos from my wedding with Annika. There were even a few Polaroids of Ted and me somewhere in Vegas, engaged in some sort of wrongful behavior. It was a large, dusty tub of memories on which I had shut the lid years ago.

I found an old photo album. It was the one Gail put together for me. I hadn't spoken to Gail in many, many years. Mazal occasionally provided me with news about her, and I also followed her on social media. If Gail was the Mole she'd done a damn good job of getting away with it, but I was never convinced it could be Gail. I felt bad for ever having allowed the business to influence our break up. She was a good person and deserved better than how I treated her.

I flipped to the next page of the photo album.

It was a picture of Annie, standing between Rex and me. I imagined Annie with a Virginia Slim dangling from her lips, sipping a Tequila Sunrise on her veranda, living her dream. I slid her most recent postcard into the Elvis biography that was in the tub. It was the book she gave me as a gift that one birthday, so long ago. I placed the book back into the bin beside the information on the Mole—the information from the F.B.I. inspector that he'd left with me that day he was in my house in Woodland Hills.

My hand lingered for a moment as I added her postcard to the other two inside the book.

Then I opened the old dusty manila envelope from Boone, the F.B.I. guy. I took out the notes.

TSV Associates—the alias the Mole used.

Hold on.

Was it really that simple—Annie's refrigerator magnet and the postcard she left—the one with the Maui landscape and the home with the veranda? The other two postcards she had mailed me—the one from Graceland and this one?

The forwarding address that the Mole gave the post office...Monovale Drive. I checked the index of the Elvis Biography. There it was! Elvis and Priscilla once lived on Monovale Drive.

Shit!

She was leaving me clues. I laughed—laughed because I had no idea how to react. She knew to leave a postcard on her fridge in Culver City. She knew I would go to her home looking for her. The two postcards she mailed to me. She wanted me to have the clues. She wanted me to know.

The elusive, Mole, *TSV Associates* was none other than Annie Wu.

TSV was code for: *Tequila Sunrise on my Veranda*.

The acronym for her stealthy side business, the one that supplied her with all that tax-free seed money, was also the acronym of her sweetest selfish dream. I laughed at the absurdity of it all.

That poor F.B.I. bastard, Charles Boone, never figured out the identity of the Mole and she'd been his state's evidence and he even relocated her.

Annie had obviously hatched a very cunning long-term strategy. She never planned to be around at the end. When she began selling information to the various sources she knew she'd have to disappear at some point. In a stroke of good luck, the Feds tapped on her shoulder, asking her to turn state's evidence. The F.B.I. offered her immunity and helped her with relocation.

So...her exit plan was created for her. Annie figured out how to win. She took care of business, just as her father had taught her.

I wanted to call somebody...anybody, to tell them what I had just figured out, but whom? The more pertinent question was WHY would I tell anyone? What would even be the point at this juncture of my life?

I knew that Annie was angry with Ken when he didn't make good on his promises to her. But, she was way too shrewd to allow the emotion of anger to cloud her thoughts. She simply resolved to make sure she took care of her own business and finish on top. Then she hatched her plan and began collecting information. Annie quickly identified that Ken Richman would have many adversaries and even more enemies. She simply determined who of those would pay good money for information pertaining to his practices. The market was established; her product was a quality one. She was off to the races. God only knows how much she earned from her little venture, apparently enough for a nice beach home in Maui.

With a veranda.

I took a moment to think about the contrast—the way Annie channeled her feelings versus the way my old friend Stan did. Stan harbored so much anger toward Ken that he couldn't think straight and it ate away at him like a cancer. It eventually broke him.

Stan's emotions were understandable to me. But, still, even to that day, I could never feel that kind of intense anger about Ken; my feelings were still that of loss and confusion, more curiosity as of late.

Mostly curiosity.

I still wondered if he meant all the things he had said to me—all the encouraging praise and the vows of friendship and brotherhood. Or, was it all just bullshit—part of his con? I hated myself a little and felt like a wimp for still wondering about all of that crap after all of the years that had gone by. I thought so much of our relationship because of what it offered me and how he got me to perform at such a high level. The thought that Ken could have regarded me as simply a marketing tool, pawn or scapegoat was crushing. Yet I still couldn't fully believe it.

For years I'd fought my need for closure. I wanted to Google search him, call him up or email him and ask him for a face to face meeting.

He owed me that much.

All of the damn nagging questions—if I could just sit down with him, man to man and ask him those burning questions. I also fought the realization that the *why he did it* hurt me more than *what he did*.

I scooped up the postcards from Annie and threw them back into the tub. I sealed up the two tubs and pushed them back against the wall, then stopped. I instinctively picked them up and walked them outside.

Trash day was the next morning.

I opened up the big black plastic City of L.A. garbage can and dumped the contents of both tubs into them. I wheeled the trashcan to the curb.

Somewhere out there, Annie and Elvis were alive and well. Yet Ken was dead to me. I would never have the chance to ask him those burning questions face to face and get straight answers.

56

Summer 2008

Isettled into the booth, loosened my tie and looked over the menu. The hotel restaurant was a convenient pause on my way home from the Great Pacific sales meeting, this one held in Newport Beach. Pretending to care and pay attention to my direct report and the other suits from our home office for eight hours had sucked most of the energy out of me.

But I smiled, knowing it would be my last sales meeting.

I was anxious to get home, but needed to let traffic die down on the 405. We had recently celebrated my daughter's tenth birthday. Our home was alive with children, family and friends that day. We hired a magician; I watched how quickly he made my daughter's eyes light with wonder. It is important to me she feels free to wonder. I want to raise a daughter who knows she can achieve anything. I guess that can happen when someone was told he was an "underachiever:" he strives to raise a child to believe in massive achievement.

My daughter herself was like one of the magician's illusions. As if by magic, ten years had vanished since her birth. Even with my busy schedule

I tried never to miss an important moment with her. My personal life no longer came second to my career; being a father was the best job I had ever been able to land.

That wasn't the case with just my daughter and my wife. I had committed to make time for all the important people in my life. Mazal and I played golfed as much as possible. Over the years, he'd suffered a few setbacks of his own—several failed businesses and a rather unexpected divorce, but I tried to be there for him: not judging, just listening, and making jokes, like we always did when things were bad. He bounced back, as tough people always do. He had a decent job and wonderful girlfriend. I worked hard at being a good friend to my best friend. He made it easy.

I was spending as much time with my mother and aunt as possible. We planned to visit them the following month to celebrate my mom's eighty-ninth birthday. It was getting a lot harder for her to travel and she didn't have the energy to talk that much any more. I wasn't sure she felt the need to. My mother and Aunt Jean were in an assisted living home in Arizona. I had grown accustomed to the six hour drive to visit them. My mother was so happy for us. She showed it in the way she focused on us. No matter what was going on around us—a birthday party, holiday, or just a baseball game on the television—her eyes were glued to my wife, her only grandchild, and me. Her smile was infectious; it felt good to visit her in Arizona and make her smile. Without speaking a word she displayed the warmth and grace that she had held her entire life. My mother, like Beth, never complained. She had never brought up the Ponzi scheme or the money she and dad had lost.

She never wanted to make me feel bad about it.

It had been a few years since Stan's funeral and Annie's last postcard. It had been more than a decade since I'd had any personal contact with anyone else connected to the MLM circus. I believed that I had buried all of my questions and regrets with Stan and the plastic tubs I dumped into the trash two years earlier.

I had been seriously contemplating retirement from my position with Great Pacific for the previous three months. Retire, quit…I wasn't sure what the hell to call it. With all of the genuine happiness in my personal life, my career position offered a delicate contrast. It felt like I was pretending to be something I wasn't.

That was not a completely unfamiliar feeling, but not one I'd choose to ignore this time around.

The phenomenal growth of our company, the continued pressures of Wall Street, and the third generation of executive management had turned us into sales-manager-bots. Any shred of entrepreneurialism and creativity at our level was being thwarted. Our voices—the voices of the people that had built the sales force—were less than important to them, and were certainly not being listened to. The high-paid outside consultants were now in charge and we, as a company, were just like Fonzie, *jumping the shark*.

The handwriting was on the wall. I saw what would come next and my choices were pretty clear. I could stay and continue to make the big bucks, be somewhat miserable in my career and eat their shit. Or, I could leave. I had made some nice money—was pretty sure I had enough to last us for a while. I could quietly step away, free fall into nothing, and try to reinvent myself.

I wasn't pissed off at the company or any of the executive management; it was just the way it was. The founders that built the great enterprise get old, retire and die. The next generation takes over and maintains the business the best way they know how. Then the third generation is ushered in. They tear things apart—tear things down. It's what they do. Things change—it's as simple as that. It would be a big decision for me financially—I'd be walking away from a seven figure annual income, so I labored over my choice.

My decision was reached the week before.

I went to an old and familiar place that day two weeks earlier to sit alone and sift through it all. I went back to that beach of my youth—lifeguard station number 11 in Santa Monica. I must have looked like quite a sight to the other beachgoers as I sat there in my pinstriped suit—crossed legged on the sand, pants legs rolled up, Lite beer in hand—wrapped in a brown paper bag.

As I closed my eyes, the sounds of the children and teenagers on the beach became the voices of Mazal and our friends as we dug for clams, chased grunion and dug holes in the sand. I was instantly transported back to the summer of 1979.

If there was a better, simpler time in my life, I'd yet to find it.

My finger wistfully drew circles in the sand. The first circle represented my boyhood, those good times on that beach and those long Valley summers that never seemed to end. I drew a line and connected it with another circle. That next circle reflected my introduction to Ken and the business that changed my life so drastically. The next line I drew in the sand led to a circle that signified my life and career choices after the carnage. I'd made some solid choices, built a damn good business and started a family.

It was the next line connecting with the next circle that I was there to figure out.

If I stepped away from my current position, who would I be and what would be next for me? What would that last empty circle I just drew in the sand become? I needed to arrive at a decision, and an answer that day.

I wasn't leaving the beach until I did.

There is this idea that you grow up to know things. That you grow up to understand the things that confused you as a child. That at a specific age the problems of your 20's became answers you finally understood. What I learned with age was with every answer came another question.

I had become more spiritual as I had become more mature. It wasn't the going to confession or praying to saints' kind of spiritual. It also wasn't the flagrant and convenient misuse of Christianity that I'd witnessed time and time again in the business. My direction was from a personal relationship with God. He didn't always speak to me in ways I could easily interpret, but if I closed my eyes and listened, the answers would eventually come.

I wiped the circles from the sand with one sweeping motion of my palm—erased four decades of my life with one swipe.

I left the beach that day. I'd made my choice. A weight had been lifted.

And there I sat, in the hotel coffee shop in Newport Beach. The long bullshit sales meeting that just ended didn't seem as dreary as usual.

As I settled into the booth and ordered I glanced around, taking in the crowd at the Newport Beach Marriott. I'd been in so many damn hotel and airport bars and restaurants over the years that they'd all started to look the same to me. As I waited for my BLT and Arnold Palmer, my mind traveled back, once again—to the business.

Every time someone ordered a Tequila Sunrise, I'd turn my head in hopes of seeing Annie. Whenever I smelled reefer, I'd fully expect to see Rex Logan emerge from a cloud of smoke. If I overheard a guy using a pick-up line on a girl, I'd recall my old running mate, Ted.

No matter how much time passed, my past was still a part of me and it would not completely let go.

I devoured my BLT and doodled on the drink napkin with my free hand. I was drawing small circles and connecting them together—something I did unconsciously. I caught myself and crumpled up the napkin—pushing it aside.

When Rex gave me Ken's address that summer day in 1982, I crumpled it up and tossed it away. I took his offer for an opportunity and threw it in the trash. I'm not sure why I reached back into the wastebasket and scooped it out that day, but I did.

I wasn't sure why that moment in time had popped into my forty-eight year old brain.

I fought off wondering how different my life would have turned out if I had left Ken's address in the trashcan. Some people say you meet who you're supposed to meet; you become what you're supposed to become. Others say you create your own future—your own luck. I believed it was a little bit of both. I'd survived by doing what I had to do to get out of bed in the morning without dwelling on my mistakes. There were days when I wondered how I would explain all of my mistakes to my daughter. When she reached the right age for such a conversation, how would I describe all of it?

Or did I even need to bother. After all, I didn't listen to my father until it was too late. It seems we learn most of the toughest lessons the hard way.

I turned my iPhone back on. It pinged nonstop as I polished off the sandwich. I ignored it. The career position that was beginning to choke me would soon be no more. Beth and I agreed that when the job was no longer fun it would be time to move on; regardless of how much money I was earning. She was glad to hear of my decision after my afternoon at the beach.

In a previous life, I'd chased the wrong things. I wouldn't do that again. I had learned that lesson well.

I gazed out the window. The sun's arc was high, reminding me that summer officially started the week before. Summers lasted forever when I was a kid. There wasn't any scheme Mazal and I wouldn't try to pull off. We were invincible and ruled our world from the seats of our ten-speed bikes. The endless summers in the Valley were the best, but they'd vanished a long damn time ago.

Fifty years old was square in my sights. I was now waking up the same time Ted and I used to stagger home.

I sipped the rest of my Arnold Palmer until the sound of air and ice cubes rattling through the straw filled the void.

All of it happened for a reason, I reasoned to myself. That's the way it worked. I'd come far. My friendships were genuine. The love of my life was chosen by me or graced upon me, I never could tell. My home was filled with love and a "perfect" little daughter—she hated me calling her that, but she was *perfect* to me. Even as I decided my corporate position wasn't worth pursuing, even a little bit lost professionally, I was still a world away from who I'd been. My values were cast in cement. Like my father's had been.

For that I could be proud.

I sent Beth a text, telling her the meeting had ended—I missed her—I'd be home in an hour or so, depending on the traffic. I asked for my check and opened my wallet. I was glad I had more than seventeen dollars in it.

I tipped the waitress well. I knew she had her own dreams to reach. I needed to hit the freeway. I started to slide out and felt the table pulsate a bit as a rather tall customer slid into the booth next to me. I looked up. And there he was, three feet away from me, wearing a smug smile, trying to wave down the waitress, calling loudly for a "Diet Coke."

It was Ken Richman.

ACKNOWLEDGEMENTS
AND AUTHOR NOTES

In the spring of 2009 I boarded a flight to New Orleans. My wife was gagging and dragging me to my first Mardi Gras. I hate unruly crowds, but she convinced me to get off our couch and it turned out to be a great adventure. I witnessed the pageantry of America's oldest parade-drinking ritual as the floats passed me by on Saint Charles Avenue. I observed that groups of outlandish characters were being taken for a fun ride, but one that would ultimately lead to nowhere in particular. There was another significant adventure launched on that trip to the Big Easy. During that week in 2009, I started putting my words to paper for this book. At times during the writing process, it felt like I was the captain of my own float, and I too, was dragging a few outlandish characters on a ride to nowhere in particular.

I had never written long-form prior to this. I'd had an article or two published in industry magazines and was famous for my long-winded emails, but had never attempted to write anything of length. Without any formal training, I began to frame the story that would become *Drawing Circles*. Six and one half years later, I cast the finished manuscript off into digital cyberspace. While plodding through those laborious and wonderful six plus years I found the energy to spit out another book. It was a non-fiction called, *The CAP Equation, A Foolproof Formula for Unlimited Success in Sales*. It was delivered to my editors in the spring of 2015 and has sold well. That book was a pleasure to write, the words seemed to pour out of me with ease. The process of writing non-fiction seemed easy after having struggled through several years of crafting a fictional account of some very real events.

I now understand why this book was so difficult to write. After I thank a few people, I'll tell you why it was so challenging.

Allow me to preface my show of appreciation by assuring you that this novel truly required a support team to write, edit and publish. I know, I know, every author says this, but REALLY, I needed every ounce of backing that was generously thrown my way, and then some. Let me first thank all of the people that graciously invested their time to read and review some of the earlier (and sketchier) versions of the book. These people actually read a first time novelist's work and were brave enough to give him their impressions of the storyline and characters. That took some guts.

To the following people (who apparently had too much free time on their hands) thanks so much: Dawn Christensen, Mollie Pearson, Janice Hill, Tim Martin, Janelle Agagon, M'Liz Kunze, Bill Topliff, Arthur Saldanha, Kandi McIntyre, Dan Bredeson, Jill Evans, Scott Blackshear, John Birsner, Doug Fox, Gary Ware, and Leslie Stevens.

Leslie's work, late in the process, was invaluable. She found a few inconsistencies that nobody else noticed. A special thanks is also due to Doug Fox, Trish Fox, Lori Ware and Gary Ware. They sent me an etched aluminum photo-plaque of Gary and Doug burning the manuscript over a trashcan after they'd both read it. This impromptu manuscript burning ceremony apparently took place on a deer-hunting trip and there may have been alcohol involved. Their inscription on that plaque read: *"No one needs to be in Joe B.'s head, except Joe B."* It's hard for me to disagree with that sentiment.

Again, the people mentioned above were brave enough to offer their ideas and comments and this input was quite helpful in shaping the story-line and characters.

About a few of those characters...obviously, when you create a story that is influenced by true events, some of the characters can live close to home, and a few of mine did. In a couple of cases, I opted to use actual first or last names. There are three female characters that are based on women that were a meaningful part of my young life. I tried to use alternate names for all three of these wonderful ladies, but it just plain didn't feel right. I'd like to thank Annika for allowing me to use her first name, but more than just that, I'd like to thank her for being honest, but yet so kind to me at such a difficult time in both our lives. I would also like to thank Gail and Stacy for not only being part of this story, but for also being such an integral part of my life.

The Mazal character was based on a real person, but I'm sure, to some, he'll sound too good to be true. Bill Mazal came into my life when I was thirteen years old and he has never left. I hope my portrayal of the Mazal character gives you a sense of what a wonderful human being he really is. I think God dropped him into my life just so I didn't have to invent a best friend for this book. When I got married for the second (and last time) Mazal was my best man, so, at least I got that right. My wish is that each of you find a "Mazal" in your life.

Hey, Mazal, if you're reading this, let's play golf up at Braemar on Thursday... our regular bet.

There is another distinct group of people that I need to acknowledge. These people are *compelled* to hang around me because they're family. The family members listed below either read one of the manuscript versions and offered critique, or they simply kept me propped up with their sincere reassurances that I'd write a "decent book." A sincere "thanks" to the following dear people: Ron and Dede Welling, Ronda and Trey Walters, Christie and Steve Kaiser, Wade and Margaret Shields, Willie and Renee

Corso and Ron and Lani DiBona. I love and cherish my family.

I want to also acknowledge the great literary professionals that were part of the support team for this project. A hearty thank you to the great Hal Marcovitz for doing such a complete and thoughtful edit on the manuscript. Hal offered me the benefit of his understanding of the legal system, amongst other things. Hal's specific input assisted me in creating a story that would be easier to follow for those not familiar with some of the nuances of multi-level marketing and/or Ponzi schemes. My sincere thanks also extends to Jerry and Michelle Dorris of Author Support. Their great cover design and interior-formatting work placed some lipstick on this pig. They are great professionals and are such a pleasure to work with, as are all of the partners of 11 Creative, LLC.

I have a talented young friend who is a gifted writer and award winning short filmmaker. Her name is Katie White. Katie was tireless in reading and re-reading early versions of the manuscript. She was brutally honest in her assessment of what was "really good" and shouldn't be touched, and also what was "okay," but needed to be fleshed out. In addition, she had the balls to tell me what sounded like, "pure crap." Incidentally, those were her actual words. Did I mention she's originally from New Jersey? I wish I had saved her handwritten editing scribbles; they would have made a humorous pamphlet on how to, or how NOT TO, critique a fist time novelist's work, depending on how thick the author's skin is. Fortunately, I have thick skin.

So, Katie, THANK YOU for hanging in there and never holding back. You taught me a great deal about the writing process and helped me develop a much more cohesive narrative than would have otherwise been written. Katie also reaffirmed that I had a solid story to offer readers. Katie, I owe you at least two birthday cocktails! (I keep missing her birthday parties, which she opts to hold in San Fernando Valley dive bars)

I have just a few more family members to acknowledge. I have NOT allowed my sister, Regina, to read or even peek at the content of this novel. It was my goal to have her read the story for the first time when she held the printed book in her hands. Regina is my *big* sister and has always watched out for me. She has a fierce loyalty to the ones she loves. Regina watched me as I made a myriad of mistakes in my life, but she never criticized me. She simply loved me and stood by my side. If Regina Buzzello is your friend you are blessed. I am truly blessed to have her as my eternal big sister and friend.

There is this cute little girl running around our house. Well...come to think of it, she's not that little any longer, but she's still cute! Alyssa Buzzello was eleven years old when I started writing this book and, as of the date of release, she'll be (almost) eighteen. She was a constant source of motivation (and nagging) during the writing process. "Are you STILL working on that darn book? How long does it take to write a stupid novel anyway?" Come to think of it, if I had a parent that took over six years to write a "stupid novel", I'd have asked the same question. Alyssa can't do much wrong in my eyes. She's a perfect little mini-me and the coolest person I know. (But not in a hipster kind of way) I love you Bear!

Alyssa made sure to remind me to add our dogs, Buzz and Ozzy, to these acknowledgements and I'm glad she did. Our two chubby blonde Labradors are the cutest and most loving boys in the world. Thanks to Ozzy for just being Ozzy. He is low maintenance, always interested in cuddling and he doesn't eat anything he shouldn't. Thanks to Buzz for not eating my manuscript, although Alyssa thinks he should have eaten a few of the earlier versions. This dog will eat anything not nailed down. I am surprised we even have a house left. I love both of these guys. They supply so much joy to our home.

Okay, one last "thanks." So, Beth...my wife. I'll start by saying there is ZERO chance of this story, this book, this novel, getting done without her. ZERO. Beth's calming voice, her ability to reach up and grab my head as it was flying off of my shoulders made the difference. I don't think there is anyone like Beth on the entire planet. Her tireless energy in reading, editing, discussing, convincing, hugging, kissing and sedating me (with a glass of red wine) was remarkable. Her contributions to this book even extend to its very title. *Drawing Circles* was her idea. As I look at the finished cover and think about the other titles I had contemplated, none of them even sound very good to me now. Thank you for this stroke of creative brilliance, Beth! Again. No chance of this book coming to life without her and, more importantly, my life would hold far less meaning without her. Beth is simply the best person I know in the world. I love her so much.

At the beginning of the acknowledgments I promised to tell you why I believe this book was so difficult to bring to fruition. Allow me to take a stab at explaining why. First and foremost, this work was loosely auto-biographical and deeply personal. Each of the characters were somehow modeled after one—or a combination of—people that were quite familiar to me. The storyline was influenced by true events, ones that affected me significantly at a rather impressionable time in my life.

In order to get the narrative right, I had to use my way-back machine. I had to re-visit times and places I didn't necessarily want to think about again. Writing this story was cathartic at times, but more often, I felt para-lyzed when recalling events that had been so painful. It was at those times I contemplated not moving forward with this book. It was at those times that Beth, and a few others close to me, *saved* me by gently saying, "Joe, this is a good story and it needs to be told."

It IS a good story, and it DID need to be told. I simply wanted to get it right and getting it *right* was about staying true to the choices and the voices used by the actual people I based these characters on. I had a deep commitment to ensure my characters mirrored what I'd observed. Hence, a happy ending or precisely closing each open loop was not my primary objective. As you know, in life, you don't always get a happy ending. Some-times, you don't get an ending at all.

People enter our lives for a reason or a season and then sometimes, they just go away, leaving unsettled issues in their wake. Irrespective of how badly we'd like to have answers to our most burning questions, we're sim-ply not owed that. Often, when we become absorbed with obtaining these types of answers, we're left with more questions about the human condi-tion than when we began our quest. I've also come to know that the thing we all call, "Karma," can bypass certain people regardless of how bad we'd like to see it cut them down to size.

Rest assured that, in seeking answers, the Tony DiBona character never learned anything more than what he already knew in his heart. I'd also like to think that the Tony character is at peace with the concept that the scales of justice don't always balance in this temporal world.

I sincerely hope that you enjoyed reading this story as much as I enjoyed the struggle of bringing it, and the characters, to life. I'd like to think that my mom and dad are reading the *Heavenly Kindle* version of this book. (If you are deceased, I'm pretty sure you can purchase afterlife copies on Amazon, as long as you still have a valid credit card)

I'd also like to believe that Buzz, Helen, Aunt Jean, Uncle Mike and Uncle Lou are smiling down upon our family and friends.

Joe Buzzello, Northridge, CA

About the Author

JOE BUZZELLO is a keynote speaker, author and nationally recognized sales and leadership expert. He has served in executive field management and Vice Presidency roles for Fortune® 500 companies. Joe has also written the non-fiction book, **The CAP Equation**, *A Foolproof Formula for Unlimited Success in Sales*, which is available on Amazon and also at:

www.CAPequation.com

Joe resides with his wife and daughter in Los Angeles, California and at his second home in Scottsdale, Arizona. Additional/bonus content and author commentary for this book can be accessed at:

www.DrawingCirclesBook.com

www.ingramcontent.com/pod-product-compliance
Lightning Source LLC
Chambersburg PA
CBHW070554260626
47161CB00002B/601